A Hand of Knaves

I0592542

edited by
Leife Shallcross and Chris Large

CS*f*G Publishing

Edited by Leife Shallcross and Chris Large
Cover art by Shauna O'Meara (with awesome help and provision of artifacts by Juliette Morley and Leife Shallcross)
Internal illustrations by Shauna O'Meara
Typesetting by Simon Petrie

National Library of Australia Cataloguing-in-Publication entry
Title: A Hand of Knaves / editors, Leife Shallcross and Chris Large
ISBN: 978-0-9775192-9-3

Other Authors/Contributors:
        Shallcross, Leife
        Large, Chris
        Canberra Speculative Fiction Guild

A Canberra Speculative Fiction Guild Book
Published by CSFG Publishing
PO Box 1533
Woden ACT 2606
Australia

Contents

Other CSfG Anthologies

Nor of Human..., 2001
(edited by Geoffrey Maloney)

Machinations, 2002
(edited by Chris Andrews)

Elsewhere, 2003
(edited by Michael Barry)

Encounters, 2004
(edited by Maxine McArthur and Donna Maree Hanson)

The CSFG Gastronomicon, 2005
(edited by Stuart Barrow)

The Outcast, 2006
(edited by Nicole R Murphy)

Masques, 2009
(edited by Gillian Polack and Scott Hopkins)

Winds of Change, 2011
(edited by Elizabeth Fitzgerald)

Next, 2013
(edited by Simon Petrie and Robert Porteous)

The Never Never Land, 2015
(edited by Mitchell Akhurst, Phillip Berrie and Ian McHugh)

Introduction

Leife Shallcross and Chris Large

If you ask Leife, she'll say this is all Chris's fault. He was the mastermind in this enterprise.

It was his idea, after all.

Yet, while Leife likes to hold herself blameless—for who could resist such an awesome idea? (Or an expert con)—a whole anthology of tales about rogues, thieves and ne'er-do-wells?—she threw in her lot with Chris willingly. And the end result—the evidence of which you now hold in your hands—is undoubtedly a product of their joint dark devising.

And what havoc has their twin evil genius wreaked? A demon-cursed adventurer, a mysterious woman recruiting an interplanetary army by less-than-ethical means, an inept assassin with a family reputation to uphold, an angry, angry schoolgirl, three elderly men forestalling the apocalypse, a pair of star-crossed scavengers, and a time-ravaged warrior who can never die are just a few of the many knaves they are responsible for letting loose in this tome of roguish mayhem.

A sympathetic soul would say the idea for A Hand of Knaves was decades in the making. We could certainly point to two lives marred by malign influences from early on, the editors having grown up loving anti-heroes such as Han Solo, Fafhrd and the Grey Mouser, Granny Weatherwax and Molly Millions. The less benevolent would point to a willing indulgence in unsavoury role models of more recent date, such as Lila Bard, Arya Stark, Tyrion Lannister and Captain Jack Harkness. Either way, its journey, from inception to the book you now hold in your hands, has been every bit as nefarious, daring and adventurous as the stories it contains.

Perhaps most concerning is the ease with which Chris and Leife were able to recruit willing accomplices to their cause. Perhaps, at the time of the submission call, back in 2017, they did not realise the chaos they would unleash. But can we really say they did not know the minds of Australia's speculative fiction authors are cluttered with dark byways and shady back alleys, Australia being entirely peopled by criminals, as we all know it is? We submit to you today that despite their protests of ignorance and dismay, the editors must have anticipated the deluge of tales of the weird and unexpected they received. They certainly should have realised, given the theme they'd chosen, that they were openly enabling unscrupulous writers to employ all means of deception, duplicity, and sleight of hand to ensure their stories would wheedle their way into innocent readers' hearts.

And there are others who have been drawn into this dark web who need to be acknowledged for their role in this wicked affair. Simon Petrie is a notable accomplice, as he not only slushwrangled all the original submissions, but also undertook the typesetting, oversaw the proofreading and generally managed all the administrative matters involved in marshalling a coterie of unruly authors. The visual appeal of this publication can be squarely attributed to the criminal talents of Shauna O'Meara, whose illustrations adorn the cover and pages of this reprehensible book. Juliette Morley's culpability extends to her involvement as publications officer, and the book has been further supported by the generosity of Kaaron Warren, Georgina Ballantine, Alan Baxter, Nicole Murphy and Rob Porteous, who all contributed perks to the crowdfunding campaign. Then, of course, there are the many souls who were convinced to support the crowdfunding campaign with their own hard earned money. You will find these generous, if misguided, individuals listed in the Rogues Gallery at the end of the book. All unauthorised apostrophes and other undesirable grammatical elements have been eliminated by our gang of tattooed, muscled-up proof readers: Todd Herzmann, Rachel Nightingale, Dave O'Connor, Robert Porteous, Alexa Shaw, and David Versace. Finally, the Canberra Speculative Fiction Guild Committee bears some responsibility as well, for having let Leife and Chris loose with this idea in the first place.

And so it comes to this: nineteen stories chosen not just for the quality of their writing, but for the daring of their characters, the wonder inspired by their ideas, and the sheer audacity of their authors. It is a catalogue of depravity kaleidoscopic in its scope. Want stories of spacefaring pirates? We've got 'em. Post-apocalyptic madness? Got that too. Double-dealing pedlars? Scientific experiments gone wrong? Cursed cities? Intergalactic drug-runners? Schools for thieves and cutthroats? Vampiric apothecaries? Canterbury Tales in space? Time-travelling mercenaries? Nefarious hackers? Psychic anarchists? We literally have it all. You won't want to skip a single story.

Throughout it all, Chris and Leife remain incorrigibly, incredibly proud of the stories in this anthology, gathered from across Australia and presented herein for your enjoyment. So as Guns N' Roses said back in 1987, in their now famous ode to those inhabiting the seedier side of life: Welcome to the Jungle, we've got fun and games. Read on friend. You have been warned.

(Not) Chris and (definitely not) Leife
June 2018

A

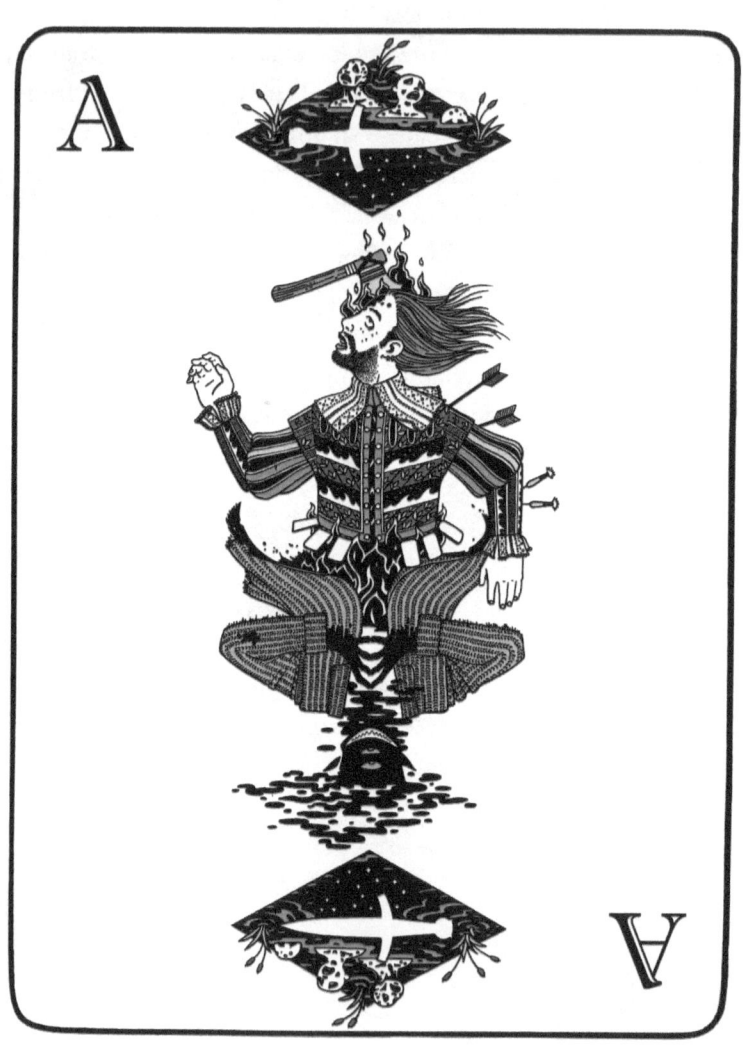

Ɐ

A Moment's Peace

David Versace

Like many seasoned travellers, I've come to distinguish cities by their scents. Chervold smells like a trap.

It's a nothing place; a muddy port coddled in the arms of peninsulas and guarded by hidden shoals, months distant from my beloved Serpentine Reach.

The demon's voice within needles endlessly. *There's no salvation here, di Sparchon!*

I don't disagree. I wish the demon would shut up about it.

This alley is wedged between an abattoir and a tannery, where pens of ophri, a hard-knuckled grazing animal, are converted to stacks of pink meat and rust-red leather respectively. A gang of thick-armed mop boys have just pumped dirty salt water over its sandstone cobbles to remove the blood. The smell could be worse.

How well you know the scent of trapped animals!

Though I confided to the dark-eyed Jarlish fisherman of my search for the apothecary specialising in demonic afflictions, I never trusted him. He was a baited hook, dangling assurances of a cure. "Go to this address," he told me, not as drunk as he pretended, "and speak Aza's name." If he was paid well to sell my foreign arse into the clutches of brigands—and he was, for the satchel he tried to hide beneath his nightstand was heavy with coins—then he was at least better company than the ceaseless scorn of the demon in my blood.

A trap! You fell for it, little merchant prince!

The alley's shadows obscure doors and ladders, loading cranes, and sealed crates. Several big men with butcher knives could hide here easily. If I stay in the moonlit street I'll soon become the subject of unwelcome Chervoldi attention. If I step into the alley, I could be discretely chopped into small pieces.

I enter the alley. *Fool!* After months of fruitless searching, I place my trust in chance. *Weakling!* Any hope of a cure is worth pursuit, be it as slender as a killer's blade. *Your hope will crush you!*

To shut out the demon's endless malice, I ask loudly, "Where is Aza?"

A cold blade pricks my flesh through the beard beneath my chin. A spice-breathed woman whispers in my ear: "Be still, foreigner. Aza dislikes sudden movements."

You see?

Her hand slithers around my waist and unbuckles my sword belt. She kicks it clattering across the alley. The woman is slightly shorter than me, which makes her unusually tall for this region. I can't be certain of anything else. The knife at my throat commands my attention.

"I want to talk, Aza. I'm no threat to you."

A second voice corrects me. "She is Corvis. I am Aza."

Another woman glides out of the darkness as if a fog has parted. She too is tall, with the squared face, red-berry-dark skin and broad shoulders typical of these islands. The armour she wears—tight slats of stiffened leather cinched around coarse, hard-wearing linen—is hardly an apothecary's stained apron. Only murderers carry that many daggers on their belt, or point crossbows at innocent men.

Innocence is a relative term in my case, I admit.

I lick my lips. "Forgive my ignorance of your Chervoldi ways. Is it customary to waylay visitors in dark alleys?"

"It's as much a custom here as anywhere," Aza says, frowning. "But we're not going to rob you."

"I'm relieved to hear it."

Corvis-behind-me presses the blade harder to my throat. "Our man says you are Dario di Sparchon. Is it true?"

Sail to the ends of the world. You cannot escape your name.

When I don't answer straight away—how can I with the demon's clamour? —Aza adds, "Di Sparchon, the demon-blooded. Are you him?"

I didn't use my name with the fisherman, nor anyone aboard the *Skipping Fix*. "Whatever rumours have reached you," I say, spreading my hands slowly, "I promise they are exaggerations."

"It's him," says Aza, nodding a signal. "Do it."

Fool!

Corvis' hand closes over my mouth. There's a flash of pain across my throat. The glint of a wet blade catches a slant of moonlight. Warmth rushes down my chest.

Things get dark.

I stand beside a stream I don't recognise, though I've been here before. Too many times. The night sky overhead is brilliant with alien constellations. Every bright point is an eye, watching for my surrender.

The stream churns around a chattering crowd of empty-eyed people, submerged to their shoulders. They babble. Their meaningless tumult drowns out the stream's insistent gurgling.

A man stands at my side.

Rather, it is something that looks like a man, wearing a simple robe with frayed cuffs and a dusty hem. I don't look at it directly. I did once and my eyes hurt for weeks afterwards, even after I came back.

I warned you, it snarls. The stream-people's noisy chatter echoes its words. *You could have saved yourself the pain.*

I roll my eyes at this. "I'm neither the author of my pain nor its chief beneficiary. If you care so much for my well-being, leave."

You hope for release, di Sparchon? You know how to earn it.

These conversations always go the same way. The demon is incapable of change.

"Surrender myself to you in return for blissful oblivion? How is it you've watched over my shoulder for a lifetime without learning to negotiate?"

The pact is the pact. Neither of us can change its terms.

"Too bad. I've never agreed to the terms and you've never made a better offer. So send me back."

The pain will be excruciating.

It honestly believes there's nothing worse than physical pain. It's a very stupid demon in many ways.

"It always is, demon. Return me to the company of honest murderers."

⊷

As always, I wake up screaming.

Suffer!

The smell of my own burning flesh fills my nostrils. The blood congealing across my throat and chest is still aflame; shadows dart like imps around the alley's industrial timbers. Someone cries in alarm; my head and shoulders wallop against the street-stones.

I get dropped a lot. Some fool always tries to move my body.

Mark these agonies, for they are never-ending.

"He's on fire." I don't forget voices during my brief death intervals; Corvis' is like a blade slipping from an oiled sheath. Memorable and apt to be the last thing you hear.

"He's alive, sister. Watch and understand his nature." I can't see Aza for the flames.

I brace myself. This is usually the point when I'm rolled up in a rug, thrown in a river or doused with a bucket. It's a sound precaution; my burning blood sometimes ignites secondary fires.

The murderesses forebear to rescue me, to my relief. In a moment, the flames dissipate like fog, leaving my bare skin intact and in rude good health. Unlike my ruined shirt.

Until the next time, and the next!

My vision clears to reveal Aza reclining on a cargo-swing; her fingers cage a slender mug. Corvis pours a warm liquid with a fragrance of dusty herbs from a metal flask into another mug, which she presses into my hands.

"Is your curiosity satisfied?" I ask with my freshly intact throat.

Aza takes a sip. "Most would not believe rumours of a foreigner who bleeds demon-fire."

"It's ridiculous how many people kill me over rumours," I agree. I recognise a businesswoman with a proposal when I see one. "Some have even better reasons."

They want your secrets! They will cut them from your flesh!

Corvis' hand presses down on my shoulder like a coil of rope. "Drink the tea."

Another test? The mug's scent is almost familiar, like something I've read about. If they hope to find my weakness, the one death I can't avoid, they're wasting their time. I've been hacked, burned, drowned, bludgeoned, chewed and, yes, poisoned. No lasting fatalities.

I will never permit your death, di Sparchon!

Meeting Aza's flat gaze, I pour the mug out on a smouldering crate. Corvis sighs and drops her hand.

Aza's lip curls at my antics. "We can help each other, di Sparchon. Do you know the Citrinian?"

It's not a name I expected to hear in Chervold.

"By reputation. A collector of antiquities and artefacts. He travels even more widely than I. He's here?"

Your curiosity will destroy you!

Aza nods. "He stores part of his famous collection in a manor house in Lichen Hole."

"I see. You think part of his collection would be better in your hands?"

Kill them and take their spoils for yourself!

Corvis spits on the ground. "He stole from us. From our mother. We want what's rightly ours."

Ah, a righteous cause. I should already be running.

"I'm no thief."

This isn't remotely true, but it's a point of pride that my most successful larcenies were technically legal under the Articles of Trade. Come see me if you want to swindle a merchant delegation from the Hephraides. Smash-and-grabs are for idiots.

You are a thief a coward a killer a betrayer a—

"Oh?" Aza sneers. She opens a book, some old journal scratched out in a language I don't know. Someone with a good eye has drawn a picture of a sword. Elaborate work about the grip and guards; markers of old Urghurgian style.

Aza's fingertips spark with power as she passes the book for my inspection. Sorcery; a warning. Disturbing, but my secret is worse.

"Great swords have many names. Our mother called this one Angry Jack."

"Who was your mother to carry Urghu metal?"

"She was a hunter of demons." Corvis leans over my shoulder, tracing fingertips across the symbols as if to make the notes comprehensible. "With this sword she killed dozens of demons, di Sparchon. Before her, it may have killed hundreds."

The fantasies of children! Demons cannot be slain.

Aza returns my sharp look with a dangerous smirk, like she knows things she shouldn't.

"Does that interest you, foreigner?"

Their plan is simple enough.

The Citrinian is a rich old hoarder, paranoid and distrustful. He employs a minimum of human guards, and none within the perimeter of his manor. Beyond that point, if the sisters' information is to be believed, he relies on deterrents immune to bribery and deceit.

All things may be deceived!

My role is uncomplicated. My indifferent martial skills are not required; my bumbling presence as an ignorant foreigner will suffice.

That, and my incapacity to die.

They exploit my gift, di Sparchon! The insult demands an answer!

As my apparently drunken stroll takes me to the manor's gate house, I laugh. The demon in my blood seethes. It's infuriated whenever I take the opportunity to turn its so-called gift to my advantage.

Two guards straighten at my approach. I see it at once—slow, reluctant, not expecting trouble. Everyone knows it would be suicide to rob the Citrinian. Everyone is not wrong.

Worse than the death of worldly flesh for you!

If only.

I swagger, heedless of the hooked spears they lower in my direction. "Ho, friends!" I drawl in undoubtedly wretched Chervoldi.

The first guard brandishes the spear tip at me and barks an emphatic string of "Be off with you," or words to that effect. I shrug helplessly and gesture at the night sky. For emphasis, I chatter in my native Serpentine, reciting the stock manifest from my first trade voyage in my father's company. Yes, he made me memorise it at the age of seven.

My catalogue of fungible assets appears to antagonise the guards. The one with the bushy moustache advances spear-first; the one with the red bandanna swaps her spear for a narrow stabbing-sword. Moustache snaps a command: "Stop," "Leave," or possibly, "Prepare yourself for presentation to whatever gods you hold dear".

No gods await you, di Sparchon!

"Try me," I mutter.

I snatch the shaft of the spear and pull myself at Moustache. While I could skewer myself on the spear—nobody ever expects that for some reason—I opt to defer the pain as long as possible.

I yank hard on the spear. It misses my midriff by a hair. Startled, Moustache lets go. I shift my grip and swing the pole up into his face. His head leaves a satisfying trail of blood and teeth as he falls.

Bandanna isn't so easily tricked. She anticipates my attack and moves off my line of sight to prepare her counter. To her credit, it's a clean strike. The blade goes in through the back and out the other side, missing the ribs altogether. The blade nicks the aorta and deflates my lung.

Yes, I can tell the difference between my organ traumas. The sign of a regrettably-led life.

You can live well, di Sparchon! Submit to me!

If Bandanna had speared me to the wall or cut a tendon, she'd have stood a chance. Fire spills from my belly onto the street. My collapse twists the blade from her hand. I hear her curse over the sudden roar in my ears. She wrenches Moustache's spear from my slack hands. Too late.

Vision fading, I hear a voiceless scuffle. The sword is pulled from my back. Someone drags me—not gently—and shoves me against a wall.

The fire in my blood flares, drowning out an exchange of Chervoldi growls. I don't think the sisters like what they see.

Who can blame them?

My demon and its submerged chorus resume the torment, mocking my swordplay and the ease of my despatch.

By my count this was my twenty-ninth fatality. Only slightly less ignominious than the time I was eaten alive by pigs.

Offal for swine, di Sparchon! Every death weakens your resolve. Every return brings you closer to—

The vicious wheedling grows distant, fading like a receding tide.

For a moment, I am alone with my thoughts.

Silence. For the first time since I was a child. Since the moment my mother—

Horrific memories rise on that alien silence.

This time, I don't notice the physical pain.

Corvis' hand is over my mouth; her thumb and forefinger pinch my nose shut. Her grey eyes stare into mine with a diamond intensity. In other circumstances, it would terrify me, arouse me, or both. But right now I can't breathe.

I hate suffocating.

She raises a finger to her lips and releases me. My mouth tastes of dust and sweet smoke as I gulp air.

Somehow we are inside the house. I'm propped against banisters at the base of a staircase rising into darkness. Corvis hunches as if shielding me from arrows. No. She's guarding the stairs.

Aza has pushed drawing-room furnishings to the walls. She turns circles in the centre of the room, like an Opekan chant-dancer's warmup. She sights along her crossbow, turning in all directions as if tracking swallows on the wing. Her nose wrinkles, emphasising a small scar between her cheek and ear. She freezes like a hunter; her attention is focused on the tip of her quarrel. It glows, pointing at a vacant patch of the plaster ceiling.

"That way," she mouths.

Corvis nods and hauls me up by my wrist. She thrusts a sword into my hand; the grip is tacky with scorched blood. I can guess whose. "This is in poor taste," I mutter.

Smirking, she pushes me up the stairs. "Lead on. Turn left if you make it to the top."

I test each step with a ginger toe, looking for traps. A squeaking joint alerting the Citrinian would be as great a danger as falling through a sabotaged stair. If I have to choose, I'll take the one that doesn't involve splintered shins.

Either the Citrinian disdains the classic expressions of extreme domestic security, or he uses these stairs himself.

I make it to the landing in one piece. Corvis is five steps behind me. Aza is at the base of the flight, pointing her crossbow at what I hope is the doorway rather than my head. She gives me a get-on-with-it glare.

I stare into the gloom while my eyes adjust. Hanging on the wall opposite is a portrait of a grim, shrivelled aristocrat with sunken eyes and a superior sneer. I'm still thinking about the Citrinian's ugly expression when a volley of darts hits me in the teeth and throat.

I spin around to meet Corvis' appalled eyes.

Then the poison hits my heart and my brain, and I'm done again.

Entering the demon's place is like the curtain lifting on a crumbling, empty stage. There's just the sense of a place, ancient and malign.

The demon is gone. The voices are silent. The threat is remote, like being in a room with a sleeping pit-dog. Asleep, it's harmless. Will something wake it?

I hate myself for giving in to that fearful silence.

"Hello? Are you there?"

… kill everything you love …

The whispered answer crushes something growing in me. Terror, despair or relief? I don't know.

"I didn't know demons took lunch breaks."

… slice your future into shreds, di Sparchon. Cut your moments into pieces, feed them to spiders …

The familiar spite, but bubbled through tar. It's so removed from a credible threat it's almost endearing.

I am struck by the horrific notion that I am closer to this thing than what's left of my family.

When I wake, we've moved again. Corvis is picking a lock hidden by a bookcase swinging on a hinge. Aza runs her fingers along the spines of shuddering books to calm them.

The hidden door opens on another poorly-lit corridor. Taking the lead, I discover the spring-loaded spiked axes mounted just inside.

Do you think I can be escaped, di Sparchon?

Why does it sound … subdued?

You are bound to me until you surrender.

What's changed?

The Citrinian values his privacy.

We follow Aza's guiding quarrel through a disused kitchen. I misstep on a pressure plate. My face is sprayed with acid.

In a bedchamber strewn with broken bones, a pack of saw-toothed menki apes leap from atop a cabinet and tear at my neck.

The false ceiling-beam in a little antechamber drops, crushing my spine.

With each death the demon's bloodthirsty threats become more hysterical.

I have no idea what's possessed it.

The Citrinian runs out of death-traps before the sisters lose their nerve. Aza's uncanny crossbow leads us to a windowless gallery at the top of the house, where glass display cases are suffused with glow-bug lights.

I could finance a trade expedition to Outer Rechoule and back with the wares on display. Jewels from every corner of every ocean. Books written in languages so old their cultures have been forgotten. Body parts from a dozen exotic creatures, some of whom once had names and addresses.

And there on the wall is Angry Jack, hooked up like a favourite saucepan.

Aza says, "Hold him."

Corvis' knee hits my back as she grabs both my wrists and pulls. I groan as my joints pop. I fall to my knees.

Corvis whispers, "I'm sorry." She doesn't free me.

Aza snaps, "This sword is our legacy. We can't risk your betrayal. But don't worry, we'll give your demon the cure it deserves."

See? You can't be trusted any more than you trust.

Thinking she's won, not expecting another trap, Aza reaches for her prize.

Before I can think about why, I swivel my legs about. My shoulders dislocate, breaking Corvis' grip. I sweep Aza's legs from under her.

She falls, snatching at Angry Jack. Her fingers sweep through the sword like it's empty air.

She tumbles aside, empty-handed, as the trap door opens beneath my arse. I hear the sisters' Chervoldi curses all the way to the bottom of the shaft.

*S*urrender. *You cannot bear this pain.*

Muscles tear. Limbs break. Skin ruptures and innards spill. Still I will not give it what it wants.

An unfamiliar voice rouses me from death. "Wake, thief."

The Citrinian is about a thousand years older than his portrait—ancient and weathered, like a stone block worn down by the steady passage of time itself. At once I know he was impossibly old before I was born.

"Who are you? Another demon-haunted fool desperate to escape a bad bargain, I suppose?"

I've been dragged like a sack of snapped branches into the oversized fireplace of another parlour. The red embers are almost cool under my burning skin.

He is fashionably dressed in a quilted tunic, clinging silk shirt, and baggy trousers cinched below the knees. He pours expensive Halwing brandy into a crystal goblet. He seems unconcerned by the bone-deep charring of his hands.

I've noticed it takes time to gather my thoughts after my skull is crushed. "You're like me?"

"You young ones always make such an unbearable ordeal of it." He almost sounds sympathetic but can't quite manage it. "You came for this, I presume?"

Angry Jack's dimly glowing blade has a slick red sheen, as if it were forged in blood. It has a presence like fury rippling through a drunken mob.

"I'm led to believe it kills demons."

He turns the blade up in mock salute and lays it flat against his cheek and brow. His granite skin ripples around the edge, like worms caught in the sun, and his eye-twitch reminds me of a dying bird. "Quite right. It cannot abide being near demons."

The hearth begins to warm me as my bones reknit. I stretch fragile muscles to roll wearily off the coals, ending up helpless at the Citrinian's feet.

"You seem at ease in your demon's company."

His ancient eyes glower. "It's not so difficult. My demon has voracious appetites. I struck a bargain to indulge them. The agreement served us both for lifetimes, but betrayal is a demon's nature. I took pains to get there first." Angry Jack is a glittering beam cutting through the smoke. "I heard of a belligerently powerful sword in the possession of an ill-tempered Chervoldi hunter. I persuaded her to part with it."

"You killed her?"

"Hardly. I tricked her child into bonding with another demon. She did the killing."

He tickles the sword under my chin. I have no strength to flinch. My demon finds its voice. *Get it away! It is poison!*

"And what of you, Serpentine? What bargain will you offer to save yourself?"

From his viper smile, I know bargaining is futile. I respond like a good merchant's son: I lie, flatter and cheat to get my way.

"Rumours of your splendid hoard haunt every port in the world, Citrinian. It called me across oceans to see it for myself." My disarming grin shows we are men who understand each other. "It took some effort to find cutthroats desperate enough to steal from you."

Is my frank admission convincing, or is he used to indulging liars? "And where are your accomplices?"

"They lacked my natural advantages against your household hospitalities. I daresay the beasts in your menagerie will eat well tonight. Their meat has already been butchered."

He sees through your lies!

I see now how Aza was tricked. The Citrinian used misdirection sorcery to draw attention to his illusory sword, powerful enough to fool Aza's spells. But she isn't stupid; she'll have figured out his magic and recalibrated her aim.

The sisters aren't coming to recover their mother's property. They're avenging a much worse crime. I just have to stall.

"Really." The Citrinian takes a long draught from his goblet, his head cocked to listen to an unheard voice.

Strike you fool! Strike if you would live!!

It's a charade. He's testing me. If I move, he'll skewer me. If he does, will it drive the demon from my blood or just kill us both?

"My demon knows your secrets, traveller. It knows the price demanded of you. You're a fool to resist."

"I've been foolish my entire life. It never tires of rescuing me."

The Citrinian's smile becomes a flat line of contempt. "It would amuse us to watch it exert itself."

He whips the blade around in an arc that meets with my knee. A crack like windswept timbers fills my ears; red floods my eyes. I blink the splashed blood away and see my foot tip sideways. My leg has slipped its moorings at the knee and drifted off.

You waited too long! You put yourself in the hands of a demon-killer! Imbecile!

Fire engulfs my leg. The pain is immense—worse than poison and burning and infection combined. I almost don't notice when the Citrinian swigs another gutful of brandy and chops my other leg in half. The sword is impossibly sharp, separating flesh and bone like soft fruit.

Clawing at the air and screeching incoherently won't fix things. I try it anyway. I grasp and wail as my lower half billows smoke. My demon drills inside my skull as if tunnelling to freedom.

It hurts! It hurts!

"You would have your uses, I imagine," says the Citrinian, kneeling by me. "But neither my demon nor I cares for companionship. Let's learn instead how many swings it takes to drain the demon from your—"

He can't finish the sentence with his throat cut. Corvis is a shadow moving within the smoke, her knives dripping.

The Citrinian turns, raising his guard, oblivious to the fatal wound. He lunges but Corvis has moved on, leaving smoke coiling in her wake. She kills with an easy grace.

"Citrinian!" Aza now, shorter and dead-eyed. "You'll die for what you did to us."

Her hands fly over her uncharged crossbow. For a wild moment I think she's forgotten to load her weapon for battle. Then I see a glowing bolt jutting from the Citrinian's eye.

"Two daughters, is it? Your mother was a good liar." The Citrinian crouches, preparing to lunge; Aza can't hope to avoid being impaled on her mother's sword.

I roll on my side, scissoring the stumps of my thighs around the Citrinian's closest ankle. The pain of the effort is almost blinding; nearly-sealed arteries rip open again, spraying fresh blood I can't afford. An ineffectual attack. His balance is scarcely upset. With the smallest exertion he could kick me away.

But he looks down, showing me his demon's enmity in too-pointed teeth and too-bright eyes. It's more than hatred. It is a tempting promise of oblivion.

Coward!

Then Corvis drives a knife into each shoulder blade, severing nerves and muscles. The Citrinian loses control of his hands. The goblet shatters. The sword falls into my lap.

The tiniest harp-note registers Aza's crossbow loosing again. The Citrinian throws back his head and now he howls. A feathered bolt sticks out of each eye.

I squeeze my legs. The Citrinian stumbles, grabbing at a crossbow bolt with one hand and empty air with the other. He falls.

I arrange a meeting between Angry Jack's point and the Citrinian's shrivelled heart.

When his body sprawls across me like a drunken sailor, it weighs next to nothing. Everything that should have withered across his unnatural span has done so.

You destroyed one of my kind without my leave, di Sparchon! No greater crime exists!

Ingrate.

I feel a tug at my fingers as Aza takes the sword. "Mother forgive me," she says. Her distant expression implies a long-delayed confession.

Corvis collects a leather sheath punched with Urghurgian lettering from the floor. She plucks the sword from her sister's fingers and hefts it like it was always hers.

Aza looks at me like I'm a festering wound. "Die, foreigner, or return to your oceans. This city is done with the demon-blooded."

She turns and disappears into the smoke. The flames have lost interest in me in favour of the wall hangings.

Corvis makes a gesture at her departing sister. "Forgive her. She can't abide the demon-haunted."

"I can't blame her." I struggle and sit up, blinking furiously at the thickening air. I'm ready for what's coming. "She hates to be reminded of what she did?"

"What was done to her," Corvis says. She taps the severed ends of my legs with the sword. "If you ask, I'll finish the job. You won't feel much pain."

Pure sincerity is a rare virtue. She'll kill me without hesitation. It would be a loving act. I'm tempted.

Don't do it.

I give her my best smile under the circumstances. "I'm grateful, but no. It's not enough for me to die. I need to outlive my demons."

She sheathes Angry Jack. "I thought you'd say that," she says. "But you did right by us. Let me return the favour."

She kneels and unstops her flask, which sloshes with a dark liquid. A familiar aroma pushes through the blood and smoke.

"What is it?"

"The tea I offered you. I concocted it to suppress my sister's demon."

"So Aza isn't the apothecary after all?"

Corvis nods.

"You made me drink it after the guards stabbed me?"

"Just a taste. Too much and your demon couldn't have brought you back." She holds it out and waits.

Don't trust her. We can—

I sip the tea. It's cold but it burns all the way down.

"Go well, Dario di Sparchon," says Corvis. Before she vanishes into the burning building, she adds, "May you find your peace."

The fire intensifies. Soon the smoke will be too thick to breathe. Likely it won't stop burning until this old manor is nothing but stone and ash.

My legs have barely begun to grow back. I can crawl, but not fast enough. Timbers rumble overhead, shifting irritably in the embrace of flames.

"Can you bring me back from this?" I ask the demon. "Can you make a man from charcoal?"

No answer. The demon's chorus is bated. The silence has returned.

I lick the moisture from my lips, cherishing the flavour. The quiet lingers.

Voiceless? Banished? It doesn't matter whether the demon's coming back.

I'm going to enjoy the moment.

David Versace lives with his family in Canberra, where he is a CSFG member, novice bass guitarist and occasional public servant. His work appears in the anthologies *Next* (CSFG Publishing) and *At the Edge* (Paper Road Press). His short story "The Lighthouse at Cape Defeat" was a 2016 Aurealis Award Best Fantasy Short Story finalist and features in his short story collection *Mnemo's Memory and Other Fantastic Tales*. He can be found online at www.davidversace.com writing a new flash fiction story every Friday morning.

A Tale of the Marriage of Gawain

Amy Brown

Have you heard the stories they tell about Gawain? They say he got his first lift off-planet working as security for a gang of Danaan smugglers: every one twice the size of him, and he terrified them all. He was a bounty hunter before Arthur took him on, and he's still got the knack. If Arthur wants you, Gawain will track you across the quadrant, maybe even the galaxy. They say he's none too picky about legal niceties along the way, and Arthur turns a blind eye.

They say he's a ladies' man. They say wherever he goes, bedroom doors are unlocked before he even lifts an eyebrow in a woman's direction. Rumour has it husbands look the other way. (Still other rumours say that certain husbands *don't* look away, if you know what I mean.) I heard he once avenged his own death. There was a period where he couldn't tell anyone his name, and he went to bed with a girl who changed her mind because he didn't look or act enough like the hologram Gawain she kept in her closet. They say he took it with good grace and backed off. When she found out her mistake, boy was she pissed, but he wouldn't give her another chance.

They say that Gawain, of all the jumped-up, gun-toting lone rangers kicking about in what passes for Arthur's jurisdiction, has his priorities sorted. They say that Gawain, in between knocking heads on Arthur's business and standing on the toes of those who get too big for their boots, has learned what women really want.

⚬⚬⚬

It happened like this: there was a person named Ragnell—let's call her a woman, That will make things easier for this part of the story, but keep in mind it's sort of a simplification. Anyway, Ragnell ought to have inherited most of the Inglewood system from her brother. But her brother, who was a useless excuse for a human being, lost the better part of the family interests in a dice game, and then got himself stabbed in a bar in the underbelly of Betelgeuse IV. And who do you suppose he lost all those land grants and stocks to? None other than Gawain, who had no business being in a dive bar on Betelgeuse IV in the first place.

Now, this person named Ragnell tried appealing to Gawain's better nature, but wherever he'd left it, it wasn't with him when he answered her messages. He left her waiting long enough before he got back to her, too. He did not, the messages said, care if her brother wasn't sober. If he couldn't hold his liquor perhaps he needed a chaperone—perhaps she ought to think about that.

The person named Ragnell did think about that, and she thought Gawain was full of shit. She told him so, too, which got a much faster response than her first message did. Gawain had won her brother's assets fair and square, he said, but he'd give her a chance: he'd let her play for them herself. Come to Camelot and challenge him: her choice of game, and he'd stake her family fortune the first round.

The person named Ragnell didn't answer this message and she didn't play fair. Arthur and his cronies were planning a hunt—again, as if they had nothing better to do—on Inglewood III, one of the very planets now in Gawain's possession. Ragnell couldn't afford to travel to Camelot, but this was her home territory: she laid plans. Inglewood III was a pleasure planet, with huge swathes of land reserved for game. Arthur and his gaggle of hangers-on were tracking deer (real, old-fashioned deer from old Earth) when they caught sight of something else, something peculiar. It slunk in and out of sight ahead of them: white, with improbably multi-coloured spots, like a tiger that had run into a paint fight (they had tigers on Inglewood III, too, but this was no tiger).

Aside from its colouring, the peculiar thing about this creature was the covetousness it inspired in anyone who saw it. Arthur caught sight of the whole length of it, glorious mane to alert, thrashing tail, and he wanted it. He wanted it for himself. This was, you understand, exactly how the person named Ragnell, who we are calling a woman for convenience's sake, had arranged things. She knew the fauna of Inglewood III well, and had put just a touch of a glamour on this one. Enough to draw Arthur away from his entourage; enough that he was loath to have any of them follow him.

Maybe she overdid it. Maybe Arthur didn't care that much about the interdiction on hunting native animals in the first place. Either way, when she stepped between the man and his prey he didn't so much as blink, just leaned past her and zapped the creature dead. Not stunned. Dead.

The person named Ragnell drew herself up to her full height—which was significant, because whatever else she was, Ragnell was not a dainty person. She drew herself up and demanded to know who Arthur thought he was.

"I am Arthur," he answered, looking irritated. "Master of this system—no, master of more of the galaxy than you can comprehend." Then he narrowed his eyes at her and said, evidently without thinking, "What happened to your face?"

The person named Ragnell was not particularly beautiful. She was, in fact, downright ugly. Particularly in the face. Arthur was more than a little taken aback.

"None of your business," she snapped, and abruptly abandoned her plans for making a sensible petition. (I suppose you want to know, too, don't you? What happened to her face? Well it's none of your business either.)

"What *is* my business," Ragnell went on, "is the slaughter of an animal under my protection!"

Arthur shook his head, once again on firm footing. "Ma'am, you've made a mistake. This planet is now under the protection of my nephew, Gawain."

The person named Ragnell pushed her cloak back so that Arthur could see she carried a hefty sidearm. "Your nephew Gawain, who isn't here to protect it," she said, "or you."

"I am armed, you know," Arthur replied, still cocky.

The person named Ragnell extended one hand, and Arthur yelped, dropping his gun as the barrel became too hot to hold. Ragnell stalked toward him, her gun aimed at his heart.

Arthur swallowed. "Um," he said. "I'm sorry about the … beast?"

Ragnell just looked at him, until he started to squirm. She may even have raised an eyebrow.

"What do you want from me?"

Here is where Ragnell might have demanded her land back. Or possibly Gawain's head on a platter. But she was feeling put out by the death of the creature, not to mention "What happened to your face?"

"Right now," she said, "I'd like to kill you."

Arthur blinked at her, as if for a second he'd been about to agree out of desperation.

"But I think I'll give you a chance. Answer me one question, and if you answer it truly I will let you live. Answer false and I will shoot you."

Arthur wet his lips. "What is the question?"

Ragnell kept her gun trained on him. "The question is: what do women want most?"

Arthur gaped at her. Honestly, he looked pretty stupid. "Honey," he said, "I've been married nearly ten years and I haven't the faintest idea what women want."

"Well, how about you go on home and ask your wife then?" Ragnell said, ignoring the 'honey'. "I'll give you a month. You come back here in a month with the answer, and I'll let you live."

"And if I don't come back?"

"I'll have you hunted down, and your wife and your nephew too." She let him think about that for a second, trying to decide if she had the capacity to take out all three of them. (She didn't, but he didn't know that.) "And," she added, "if you bring me a good answer, I'll let you keep the pelt." She didn't look at the not-really-a-tiger—she didn't have to.

Arthur called off the hunt and went back to his ship, and then back to his planet. The person named Ragnell waited, and collected gossip. They said Arthur had gone home and there had been some kind of row between him and his wife. They said Arthur and Gawain had been sulking and drinking together for days. Then, and this part made her happiest, the rumour was that Arthur and Gawain were each, individually, traipsing about the palace— then the planet, then the quadrant—asking people if they knew what women want. It was widely supposed that Guinevere had given Arthur some kind of ultimatum (the person named Ragnell felt a little bad about that, but maybe the girl would thank her. A husband like that could do with some shaking up).

They collected their answers and assembled a spreadsheet. I tell you, I have seen this spreadsheet and it's a work of art. Some people said to them that women want gold, or jewels, or fancy landspeeders. Someone suggested what women want most is a cure for menstrual cramps, which sounded pretty reasonable to me. More than a few said most women wanted land, or money, or a stake in the family business (the person named Ragnell would have approved). Some said women wanted children; some said women wanted better ways of avoiding children. Gawain asked some of his more flamboyant friends—and who knew Gawain had such friends?—and the answer there was that everyone, man, woman, or not otherwise specified, wants a truly waterproof mascara. Arthur consulted the locals on Sirius V, who recognise no gender, and dutifully wrote down 'concept "woman" not recognised'. Gawain got a similar response in the Rigel system, where the locals recognise no concept of desire.

In the fourth week after their encounter, the person named Ragnell heard that Arthur had set course for the Inglewood system, apparently having decided to narrow his search down to women his enemy might conceivably have met. She set about preparing her next step.

Somewhere out in the orbit of the Inglewood star, Arthur's ship was hailed by a short-range transport, a little one-person affair which wouldn't cope well in deep space. The transport contained a young man: small, dark, and somewhat effeminate. He wore white and carried a blaster, but you got the feeling that he might never have used it. He looked, to Arthur's eyes, like the kind of young man who had a lot of women for friends.

Just as Arthur was pondering how quickly he could introduce the topic of 'what women want' without seeming like he was typecasting, the young man brought it up himself.

"I know the answer you're looking for," he said. "And why you're looking for it."

"Who are you?" Arthur demanded, and then, "What do you know?"

"Let us say that I am no friend of the lady Ragnell," said the young man who probably could not use a blaster. "I cannot protect you from her, but I can give you the answer you seek."

Arthur digested this information. He'd heard about the woman pestering Gawain over a land contract or something. "*That* was Ragnell? The one whose brother lost all his property in a dice game?"

"Yes," the young man said, flipping his hair. "That's her. She skinned that tiger herself, you know." Here he shuddered theatrically. "She says she'll use its pelt as your shroud."

For a moment, Arthur hesitated. After all, that would be going out in style.

"Do you want to know the answer, or not?"

"What happened to her face?" Arthur asked.

The young man glared into the camera. "None of your fucking business." Then he seemed to recover his poise, and his coy demeanour. "Nosy, aren't you? I'll give you a choice: you can have the answer to that or you can have the answer you really need."

"Oh, um," said Arthur. "The answer to the woman's question."

The young man smiled, and said, "Well, darling, I know Ragnell and I know the answer she does not expect you to give. I will tell it to you, on one condition."

"What now?" said Arthur, with a sinking feeling.

"Your nephew Gawain," the young man said.

"What about him?"

"I want to marry him," the young man said. "I want to be married before all your people, on board your ship, in orbit over Camelot. Is that clear? I will tell you the answer to the question you seek once I have your nephew's hand in marriage."

Now, Arthur was no stranger to marrying off his friends and relations for political gain, but this was the first time anyone had demanded Gawain's hand. In the ordinary way of things, Gawain was a little too powerful in his own right for Arthur to run his personal life for him.

Nevertheless, it seemed the simplest solution, so he took the young man's name and turned his ship toward Camelot.

He called up Gawain.

He called the young man back.

Gawain called the young man.

Guinevere called Gawain.

Arthur called Guinevere.

By the time Arthur's ship took its customary place in orbit over Camelot, the marriage was arranged, and a fast ship sent back to the Inglewood system to collect the young man, who had given his name as Inconnu. Arthur was pretty sure that wasn't his legal name. It sounded like something you'd see on a night club poster:

"DJ Inconnu, here for one night only."

I have to say, for a man who'd been strong-armed into an abrupt wedding, Gawain was positively gracious. If he had a problem with the situation, he wasn't letting it show. And he was dressed—well. The fabric alone must have cost a fortune, and then there's a premium to pay to get your pants to fit your ass *that* well. I thought I was a master of a certain kind of couture, but here I was being outdone by a man best known for out-drinking half the bruisers in the outer planets.

He carried my bags off the shuttle, and kissed my hand—not smarmily, you know, but like he really meant it. I almost felt bad about what was coming. We were married in the finest style that could be rustled up at short notice. Guinevere loaned me a veil, and Gawain gave me one of his own outfits from when he was younger—a really nice one, all in jewel-green. It had to be taken in, but he didn't seem to begrudge it. There was a feast, of course, and I sat beside my new husband with Guinevere and Arthur on either side of us. There was little opportunity for talk, least of all a private word between husbands, but Gawain seemed pretty laid-back about it all.

"I'm sorry," I said, laying a hand on his arm and leaning in, while Arthur was talking to the bruiser on his other side—Karl or Kay, or something like that.

"For what?" Gawain asked, just as quietly.

"Springing this on you," I said.

Gawain shrugged. "I gather you needed an escape route," he said. "Especially if you're going to give us that answer, you wouldn't be safe in the same system as Ragnell." He glanced sideways, eyes skimming over my face and lingering a little on my waist where the tunic nipped in. "Besides," he said, "I'm sure I can make the best of it."

Now I really did feel bad about what was coming next. But first I had to deal with Arthur, who, sure enough, cornered me shortly before we were due to beam down to the surface.

"The answer, young man?" he asked. Gawain might be sympathetic, but Arthur didn't like me. Fair enough.

I leaned in, my lips close to his ear, and whispered: "R-E-S-P-E-C-T." I didn't sing it, but it was a serious temptation.

I left him there, puzzling that one out, and went to join my new husband in the transporter room. I wanted to ask him to give me a few minutes, let me go ahead and compose myself, but I didn't know the layout of his house. So we went down together, and as we stepped off the transporter pads, Gawain turned to me and visibly recoiled.

Predictably, his first question was "What happened to your face?" Then, as I glared at him, he put two and two together and followed that up with "Who exactly are you?"

I told him the truth: "I *ought* to be baron of the Inglewood system right now."

"Baron ... ess," Gawain said.

"Doesn't matter much to me," I told him. "What does matter, is my fool of a brother gambled away my inheritance, which he had no right to do, and got himself shot. And," I added, poking him in the chest, "you said I could challenge you to a wager to win it back."

"I did," Gawain said. He seemed a little dazed.

"Well, this is it. You call for an annulment, I get my property back." I expected him to accept it at once: I would've, if I were him. Instead, he frowned at me. He was, I noticed, rather cute when he was thinking.

"And what was that up there?" he asked, gesticulating toward the ceiling. "Some kind of ... glamour? You were ... smaller." *Not hideous*, he didn't say. He also didn't say *less female*, which was nice of him.

Because he didn't say either of those things, I told him the truth again. "Some kind of glamour, yes. Or this is," I gestured vaguely toward my body, which was once again bigger and less graceful and distinctly ill-favoured in the face. "Long story, involving a pissed-off magician, me as a baby, a transporter drive, and my mother's untimely death. End result is my brother inherited the family estates and I got a shape-shifting curse. I get this face and the body that goes with it, any time I'm planetside, and the other one when I'm off-planet."

Gawain considered this for a few seconds, and then said, "Bugger." He didn't seem all that concerned.

"Sorry about that," I said. "It kind of ruins the wedding."

He tilted his head at me. "I dunno," he said. "You're not going to kill Arthur, are you?"

"No," I conceded. And, reluctantly, I added, "I've got a tiger pelt for him in my transport: he earned it fair and square."

"Then that's marriage objective one achieved." He turned and headed for the door into the main part of the house. It took me a moment to move after him, and a few more moments to speak. In my defence, you'd have trouble remembering what you were supposed to be doing, with that ass in those pants in front of you.

"Look," I said, feeling distinctly unnerved, "all you have to do is sign over the estates and I'll get this annulled. No hard feelings."

"Last I checked, if you're my husband—er, wife?—then we hold all property in common," Gawain countered, stopping in the middle of the first room, which was—to be honest I still don't know what it was originally intended for. Gawain uses it to host large holo-gaming parties.

"You can't honestly tell me you're going to keep me like this?" I said, incredulous. "That is the very opposite of a trophy husband! Do you want to repulse all your friends and relations?"

He thought about that for a moment. "Arthur's going to be pissed," he said. "But he's going to be pissed for bigger reasons than your face." He wandered off to one side for a second, rummaged under a counter, and came back with beer. Cold beer, at least, but the sort of canned stuff you find in the outer planets, not in the expensive gaming rooms of Arthur's chief henchmen.

"Oh, wow. Thanks," I said, taking the can and examining it with suspicion. "You do recall the part where if we're married we're supposed to be having sex?" That daunted him, I could tell. Gawain the ladykiller; he could get any pretty girl he wanted. "And if I find you're running around behind my back I'll have you poisoned, and not with the quick kind of poison," I added.

"See," he said, pointing at me, "I like that in a woman!"

"What? Threats of murder?"

He shrugged, pulled the tab on his beer. "You probably could kill me," he said. "It's kinda hot."

"It'd be hotter if I didn't look like ..." I gestured helplessly at my physical form, improbably-sized feet to unfortunate face. The funny thing is, I don't actually like the other one much better: people are nicer to it, I suppose. But it's too small, and in it, I'm constantly under-estimated, which is nearly as bad as being treated like a freak.

"Well," he said, "what do you want to do about it? I'll sign over the estates and get the annulment, if you really want."

"Or?"

"Or we stay here, explain shit to Arthur, and then get ourselves a ship and go adventuring," he said, with a shrug.

"So you get my pretty body back," I said. Not that it was even a particularly beautiful body: just the more pleasant of my two. "You realise every planet we dock at, you get this one back again?"

He gave me a look that said *Well, duh.* "And also every time we come back here," he said. "Which we will have to: I have responsibilities to Arthur."

"I don't," I snapped.

Gawain frowned for a second. "You could," he said, carefully, "stay space-side, if you prefer. If that's the problem."

"No!" I was in danger of rupturing the unopened beer can, I was gripping it so tightly. "I just didn't expect you to want to stay married!"

"Then shall I call my lawyer and have separation papers drawn up?" he demanded. He looked flustered, a little red in the face. It was a good look on him. I considered the very many good things I had heard about this man's talents.

"Not if you'll take me to bed," I said. "Now. Like this."

He looked me over, and said with faint awe, "You could probably kill me with your bare hands." They were big hands, even compared to the general immensity of the body I was wearing. "Come on then," he said, and held out one of his own, equally big and far lovelier hands.

———

There are plenty of stories about Gawain. Some of them say he travels with a young man who looks like he'd be more at home with a curling iron than the blaster he carries, but whom Gawain seems to adore. Some of them say he married the ugliest woman in the galaxy, and no one knows why, but he seems to find her witty. Everyone agrees on the fact that Arthur dislikes this person whom Gawain married, regardless of their gender. It's also generally agreed that Gawain's spouse, whoever it is, and Guinevere are on suspiciously good terms.

They *say* that Gawain has learned the secret of what women really want. I wouldn't know: it's only as a matter of convenience that we're calling me a woman in the first place.

Amy Brown once promised her students she would write an Arthurian Space Opera. She hasn't managed that yet but hopes that quirky space cowboy retellings of medieval literature is a start. She has taught medieval literature in Sydney and in Switzerland, and normally writes dry academic prose. Her less crusty writing has appeared in *Semaphore Magazine* (NZ) and on theconversation.com.au.

The Best Heist Yet

Cassandra Page

"**Y**ou sure this is a good idea?"

Cherra didn't look at me, her dark eyes fixed on the grated vent six feet above our heads. "The contract is legit—I had Shoal check it out. And govie work means good pay. Plus we don't have to worry about being rumbled by fedpol if we pinch anything, 'cause they sent us here in the first place. This could be our best heist yet." She skimmed a hand back over her ear: a reflex, not a necessity. She'd already caught her wild curls up in a dark cap before the run; fluoro pink would show up too easily in low light.

The wan glow from a dying bank of neons above our heads glinted off the new, glossy black BCI port behind her ear. My soft-soled shoes whispered on concrete as I stepped up to her, tugging the cap down to cover the port—and not just because it might give us away. "Yeah," I said. "It just doesn't sit right with me is all. Why don't they use govie suits? They've got plenty of them."

Cherra flashed me a grin that lit up my insides like a megamall before Xmas, even after all this time. "You worry too much, baby girl," she said, giving me a kiss that tasted like lemon drops. Her lips were soft, and brushed against mine as she spoke. "Of course they want us. We're unbeatable."

She stepped back, and I sighed, smiling my surrender. A kiss was all it ever took for her to win me over. Besides, while this job was strictly recon, who knew what we'd find inside? CYTek had manufactured implants and bots before the company went bust in the downturn, leaving this plant an abandoned cubic shell in the middle of a dead industrial zone on the edge of an ailing city. Still, maybe we'd find some old kit lying around—it might be dated, but there was always a market for that. Not everyone could afford cutting edge bionetics. Almost no one could. And most people didn't shudder at the sight of a BCI port like I did.

Cherra stepped forward, placing her hand on the dull steel wall. "It's vibrating. Guess the govie folks were right. Someone's squatting after all. What do you say, baby girl? Let's take a peek."

●

Swallowing, I shove the memory away. Last time I was here my pulse had raced with the thrill of the job, of being with *her*. Now I am a taut wire, humming with dark anticipation, not daring to hope. The scar tissue over my left breast and on my palm itches sometimes, not quite healed. After forking out for the expensive implants, there hadn't been much left over for installation. I'd finish healing the old-fashioned way.

I still hate bionetics. Knowing there's tech inside me makes my fingers twitch, eager to dig it out like a splinter. But I restrain myself. I need the tech.

The grate is pulled to, the holes where bolt heads should be a row of empty eyes. No one re-secured the grate after ... after. Last time, Cherra had boosted me up. This time, I am alone. I wouldn't risk anyone else on this job. Not that anyone would come. A pay-free suicide run, Shoal had called it.

Tugging my sleeve down over the awkward lump of my utility bracer, I reach for the holster at my belt and pull out the single-use grapnel, snug in its launcher. The device is light in my hand and, when I pull the trigger, it makes the barest sound of puffing air as the grapnel fires, microfilament shimmering behind it. The projectile hits the steel beneath the grate with a *tink*. I tug on the microfilament to set the hook, and scale the wall.

A gentle spray of mist from the tiny aerosol bottle I retrieve from my bra ensures that the hinges are smooth and silent when I lift the grate. I peer along the short shaft, searching the shadows for signs of movement. Nothing. My shoes whisk against steel as I slide in, pulling the microfilament up behind me and easing the grate closed.

At the other end of the shaft is another grate, artificial light seeping in through its bars. This one is also unsecured. *Maybe they never figured out how we got in.* I ease my hand through the bars to oil these hinges. *Or they know and they don't care.* I set my jaw and climb down into the room beyond.

Once, this space would have been a bustling office. I can see hints of long-ago office workers in faded posters, a GMO pot plant still perky despite the lack of natural light, a superhero desk ornament whose plastic fist punches the air as I walk past. But signs of long abandonment abound. Overhead, one of the neons flickers, ticking like a beetle pounding itself to death against a window. A piece of fruit has gone right past desiccated and on to mummified, and all the desktops bear empty spaces, outlined by dust, where Tabdroids and projectors would once have sat.

Cherra had pouted the first time we'd crossed this room, leaning towards me to whisper, "Someone's looted the kit already."

"Tabdroids are too bulky to be worth stealing," I'd told her. "We couldn't fit more than six or seven in my pack."

The room has two exits: the one to my right leads to the old CYTek reception and the shuttered main entrance. The other, deeper into the factory.

The faint, high-pitched hum of a fan is all the warning I get. I freeze halfway to the second door, my feet glued to the sturdy carpet underfoot and my breathing shallow, as a whirring drone whisks into the room. It's a tiny thing with a rotor on top, a glossy black sensor on the front, and an antenna protruding from its rear like a stinger.

The sawbones who'd installed my implants, Doc Axel, had assured me the cloaker would make me undetectable to this type of bot sensor so long as I stayed still; the effect wasn't total invisibility, but the cloaker did scrub my infra-red emissions. Or something. I narrow my eyes to slits so I don't need to blink so often, watching the drone as it passes before me on its sweep of the room. It comes so close I felt the breeze from its passage and almost bite my lip, afraid it will smack me in the head.

But it doesn't. And it doesn't show any sign it has detected me—no pause, no change in the sound of its internal cooling fans to indicate it's doing a deeper scan. Either my cloaker worked or I'm so bleeding obvious it didn't need to take a harder look. I feel like an emperor in new clothes, but what else can I do but trust my tech? I'm already here.

·

After the drone buzzes away, I count to sixty and begin to move.

The doorway opens out onto a corridor that runs along the outside of the office. There's more of that sturdy carpet, almost as hard underfoot as the concrete had been outside. The lights here are dimmer than they were in the office; several of the neons have blown out. The opposite doors have cartoon silhouettes on the doors, the universal symbols for bathrooms: male, female, other. Cherra and I didn't bother searching them last time, and I give them a miss again now. Glass-walled offices provide a glimpse into the cupboard-like kingdoms of the low-level managers. In one, a tenacious vine on top of a filing cabinet has sent tendrils up the wall towards the light fitting. New green shoots uncurl like fingers towards the sun, a refreshing burst of colour in an otherwise drab space.

The corridor hooks right at the end, and now I'm starting to wend my way into the factory part of the complex. The carpet yields to steel flooring, and I slow my step so as not to make a sound. I can feel the faint tremor of working machinery through the thin soles of my shoes, though it is still distant. Windows reveal dimly lit workshops; many of them have been scavenged for equipment too.

After several minutes, the corridor terminates in a T-intersection. A pair of heavy double doors looms before me. The sight of their familiar, unadorned greyness makes my heart kick against my ribs—an uncomfortable feeling given my recent surgery. My hands begin to tremble and I pause for a moment, taking several deep breaths. *Get it the feck together.*

I hold my breath to listen for rotors, and when I hear none I risk a peek down each side corridor. All clear. I creep over to the doors and press my ear to the steel. Silence.

Finally, pulse racing, I ease one of the doors open and slip inside.

"About time," Cherra breathed, her eyes widening as she took in the workshop. On one wall stood a tall server in a nest of cables. A flickering green light in the front panel indicated it was powered. A long bench dominated the centre of the room; a conveyer belt was inset along its spine, robotic arms poised idly above it,

giving the appearance of a dead centipede lying on its back with its feet in the air. Conduits ran overhead and along the far wall. Interspersed between darkened corridors were individual assembly stations and a supervisory workstation on an elevated platform.

The Tabdroids were missing from those stations too—although, in here, there was no dust film to outline their ghosts. This room seemed abandoned, but it was too clean.

"Still no sign of who's running this place." I grimaced.

"The schematics say there are management offices on the second floor," Cherra replied, her gaze fixed on something in the centre of the conveyer belt: a fist-sized device of some kind, left abandoned on the centipede's belly. "I expect they're holed up there. Hello, gorgeous."

She stepped forward, reaching between the robotic arms. A sick feeling tightened my gut. I opened my mouth to object, but—

The implant moved, unfurling like a spider, the shining spike of a needle jabbing at Cherra's hand. She gasped as it pricked her flesh, turning her palm over to reveal a spot of blood. "Oh, feck. I hope that's not t-to ..."

She collapsed, her head striking the edge of the bench with a nauseating thud. Her hair tumbled free in a pink wave as her cap was knocked aside.

"Cherra!" I dashed to her side. The robotic arms whirred to life, rotating on their gimbals to face me, rearing up like snakes preparing to strike. Ducking, I reached for my wife. The back of my head exploded with pain as something clobbered me. Stars danced before my eyes. I caught Cherra's hand as the arms thrashed overhead, my fingers seeking her pulse. Still strong.

Scuttling drew my gaze as the spider-like bot crawled down the side of the bench and hopped onto Cherra's shoulder. It had a reflective green cross on its side. An aid bot? But it didn't look right. Its dome-like sensors studied Cherra's exposed BCI port before fixing on me. The stinger darted forward. I scrambled out of reach, grabbing the expandable baton at my belt. "Get off her," I snarled, flicking my wrist to extend the weapon. Its tip sparked red. The sharp stink of ozone prickled my nose.

"Baby girl," Cherra said, her voice slurring, her pupils dilated and fixed on something over my shoulder. "Run!"

I glanced behind. A swarm of tiny bots seethed from an open grate beside the server. Many of them bore the same green cross as the bot on Cherra's shoulder, although their forms had wild variation. Some buzzed towards me, slow and ponderous. Others plopped to the ground and inched closer on tracks.

The bot on Cherra's shoulder jabbed her again, this time in the throat. "Run," she breathed as her eyes rolled back in her skull.

I didn't run.

I fought.

I lost.

I'd woken up in an underground garbage dump, groggy and aching from a dozen bruises and cuts. Cherra hadn't been there—though, afterwards, she was there in my nightmares, as I waded through sludge, vomiting from the stench and crying at her directionless screams.

—◆—

I ease the heavy door shut behind me and turn.

My jaw falls open.

The room is exactly the same. *Exactly.* The workbench, the idle robotic arms, even the furled, tempting shape of the aid bot. My gaze flicks down to the place Cherra fell, but there is no sign of her. Despite myself, my stomach clenches. I didn't really think I'd find her there, waiting for me to save her, did I? It's been weeks.

Still, when I blink, a tear slips out, leaving a line on my cheek. The cool air bites at it.

I look again at the aid bot. Is it the same one? I can't tell, but my jaw clenches and my hand drifts towards the baton at my waist. I am faster now. I could smash it to fragments before the robotic arms got me. Couldn't I?

A whirring to my left makes me whirl, heart in my throat. A drone hovers before the server. *Where'd you come from?* The black sensor on the front of its spherical body is pointed at me and I get the impression it's studying me. *It saw me move. Feck.*

We stare at each other. My pulse thunders in my ears, and my fingers clench around the baton's handle, but then I grow aware of a faint noise, a series of chirping beeps. It's coming from the drone. Not an alarm. More like rats squeaking to one another. Is it talking to one of its fellow bots? Is it talking … to me?

I finger the tiny switch beside the BCI port on the palm of my hand, activating that implant, and the squeaking translates into a single word, repeated over and over: <IDENTIFY. IDENTIFY. IDENTIFY.>

I don't know how to reply in machine language. I know the port is translating, but replying the same way is beyond me. I don't even know if my implant can do that, and the memory of Shoal urging me to read the goddamn manual curls my tongue. That would've taken weeks, and I'd lost too much time already. So I just stare back, my gaze going between the drone and the black rectangle behind it. Waiting for the swarm to reappear.

<IDENTIFY. IDENTIFY. IDENTIFY.>

Does it want my name? My AusCard number? That's not going to happen.

The drone drifts from side to side, the sensor staying fixed on me. It reminds me of the way Doc Axel had walked around me, assessing my proportions and requirements in a way that would've been creepy if he hadn't been so clinical about it.

<FORM: HUMAN> the drone says. <HEAT SIGNATURE: EIGHTEEN POINT THREE DEGREES. DECEASED HUMAN? ERROR. SIGNIFICANT MOVEMENT DETECTED. INCONSISTENT WITH POST-MORTEM ACTIVITY. COMPATIBILITY: UNCERTAIN.>

I blink, my thoughts tumbling over themselves. A memory surfaces, of me pulling Cherra's dark cap down to cover the BCI port at her throat. The cap knocked free as she hit her head. Her, taken. Me, implantless, dumped out with the trash.

Before I can reconsider, I raise my hand, showing the bot the gleaming nodes of the new BCI port on my palm, the skin around it pink and shiny.

<SIGNIFICANT MOVEMENT DETECTED. COMPATIBILITY CONFIRMED,> the drone chirps. <REQUEST RETRIEVAL. UNIT SD23 TEMPERATURE SCANNER MALFUNCTIONING. REPORTING TO SERVICING.>

The drone buzzes from the room, and I have to remind myself not to anthropomorphise the soulless little thing—even though the cant of its propellers tips its sensors forward to give it a hangdog look.

The seething, clattering racket emerging from the dark rectangle beside the server sends my heart right back into my throat, and I pluck a small ovoid pod from my utility bracer with the sound of parting velcro. I pop the lid back to reveal a glittering pin, affixed to a silicon bulb of liquid. *This better work.*

I jam the pin into the soft skin of my wrist and squeeze the bulb just as the bots boil from the rectangle, surging towards me. On the conveyer belt, the aid bot that got Cherra unfurls and skitters down the side. My heart thunders and I backpedal despite myself, snatching my baton from my hip. Ignoring the oncoming swarm, I wait for the little aid bot to pass outside the arc of the conveyer belt's arms. Then I dart forward, swatting at it. The baton connects with a satisfying crunch and a flaming jolt of electricity. The thing flies through the air, hitting the wall with a crash and a spray of sparks.

The other bots surge over me, several jabbing me with needles. Smiling, I fall bonelessly to the ground, eyes sliding shut.

My throat, thigh and outer arm ache where the bots stabbed me, and my scalp burns where a lock of hair was torn out after getting caught in the tracks of the one supporting my head. But my blood is filled with a saline coolness as the drug labours to neutralise the bots' sedative, and my mind works furiously as I attempt to map our path through the facility.

The swarm takes me through the workshop, past the places the schematic labelled the canteen and staff room, and towards the main factory. Most of the machines are underneath my body, holding me up like ants carrying a prize from a picnic, but one aid bot perches on my forehead, and I nearly start when it slides a cool probe into my ear. After a moment, it chirps. <Temperature: thirty-six point seven degrees. Unit SD23 malfunction confirmed. Disassembly authorised.>

Poor SD23.

I struggle to keep my breathing even and slow as the bot crosses my face, its cool feet pressing against my cheek, my lips, my throat. What if it takes a blood test and realises I'm not sedated? It pauses at the point where the scar tissue is visible above the low collar of my shirt, and I almost shudder as it prods the site and whirrs to itself. I soothe myself with the memory of the other aid bot and how one of its legs had flown off when it hit the wall, spinning through the air in a graceful arc.

Eventually, the light pressing against my eyelids changes from the dull grey of intermittent neons to something brighter. The swarm eases me to the ground, the aid bot hopping off my chest and scuttling away. The floor vibrates under me, the sensation tickling my inner ear. We're here … wherever here is. Now I will find out who the CYTek squatters are. I will tear them apart for taking Cherra from me.

I crack my eyelids slightly, peering through the smudge of my lashes at the new room. The ceiling glows a bright, uniform white, unbroken by conduits or fixtures. My ears strain, but all I can hear are the sounds of the bots whirring and clanking as they withdraw from the room. A deeper hum, further away.

I let my head loll to the side as if asleep. At the edge of the ceiling, the white light of the diffuser gives way to a blue-grey wall, a bank of computers, a narrow bench encircled by a scanner on a track. Cables and tubes snake along the floor to the bench, their ends disconnected. An aid bot scurries to and fro nearby. A sick bay, then, for CYTek staff who got injured on the job?

The machine chatter is lower in pitch to my ears, but the implant interprets it just fine. <Beta waves detected. Subject is conscious.>

Feck.

Wishing I hadn't dropped my baton when the bots swarmed me, I leap to my feet. The room sways a little and I grit my teeth, willing the anti-sedative to work harder. I can't keel over now.

The room is bigger than I first thought, stretching away to my right. More of those medical benches line the walls, but I catch only a glimpse of them, because the centre of the room is occupied by the biggest nurse bot I've ever seen.

Built on a heavy, tracked base like the cleaning bots that sweep the streets in the city's first-class district, the thing stands easily seven feet tall. Heavy arms on gimbals protrude from its sides and are fixed onto vertical tracks. The ends of the arms are affixed with flat paddles designed to slide under a patient so they can be lifted. Smaller arms dangle like dozens of cilia along the front of the bot, running parallel to chrome panels painted with reflective green crosses. Its head is a rotating sensor nub that is dwarfed by the bulk of its body.

As I stare, one of the panels buzzes open to reveal rack upon rack of opaque black bulbs, each with an unsheathed pin at the top. A tiny arm adjacent to the panel retrieves one of the bulbs, passing it to a larger central arm. The panel clicks shut.

"Please remain still." The soothing feminine voice issues from a small speaker by the bot's left shoulder. "This may sting a little. Your cooperation is appreciated."

I sidestep the machine as it rolls forward, leaping up onto the empty medical bench. One of the large arms pivots towards me, its paddle swatting the air as though at an annoying insect. It glances across my shin as I step over the scanner, and I curse. "Oi, nurse bot," I say. "I don't grant my consent for this procedure. Do you hear me? Consent denied!"

"Consent for wetware conversion is automatically granted on entry to this facility and may not be waived," the bot's friendly voice says. The bot rumbles around the side of the bench, its paddles reaching towards me. I slide down the other side, my foot turning as I step on the small aid bot that had been working with the cables. Something sharp slices through my soft-soled shoe, and I kick the thing away, limping out into the centre of the room. Blood splotches the floor behind me.

Seeing the room unobstructed for the first time, I freeze, mouth hanging open.

There are at least a dozen medical benches along the walls of the room. Almost all of them are occupied by reclining human figures. Most are tall, homogenous men, dressed in black business attire sliced at the arms and crotches to allow each man to be connected to a drip and catheter. Their identical chiselled jaws and dark hair are telltale signs that they are govie suits, fresh off the clone rack. Another bench is occupied by a tattooed woman who wears the vinyl and leather plates of a cypherpunker. And there, in her black catsuit, now torn in several places, is Cherra. The fattest cable is connected to the BCI port at her throat; other tubes are hooked to her wrist and … elsewhere. Rage fills me at the indignity of it.

The nurse bot slams into me, paddles pressing my upper arms into my sides. "This may sting a little," it says soothingly as its cilia clutch at my clothes, pulling me closer. I grunt as I feel the cold heat of the needle slide into my stomach. It doesn't sting for long, though, the sensation quickly numbed as the contents of the bulb begin their war with the anti-sedative already in my system.

The fingers of one hand reach for the utility bracer on the other wrist. I pluck the last of the anti-sedative pods free, but my hand is tingling, beginning to lose sensation, and I fumble it, dropping the precious pod to the floor. It clatters away. My fingers stretch towards the last, heavy lump in the internal, sealed compartment, but I can't quite reach it.

The numbness spreads, and my hand drops to my side.

"Why?" I whisper through lips I can't feel anymore.

"Because it is required," the nurse bot replies, sweeping me up with its huge arms and rolling towards the vacant bench. The scanner rumbles along its tracks as the nurse bot nudges it aside and eases me onto the padded surface. "Insufficient parts require improvisation. Wetware is required to sustain processing power."

The bot rolls around the foot of the bench, and I turn my head, my gaze finding Cherra. She is on the bench beside me. *At least we're together again.* The thought is muzzy, and my wife's figure seems to blur as the nurse's stronger sedatives begin to overwhelm my own, street-grade drugs. I blink, bringing Cherra back into focus. I don't want to let her out of my sight. Not again.

Her hair trails in a torrent of pink down the side of the bench. Her lips are parted and her chest rises and falls. *She's alive!*

The thought is electricity in my veins. My arms are leaden, but I manage to lift them onto my belly. Again my fingers scrabble at the utility bracelet, digging into the sealed compartment for the heavy round ball of the Emp.

As the nurse bot lifts the heavy cable with the whine of moving parts, I pull the ball from its pouch. As the bot snatches my hand back, I grip the ball in my other hand, prising open the panel with a nail. As it connects the cable to the BCI port on my palm, I push the small, round button.

For a heartbeat, I am everything. I am the giant server cluster, sweltering in the poorly air-conditioned room next door. I am SD23, patient and still as I am cannibalised for parts by my fellow bots. I am Cherra and the govie suits and the cypherpunker, dreaming of code and revenge against the humans that attempted to decommission me.

The device thrums in my hand, and with a flash of ozone and sparks, the room is plunged into darkness.

I am myself again. And I am so, so tired.

◉

"Baby girl?"

Something tugs at my hand, and I drag my eyelids open. Cherra's face fills my vision, lovely even lit from below by the faint green glow of a biostick. She is frowning, her expression worried as she studies me. When she sees the recognition on my face, a smile crinkles the skin around her dark eyes.

"Hey, beautiful," I say, the words so slurred I can barely understand them.

"You used an Emp?"

"Mmmm." I rub my face, trying to brush away the artificial cobwebs of sleep. "Implants shielded. Doc Axel said."

"Not all of 'em," Cherra says, glancing over her shoulder at something I can't see. "That cypherpunker clearly had dodgy tech."

I grow cold as I realise what I might have done. Doc Axel had assured me my implants would be fine against an electromagnetic pulse, which was why I'd asked Shoal to get me an Emp, just in case. If Cherra's hadn't been shielded, if the shielding had fritzed …

"Don't worry about it," Cherra says, helping me stumble to my feet. A stab of pain reminds me of the cut on the bottom of my foot, and I wince.

"Let's get the feck out of here before the suits come around," she says. "I don't feel like spending the rest of the day being debriefed. Or worse."

As we stagger together across the dark medical room by the light of the single biostick, I can't help the smile that splits my face.

"What?" Cherra glances at me. Her arm is around my waist and mine around her shoulder, each of us leaning on the other for support.

"You were right," I tell her. "This was our best heist yet."

She snorts as we pass out of the room and into the corridor. It seems longer in the poor light, and even though my aching body hates the idea of trudging along it, my smile grows wider. "All we got was shanghaied," she points out.

"Nah, that's all *you* got," I say, squeezing her arm. "I got some seriously sweet loot."

Cherra's speculative gaze runs over me as though expecting my backpack to materialise, stuffed with goodies. "Tech?" she asks.

"You."

Her lips are dry and she hasn't had a lemon drop in weeks, but it is still the most passionate kiss she's ever given me: deep, grateful and full of desire. The dizziness that sweeps over me has nothing to do with the drugs. "You're right," she says, studying me from an inch away. Heat flushes my cheeks. "This was your best heist ever."

Cassandra Page is an author, editor, public servant and geek who lives in Canberra with her son and two Cairn Terriers. She has serious coffee and gaming addictions, and has loved to read since primary school, when the library was her refuge. She reads and writes across the speculative fiction spectrum—although urban fantasy is her favourite. When she's not doing either of these things, she engages in geekery, from *Doctor Who* to AD&D. Because who said you need to grow up? You can learn more about her books at www.cassandrapage.com.

The Pedlar

Rebecca Fraser

Calypso Reeves crested the last of the loose-rocked, burrow-pocked, ankle-twisting hills. He dropped the handles of his cart to the moss-soft ground with a sigh of exhausted triumph. The waning sun bathed the valley below in a golden sheen as it made its slow retreat behind the distant craggy ranges. Calypso stood, hands on hips, and surveyed the peak-roofed hamlet below until it was nothing more than a flint-hued silhouette in the dying light. He would ply his trade there on the morrow.

But first, preparations. He undid the knots that secured his bedroll and shook it out. He selected a spot next to a small grassed hillock that would serve nicely as a pillow. What with the velvet sponginess of the ground and the clean mountain air, Calypso reckoned sleep would come easy tonight. A sight more comfortable than the outskirts of the last town had offered at any rate. Godforsaken dust-blown hole. It was almost a blessing he'd had to leave there in a hurry.

Calypso pulled one long, heel-worn boot off, then the other. He threaded each one onto the handles of his cart. Keep the snakes out. Travelling men get to know the ways of the road. He flexed his toes and rubbed at his stockinged feet. The flatlands might be rock-hewn wastelands freckled with ugly towns and even uglier townsfolk, but the roads sure were easier on the feet than the steep trails that twisted through the mountains. Especially when you were pushing a wooden cart heavy with wares in front of you, mile after sweat-stained mile. Still, nothing to be done about it. He'd have to get used to the highlands for a while. The road at his back was sure to be less than welcoming for quite some time.

He pulled the sacking cover from his cart now, and did a quick inventory. He knew his stock well—a place for everything and everything in its place. Even in the vestiges of dusk he could identify the familiar outline of his wares. A bundle of candles here, a copper kettle there. Next to them, a skein of silk thread, a tin of boot polish, a mortar and pestle, clothing pegs, a set of ivory-handled teaspoons. Something for everyone, whether they knew they wanted it or not. A bundle of hair ribbons, a collection of door knobs, glass bottles filled with boiled sweets, jars of ointment for maladies various, books of matches, bolts of fabric—Calypso Reeves had it all.

Next, he reached into the folds of his overcoat. A patchwork shroud of leather and suede, scarred from years of mending and re-patching, his coat told the tales he had worked so hard to keep from showing on his face. Deep from within its purple lining he withdrew a slender parcel wrapped in otter hide. He opened it reverently, peeling back the supple layers to reveal a long spiral flute.

Calypso picked it up and brought it to his lips. The flute's bone-white surface gave off a faint ethereal glow, making shadows dance across his face. He blew into it once, letting the crisp note linger for a moment in the mountain air, before breaking into a melodic tune. He circled his cart as he played, fingers working the holes spaced along the spiral's hollow. The tune picked up speed as he went, and his circling dance turned into a whirling-stomping caper. Around and around he went, fingers flying, his coat swirling around him, until finally the frenzied music reached a crescendo, and he sank to the ground, panting and wild-eyed.

Once he'd caught his breath, he tucked the cover back around his wares, secured his cart, and sat cross-legged on the bedroll. A star-peppered galaxy now revealed itself against the blue-black canvas of night, and beneath the starshine of ancient constellations, Calypso played his flute again. The tune this time was soft and slow, filled with a tragic beauty that could moisten the eyes of the hardest of men. The music wafted across the valley, drifting down, unheard yet felt, to the township below. That night, babies cried out in their sleep, dogs barked and snapped at things unseen, and townsfolk sniped and bickered at each other, gripped by emotions they couldn't explain.

With his tune complete, Calypso replaced the flute in its wrappings. He stroked it gently before rolling it in the hide. He admired the smooth polished twists of its spirals, his fingers tracing the bumps and turns. To the untrained eye it resembled a narwhal's tusk, a treasure claimed from a denizen of the deep. But Calypso knew from whence its enchantment came—his flute was carved from pure alicorn.

He'd had to pay a fitting price for the unicorn's horn—oh, cursed day—was still paying it. Who was foolish enough to steal from a warlock? That was the question that chased its tail through his head mile after mile, town after town, year after year.

So too did the warlock's incantation that had roared after him like wildfire as he fled the warlock's cave, clutching the stolen flute.

"Wander, thief, that is your fate
Carry your greed, and feel it's weight
The flute will serve, it knows its role
In sustaining your misguided goal
A pedlar's life, caveat emptor
Until reversed forevermore
When reparation befits your crime
Until then roam, 'til the end of time."

He sighed and returned the flute to the depths of his coat, then lit a thin cigarette of hand-rolled tobacco. He smoked it slowly and stared at the flickering lights of the town below. He didn't know its name. What did it matter? It was always the same. Day in, day out. His hands calloused from gripping the cart handles as it bounced and buckled over potholes and puddles, high roads and low. *Wander, thief, that is your fate.* Wander. What else was there when he'd tried everything to elude the curse? No matter how far he ran, how many beds he warmed, or how many taverns he tried to lose himself in, when he woke it was always the same. A road. The cart. Always the damned cart.

And so, *carry your greed*, he'd learned to make the best of it.

The cigarette's tip crackled and flared with every drag, making Calypso's eyes appear a deeper shade of amber, and exaggerating the sly smile that spread across his face.

Calypso was right; sleep came very easy that night.

━

A veil of dew had settled across his coat and bedding overnight. It twinkled in the thin morning sunshine as he rose and brushed himself down. In the hush of early dawn, he could hear very faint sounds of life from the township, borne upward by the valley's natural acoustics. The dull clang of cow bells from fringe dwelling livestock; the clip-clop of hooves on cobble accompanied by a honking bray; a hearty exchange of greeting—milkman? baker?—between early morning traders.

Calypso opened his knapsack and withdrew a razor, a knob of soap, and a cracked piece of glass. He set about lathering up his face and shaved clean a week's worth of stubble. When he was done he checked himself in the glass. Void of facial hair, he could be any age. His high cheekbones and angular nose offset the tumbling curls that fell about his collar, the same intense colour as his eyes. He smiled at his reflection—a different smile from last night. This one was as warm and welcoming as a hot stew on a cold winter's night. It reached his eyes and gave the creases around them a charming character. For the finishing touch he put on his broad-brimmed felt hat and adjusted it to a rakish angle. Perfect.

Calypso rolled up his bedding, put his knapsack on his back, seized up the handles of his cart and began his journey down the winding trail to the town below.

By the time he reached the grasslands of the valley, the sun had risen fully and placed its warm hands on his shoulders. He passed through lavender-filled fields that rippled in the breeze like a purple perfumed sea. They gave way to agricultural plains neatly divided by wooden fences; freshly tilled soil in some, crops of dark-leaved vegetables filling others. Farming folk. Good. They were always the easiest to—

"Ho, there!" A cheerful voice from behind interrupted his thoughts. He turned to see a chestnut horse making its way along the path toward him. Astride it sat a ruddy-cheeked youth in the check-shirt uniform of countryfolk.

"Ho, yourself, my good man," replied Calypso. "A magnificent morning for a ride, I warrant."

The youth beamed at Calypso in the manner of a boy unused to being referred to as a man. "Yessir, although more work than pleasure. I've got a rambling of sheep to corral before lunchtime."

"Ah, no doubt work for only the most experienced of riders," Calypso nodded respectfully. The youth sat up a little straighter on his mount, puffed out his chest.

"Tell me," Calypso continued. "What town am I about to reach? I've got a cart loaded with quality wares I'm eager to sell. Do you think a weary pedlar will be well received?"

"It's Lavendale, sir. And yes, I'd think so," the boy leaned forward on his horse to better see the cart. "We don't get many travelling folks out our way, that's for sure."

"Excellent. A mile further? Maybe two?

"No more than a mile, sir. But mayhap it will feel longer pushing a cart as heavy as yours. I've got some cornbread." The boy reached into a saddlebag and produced a cloth-wrapped hunk of bread. "I'd be happy to break it with you. Some extra sustenance for your journey perhaps?"

Calypso was briefly touched by the boy's gesture. He couldn't remember the last time he'd been offered anything with such open generosity. The flatlanders jeered at the mountainfolk's simple ways, but they'd never offered him a crumb he hadn't had to … play for. "Very kind, I thank you, but keep it for your toil. Lavendale, you say?" Calypso fixed the boy with his most winning smile. "You've been most helpful. And now you're going to forget you ever saw me as you go on your sheep-wrangling way. *Do you understand?*" He locked his amber eyes on the boy's grey ones as he spoke the last words, holding them with an intense stare.

"Yes. I never saw you. Good day." The boy's face was slack as he dug his heels into his horse's flank and steered it down a narrow path between two fields.

Calypso pushed his cart onwards, its wooden wheels turning smoothly on the pressed dirt road that led towards town. He whistled as he walked now, a jolly tune that took him all the way to where the narrow, cobbled streets of Lavendale began. He wheeled his cart between them, whistling his way past the curious stares from onlookers until he reached the town square—a wide cobblestoned space framed by a collection of shopfronts, an inn, and several shuttered-window dwellings.

He guided his cart to the centre of the square, and removed the sacking cover with a flourish. He felt the eyes of the town on him as he went about his theatre. It wouldn't be long before they started gathering around his cart. It was all so predictable—the towns might change, but the people never did. It always started with a nonchalant inspection of his cart. A picking up and setting down of various items. An indifferent query as to price. A clucking of the tongue.

But he knew how to clinch the deal. And maybe, just maybe, this time would be the last.

While he waited for the townsfolk to decide who would be the first to come forward, giving unspoken permission for everyone else to follow suit, he warmed them up with a song.

"Oh, life on the road can be hard on your soul
When it rains in your heart, and the sun burns a hole
In the memory of the girl you loved long ago
No matter how far you travel, she won't let you go."

His voice rang out honest and true across the square, as he went about arranging his wares. It was weighted with the right amount of emotion, and it wasn't long before the first of the womenfolk hovered around his cart. They were joined by others and soon a bustling throng inspected his merchandise.

"Good people of Lavendale," Calypso spread his arms wide. "Welcome to my humble cart. I have heard tell far and wide of your generous hearth and industrious heart. Perhaps you might permit a travelling man a little business as he passes through."

"'Ow much for this 'ere kettle?" A sharp-faced woman brandished the copper kettle and thrust it at him.

"What do you want with a kettle, Bernette?" said a plump woman next to her. "Emille fashioned you a perfectly good one last year. Makes a fine brew, it does."

"My dear lady," Calypso addressed Bernette directly. "While your Emille is no doubt a gifted smith, I venture you've never tasted tea from a copper kettle such as this. It's like drinking warmed nectar." He met her gaze. His amber eyes flared.

"I'll take it." Bernette hid the kettle under her apron, and glared about fiercely as if anyone dare challenge her. "I saw it first. 'Ow much?"

"But, of course you did, my dear," Calypso's voice oozed sensuality in her ear. "The price is ..."

Bernette didn't even balk. She opened her purse and dug about, then thrust a collection of coins into Calypso's palm and hurried back through the square, clutching the kettle. Nobody noticed her leave; they were too enthralled with the pedlar's wares.

"These doorknobs, full set are they?" asked a ginger-bearded man.

"But of course. Enhance any set of drawers they will, sir."

"Eh," the man grunted, "What's your best price, pedlar?"

"My *only* price," replied Calypso, "is two hundred madeiros."

"Two *hundred*?" blustered the man, his face taking on the same hue as his beard. "I've never heard such a—"

"Two hundred madeiros," repeated Calypso evenly. "A fair price, wouldn't you agree?" He locked his eyes on the man's until they cleared with a new understanding.

"Yes, very fair. Very fair indeed, thank you." The man produced an assortment of coins from a leather pouch and began counting them out. "Eh, I've only got seventy, it seems," he shot Calypso a desperate look. "Would you take a credit note? I've got to have those knobs." His voice took on a wheedling tone and he seized Calypso's arm. As he did, his coat shifted to reveal an expensive-looking pocket watch on a golden fob.

"I tell you what," said Calypso, "seventy madeiros, and your timepiece, and we'll shake on the deal."

The man pumped Calypso's arm rapidly, before tearing the fob from his buttonhole and shoving it along with the money at the pedlar. He disappeared into the crowd holding the doorknobs to his chest as protectively as if he held a newborn baby.

And so it went on. One by one, the items on Calypso's cart disappeared. Occasionally a spat broke out between townsfolk as they scrambled to claim ownership over sealing wax or boot laces or a card of buttons. Calypso smoothed them over with ease.

"Young lady," he said to a stooped crone who had snatched the buttons away from another. "Perhaps these hair ribbons would be more to your liking? The blue would look bewitching against your peachy complexion, if I may be so bold."

"Oh, you," said the woman, blushing and flapping her hands at him. "Young lady, indeed!" She made the mistake of eyeing him coquettishly from under her bonnet, before handing over her entire pocketbook in payment for the ribbons. Her friend did the same for the buttons.

When everything down to the last bottle of boiled sweets had been sold, and the frenzy that had gripped the townsfolk subsided, he knew it was time to make his exit.

He doffed his hat, and made a low sweeping bow to the crowd. "People of Lavendale, it has been an absolute pleasure. I thank you humbly for your business, and I bid you good day." He picked up the handles, and began pushing his now empty cart through the square.

He navigated the laneways and side streets until he reached the other side of town, allowing himself a sigh of relief as the narrow roads gave way to the wider stretch of open road surrounded by pastures. The craggy ranges he had spotted the night before beckoned to him from the horizon.

It was close to midnight by the time he'd scaled the highest peak. His boots had slipped and scraped on the loose shale path that snaked slowly upwards, and his neckerchief was dark with sweat, but with a lighter load the going was always easier. He found a sheltered spot to pass the night, and once again shook out his bedroll. Again, he uncovered his cart. Last night it had been laden with wares, but now it was bare.

He reached into the purple lining of his coat and withdrew his alicorn flute. He unwrapped it, put it to his lips and blew. This time, he thought bitterly. This time. The tune it played was not the fevered music of last night, nor was it the mournful melody that had followed. This time, it was a series of short, sharp notes that varied in pitch. Some were so low they could have been mistaken for the sighing of the harvest breeze through the valley; at other times they reached a strident note audible to nothing that was human.

But, as Calypso played, a succession of items flew through the darkness from the direction of Lavendale to take up their place on the pedlar's cart. The copper kettle arrived first, landing with a clanging bump on the cart's wooden tray. It was followed by the doorknobs, the mortar and pestle, the hair ribbons, the jars of ointments, and so on.

When the last item had returned, he sighed heavily, pulled the cover back over the cart and tucked in his wares. A place for everything and everything in its place. Then Calypso Reeves returned his flute to the lining of his jacket, lit one of his hand-rolled cigarettes, and stared off into the lands that lay ahead. Somewhere over the horizon lay another town. He didn't know its name. But what did it matter? Nothing really mattered anymore. He bellowed his frustration into the night.

As the echoes died away, Calypso's stomach growled with the stirrings of hunger, and he remembered the youth's offer of cornbread that morning. Thinking of the exchange, something besides hunger began to stir inside him. He turned it over in his mind, the forgotten cigarette winking in the darkness.

And then a fragment of the warlock's curse crashed into his mind like a thunderclap:

A pedlar's life, caveat emptor
Until reversed forevermore
When reparation befits your crime
Until then roam, 'til the end of time.

When reparation befits your crime. Sharing. Giving. Had the means to lift the curse been there the whole time? Instead of deceiving people into buying his wares, had he simply to give them away? It was the only thing he hadn't tried.

Calypso Reeves leaped to his feet. No time for sleep. He seized up his bedroll and stuffed it into his cart. Then, with moonlight as his witness, he steered his cart down the moss-flanked path that snaked down into the next valley. He gathered speed as he went, until he was running, bootheels kicking up clods of soil, his cart bumping along in front.

He would reach the next town as soon as he could. There he would give his wares away to the townsfolk, every last item. And maybe, this time, they wouldn't come back.

The energy of this thought carried him through the night until the thin light of early dawn probed at the landscape with golden fingers, to reveal the dark outline of trees. Their spindly, outstretched branches swayed in the breeze like the arms of capering skeletons against the morning pale.

With the light came a clarity of thought the midnight hours had rendered mute. If he were to give his wares away, how long would he last? He had coin in his pocket from Lavendale, of course, but that was the sum total of his wealth. He'd never considered saving his spoils before; he'd never needed to. There was always another town to fleece. And in between there was ale, and gambling, and women. As much and as often as he wanted.

He lay the handles of the cart on the ground and rubbed his hands together slowly, the callouses bumping against each other like old friends. He would need money to settle down at his time of life. Enough for a house, or perhaps a small shop, or a farm … work. Yes, he would have to work once he absolved himself of the warlock's curse.

He squinted ahead to a where a far-off curl of smoke heralded the next town. Perhaps one more round of the cart, just to build up a nest egg. Maybe two. Yes, but why stop there?

He picked up the handles of his cart and began pushing it onwards to where the smoke curl beckoned. He whistled as he walked, a jaunty tune the breeze carried ahead as if to announce his arrival. Calypso's amber eyes gleamed in the morning light.

Rebecca Fraser is an Australian author based on Victoria's Mornington Peninsula. Her short stories, poems, and flash fiction have appeared in various anthologies, magazines, and journals since 2007, and her first novel *Curtis Creed and the Lore of the Ocean* is due for release in 2018 through IFWG Australia. To provide her muse with life's essentials she supplements by freelance copywriting for the corporate world, however her true passion lies in storytelling. rebeccafraser.wordpress.com

A Fair Wind Off Baracoa

Robert Porteous

All roads lead to Baracoa. If you wait long enough, everyone passes through. Everyone you ever wanted to see … and, well, plenty more you'd never want to see again.

The evening tide had brought in the *Montserrat*, and Captain Nevis with it. Black Nevis to his crew, on account of his foul moods, but Ruby wanted to see him very much.

Nevis was waiting in the Governor's Ruin, the finest suite in Crack Jenny's Teahouse. The door was ajar and she peered through, steeling herself. He was nothing fine to look at. A bloated travesty of a man, all rigged up in his captain's finery—his long blue peacoat garlanded about with so much gold braid you might take him for an Admiral of the Fleet rather than captain of a scruffy merchantman.

Putting on a sweet smile, she backed in, pushing the door open. The parrot on her shoulder squawked in alarm, forced to duck under the lintel. She pirouetted round, juggling her tray, glass clinking against bottle.

"Who're you?" Nevis turned to watch her come in, his frown darkening. "Where are those girls I ordered?"

"I'm Ruby, sir." She walked across, setting her skirts aswirl with each flick of her hips. "They've taken ill."

"What, both of them?"

Ruby shrugged, "That's how it falls, sometimes, with women's issues."

They were red-headed twins, of course—everyone knew about Nevis' proclivities. Crack Jenny's Teahouse had a name for procuring whatever her clients demanded, with little regard for the merchandise, an ill-repute that drew the likes of Black Nevis to her door rather than somewhere more salubrious. Ruby had intercepted them in the corridor, pale faced and trembling. Hopefully, by now, they were far from here with her coin in their pockets.

Nevis' face darkened, gathering himself for some bluster.

"I've brought you some rum," she purred, leaning forward to set down the tray, her blouse falling open.

Distracted, Nevis' eyes dropped to the decanter, the rum as red as Ruby's hair, with evident suspicion. "I didn't ask for the top shelf. I won't be paying extra."

"With Crack Jenny's compliments, Captain. From her own cabinet." Crack Jenny wasn't aware of her generosity yet. With any luck, she wouldn't come to till morning, nursing a sore head. "Amaretto cherries steeped in the finest Baracoan rum. But first, let me get you comfortable." She sat on a stool opposite and took up his left boot, pushing a bare foot into his groin for leverage, letting her skirt ride up her thighs. She pulled the first grav-boot off with a jerk and felt his crotch firm beneath her instep. Good, his tastes extended beyond skinny young redheads. Her business might go a little easier.

"You be careful of that other—" he began, but Ruby had already slapped the neural-servo release with her palm and untoggled the prosthetic lock. "You know your way around," he admitted grudgingly.

She set the artificial leg down. A writhing mass of fibres churned at the stump. The parrot cocked his head and watched them retract. "My daddy, Kaiton rest his soul, was a merchant marine. He survived the wars, but he ended up more mech than man. I'd help him get dressed."

The parrot flew across to Nevis' chair, landing clumsily on the armrest.

"He's called Calico. He used to be my daddy's bird."

"Is he AI?" asked Nevis, watching the parrot sidle up to him.

Ruby spread her arms and laughed. "Do I look like I could afford an AI? No, he's just a dumb mech. Tell him your name and he'll talk to you."

"I'm partial to parrots," admitted Nevis. "Had one as ship's mascot when I was in Fleet." He turned to the bird, "I'm Captain Nevis, of the *Montserrat*."

"Aye, Aye, Cap'n Nevis!" squawked Calico, bobbing its head. It leaned in towards Nevis' face and twisted its head to inspect him closely with one green eye. Its pupil pinched in and then dilated again. "There's a fair wind off Baracoa!"

"I think he likes you," Ruby said, smiling. With practiced deftness, she squeezed half a blue Baracoan lime into a glass and topped it up with golden cane syrup and ruby amaretto rum, careful to keep the colours separate. "There you are, house special," she leaned forward to hand it to Nevis, watching as his eyes slid down to her chest again. "That'll stir your blood."

"Let me check it first." He pulled back one sleeve of his coat, revealing a strip of dark crystal set into his arm. He dipped a finger into the glass and tapped some of the liquor onto the crystal. Calico cocked his head to watch. The fluid wicked into the analyser, a light within flickered amber then a row of green lit along its length.

"No need," said Ruby, handing him a swizzle-stick coated with a strong hypnotic. "No one tampers with our bottles." She looked on with affected nonchalance as he stirred, held the glass up to see the colours swirl, and took a draught.

He'd be asleep within the hour and eminently suggestible in the interim.

"You're lucky, being a spacer." She rubbed at the ring on her finger. Her eyes took on a far-off expression, as if she were looking straight through Nevis, toward the *Montserrat* floating in orbit behind him. Nevis took another swig of the rum and reached for her, pulling her onto his lap. "Now, my lovely. We've some business—"

With a sudden flare, a holo-image of two girls appeared, hovering over Ruby's hand. They clung to each other, long red hair cascading over their plain white dresses. "Oh," she gasped, stepping back off Nevis' lap and frantically twisting at the ring. "I didn't mean … I was just thinking of never seeing my sisters again."

"Pretty young things," said Nevis leaning forward. "Where did you say they were?"

"My uncle took them to Cayenne, when our mother died." Ruby rekindled the hologram and sighed deeply as the little image reappeared. "I can't afford passage, so I don't expect I'll ever see them again."

"I'm on my way to Cayenne," said Nevis. "After we take on a load of lanthanides in Puerto Cabello. We're loading stores here, for their mines."

"Oh," said Ruby breathlessly. "Perhaps you could take me with you." She stared down at the girls. "They're twins, so at least they have each other. But me ... I'd be so very grateful."

"Ah, yes," Nevis said, licking his lips, his eyes fixed on the siblings. "Twins, eh? I expect they'd be rather grateful too."

"How could we ever make it up to you?" Ruby asked, extinguishing the hologram, her hands clasped.

"I'm sure something ..." Nevis stifled a yawn "... could be arranged." He blinked wearily and stared at his empty glass. "This rum has a bit of fight in it."

"A bit. A bit of a fight," screeched Calico. "All hands to the laser cannons!"

"Shush, Calico!" Ruby stood and unwound Nevis' fingers from the glass. Still holding his hand, she put the glass down and slipped her blouse off one shoulder.

"Come to bed." She pulled on his hand, one eyebrow cocked teasingly. "Let me show you how grateful I can be."

"Captain Nevis!" Ruby shook him by the shoulder. "You have to wake up."

Nevis lifted himself onto an elbow, rubbing his bleary eyes with the back of a hand. Ruby pulled on the navy peacoat over not much else and went to the door.

"There's a boy. Says you're needed urgently on the *Montserrat*." She dropped to kneel in front of him, holding his prosthetic leg. "You'd better get dressed."

"I told them I wasn't to be disturbed!" He rubbed his head and watched as she buckled on the leg. "What happened last night?"

"You were wonderful," Ruby smiled, passing him his trousers.

"I don't remember a thing." He grabbed her roughly by the chin and leered greedily. "Damn rum. We'll just have to do it over."

There was a firm knock at the door. "A moment, dammit!" called Nevis, standing and buttoning his shirt. He stopped to stare at a red plasteel travelling chest on the floor by the door. "What's that doing there?"

"It's mine. You sent for it last night," she said, pulling on her skirt.

Nevis turned back to look at her, frowning.

"You said you'd take me with you. To Cayenne."

"Cayenne," said Nevis blankly. He blinked, then nodded. "Yes, Cayenne. To reunite you with your sweet young sisters."

Another hard knock. Nevis opened the door sharply. The young man outside was caught in the act of knocking again. He pulled his arm back and saluted smartly.

"Ensign Torbeck, sir! XO requests your presence on the bridge!" He glanced nervously over Nevis' shoulder at Ruby. "The cargo's loaded and the … *customers*," he hesitated over the word, his eyes flicking back to Ruby, "have requested that we dispatch the *Montserrat* with all possible haste."

"I ordered that I not be disturbed," said Nevis icily. "I'll come up to the ship when I'm good and ready!" He moved to close the door but the ensign stepped forward.

Nevis drew breath, clearly fit to explode but the ensign interjected desperately, "Sir, there's a message. A threat to the *Montserrat*. You *have* to catch the morning hook-tide, sir."

"Don't you ever," Nevis bellowed, "tell me what I have to do!" He elbowed the boy out of the way and strode down the corridor. The ensign regained his balance and scurried after him.

Ruby looked at her travelling chest and sighed. "No, not at all, gentlemen. I'll carry it myself." She hefted it up by a handle on one end and balanced it on her shoulder. "Come on, Calico, we've got a shuttle to catch.

"Time and tide wait for no one."

‌⸺❦⸺

Dawn was concocting its own ethereal cocktail. The heavens above the space port were turning sky blue over lemon, blushed with apricot. But it was still cold, and Ruby was glad of the heavy peacoat.

Three giant tenders lay in a line at the foot of the port's rail gun, waiting to be launched. The gun's rails were perfectly straight, tapering off to invisibility somewhere just above where the sun would shortly appear. Clusters of cargo-bots and ground crew in mech suits laboured in and out of the tenders, finishing the loading.

The *Montserrat's* shuttle was the last of the three. Ruby paused at the bottom of the entry ramp, feeling more than seeing its bulk looming above her.

"Miz, can I help you with that?" It was the ensign, Torbeck.

She handed over her chest and stretched her neck, glad to be rid of the weight. "Thank you, that's a kindness. And it's Ruby."

"Jacmel." He hefted the chest onto his own shoulder with ease. "Actually, everyone on board calls me Jac." He turned and began climbing the ramp. "Come on. Mustn't keep the captain w—"

His words were drowned out by a rising scream as the next tender up the line tested its engines. They flared orange, sharpened to a hard blue then winked out as quickly. Ruby was buffeted by the blast of warm air. Jac had disappeared into the shuttle so she pulled Calico tight to her chest and followed him.

Captain Nevis was already in the officer's cabin. He had pride of place, in a high-backed pilot's chair in front of the main screens. An empty honour—the shuttle's computer would fly the arc. Had to, as hitting the sky-hook was a matter of split seconds.

Jac sat behind Nevis and pointed Ruby into the seat beside him. She made a show of tangling the webbing and smiled in mock-relief as Jac sprang over to help her. Nevis remained hunched over the screens and gave no sign of paying attention.

There was a rumble as the first of the shuttles was fired down the rail.

"We'll be going in a few seconds. You'll have to brace yourself. The acceleration is pretty intense for a landlubber."

A second rumble, louder. Ruby pursed her lips in concern.

"Don't worry. It'll be over in less than a minute. Just remember to breathe." Jac smiled encouragingly.

There was a soft beep, the cabin lighting went amber and Ruby was thrust back into her seat. Calico pressed hard into her stomach. She closed her eyes and relaxed, counting out the seconds in time to her breathing.

"You see, it wasn't so bad." Jac, pale-faced, had forced a smile. "But best leave your harness on. We'll dock with the sky-hook in about ten minutes." Behind them, the reaction engines cut in with a stutter.

The hooks were tethered to a big asteroid in orbit a thousand kloms up, spinning round like the spokes of a wheel. A hook aligned with the space port twice a day—the hook-tides, the spacers called them. It was the only thing that made inter-planetary trade affordable. That and the Trajan Pinch, the trans-dimensional portal in orbit even further out.

The tender had matched speeds so perfectly that the hook seemed to drop straight down from the sky above. They docked with a jolt and a rattle of magnetic clamps. The sensation of gravity was restored with a jerk as the hook snatched them skyward. Not long now and she would be aboard the *Montserrat* and through the Pinch.

If all went well ...

"Smooth as silk." Jac unbuckled his harness and reached over to help with hers. "Why are you looking so serious?"

Careless! She groped for an excuse, opening her eyes wide. "Do you think the pirates will come back? The ones who ambushed the *Les Abymes* here last week. If they can take down an imperial cruiser, what chance do we have?"

Nevis had not seemed to be paying them any attention. But, at the mention of pirates, he spun his chair round to face them. "Pirates? Petty muggers, more like. They popped out of the Pinch straight after the *Abymes* came through and fired off a few torpedoes. As soon as they saw what they were up against, they turned tail." His face twisted into a sneer, "By now, they'll be hiding their sorry arses half a galaxy away."

"But they crippled her," Ruby protested.

"A lucky shot. Hit both main thrusters, somehow." Nevis shrugged dismissively. "It was all a coincidence. There's no way they could have known ..."

"Known what?"

"Nothing." He frowned, "I mean, they couldn't have known they were taking on a cruiser."

"So, you don't believe that the *Abymes* is a treasure ship?" asked Ruby.

"A cruiser carrying treasure?" Nevis' faced folded back into his familiar sneer. "Bunkum. Where did you hear that?"

"It was all over Baracoa, Captain. They say that's what the pirates were after."

"You sharecroppers are too gullible. Look, all these stories about treasure and piracy are sheer fantasy. It's just petty thievery, wildly exaggerated by the entertainment vids."

Jac looked shocked. "But sir! Not the Scarlet Corsair. I've seen vids about the ships she's captured. And none of the crew harmed. She must be real."

"Listen to yourself," laughed Nevis. "Any fool can see she's a rouged-up synth straight out of the romance feeds." He turned away, chuckling, "As if a woman could take a ship single-handed!"

⊶═

They were met on the *Montserrat* by the executive officer, a severe looking woman flanked by two armed escorts. All three saluted smartly as the ship's computer piped the three-note alert to the crew, 'Captain on board'.

"I'll deal with you on the bridge in ten," snarled Nevis at the XO. "I'm going to unfrock." He pushed past the escorts. "And put that Miz in my cabin once I'm dressed."

The XO fixed the ensign with a cold stare. "What were you thinking, Torbeck, bringing her along?"

Jac cleared his throat nervously, "Cap'n's orders, mam."

"And you, girl, got a name?"

"Ruby, mam."

"Well, Ruby, I run a tight ship. Tight does not include scantily clad young women. Give me any grief and I'll flush you out the nearest airlock." She peered at Ruby more closely. "Why *are* you here?"

Ruby wrung her hands, "I ... I always dreamed of going into space."

"Dreamed of being a captain's whore, more like. Well, you should've been more careful what you wished for." The XO turned to the escorts. "Take her to the Captain's suite and guard the door."

Jac picked up the travelling chest and moved to follow the escorts.

"Wait," called the XO. "What's that? Torbeck, did you screen it before bringing it on board?"

"No," stuttered Jac. "There wasn't time."

"You must learn to make time, Ensign." Her tone promised unpleasant lessons ahead. "Open it," she ordered Ruby. "Tip it all out."

Ruby bit back a protest and opened the chest, tipping it on its side. There wasn't much. A few clothes, some lacy underwear and cosmetics, her vid tablet. A cylindrical perfume spray rolled across to stop against the XO's boot. The XO toed it disdainfully.

"It's perfume," explained Ruby, on her knees, reaching to snatch it back. "It's expensive."

"No," said the XO, sniffing the air. "I think you'll find it's cheap."

"Clean this mess up," she ordered. "That parrot, is it AI?"

"Hardly," said Ruby wearily. "Just a dumb mech."

"Who's a pretty boy?" squawked Calico.

Nevis' cabin was well-appointed and tidy. His discarded frock uniform tumbled over the foot of the bed, the only thing out of place. Ruby waited to hear the door lock before turning to the large screen console. She lifted Calico up to the desktop.

"See what you can make of that."

The parrot bobbed his head for a moment then said in Nevis' gruff tones, "Ship, activate secondary control console."

"Authorisation required," responded the ship's computer. A scanner popped up from the console.

"Captain Nevis of the *Montserrat*." Calico said, putting his eye to the scanner.

"Biometric identification confirmed."

"I'm in," squawked Calico.

"Nice work with Nevis' retina."

"Too easy. He couldn't take his eye off me. Who's a pretty boy?" Calico squawked triumphantly then adopted Nevis' voice again, "Ship, bring up the bridge on vid. No visuals or voice from this console."

"Good. I'll eavesdrop on the XO's briefing while you work out how to control the ship from here." Ruby emptied the chest onto the floor. "But first, I'm going to dress for work."

She pushed the clothes to one side and pressed a hidden control. The chest collapsed into a heap of plasteel slabs. She picked up her vid screen and spoke a code word that activated a morphic radiator. Beneath its rays, the plasteel began to warp and flex like a waking sleeper. Some of the mnemonic alloy plates rolled into cylinders, others stretched and buckled to form a helmet and breastplate.

"Bridge on screen," squawked Calico.

Ruby came across to watch, stripping off her clothes. "Eyes front, old man."

Calico made a show of hiding his head behind a wing, complaining in Nevis' voice, "Nothing I haven't seen before."

"Stop being Nevis," said Ruby as she sprayed adhesive foam from her 'expensive perfume' over her arms and chest. "It's creepy." She began to apply the hardened, brick-red armour.

On screen, the XO was standing stiffly while the rest of the bridge crew kept their heads down over their consoles.

"Captain on the bridge," announced the ship.

"Right. What's so important?" growled Nevis, frowning, his eyes sweeping the bridge for anything out of place.

"Pirates, sir," said the XO, chin up. "The Fleet comms-link at Cayenne has been compromised. Routine maintenance found evidence of a pirate fibre-tap."

"All of *Les Abymes'* reports to Fleet went through Cayenne," Nevis cursed.

"They'll know our every move, sir. We have to move quickly."

"Damn," said Nevis angrily. "This was meant to be a milk run. What's our status?"

"The cargo's been transferred from *Les Abymes*, all in plasteel pods. I reckon there must be 8,000 tonnes of pure lanthanides."

Nevis gave a low whistle. "So that's what's got everyone so excited. That's more than the whole Empire uses in a year. It must be worth a fortune."

"Eight thousand, two hundred tonnes at 130,000 credits per kilo, to be precise," murmured Ruby. "A trillion credits, all neatly packaged to go."

"We've welded it into the cargo bay, sir," added the XO. "Even if we do get boarded, they'll never get it off the ship before Fleet arrives."

"And where, precisely, is the fuckin' Fleet now?"

"They're on their way but they're still a day from the nearest Pinch. We're supposed to get out of here and meet them there."

"A day? If someone's coming after us with torpedos, I could use a couple of dreadnoughts in close convoy right now."

The XO shrugged apologetically. "At least *Les Abymes* has sent us two units of marines for protection. We've got fifty space marines and all their gear bivouacking in Hold 2. They're pretty cramped. Permission to bring half of them across to Hold 1."

"Do it. Just keep them out of my way." The captain turned to the main screens. "Helm, prepare to move us to the Pinch."

"Qué desmadre! Fifty marines!" cursed Ruby, pulling on the last of the armour and slapping it down hard to make sure it was properly bonded. "This print-on-demand armour can take a couple of shots but it won't last a fire fight."

"We've got to call the *Corsair* off," squawked Calico. "If they try to board, it'll be a bloodbath. And then we have to figure a way to get off this ship."

"Bajo and his team should have boarded the Pinch by now. Can you send a tight-band message there without the bridge noticing? Tell them to relay a warning to the *Corsair*."

There was a pause before Calico replied, "Bajo confirms. He's taken control of the Pinch and is standing by."

"You can always depend on Bajo. Can you locate the shuttles?"

"Two small shuttles and the tender in Hold 1. Two military shuttles in Hold 2. But we'd have to get past the marines."

"Escape pods?"

"Some on every level. But drop one of those and the bridge will light up with alarms. Hardwired, so I can't stop it. The pods aren't powered so they'd scoop us back up before Bajo could get near."

"Well, if we can't get off alive," said Ruby slowly, "we'll just have to persuade everyone else to leave."

"Sure. And leave us with the treasure. Very likely." Calico tried to snort but ended up making a strangled sneezing noise. "Did you happen to pack a tactical nuke in your cosmetic kit?"

"No, but I've an idea to frighten them off. How much control of the ship do we have from this console?"

"Not much. Captain's console is for comms, not helm."

"Can you hack into the engines from here?"

"Yes, or at least the fusion drive. But I can't recognise anything that looks like attitude controls, so I can't steer her."

"What's our heading?"

"Towards the Pinch, just ticking over on reaction thrust. They won't risk using the fusion drive so close."

"So, let's give them a fright and make them show us where the attitude controls are. Ignite the fusion drive, full thrust."

"But cap'n, not from cold! They'll go unstable and either burn out or shut down."

"Precisely. But not before they've given us a kick like Kaiton Almighty."

"Cap'n, I don't think this is a good idea, not so close to the Pinch."

"Noted, Mister Calico. Now ignite when ready." She flexed her gloved fingers. "I'm going out to have a chat to our guards and borrow a couple of slug-chuckers. Don't forget to watch for the attitude controls."

The whole bridge rocked. The sensation was as if the Montserrat had just tipped up its nose. Anyone not harnessed was thrown to the back. Nevis fell on his arse. It took the metagrav a few moments to adjust and restore a proper sense of 'down'.

"Helm! What the hell are you playing at?" roared Nevis, clambering to his feet.

"Nothing, sir." Helm threw both hands up in the air as evidence.

"Warning. Fusion drive is at full thrust," said the ship.

"Who the hell's driving my ship!" shouted Nevis. "Cut the engines!"

"I can't," said Helm. "They're not responding."

"Captain," said the XO sharply, pointing at the image of the blue-lit ring on the main screen. "We're heading straight at the Pinch. We're going to hit it!"

"Damn and blast," swore Nevis, his eyes wide. "If we hit the Pinch while it's warping space, they'll see the flare in Puerto Cabello!"

"Helm," called the XO, "have you got attitude control?"

"Yes, mam."

"Then steer us clear."

It seemed as if the whole bridge crew were holding their collective breath, eyes glued to the main screen. Slowly, the Pinch ring began to move off centre.

Two floors below, Ruby and Calico watched equally intently.

"Kill the fusion drive, like it flared out," ordered Ruby, sticking two borrowed pistols into their holsters and bracing herself. "Did you get the steering controls?"

The fusion impulse cut out abruptly, throwing everyone forward.

"Aye, cap'n," said Calico, wings flared, metal claws scrabbling for balance. "Clear as daylight."

"Then kill all engines and thrusters," said Ruby, watching the growing consternation on the bridge.

"I've lost control," called the helmsman, punching frantically at his console. "Nothing's responding."

"It doesn't matter now," said Nevis, looking relieved. "We're not going to hit."

"No, wait, we're spinning," shouted the XO, staring at the screen. "Helm, what's our course?"

"Still on collision course, but slewing sideways. We're gonna hit the Pinch broadside."

"How long to impact?" demanded Nevis as the helmsman worked frantically at his console.

"Eight minutes and twelve seconds to impact," announced the *Montserrat* calmly. "Recommend immediate evasive action."

"I'm trying, you fool ship," yelled Nevis. "All hands abandon ship!"

—◆—

"**E**ight minutes," said Ruby running to the door. "I'll drag these guards into escape pods. Once the bridge clears, restore helm control. We'll finish this up there."

She entered the bridge at a run, Calico on her shoulder, wings spread for balance. She dropped him on the helm console.

"Status?" she demanded.

"Five minutes and forty-three seconds to impact," the *Montserrat* responded. "All remaining crew should move to the escape pods."

"Not you. Calico?"

"She's twisted almost halfway round. There's no time to turn her back, and I can't restart the fusion drive that quickly either." Calico bobbed his head in agitation. "We're not going to make it."

"I don't want you to bring her nose round. Straighten her up. We'll go through arse first." Ruby pulled off her helmet and ran her fingers through her red hair. "Ship, bring up the stern vid and get me a screen to the Pinch."

The Pinch filled the screen, rotating slowly. The starfield framed by the ring flickered and a sleek pocket-destroyer came into view. It glinted red in the light of an unseen sun.

The *Scarlet Corsair*.

Bajo's face came up on a side screen. "Cap'n Scarlet! Glad to see you. You're tumbling in bloody fast. I hope you've got a plan that doesn't end with us all tuning our harps at Kaiton's feet."

"Mister Calico has the helm. We're coming though breech. Set the timed charges and get out of there as soon as we're through. We'll see you on the other side."

"One way or another!" Bajo agreed. His screen went dark.

Ruby stood behind Calico, feet apart, one hand behind her back, the other resting lightly on the butt of a pistol.

Every inch Captain Scarlet, the renowned corsair.

The Pinch swept towards them, expanding to fill the screen.

"One minute to impact."

"Take us through, Mister Calico. It's either more money than we ever dreamed of or we go straight to hell."

"You? The wench from the teahouse!"

There was a sharp crack and Ruby was slammed in the shoulder. She pitched forward, dropping to take cover behind the helm, spinning round, her pistols in her hands.

"I'll kill you, you poxy rogue!" spat Nevis, firing wide. "You're stealing my ship!"

"As if a woman could take a ship single-handed," Ruby said calmly, taking a careful shot. Nevis staggered back, his shoulder bloodied. "I merely found this ship abandoned and claimed salvage." She fired another shot, knocking the pistol from Nevis' hand.

He fell to his knee, scrabbling for the weapon. Picking it up with his left hand, he aimed at the helm.

"Drop your weapon or I drill the parrot. Better we all die than you get my ship."

Ruby stood slowly, her pistol aimed directly at Nevis.

He laughed. "You don't scare me. You never harm a soul."

"I think you'll find that story has been wildly exaggerated by the entertainment vids," Ruby said coldly.

Nevis's eyes widened. He opened his mouth as if to protest but Ruby fired before he could say a word. He slumped forward, his pistol falling from limp fingers.

***

"Bajo docking now," announced Calico. "The Pinch set to detonate in five minutes."

"Bring the fusion drive back on line and get us out of here, Mister Calico," said Ruby, rolling her bruised shoulder. "I understand it's very spectacular when a pinch destabilises but I'd like to watch from a safe distance."

"It was a clever call, cap'n," observed Calico as the ring receded in the stern vid. "But how did you know they'd try and ship the hoard out on the *Montserrat*? Why not bring in a dreadnought?"

"Because even a grifter like Nevis would be cheaper." She sighed. "And Fleet is run by accountants these days."

"Their loss. A sweet trillion credit loss, to be precise."

"What'll you do with your share?"

"I've an eye on moving to a bigger body—something with opposable thumbs. What about you, cap'n?"

"It's not about the money, Mister Calico. It never was."

She moved to stand behind the helm. Silently, the star field warped in and released. A rainbow corona flashed and writhed where the Pinch had been.

"All I ask is a fast ship, a fair wind at my back, and no man my master."

Rob Porteous is a Canberra writer who isn't very good at making things up. Accordingly, this story was inspired by the mysterious 16th century pirate, the Red Lady, famed for cunningly taking ships single-handed through guile and subterfuge. All the names were inspired by real places and pirate people from the Caribbean and even Ruby's cocktail is an homage (i.e. blatant copy) of Hemingway's eponymous Cuban cocktail, the *Papa Doble* daiquiri!

A Widow's Worth

Louise Pieper

"A dead merchant means a rich widow," the Vod said.

The head of clan Emis-Var was as dark-haired and cold-hearted as all Varlords of the Nos. He stood with his three sons on the wide stone steps which descended from his mansion to the murky waters of the Else Canal. It was not as prestigious an address as those which fronted Babynyk's Grand Canal, but it had its benefits. The four men stared at the corpse of Micho Oblinka, which the tide had obligingly brought them.

"He took a new wife with the Flower Moon," the eldest Emis-Var son said. Jurik was broad and blunt, happy to mirror the Vod in all things.

"No heirs," Svan added, straightening his cuff. The second son was a thin blade sheathed in dark velvet. He looked bored, which was to say dangerous.

The Vod smiled. "Thirty years of ploughing a barren field, and dead within four moons of putting a new mare to harness."

The youngest son, Tomni, could picture Reba Oblinka's face—she'd graced several Varlord events because of her husband's wealth—but he couldn't imagine her mourning the old merchant's death. Rumour said her father had traded river pearls, flax cloth and his pretty daughter for Micho Oblinka's gold.

"But, Father—" he said, and their sire's hand lashed out, striking Tomni's mouth. He bit back a cry, as his brothers straightened, eyes gleaming.

"Respect," their father murmured. "Obedience."

"I am sorry, my Vod." His mouth flamed, but he knew better than to raise his hand to see if it bled. Their mother's death had brought an end to what the Vod called Tomni's cosseting. He'd seen seventeen Gift Moons; he must behave as a man. He raised his chin and said, "She'll not, with respect, yet know she's a widow."

"Exactly." Their father's eyes lit with avarice. "And being newly from Awlensk, she won't understand the Nos custom of pannyk."

Svan laughed, and put his hand to his sword hilt. "An easy matter then."

"I've only to snatch her before she learns of Micho's fate," Jurik said.

"You, brother?" Svan sneered.

"But he's still wet," Tomni protested. "You can't—" He snapped his mouth shut. Of course they could steal the widow. Steal her, and wed her, and bed her, before she knew she'd lost the protection of her husband. Without a witnessed repudiation, pannyk allowed a bride, or a groom for that matter, to be taken at sword point. But how often was a groom forced, when Babynyk's boys were trained in swordplay as soon as they could walk? Even Tomni could defend himself with the sword at his hip. His father had made sure of that.

"I wonder which of you will prove himself, and take the prize?" The Vod's gaze fell on his oldest son. "Jurik, go to the Oblinka residence. Find our widow, if she's there."

"And if she's not?" Jurik asked.

Their father bared his teeth. "Then steel yourself to give Svan your blessing." He tapped his second son's chest. "She may have realised Micho is missing, and gone to find him. Search his warehouses, and the mill in Ostez."

Svan swaggered up a step, checked the draw on his sword, and said, "Might as well bless me now, brother."

"You need more than boasts for pannyk." Jurik spat.

The Vod stepped between his two eldest sons and grasped their shoulders.

"You need speed and discretion. We've little enough advantage before we must report the corpse. Piko, saddle my sons' horses. Lark, fetch a vow-sayer."

The servants, waiting at the top of the canal steps, stiffened as he named them, and dashed off on their errands. Svan and Jurik followed, still arguing.

Tomni welcomed their bickering and their father's diversion. Let them chase after the widow, if only he might go to the Trovisk, and the bookshop hidden in its winding streets. The tips of his fingers brushed the note in his pocket. The bookseller had agreed to send him word as soon as Degza's *Alchemica* arrived. He'd waited patiently, but now that it was within his grasp further delay seemed intolerable.

His father tapped one thick knuckle against his mouth and considered Tomni.

"Where shall I send you? Perhaps ..."

"Perhaps, my Vod," Tomni said quickly, "she'll be in the Trovisk?"

"Shopping," the Vod said, with distaste. "Then look there." He strode off, dismissing his youngest son's chance of success. Tomni nodded. He'd search for her, of course, although he doubted he'd find the widow between the pages of his book.

"**I**'ve only one copy of Degza's *Alchemica*."

Tomni threaded between stacked tomes towards the bookseller's familiar voice. The lanes of the Trovisk were narrow and twisted, and the bookstore had once been a blind alley, now roofed and lined with shelves. The recessed stoop at the far end of the store was the only area wider than his outstretched hands. There sat the counter, and a door against which the bookseller leaned his chair. Tomni suspected it led to the old man's dwelling.

"Then sell me that copy." The customer's voice was low but insistent.

"He cannot," Tomni said. He hurried the last few steps, eager to secure his claim. "It's promised to me."

His rival for Degza's secrets whirled, and Tomni's hand went to his sword hilt. Then he stared, for not only was the customer a woman, with an indignant flush to her cheeks and hair as dark as shadowed sable, she was also Reba Oblinka.

"P-p-pan Oblinka." He took his hand from his sword and pressed it to his chest.

"Ser Emis-Var," she replied, politely enough, although she tucked her hands in the folds of her skirt and didn't cross her wrists at her waist, as she might have done for a higher-ranking Varlord.

"You study alchemy?" Tomni asked, and cursed himself for the surprise in his voice.

"Not at all, ser." Her face was a mask of courtesy, although he fancied her cheeks had grown pinker. "I merely have an affection for authors whose names begin with a 'D'."

It was a clever reply to his foolishness, and he sought a response to acknowledge it.

"Dal-Var, and Deshek, and Do—" He stumbled over Donola, whose early works on anatomy were respected, but whose later volumes had wandered down the dark paths of necromancy. "Do—Dovinzja. All are worthy of affection."

A smile flitted across her lips.

"I've waited three moons for the *Alchemica*," he added, by way of apology.

Her shoulders drooped. "Then I must do no less." Her gaze followed the book as it passed into his care. "I shall place my order, and go home to console myself with Dovinzja's *Botanica*."

She looked unhappy with the idea, and had more unhappiness to come. Someone must tell her of her husband's death. Someone must warn her of pannyk, so she knew her danger. She must understand before she went home and found Jurik waiting for her. That someone, Tomni realised, must be him. He ran his hand over the soft leather binding of the *Alchemica*. His fingers itched to turn the cover, touch the thick pages, learn their secrets.

"Pan Oblinka?" he said, before he could change his mind. "Would you let me make you a gift of the Degza, and spare me a few moments of your time?"

She stared from his face to the book. She had eyes like a forest; mottled green and brown, with flecks of sunlight glancing through the leaves.

"That is … kind," she said, as if to say suspicious. He held out the book, and she took it awkwardly, with one hand.

"Might we speak somewhere more—" Again, he faltered. "Secure?"

"Vaval?" she said.

The bookseller nodded, although he also frowned. He rose and opened the door, waving them through. Tomni's guess proved correct, although the old man's room greatly resembled his shop, for its walls were also book-lined. Only a bed, a simple kitchen with a table and stool, and a reading chair before the fireplace betrayed the room's domestic purpose. Vaval left the door ajar, and resumed his seat.

"Pan Oblinka, will you sit?" Tomni waved her to the soft chair, trying to imagine how he might tell her the news.

She perched on the edge of the seat, like a bird ready to startle into flight, and said, "Will you call me Reba?"

He dropped onto the stool, surprised by her offer. The impact jolted his next words from him. "Your husband's dead."

She raised a hand to her mouth, and he rushed on. "I'm sorry! He drowned. The tide brought him to the steps of my father's house."

"Micho hated water," she murmured, and Tomni found himself apologising again, although he scarcely knew for what. He had not chosen the manner of her husband's death.

"I don't wish to distress you, er, Reba, but do you understand the custom of pannyk?" She nodded and he huffed out a breath. "Then you realise you're in danger?"

"From you?" she asked.

His first impulse was to deny it, but a scholar must value truth.

"Yes. My father recognised the opportunity. He sent my oldest brother to your house, my second brother to your warehouses, and me to the Trovisk, to find you."

"How did you know I'd be at Vaval's?" she asked, and he marvelled at her calm.

"In truth," he said, "I came for the *Alchemica*."

"But you gift it to me." Her fingers pressed white against the leather of the book. "You don't try and drag me at sword point to a vow-making?"

"Would you rather I did?" he said, still smarting from the *Alchemica*'s loss, although he knew he shouldn't blame her. He bit his lip and flinched. He'd forgotten his father's blow.

She tipped her head, studying him, and tapped the book. "Do you think to woo me with it?"

"No!" He jerked to his feet, and she raised the *Alchemica* like a shield between them.

"No," he repeated, more moderately. "I think pannyk no better than rape. I wouldn't wed by force, and I wouldn't try to woo you before your husband's even cremated." Her eyes widened. "I'm sorry. I only thought Degza might bring comfort to you in the days to come."

"So you're—a friend?" she said, as if she didn't quite believe it. "Tomni, yes?"

He hadn't offered his name in return for hers, as any child knew to do. He hoped his nod hid his blushes. "You should hire a bodyguard. My father's not the only one who will covet the Oblinka fortune."

She stood, and her lips curved into a smile. Tomni forgot about her fortune, his father's anger, the *Alchemica*—forgot everything as her smile lit the sunshine in her eyes. She stepped closer, bringing the scent of tansy and pennyroyal with her. She raised her hand, and almost touched his bruised mouth, and he forgot the ache of it, lost in imagining the cool press of her fingers.

"It's wise advice, my friend," she said. "You also should take care." He watched her leave the bookseller's room, unable to think for the sudden roaring of his blood.

For three days, Svan and Jurik squabbled and scoured the city for the widow, but Reba Oblinka had disappeared. When she emerged—weighted by the tarnished silver trappings of grief—she had a new shadow.

Osken Marl, whose finances made him desperate enough to risk public censure, attempted to seize her as she left the cremation terrace. Perhaps he thought she'd be blinded by a widow's tears. Perhaps he hoped the mourning plate would slow her escape. In any case, he snatched for her.

"I reject thy suit, Osken Marl," Reba said.

Witnesses agreed she spoke the necessary repudiation before she swayed, supple as a willow, and the dark-clad man behind her stepped into the breach. Her Shadow's arms opened, welcoming her abductor with an embrace lengthened by twin blades. They were ugly weapons, more like butcher's knives than the elegant swords of the Varlords, but sharp enough. Before Marl's hand closed on the air where Reba's shoulder had been, his head was bouncing away across the cobbles.

Tomni didn't see the incident, but he heard of it. Everyone heard of it. Within a day, the Widow Oblinka had sent the severed thumbs of three hired thugs to Vod Roch-Var. It was said the vow-sayer who waited with the Vod fainted at the sight of the digits, sealed in a box with a blood-soaked missive which read: 'I reject thy suit, Cazil Roch-Var'.

Tomni wondered what progress Reba made with Degza's *Alchemica*. He re-read the *Botanica*, as she'd intended to do, while rumours about her Shadow grew. It was whispered he was troll-kith and more than half beast. It was said he'd been raised by dark sorceries from the fanged caves of Csillek, and that her father had sent him to her in a tallow-lined barrel packed with mouldering shrouds and crushed bone, all the way from Awlensk. Lists were made of those he'd killed: Osken Marl, Vod Brok-Var's second son, three rival Taturk cousins, and at least eight mercenaries, sent by other suitors.

The bachelors of Babynyk took pause.

"He's a half-blood reaver," Svan muttered. "I heard that his father's a Dybleki."

"And his mother's a sea witch?" Jurik mocked. "He's just a mercenary. She's wasting coin, trying to avoid the inevitable. Stupid girl." It was coin Jurik already considered his.

"She'll be at Pan Erden-Var's festivities for the Love Moon," the Vod told his sons.

"So will her Beast," Svan muttered, kicking the leg of Tomni's chair.

"Everyone will be there," Jurik said. "Hard for the Shadow to stay close."

"Their mistake was to leave the widow conscious, to reject them." The Vod wagged one finger. "It gives her bodyguard free rein. Without the repudiation, an attack is murder."

"You'll still be dead," Svan sneered at Jurik, "but the Beast will be in the wrong."

"We drug her," the Vod commanded. He stalked around the table to cuff the back of Svan's head, then paced to the windows, not caring that his second son passed the cuffing on to Tomni. "Jurik?"

"White poppy juice," that son suggested.

Tomni's ears rang, but he found his voice. "Fa—my Vod? Poppy scent is hard to mask. Won't she be alert for it?"

His father frowned. "Svan?"

The second son grinned across the table at his older brother, and said, "Wild rue."

"Too bitter," Tomni countered, ducking his head. The thought of Reba, unconscious and at Jurik's or Svan's mercy, was worse than any retribution from his brothers.

"What then?" the Vod demanded of him.

"Passionflower?" Tomni hazarded.

His brothers snorted their derision, but the Vod held up his hand.

"Enough. It's not as fast-acting as the poppy, and she'll have to drink more of the syrup, but it will work."

"My Vod," Tomni said, dipping his chin. The *Botanica* listed the extract of passionflower as an aphrodisiac, a narcotic, and a soporific. It mentioned zinziver root as an effective counter to the drug. He would send Reba a note, directing her studies to the relevant page of Dovinzja's text.

⚊⚊❦

Across the Erden-Var's great hall, Tomni watched Reba accept a drink from Jurik. Had she received his note? Had she understood? Her Shadow stood nearby, but his presence wouldn't counter the passionflower's dose. Reba raised her glass, and something in her smile let Tomni breathe easier.

"Make sure you do your part," the Vod hissed in his ear.

Tomni nodded and took care to speak to Reba before Svan; took care to offer her a glass of honeyed grape juice. It was one less thing his father might criticise him for.

She wore widow's grey, but what would render another drab made her glow like the full moon reflected on the dark waters of Babynyk's Grand Canal. Tomni's throat tightened, and he wished he'd gathered a drink of his own, although then he wouldn't have had a free hand to add the syrup to Reba's glass.

"How kind you are." She sipped and smiled. "It's quite delicious with zinziver."

He dipped his chin to hide his smile. She drained the juice, and handed the empty glass to her Shadow. He was neither tall nor broad, but he possessed a coarse ugliness and a lethal stillness which prickled at the skin on the back of Tomni's neck.

"Led," Reba said, "this is my friend, Tomni Emis-Var."

The Shadow bowed his head, but not before one side of his thick eyebrow rose. No wonder they called him the Beast. A folk belief said those with a single brow became wolves with the full moon. Despite himself, Tomni's gaze stole to the windows, where the moon hung low, a ripe and luminous fruit.

"May I ask," he said, struggling to keep his voice steady, "how you advance with the *Alchemica*?"

"I thank you again. It's very good."

He almost managed a smile. Reba gave voice to a delighted laugh, and those around them turned to see the cause. Svan glared at him, but Tomni forgot his brother as Reba laid her hand on his arm.

"You know," she murmured, "your gift means more to me, because you value the Degza so highly. Might we discuss books someday?"

"Yes," he said. The word broke from him on a groan. His skin prickled with heat, as the scent of Reba's hair mingled with the honeyed sweetness of her breath. She leaned closer and the firm swell of her breast brushed against his arm.

"Degza for alchemy," she whispered against his ear. "The so-helpful Dovinzja for botany, and Donola—"

"Donola?" he gasped. What did she know of those grim works?

"—for anatomy." She drew back, but her grip tightened, and laughter sparkled in her eyes. "You *have* studied anatomy, ser?"

"Yes." He choked out agreement, caught by the teasing promise in her voice. She looked as young as he, but she was a widow, and while he'd read of … anatomical matters, she'd probably, doubtlessly, wondrously applied what she had studied, rather than only imagined. That knowledge flamed in the golden sparks of her eyes and scorched him. She lifted her hand from his arm, her fingertips lingering on his sleeve.

"I must speak to others, Tomni. Your brother, in particular, looks aggrieved."

"Yes," he repeated. "Will you—"

"I shall leave word with Vaval," she promised.

<hr>

"**U**seless," Vod Emis-Var said. "Three doses!"

"She never so much as staggered," Jurik complained.

Svan bared his teeth at Tomni. "Did you even remember to add the dose?"

"Of course," Tomni said. He couldn't lie to fool his brothers, so he'd learnt to make truth his ally. "I smelt zinziver on her breath, my Vod."

"Cunning vixen." His father sounded almost admiring.

"What did you talk about?" Svan demanded.

"Oh, books," Tomni said.

Jurik grunted his disgust.

"No wonder she laughed at you." Svan's lip curled. "A chance to get her alone—"

"Gone begging because of a moonstruck bookworm," Jurik finished, in rare accord with Svan.

Tomni hung his head. "Your pardon, my Vod."

His father sighed. "Get out of my sight, boy."

He hurried to obey.

<hr>

As the Love Moon waned, his admiration for Reba grew, nurtured by notes exchanged through the bookseller. She'd read widely, and knew much.

Her tinctoria theory on the alchemical importance of dye plants took his breath away. When she proposed they meet, so she might give him the Degza, Tomni realised he looked forward more to seeing Reba than to reading the *Alchemica*. He mumbled excuses after dinner, and went to his room, before slipping out and hurrying to the Trovisk.

The bookseller's door was unlocked. Had the old man shut himself in his room, as he had promised, leaving them the privacy of the book-lined passage? It seemed a softly-lit, humble paradise.

"Tomni," Reba said, stepping from the recess. His heart leapt at the sight of her, and he opened his mouth, although he didn't know how to tell her all he felt.

"I don't believe it," Jurik said, shouldering through the door behind him, a dark cloak draped over his arm.

"Tomni?" Reba's voice pitched up, full of hurt.

"I didn't—"

"That's two kronik you owe me," Svan said, shoving his older brother as he followed him into the bookstore. "I told you the worm was lying." He drew his sword. "Get out of the way, Tomni. Father's fetching a vow-sayer. By my blade I claim the widow."

"You claim?" Jurik cried.

"No," Tomni said.

"I reject thy suit, Svan Emis-Var." Reba clenched her fists. "And before you presume, I also reject thy suit, Jurik Emis-Var."

Svan shrugged. "There's none to witness the repudiation."

"Led," Reba called, and her dark-clad Shadow stepped from the recess beside her.

"Witnessed," Led growled. He didn't seem to move, but his blades were in his hands.

"Witnessed," Tomni said. He turned, and drew steel on his brothers. "I won't—"

"Shut up, idiot." Svan pulled the cloak off his brother's arm. Jurik raised the crossbow and fired. The quarrel buried itself in Led's chest. Reba's bodyguard tilted his head, as if to look at the bolt driven into his heart, and toppled to the floor.

"I claim—" Jurik began, drawing his blade, but Reba raised one hand.

"No," she said. "*Ahlgard f'thessig im brahn Ledjek'hihl, des ialj'url.*"

The tortured syllables scraped at Tomni's ears. He shook his head, and blinked, then blinked again. Her Shadow had risen into a crouch.

"Stay very still, Tomni," Reba said. "*Krgh'ehim.*"

It wasn't possible. Led flowed past Tomni, although the bookstore was too narrow. Jurik's sword leapt, deadly and capable, but there was no room to display his skill. He cursed instead, turned his wrist to parry one of Led's short blades, and grunted as the other slid between his ribs. He shuddered like a fish on a hook, driven onto his toes by the force of the Shadow's blow.

Led tipped his knife and Jurik's carcass dropped at his feet. He kicked it aside.

Svan stumbled back, scattering books as he retreated into the Trovisk. The lamplight caught his grin and painted it a feral yellow. His arms swept wide—sword flashing and cloak swirling—but his eyes betrayed his false bravado. He knew he faced death.

Led leapt after him, blades outstretched as if he was nothing but an arrow's dark fletching, sending the strike true. With a cry, Svan flung the cloak and lunged, but the cloth failed to tangle his foe. Instead, the Shadow twisted like smoke, rising up beside the cloak and driving both of his long knives into Svan's unprotected torso.

Tomni blinked.

Jurik.

Blink.

Svan.

Blink.

His brothers lay broken in a tide of blood.

Led turned his cold, dead gaze on Tomni, who didn't dare to blink again.

"*F'szekid Ledjek'hihl,*" Reba whispered, and Led's blades returned to their sheaths.

"I d-d-didn't—" Tomni couldn't seem to harness his thoughts and his tongue to a single purpose.

She held up her hand. "I know, my friend."

"He, but, but, he was dead, but how—" Still he babbled.

"Hush," Reba soothed. She waved him closer, and he moved away from Led, away from what remained of his brothers. "It's simple enough. Before I became Reba Oblinka, I was Reba Donola."

"Donola? The Donola? The—"

"Necromancer." She nodded.

Tomni swallowed. "Donola was your father?"

"My friend, a woman is quite capable of writing books."

"Your mother?" He couldn't imagine such a thing.

She sighed. "I am Donola. They're my books."

He stared. "But you—you're too young." It wasn't possible.

"Alchemy, Tomni." Reba sighed again. "I learnt the secret of eternal youth. I'm older than I look."

"But your father was a merchant from Awlensk—" Words spilled from him, even though he knew they were the wrong ones.

"Hush."

She laid her finger on his lips, and the babble ceased, replaced with wonder at her touch.

"I needed to be in Babynyk. Micho proved less amenable than I'd hoped. But you're young and clever, and you know how to do what you're told, don't you?"

Tomni's mind reeled at the warmth of her fingertips, and the scent of her as she swayed closer, but his father had taught him obedience and respect.

"Yes," he said.

Her hand caressed his cheek and slid to press against the back of his neck.

"Then kiss me, Tomni."

Obedience and respect and the dizzying sunlight in her eyes. He did what he was told.

Reba eased the sword from his loose grip as their lips parted. She murmured, "Shall we go and find a vow-sayer, or shall we wait for your father to bring us one?"

His senses spun, but he managed to reply, "We'll do whatever you want, Reba."

Then he kissed her again, as she smiled.

Louise Pieper has been accused of having been born in a tent; having too many books, a weird sense of humour, an unsophisticated palate, and no soul; of being too smart for her own good; of reading too much; laughing too loud; wearing too much black; and referring to herself in the third person. Of course, it's just feckless scandalmongering—she was born in a hospital. She's a card-carrying librarian who lives halfway up a hill in Canberra, and half the time in imaginary worlds. She's never knowingly aided or abetted a zombie.

Ace Zone

Eugen Bacon

SHOWERS. LIGHTNING. The night is momentous. She flirts with it: dusk. Drizzle joins forces with the black sky. Nightfall transfigures her. She is Ace Zone. Beautiful … in a subterranean way.

Her arrival into the land of Meteor is seismic, as is the downpour she commands. Rain: she loves rain. *Step … swish … step … swish.* She walks in its curtain. She has beckoned winter; a night so dark, it chases poltergeists. She cannot tolerate summer. Not since the battle in Sanz, when Ur butchered his own brother Opac, her husband.

Ur's cruelty has urged Ace Zone to respond. She remembers the good judgment of Opac, may the gods rest his spirit. But she also knows that to triumph in her war, to depose Ur and his iniquity, she must fight blackness with blackness.

A tongue of lightning. Wind spits a wet spray from the tip of Ace's hat. Moisture finds her nose inside a veil. *Splash!* A slipshod road shuttle swerves. Rain like flecks of silver. She crosses Kings Plaza. *Step … swish … Step … swish.* She comes to a Y-junction. Traffic, shuttles headed to the city, to the mountain, to the marina. On the other side of the intersection she follows the *Bridge Ahead* sign. She goes up a lone alley. Her hips sashay to the music of fat rain.

She waves a hand, and rain fades. A purple cloud swells on the horizon. It draws near, nearer still, pushes the last droplets of drizzle away. Bats drift across the firmament. Twin moons peek off the cloud; tentative honey-gold eyes in a lilac spread above.

Ace walks under a banshee tree with foliage that twists into the sky. Remnants of rain whisper in the dark leaves. Lowermost branches hang leafy fringes to the ground. The bough trembles. A lost spray slides down Ace's forehead. Puddles, more puddles. A baby cries in the distance. A hinge groans. The lane is fogged, deserted. North east, a group of girls is bunched around a streetlamp. Bohemian tops; pencil shorts. They quit talking, stare at her. A door slams. *Step ... swish ... step ... swish.* Ace skirts around the hoarfrost women.

She finds him at the end of the road, at the corner of Little Boulevard and Stellar Street. He is standing outside Saturn Inn. His eyes are loud. They shout interest.

"What are you, sixteen?" he says.

"Ace," she says. "Ace Zone."

He is visually pleasing: fine height, muscle and focus. Marks of a soldier. His burgundy waves are drenched. His smile is bold.

He does not understand her kind. His eyes seek only pleasure.

She loosens her hat, removes her veil.

He sizes her toe to lip, takes in the ankle-length boots; the dark cloak. Her tourmaline eyes are the colour of water melon; they shift between rubicund and jade. She knows he is stunned by the rubellite in her hair: how it casts light from tresses that fall to her hips. She opens her cloak.

"You are wet," he says.

She is beautiful ... in a subterranean way.

She rubs her hands. "Take me somewhere."

"Saturn ..." he glances at the inn. "It has ... rooms." He licks his lip.

The inn's rowdiness explodes behind the doors. A shout of ribald laughter.

"The river crossing," he says quickly. "There's Maunder. It's 7-star."

She smiles. "Show me."

He leads in silence. Squish. Squish. Squish. His wet shoes.

Step ... swish ... Step ... swish.

"Do you have a name?" Her voice is like an oboe.

"Selenius."

"Good," she says.

Selenius finds the foot of a tunnel. Down stone steps, then up, up in a twist into a gust of fresh air. Hotel Maunder is like a castle: it climbs. Vultures emboss its marble walls. A velvet carpet stretches long.

U p a gilded balustrade, dragons crown the parallel pillars in the suite. A bronzed effigy, naked, glorious, holds a chalice.

"Drink?" says Ace.

She digests his youth, his magnificence in the play of chandelier light. A careless fringe sprays down one side of his forehead. His nose is fragile. His mouth can be mean.

She steps out of her gown. His lust for her: the energy of its score fills her with chaos. Creation. Chaos.

Later, much later, she holds out a hand. "Dance," she says.

"I can't."

"Wagner."

"Please—"

"Imagine Wagner. Tchaikovsky. Brahms. Chopin. Verdi. Einaudi." They dance to Earth music.

Complete strangers. Or are they?

She glides in and out of his arms. She twirls, twirls, twirls ... His face is softer now, the meanness in his lip gone. He sees a future: his and hers. He caresses the rise of her cheekbone; the flute of her nose ... She glides in and out of his reach.

"Pharaoh," she whispers. "You look like a Pharaoh."

He is hesitant with her play. "Are you hungry?"

"Famished."

They gobble scorpiurus flowers and amethyst worms with saffron rice. They wash it down with wine and russet cheese, grilled and served with sweet radish.

He is to her more than a seasonal interest. He is a prospective soldier.

She is unrushed. She feeds him a truffle. Port. She swings a leg over him. He trembles as she strokes him. Her eyes blaze like comets. She bares teeth, injects her potion.

When he wakes, she will be gone; perhaps already to Planet Ishtar, or Lune, or Rigolith. She has little time but ample to do, drafting soldiers into her battalion. Selenius might note the bite mark on his neck, but he will not comprehend it. He will remember little of the night, nothing of Ace Zone. But for Sanz, its new emancipation battle, he will give everything, *everything*, when Ace commands it.

Eugen M Bacon is a computer graduate mentally re-engineered into creative writing and has published over 100 short stories. Her work has won, been shortlisted, longlisted or commended in national and international awards, and creative articles nominated for the Aurealis Convenors Award For Excellence. Eugen's work has appeared or is forthcoming in *Award Winning Australian Writing*, *AntipodeanSF*, *Andromeda*, *Aurealis*, *Bards and Sages Quarterly*, *Breach*, *Bukker Tillibul*, *Every Day Fiction*, *Farther Stars Than These*, *Horrified Press* anthologies, *4 Star Stories*, *Mascara Literary Review*, *Meniscus*, *TEXT*, *Parentheses*, *The Victorian Writer* and through Routledge in *New Writing*.

A Question of Identity

Grace Maslin

Lesden cast about one more time, fingers poised over his left charger, but there were no leather-clad droids marching through the foliage to arrest him. He relaxed and stepped into the alcove, hoping its other occupant wouldn't notice he was out of breath.

Jax scowled at him as he tugged down his hood. "Trouble already?"

"Only a little." Lesden sat next to him and rummaged around in his bag for a wipe. "The Mono staff tried to shut the station doors with me inside." He started rubbing the sunburst makeup off his face: waste of good artwork, really, but far too recognisable. "Simple misunderstanding, mate. I already Changed my leggings, don't—"

"Fuss?" said Jax. "Didn't I stress the importance of this job enough?"

"Hey, ease up! I'm here, aren't I?" Lesden flexed his fingers, flashing the blue panels of his gloves at his friend. "Fastest techie in the 'Sink, at your service."

Jax snorted and flipped open his own bag.

"I nearly didn't come," Lesden added, a little stung by this response. "You know I don't like working in the open, Jax. If I wasn't goddamn skint ..."

"Here." Jax dropped a heavy secbox in his lap. "Stop complaining and get cracking."

Lesden whistled in admiration as he examined the secbox, its smooth metal making his blood fizz with anticipation. "An Atlas! Where'd you get this?"

"You don't want to know."

"Ha." Lesden squinted at the serial number underneath and froze, his pulse thudding in his ears. "Oh, shit. Tell me you didn't."

"What?"

"It's a 6000, Jax. Only the Council has that model!"

"So?" Jax folded his arms and tried to look impassive, but Lesden saw the flicker of guilt in his mod-gold eyes. "High pay means high risks, mate. If I'd told you up front you wouldn't have shown up."

"No shit! I don't have a death wish, unlike some people—"

"Please, Les," said Jax softly, touching his knee. "I need this just as much as you do."

Lesden stared at him. Begging was a new tactic. "This better make us shiny rich, Jax …" He stopped, icicles jabbing into his stomach as he remembered what else a 6000 Atlas meant. He wedged the secbox between his legs, upside down, and scrabbled for the access panel.

Jax leaned over. "I cut off the tracker. I can do that much."

Lesden shook his head. "This bastard's got a backup." His fingertips found the catch and he ripped off the panel to gaze at the circuitry. Standard layout, thank the archangels. He pulled out his probes and got to work. No flashing light to point the way, but the battery diode was simple enough to disable.

"There." Lesden leaned back, willing his heart to slow down. "I don't suppose we can move?"

"Too hot." Jax's eyes were wide, but his voice was steady as ever. "We wouldn't make it out of the park."

"Great." Lesden unwound the wires at his wrists and started to plug himself in. "So now I have to race some squad of Council droids, is that it?" The glove panels lit up, and he couldn't help grinning like a dosed-up patchie. "Alright then." Time to take the vengeance his father deserved, but had never had the guts to seek for himself.

Lesden tapped his fingers against his palms, sending commands down the wires to the secbox, and following his progress on the panels. The text was much smaller on the gloves than on his workshop screens, but not so small he missed the tripwire activating a few minutes in.

"C'mere, you naughty thing," Lesden muttered, chasing the code and scrambling it before it could trigger a lockdown. Nothing he hadn't anticipated, but he rarely handled secboxes this hardcore. Lesden swallowed and shook out his fingers, trying to ignore the sweat prickling his palms. He could do this.

"You okay?" said Jax, now hovering at the alcove entrance. "Not to rush you, but—" He broke off, looking over his shoulder, and then ran towards Lesden. "Hide it," he hissed. "Gloves off!"

Lesden just had time to put the secbox in his bag before Jax sat on his knees and kissed him. He grunted in surprise, but Jax just tugged at his gloves and kept going. Lesden thumbed the gloves into standby and carefully pulled them off, more than a little distracted.

"Citizens!"

Lesden jumped, breaking away to suck in much-needed air through his tingling lips. Jax squeezed his hands and slid sideways off his lap, taking Lesden's bag with him.

"Problem, officer?" Jax asked, with just a hint of impatience.

"Yes."

Lesden looked up and saw a woman in Mono red aiming an electric gun at his face. He squeaked and raised his palms in surrender, and then had to fix his gaze on the gun instead of staring at the exposed chip burns on the backs of his hands.

Shit. His head spun with noise and images like a Gen overdose. Metal shafts —blood red—why hadn't he bought more skin patches? Jax's voice protesting his innocence, they'd been here for an hour …

"Of course *alone*, officer, don't be crude," said Jax, leaning into Lesden's shoulder. Lesden blinked the world back into focus.

"He does bear a remarkable resemblance." The Mono woman was still pointing the gun at him, and now had security footage playing above her other hand. "Green hair, blue hood—"

Jax tsked. "I knew green wasn't your colour, darling."

Lesden did his best to look affronted; he could play cool well enough, but full-blown acting was Jax's area of expertise. "I thought you said you liked it."

"I did until it made you look like a criminal."

"Citizens …"

"Give me that." Jax stretched forward and snatched the holobot from her other hand. "Oh, no," he said, swiping through the footage. "You're searching the wrong database, officer. *This* man has got pink pants." He slid his hand between Lesden's denim-clad thighs, and smiled as Lesden twitched. "I don't date lorikeets. I'd rather get a tattoo on my dick."

Lesden hastily turned his smirk into a grimace. "*So* not my style," he drawled; he could feel Jax's confidence easing his nerves. They might just get out of this, if Jax didn't take his theatrics too far.

The woman retrieved her holobot with a scowl and clipped it to her belt. "Fashion can be fickle," she said, and reached for Lesden's right hip.

He felt Jax stiffen beside him, but Lesden made himself laugh and let the Mono officer search for the control panel. "Easy, love." He rolled his hips beneath her hand and glanced at Jax. "He gets jealous so fast."

The woman huffed and stepped back, holstering her gun. "They're not Changecloth."

"Retro all the way, darling," Lesden lied, and gave her a wink.

Her lips thinned. "My apologies, citizen." The officer turned on her heel and walked out. Lesden sat back, enjoying the look on Jax's face while they waited for the officer to get a safe distance away.

"What the hell?" Jax punched his shoulder. The camp mask had fallen abruptly away. "Why don't you have patches on? And how—"

"I switched the controls." Lesden touched his left hip and let out a shaky laugh at the sheer dumb luck of it. "And I can't put a skin graft on while I'm working, idiot, what if I have a chip surge?" Not to mention how bloody expensive the compatible ones were.

Jax shook his head and gave him back his bag. "Just find the damn combination and get this open."

Lesden smiled as he took out the secbox. "I'm not going after the combination," he said, putting his fingerless gloves back on.

"The hell are you doing then?"

"Something better." Lesden's fingers danced as he made up for lost time. "It's like a safe with an armed guard standing in front of it. You can't guess the code with him breathing down your neck. So most people try to sneak past and lever it open – but he's expecting that, and there's sensors everywhere."

"So what does my Lucky Les do, then?"

Lesden stared at the directory blinking on his panel, and felt his mouth pull into a savage grin. "He walks up to the guard and makes *him* open it." A few seconds of searching, and there it was. "Emergency protocol. Say the right words, flash the ident, and he'll evacuate the safe contents for you."

Jax chuckled and stood up. "Nice," he said, walking back to the entrance.

"Hmm." If only it were as simple as saying it aloud. The ident was the killer: if he got that wrong, the game was up. And Lesden had never tried to fake a Council ident before.

He unplugged his gloves, tucking the wires away and gently moving the secbox on to the bench beside him. "Nearly there," he told Jax, flicking through the filters on his left glove. His master chip was quite old, but he'd built overlays to make up for that. How much use they'd be now, though …

Lesden decided simpler was better, set the filters and took a deep breath. "Here goes." He screwed his eyes shut and pressed his left fist against the secbox. One heartbeat passed, and then a bolt of energy seared through his glove as his ident was rejected. Lesden howled and snatched his hand away, cradling it in his lap.

"Shit." Jax ran towards him, his face white. "We're out of time." He reached for the secbox.

"Don't—"

Electricity crackled, and Jax fell backwards, stunned by the secbox's lockdown shield.

"Jax!" Lesden cried, crouching next to him.

"Freeze!"

Lesden looked up and saw the Council squad they'd been hiding from, stepping forward with guns raised. He clenched his fists, activating his gloves' own lockdown protocols, and the leading droid tilted its head.

"Unknown tech detected," it said, and shot him.

———

"He's waking up, Marcella," someone said, from far away. "Better get in here."

Lesden groaned. The owner of the voice was being overly optimistic: he didn't feel at all awake. His ribs throbbed, his head felt like it was filled with cement, and his hand …

He couldn't move his hands.

Lesden's body jerked, his eyes cracking open. He was seated at a table with his very naked hands cuffed in front of him. "No." Panic squeezed at his chest, and he tugged uselessly against the magnetic plate. "Where are my gloves?"

"With Marcella." The man sitting opposite him spared Lesden one bored glance before returning his gaze to the monitor in his hands. "Head of Tech, and she's been cooing over those things like a kid with her first skimboard."

Lesden twitched, trying to quash a spike of childhood anger, and the man looked at him sharply. Not so disinterested, Lesden thought, staring into his crystal-blue eyes. Watch your step.

"She's quite fascinated by them," the man continued. "Especially since the Mono footage came through."

Damn. Lesden slumped. Those gloves were his livelihood, his protection: and he'd never get them back. Not now they knew he'd weaponised them. He shifted in his seat and noticed a pair of thin wires in his lap. Frowning, he followed them up his chest and realised, with a flash of nausea, that they were attached to his neck.

Lesden looked at the monitor, where the wires' physio data must be streaming, and then at the man's padded grey jacket. "Where am I?" he said quietly, hoping he was wrong.

"Council's Intel division," the man said, and Lesden caught his breath. Everyone in the Heatsink knew the spooks were worse than the police. His reaction must have shown on the monitor; the man looked up again and smiled unpleasantly.

"That's right kid, you're in deep shit." The man leaned forward and patted Lesden's scarred hands, making him flinch. "Caught with Council property in your freshly cooked hacker's hands, no less. But your sentence depends on how much you know about said property."

"Nothing," said Lesden quickly, blessing Jax's paranoia as he watched the man's eyes flick down to the monitor. "Honest."

The Intel man stared at the monitor for another moment, then grunted. "Better hope your friend's story matches yours."

"He alright?" Lesden blurted, before he could stop himself. The man raised his eyebrows and Lesden looked down, wishing he could break his own jaw and stop anything else slipping out.

"He's fine—assuming he's cooperating." The Intel man sounded smug; no wonder, Lesden had just handed him even more leverage. How could he be so stupid? "So you were happy to just open a secbox for him, with no idea of its contents?"

"Well, yeah." Lesden relaxed a little; this was safer ground. "I was skint, it was valuable, that's all I needed to know. I didn't even realise it was Council 'til I saw the box."

"What gave it away?" asked a new voice.

Lesden twisted around in his seat to see a tall, dark-skinned woman entering the room, door panels hissing shut behind her. She walked around and sat beside the Intel guy, laying a pair of black gloves on the table. "Sorry I'm late," the newcomer said.

Lesden gazed at his gloves, his thoughts churning. This must be Marcella: how long had she been the boss of Tech division? Had she known his father?

Brown fingers hid the gloves from view. "Well?" Marcella prompted. "How did you know?"

Lesden pushed his memories aside, calling up the nonchalant mask he used for payment negotiations. "Non-commercial model." He shrugged. "You wouldn't give the companies the 6000 'til you'd developed another one."

Marcella's teeth flashed as she laughed. "Damn, kid, you've seen right through us." She sobered, leaning back and folding her arms. "Not to mention all our security features."

"I've seen 5000s before," said Lesden. "It wasn't that different."

"Not when you bypass most of the defences and go after the emergency release."

Lesden blinked. They'd run diagnostics on the secbox, then. How long had he been out?

Marcella was staring at him like she was running a deepscan. "Ingenious," she said slowly. "Most people don't even know that protocol exists."

"I'm not most people." Lesden had found it by pure luck, trawling through a busted secbox he'd picked off an incinerator van, but this woman didn't need to know that.

"Did you actually expect it to work?"

"Uh ..." Lesden hesitated, taken aback. *Please, Les.* He swallowed and dropped his gaze. "Not really." It had only worked once before, when he'd stolen the ident to match. But, thanks to the secondary tracker, it had been his one shot at opening the secbox for Jax before the squad found them.

"I see." Marcella drummed her fingers on the table, seeming lost in thought. "What's your name?"

"What?"

Marcella chuckled at his expression. "Not your real name, kid, we'll get that off your ident chip soon enough." Lesden suppressed a scowl as Marcella winked at him. "I hope you didn't pay too much to have it corrupted. They did a pretty poor job of it."

Lesden looked away, breathing hard. He had to calm down; they could see his every reaction, hooked up as he was to a body monitor. He sighed, forcing his muscles to relax, and met Marcella's dark gaze. "Lesden."

"Never heard of you," Marcella said at once.

Lesden rolled his eyes. "Course not. Can't put out a warrant if you don't know I exist, can you?"

Marcella cocked her head, considering. "Practical," she said at last, as if to herself. "And yet you certainly dress the part of a glory-seeking techie."

Lesden kept his mouth shut. He didn't see why his clothes were important, but the Tech boss looked like she was on to something, which did not bode well.

"Ell." Marcella flicked the syllable off her tongue, her eyes far away. "Knows all the system's secrets, but doesn't want to build a reputation." Her focus suddenly shifted, like a missile locking onto its target, and Lesden gulped. "You're the one who broke into the Acauldon Company safe last year."

Lesden froze, his heart skipping a beat before going into overdrive. Holy shit, he was in for it now. He never should have let Tahlie talk him into leaving a calling card; but it had been his first big job, and he'd liked the idea of showing off a little.

Marcella glanced at the monitor and grinned. "That's been bugging me for eleven months, Lesden. Thank you for clearing that up."

"Prove it," Lesden spat, trying to stem his panic. Acauldon had a ruthless history of dealing with hackers; not that he'd stopped to think about that when Tahlie had approached him, high as he was on Gen and vodka. A mate of hers was running the heist, she'd said. They'd never failed yet, and *everyone* would want Lucky Les to work for them after he pulled this off. He'd never go hungry again …

Being kidnapped for a job interview with a particularly security-conscious gang had rather taken the shine off his fame, though. Now the money was almost gone, and he was mired neck-deep in Council secrets.

"We don't need proof," said the Intel man. "Not when you can't afford legal representation."

Lesden glared at him, anger drowning out his fear. So these elitist bastards had rigged the system: no surprises there.

Marcella stroked Lesden's gloves thoughtfully. "I'll make you a deal, kid," she said. "You tell me how these beauties work, and I'll forget about contacting Acauldon."

"Bullshit," Lesden said. He knew better than to believe Marcella; but the Intel man seemed uncomfortable, which was interesting.

"Marcella," the Intel guy began.

"They got the money back on insurance, Georg. You know that."

"That's not—you don't have to bribe him to get him to talk." Georg gave Lesden a measuring look that sent ice down his spine. "We have other means."

Lesden swallowed, silently praying that Jax wasn't being too stubborn.

"No," said Marcella. "The kid's under my jurisdiction."

Georg shrugged. "As you like."

Lesden dug his nails into his palms as Marcella looked at him again. He knew his fright would show on the monitor, but he didn't want it written all over his face.

"Do we stand?" said Marcella, like any Heatsink gangster sealing a contract.

"Straight and true," Lesden replied formally, and then wiggled his fingers. "You'll need to let me unlock them, first."

Marcella's eyes narrowed, though Lesden was sure he saw her mouth twitch upwards as well. "I can do that. Just tell me—"

"They're print-sensitive, mate." Lesden shook his head. "I spent months working on them, you think I'd leave them open for public use?"

Marcella stared at him silently, and Lesden hoped his pulse was good and steady on that damn body monitor. But before Marcella could make a decision, she blinked and lifted a hand to her ear. "Go ahead," she told the caller, turning aside.

Lesden fidgeted as Marcella took a slender holobot from her pocket and activated the screen. "Got it. Nice work, Kath." She sat and read the message for a few moments, and when she looked up at Lesden, she was grinning.

"Mister Savansie," she said, and Lesden felt his mouth go dry. He'd been expecting this, but it was still a nasty jolt to hear his name.

"Nikales Savansie," Marcella read. Lesden's fists clenched. "Twenty years old, Eurasian, blood type O positive. Reported missing five years ago by his father, Aleksei Savansie, with no further—"

"Don't you fucking dare." Lesden's hands were aching, but he couldn't relax them. "Don't say his name like you've done nothing wrong!"

Marcella frowned and flicked through the data on her screen, and Lesden watched her face change when she found his father's entry. "Discharged from the Council for policy violation and reckless endangerment," she recited.

"Thrown out for saving someone's life," Lesden snapped. "One functional hand, shit job prospects and a child to raise." But never a complaint about his former employers, to his son's increasing frustration.

Marcella looked like she'd bitten into a priceless fruit and found it sour. "He entered a B Zone restricted area ..."

"We were starving!" His view shifted, and Lesden realised he was on his feet, bent awkwardly over his shackled hands, shouting over the roaring in his ears. "We lived off algae bars for months 'til I started selling gadg— ah!" Agony flashed down his body as fingers dug into his shoulders, and the droid guided his buckling legs back into his seat.

Georg gestured. "Easy, F-18." The pressure eased from unbearable to uncomfortable, and Lesden gasped in relief.

"Have you finished?" Marcella asked calmly. Lesden said nothing, still shaking in the droid's grip. Marcella sighed. "Let go, F-18. I understand how you feel, Mister Savansie. Your father exposed a gap in our safety protocols, and then ended up being blamed for the accident. He did not deserve such treatment."

Lesden stared at her, wavering between suspicion and shock. He'd dreamed for years of confronting the Tech division, and he'd never imagined someone like Marcella would admit fault so quickly.

Sure enough, her next comment struck deep. "I don't think he deserved to be abandoned by his only son, either."

"Shut up." Lesden's throat went tight. "You don't know anything about it."

"So enlighten me, Niki."

Lesden flinched violently, phantom pain stabbing at his temple. "Don't call me that." His voice came out thin and trembling, like a goddamn child's. Fuming at his weakness, Lesden kept his eyes shut against the tears, and the ghosts.

"Alright." Marcella gently broke the silence. "I didn't know him, but judging by these older reports, Aleksei was a good man. And I'd hate to see those talents wasted a second time."

Georg groaned. "Not again, Marcella."

"Ignore him," Marcella told Lesden. "Usually, you'd only get two options: pay the fine, which won't be cheap, or spend some time in a high security prison like Damanth—which won't be pleasant if you can't pay for the extras."

Lesden shuddered despite himself, remembering the stories he'd heard pinging around the Heatsink about Damanth.

"In honour of your father, I'm willing to offer you something else. Work off your sentence in Tech, with me." Lesden glanced up at that, and Marcella looked quite serious. "I'll even let you keep the gloves. See if we can't put those wicked fingers to good use."

His *gloves*. Lesden bit his tongue to stem the wave of excitement. What would his friends think if Lucky Les could be bought so easily? He couldn't just roll over and start working for the people who'd ruined his life!

But that left prison, with no way to defend himself ...

Lesden dithered, trying to weigh his pride against his fear. A thought crept up from the darkest corner of his memories. Which path would Aleksei Savansie, with his unwavering loyalty to the Council, want his runaway son to take?

Lesden looked up. "What's the catch?"

"Smart kid." Marcella smiled. "It's an extended parole: well over a year, on your charges. You'll be essentially chained to your desk by an anklet, during the day, and locked up at night."

"Sounds like prison." It also sounded suspiciously well rehearsed.

"But the food's much better." Marcella winked. "Not to mention your co-workers."

Had Marcella been leading up to this the whole time? If that was the case, Lesden wasn't going to make things too easy for her.

"What about my friend?" he asked.

Marcella spread her hands and looked at Georg, who leaned forward. "He actually does know what was in that secbox," said Georg. "*And* when we were moving it. You'd need some bloody impressive intel to buy his release, kid. So unless you know the headquarters or future plans of any big gangs ..."

Lesden's heart sank. He knew where Jax and Tahlie lived, that was about it; the gangs didn't trust the freelancers with important intel like that.

Georg nodded at his silence. "I didn't think so."

Lesden shut his eyes, remembering the touch of Jax's mouth against his, the easy arrogance in his smile. Maybe if he played along, they would let him visit Jax. And later, when they gave him access to the network, he could find something to bargain with—

"Lesden." Marcella's tone was almost kind; Lesden looked at her in surprise. "Your friend got himself into this situation—it's not your fault. What I'm offering is a fresh start, if you want it."

Lesden frowned at his hacker's hands, still cuffed in front of him. He'd be a goddamn sellout ... but that was Heatsink thinking, the opposite of what his father would do. He'd spent the last five years making himself as unlike his father as possible; he wasn't sure, now, which way he wanted to jump.

"Time to grow up, kid," said Marcella softly. "Make your choice."

Lesden or Nikales? If he went to prison, things would only get worse for him, and it wasn't like he could do anything for Jax from there. If he followed in his father's footsteps, maybe he would finally understand why Aleksei had made his peace with what had happened. *A gap in our safety protocols*, Marcella had said. As an insider, perhaps he could find a way to set the record straight, and even get his father some long-overdue compensation.

He met Marcella's eyes. "That anklet better be damn comfy."

Marcella laughed, releasing the magnet, and grasped his hand. "Welcome to the Council, Mister Savansie."

Grace Maslin was first inspired to write stories by her grandfather, who wrote and illustrated stories starring Australian wildlife for his grandchildren. Her work was shortlisted in the 2011 LitLinks writing competition. She enjoys speculative fiction the most because she loves the freedom to imagine other worlds and possibilities. A student biologist by day and a Marvel fan by night, Grace enjoys ice skating and playing music as well as reading and writing.

The Apothecary's Apprentice

Isobel Johnstone

The Abbey Theatre, Dublin, October 1773.

Lavinia stepped out into the cool street, hopped daintily over an oozing brown puddle (she preferred not to think about the contents), and inhaled deeply. It was a relief to escape from the musty, moth-eaten, sweaty smell of the theatre. The stage had always been the one place she felt free and unfettered, but today it was as if the walls of the newly painted set—her character Clarinda's 'charming' bedchamber—were closing in on her.

Unfortunately, the air outside was not much of an improvement. There was a warning shout from one of the apartments above her head and Lavinia neatly sidestepped a torrent of filth issuing from one of the top floor windows.

She took another breath, and instantly regretted it.

The comfortingly familiar routine of rehearsal had steadied her nerves, but she remained acutely aware of the unread letter tucked inside her evening gown, the parchment burning against her skin. The unwanted missive had reached her that morning at the port as the company disembarked, delivered by an ashen-faced boy who scampered away before she had recovered herself sufficiently to question him.

Lavinia drew the envelope out slowly, first checking discreetly over her shoulder to ensure that none of her fellow performers were in sight (the last thing she needed was for her private life to become the subject of fevered company gossip), and broke the wax seal with trembling fingers. The yellowing paper crackled slightly at her touch, as though it might crumble into dust at any moment.

"*My dearest Constance*," she read, suppressing a shudder at the sight of the spidery lettering, the ornate '*C*' unnaturally curled and elongated. She steeled herself to continue.

You will forgive a fond old man for addressing you by your long-discarded name. Constance, my beloved daughter! I have watched your progress from afar with fondest devotion, and (dare I say it?) pride. You have led a vibrant and successful life, and now—so soon!—the bloom of your youth begins to fade. You must understand that I have no choice but to "strike while the iron is hot", to adopt a vulgar expression.

Twenty years have elapsed, almost to the day, since you abandoned our life together with such unaccountable suddenness! I have been patient, my dear, but my patience is not infinite.

You may expect me a week from Friday, at the final performance of The Dissembling Daughter. *I shall demand my payment then—in full.*

In warm anticipation of our long-awaited reunion,
Your Loving Father (Aurelias Fitzherbert)

Lavinia read the letter a second time, imagining she could hear the words spoken out loud in Mr Fitzherbert's thin, tremulous voice.

The Apothecary! After all these years, her erstwhile employer and protector, the man she had once called Father, had re-emerged from the shadows, ready to claim his recompense for feeding and clothing her, for 'keeping her off the streets'. Never mind that she had been expected to work for her bread and butter. Unnatural, unspeakable work.

Lavinia closed her eyes, allowing herself a full minute to empty her mind and regain her composure—no more, no less. It was like managing stage fright.

She was no longer a slip of a girl, beholden to her macabre Master. She was the great Lavinia Lamont, the most celebrated actress of the age! She had worked hard to fashion a new life for herself, and she was resolved not to let go of it without a fight. Not while she was at the very pinnacle of her dramatic powers! Mr Fitzherbert would have to wait a little longer before exacting his payment. A lot longer, if she had anything to do with it.

Her first task was to reply to the letter, however distasteful the prospect of putting pen to paper. Her second task was to procure help. Fortunately, Lavinia still kept her ear to the ground. She had not been idle all these years, but worked to cultivate a host of shadowy connections in case of precisely this eventuality.

The greatest drama of her life was about to unfold, and tonight she would set the first act in motion.

Her dressing room was much smaller than in London, and under other circumstances she might have resented the compact space. As it was, she was grateful for the privacy her modest room afforded. Lavinia sat in front of her mirror, removed her elaborate wig, and started to comb her nut-brown hair—still thick and glossy, she noted with approval. She was not so old, yet! It was a soothing ritual, distracting her while she waited for her Rescuer-for-Hire to materialise.

Lavinia had seen him in the audience, watching her intently: a tall, straight-backed man in a black mask and long velvet cloak. The man she knew only as the Masked Gentleman.

The note, which she had found slipped under her door that morning, was executed in a bold, flowing hand, refreshingly different from Mr Fitzherbert's quavering script. The missive had seemingly been composed in some haste, as the paper was generously scattered with ink blots. It read simply 'the stroke of midnight'—a touch melodramatic, but she supposed it was the lure of romance and adventure that drew young noblemen like the mysterious Masked Gentleman to life on the outskirts of the law in the first place.

She was so lost in thought that she jumped when the knock finally came: three times in rapid succession.

Enter the Masked Gentleman, Lavinia thought, opening her dressing room door.

She was surprised to find that that her rescuer was considerably younger than she had anticipated. His mask could not conceal the roundness of his face, the plumpness of his lips, the baby-like softness of his skin. He could not be more than two- or three- and twenty. Lavinia suppressed a twinge of guilt.

"Miss Lamont!" The visitor swept off his hat and bowed with an effortless theatrical flourish. "Allow me to present myself. You will forgive me for not removing my mask." He gestured to the black band that covered the top half of his face. "Secrecy, you must understand, is of the utmost importance to men of my calling. Do not think to learn my name! You may call me"—he paused a split second for dramatic effect, a technique Lavinia was well-acquainted with—"*the Masked Gentleman*."

Lavinia suppressed the urge to laugh at the young man's earnestness—had she ever taken a role so seriously in all her life? She was grateful for the professional training that allowed her to keep a straight face.

"I understand perfectly," she replied, careful to keep all trace of amusement from her voice. "A man in your position has, I am sure, many enemies. Your caution is perfectly understandable. Won't you please sit down?"

The Gentleman flopped into a chair like an ungainly schoolboy. "Anything for the great Lavinia Lamont!" He leaned forward confidentially: "I am an ardent admirer, Miss Lamont. Your Rosalind was the most charming I have ever beheld; your Cordelia moved me to tears with the purity of her filial affection!"

"You are far too kind, sir. I trust you enjoyed this evening's performance?"

Lavinia began to regret her polite enquiry as the Gentleman launched into a rapturous monologue about dramatic virtues of *The Dissembling Daughter*. After five full minutes she coughed politely, deciding it was high time to cut the young man short.

"Forgive me, sir, but the evening's business awaits. This dreadful affair has left me quite distracted." She gave him an appealing look.

"But of course, Miss Lamont," said the Gentleman, suddenly brisk and business-like. "Let us get down to work! You have the evidence to hand?"

Lavinia handed over Mr Fitzherbert's letter, watching carefully as the Gentleman perused its contents.

"Mr Fitzherbert took me in after my father died," she said, "when I was but a child of eight. He ran a small apothecary's shop in Norton Folgate—the usual remedies. But he had another business on the side, catering to a wealthier clientele. He would supply them with certain ... restoratives ... of a less traditional kind."

"I see," said the Gentleman gravely. "And you assisted him in this… unconventional line of work?"

"Under duress, sir! I fled in search of a new life at the tender age of fifteen. Mr Fitzherbert believes I remain indebted to him, and wishes to take advantage of the modest success I have achieved in my chosen profession. He will be in the audience tomorrow, for the final performance of *The Dissembling Daughter*, waiting to claim his recompense."

The Gentleman drew himself up proudly. "Fear not, Miss Lamont!" he cried. "You have done right to seek my help. My fame has spread far and wide, from Dublin all the way to London! Liberating a helpless woman from the clutches of a sinister Apothecary with a side-line dabbling in the occult? Such a feat is all in a day's work for the Masked Gentleman! The satisfaction of ridding the world of such a scoundrel shall be my reward."

"That—and the money," Lavinia reminded him tartly.

"Why yes, and the money, of course," he agreed breezily.

"It is settled, then. Act IV is the time to strike, when the enraged Lord Warburton leaps over the footstool—let this be your signal! You have procured the weapon?"

By way of an answer, the Gentleman withdrew a small parcel wrapped in a white silk handkerchief (monogrammed *P*, Lavinia couldn't help noticing) from underneath his cloak, and lifted the corner to reveal the point of a gleaming dagger.

"A single blow straight to the heart," she heard herself say mechanically. "It must be swift and silent. And you must dispose of the body discreetly. If my relation to Mr Fitzherbert were to become public knowledge—"

"You can rely on me, Miss Lamont," said the young man earnestly.

"I cannot thank you enough, good sir," said Lavinia, lowering her eyes modestly with a practised flutter of her long lashes. Men were wont to swoon at this look, and she thought she saw the Gentleman's cheeks colour beneath his mask.

He paused just as he reached the door. "Will you satisfy my curiosity on one further point, Miss Lamont? Of the many characters you have inhabited, which is the nearest to your true self?"

"Ah, now that would be revealing *my* secret, sir," Lavinia replied smilingly, suppressing another twinge of guilt.

✹

Shop 362, St James Street, Norton Folgate, London, July 1753.

The scream hung in the air, high-pitched and quivering, like a piece of string stretched to breaking point, before—SNAP. The sickeningly familiar sound of a metallic lid clicking shut.

Mrs Bracegirdle swayed on her feet before collapsing onto the floor, limbs askew. The Procedure was no less agonising for being bloodless. Mrs Bracegirdle's plump, pleasant face was grotesquely distorted, her eyes bulging, her mouth frozen wide open in a final scream of terror. Her jaw was so painfully twisted that Constance wondered if it had been dislocated.

"Hurry up, my girl!" Mr Fitzherbert wheezed, clicking his bony fingers in agitation. "The bottle, if you please!" His pale bulbous eyes were starting out of his head, his yellowing teeth bared in a snarl of anticipation at the prospect of bottling yet another rare specimen.

Constance retrieved a rounded glass bottle from a shelf filled with empty vials of varying shapes and sizes, and held it out towards Mr Fitzherbert, concentrating on steadying her trembling hands. The final stage of the Procedure never got any easier, but over the years she had learned to adopt a mask of relative composure, detaching herself from the gruesome reality of her work. She had even begun to take a degree of pride in her efficiency, her studied unflappability in the face of horrors that would cause more sensitive souls to take leave of their reason. She was fifteen years old this very day, practically a woman, and Mr Fitzherbert hardly ever had need to chastise her for weakness anymore.

Why, then, was she shaking like a leaf, sick with fear and revulsion as though this was her very first Procedure?

"Observe the variegated colours, my girl, the richness of the crimson and purple hues!" cried Mr Fitzherbert gleefully, as he transferred the viscous substance from his ornate silver "holding box" (which reminded Constance of a very large snuff box) into the rounded flask by means of a small spout. When the last drop had been transferred he fixed the stopper with a pop, and handed the flask back to Constance.

"The consistency is fluid," Mr Fitzherbert commented approvingly, "no unsightly lumps and bumps. You reeled in a pretty fish for us this time, Constance my sweet."

Constance felt her cheeks flush at this rare compliment from her irascible Master. To distract herself she held the flask up to the light and admired the contents, which reminded her of softly swirling clouds. Mr Fitzherbert was right: the colours were particularly bright this time. Deep purples, soft mauves and vivid pinks, like a sunset in a painting. Mrs Bracegirdle must have led a more vibrant and adventurous life than Constance would have given her credit for.

"We'll fetch a pretty penny for this old crone," cackled Mr Fitzherbert, rubbing his bony hands together. "I have several interested parties lined up already. Lady Denholm"—he pronounced the name with the special unctuousness he reserved for his wealthiest clients—"is gracing us with her presence this afternoon. She has a predilection for richly-coloured souls. "None of your delicate pastel do-gooders for me, Mr Fitzherbert!" she always says. "I long to experience the unbridled passions of a woman who has truly lived!""

The discerning Lady Denholm was a regular customer, demanding a freshly bottled soul two or three times a year.

"I'll shelve Mrs Bracegirdle with the Category III souls," said Constance, feigning a briskness she did not feel, "and dispose of the body before Lady Denholm arrives."

"Excellent, my dear," murmured Mr Fitzherbert distractedly, as he edged his way creakily out of the Procedure Room, fastidiously sidestepping Mrs Bracegirdle's slumped body. Constance waited until she could hear Mr Fitzherbert busying himself in the shop overhead before she allowed herself to sink to the floor, her arms around her shaking knees. Mrs Bracegirdle's death had left her more perturbed than usual.

Constance had lured the unfortunate woman into the shop under the usual pretext of a miraculous new treatment for persistent toothache. As they waited for Mr Fitzherbert to materialise with the promised remedy, Mrs Bracegirdle had offered Constance sweets and regaled her with tales of her travels in Europe and the East, not seeming to mind that her companion was a mere serving girl. Surely such a generous-hearted woman had not deserved such a miserable fate?

As Constance sat trembling on the hard wooden floor, remembering kindly Mrs Bracegirdle's agonised last moments, a new resolve took hold of her. She would dispose of the body as usual, carving the dead woman up and depositing her remains in the Thames in several grisly instalments. But this time, after she was finished she would make her escape, as she had so often dreamed of doing.

Constance no longer doubted that she had the skills to survive in the outside world. She could defend herself if need be—Mr Fitzherbert had taught her well.

The Abbey Theatre, Dublin, October 1773. Closing night.

Lavinia was only dimly aware of the audience's laughter as she cast her eyes anxiously upwards. She had received a note after Act I in the Gentleman's bold, flowing script, which read simply 'Box 4'. She had been discreetly scanning the box's occupants ever since. She could see the Gentleman, masked and cloaked, seemingly intent on watching the onstage action unfold. She only hoped that he was rather less enthralled by the escapades of Clarinda and the unfortunate Lord Fopsworth than he appeared to be. At the front of the box were three macaronis with powder-white faces and towering hair, adorned with what Lavinia could only describe as 'plumage'. They looked like exotic parrots, which was advantageous as it drew attention away from the peculiarities of her rescuer's attire.

To the Gentleman's left sat a small, wizened old man with yellowing skin and sharp, beady eyes. The sight of him, even at such a distance, made Lavonia's stomach lurch.

"Good sir," Lord Fopsworth protested, "allow me to explain——"

Lavinia quietly exited stage left. She was not required for the remainder of the scene, and if she made haste, she could observe the far more compelling drama unfolding in Box 4 from the opposite side of the theatre. She threw a dark grey cloak around her shoulder to conceal Clarinda's brightly-coloured dress and made her way as quickly as she dared into the public gallery, heading towards the staircase that wound its way up to the boxes. She took the stairs two at a time, pausing outside the box directly opposite Box 4, and discreetly parting the red velvet curtain. The box was occupied by a young man and woman who were evidently more enamoured of one another than the action taking place on stage, and paid no attention to Lavinia. She sank quietly into an empty seat, retrieved a small pair of opera glasses from the folds of her cloak, and peered breathlessly at the Gentleman and Mr Fitzherbert. The moment was drawing near.

"You artful, good-for-nothing rogue! I am not yet so old that I have forgotten how to fight——come, will you defend your honour like a man, or flee like a coward?"

At the precise moment that Lord Warburton drew his sword and leapt over the footstool, the Masked Gentleman leaned in swiftly and silently for the killing blow. Lavinia had to admire his reflexes——evidently his absorption in the play was not as complete as it had seemed. If Mr Fitzherbert had been any other man, the plan would have gone off perfectly.

Unfortunately, Mr Fitzherbert was no ordinary man.

The Gentleman plunged his dagger into the older man's chest, a direct blow to the heart. Mr Fitzherbert shuddered and went still, and Lavinia found herself holding her breath and hoping against hope that the Gentleman had succeeded, though she knew it was impossible. In an instant, her irrational hope was dashed. Mr Fitzherbert sprang upright as suddenly as a demonic jack-in-the-box, breaking into a sharp-toothed smile and removing the dagger from his chest with a single swift and fluid movement.

The Gentleman stared in open-mouthed bewilderment at his would-be murder victim. His astonished reaction would have been comical had the situation been less grave. Lavinia wondered what was going through his mind. Did he assume that she was ignorant of the Apothecary's demonic regenerative abilities? Or did he see the look of deranged triumph in Mr Fitzherbert's face and understand in that moment that Lavinia had double-crossed him?

Another minute and it was all over. Mr Fitzherbert performed a complicated trick with his fingers, weaving them back and forth in front of the Gentleman's nose, and the younger man slumped forward in his seat. Lavinia watched in horror (and reluctant admiration) as the elderly and seemingly enfeebled Fitzherbert effortlessly drew the Gentleman up, slinging one arm across his shoulder, and shuffled out of the row. The performance looked convincing, but Lavinia knew how frail Mr Fitzherbert really was. Surely he had performed a levitation spell. She watched him pause and make some excuse to the startled macaroni. Then he bowed his head politely and exited the box, the unfortunate Gentleman in tow.

Lavinia glanced distractedly at the stage. Act V was about to begin—she needed to get back! And act as though tonight were a night like any other ...

She made her way back down the winding staircase, trying without success to banish her guilt over the Gentleman's fate. He was so young, and so endearingly earnest! It was his misfortune that he had chosen to pursue the life of an adventurer—a vibrant life. The insatiable Lady Denholm would devour his soul with glee.

The Masked Gentleman's soul in exchange for hers: that had been the bargain. The Gentleman was at the very top of Mr Fitzherbert's treasured Procurement List, and his eyes had lit up when she suggested using her current predicament as bait to reel the young man in.

Mr Fitzherbert, cunning as ever, had agreed to spare her, on the condition that she would once again act as his Procurer. Surely this was preferable to the hideous alternative of de-soulment and death? She had not worked for twenty years, ascended to the very apex of her profession, only to end up as another bottled soul in Mr Fitzherbert's collection. A spiritual 'restorative' for wealthy clients with idle, sedentary lives. The very thought made her skin crawl. Come what may, her memories and experiences would remain hers alone.

During her audience with the Gentleman, Lavinia had found herself wishing that this engaging stranger really *did* have the power to liberate her from her former 'protector' with the stroke of a knife. A fairytale ending,

But she knew the Apothecary's secret—a secret that the Masked Gentleman could not possibly guess at. Mr Fitzherbert could not be killed like an ordinary man, because Mr Fitzherbert could no longer be said to be truly alive. His existence had been artificially prolonged by imbibing soul after soul for decades on end, until he was as wan and emaciated as an opium addict. It had made her blood run cold the first time she had witnessed his apparent death (at the hands of a desperate former client who had fallen on hard times, and could no longer afford payment for the restoratives he craved), and his instantaneous 'resurrection'.

Lavinia shook herself. Dwelling on the Gentleman's fate, however cruel and undeserved, would accomplish nothing. If all went according to plan, the Apothecary would vanish from her life forever. Nothing else mattered.

She paused in the wings to throw off her cloak, held her head high, and stepped out onstage.

"Oh Kitty!" Lavinia exclaimed as the curtain rose on Act V of *The Dissembling Daughter*. "My most loyal and beloved companion! You once said you would do anything in the world to help me, your mistress and only friend. Well then—the hour has come! My father is quite mad with rage, and I must prevent him from doing grievous injury to my dearest William. Yet I am cruelly confined to my bedchamber, with the servants instructed to prevent me from passing the threshold! Kitty, will you consent to switch clothes with me, that I may escape in the guise of a common maidservant, and thus attired pursue my enraged father and the unfortunate Lord Fopsworth?"

"Lord save me, mistress, you know I'd do anything to 'elp you!"

Lavinia paused, flustered. Was it her imagination, or had Kitty's voice suddenly dropped a register? Young Lydia had been complaining of a cold at rehearsal yesterday …

Slowly, she turned around to take a proper look at Lydia. It took all her professional training not to let out a cry of surprise and alarm—or was it relief?

Standing before her in a serving girl's cap and apron, his round face powdered and his plump lips rouged, was the Gentleman—this time without his mask. He was alive, and still in possession of his soul! And, for reasons she couldn't quite fathom, he had decided upon this precise moment to fulfil a secret ambition to take to the stage.

But if the Gentleman was alive … then where was Mr Fitzherbert?

She could sense the audience members shifting uncomfortably in their seats. Not only had the actress playing Kitty unexpectedly gained five inches in height and a considerably deeper voice, it was unheard of for the great Lavinia Lamont to come in late with a line. Her timing was universally agreed to be impeccable.

"It is settled, then!" she said, assuming a decisiveness she most certainly didn't feel, and envying Clarinda the relative simplicity of her predicament. "We shall switch places, and deceive these silly, unsuspecting men!" Lavinia grabbed the Gentleman by the arm and dragged him behind a decorative screen.

"What do you think you're doing?" Lavinia hissed, when they were safely out of the audience's sight.

"What do *you* think I'm doing, Miss Lamont?" the Gentleman returned. "I'm buying myself time! Hiding in plain sight from your demonic soul sucker friend. Nicely played, by the way. He's a Soulcatcher. I should have guessed!"

"He isn't my friend," Lavinia spat. "I despise him! And how do you know what a Soulcatcher is?"

"You have a funny way of demonstrating your dislike," said the Gentleman, ignoring her question. "If it were up to you I'd be lying dead backstage with my soul in jar, and Mr Fitzherbert would be celebrating Christmas three months early. Luckily, I keep a miscellany of demon-repelling charms to hand. Now get out of that dress, Miss Lamont, and quickly!"

He was already halfway out of his pinafore, and was struggling with his pantaloons. "It took me an age to get these on in the first place," he grumbled.

"Oh, for heaven's sake—" said Lavinia, helping to pull the pinafore over the Gentleman's head and bumping the flimsy screen as she did so. She could hear the audience convulse with laughter—at least the locals seemed to be enjoying the show.

"Where is Fitzherbert?" she demanded, as she slipped off Clarinda's bright blue evening gown and flung it at the Gentleman.

"I transfixed him with an Oculus charm and dealt him a mighty blow, enough to fell a man half his age. Yet I suspect it will not be long before he recovers. Is there any way to destroy him?"

"If there were a way to destroy him, do you not think I would have found it by now? You understand that he will come after us."

"One predicament at a time, Miss Lamont. Let us get through the evening's performance first."

"Do you even know your lines?"

"I have been to see this play every night since it opened. I am intimately acquainted with the plot. And if I get stuck—I shall improvise!"

Lavinia groaned inwardly, and stepped out from behind the screen, now dressed in Kitty's pinafore and cap. She could not help smirking at the thought that Clarinda's evening gown suited the Gentleman rather well.

"Quickly, Mistress," he cried, pointing towards the door. "There is no time to lose! You must pursue your father and Lord Fopsworth, before—"

The Gentleman stopped speaking abruptly. Lavinia, fearing that he had forgotten Kitty's lines despite his earlier bravado, opened her mouth to come to his rescue—but no words came out. With a mounting sense of dread, she looked towards the audience expecting laughter, jeering, rotten apples being pelted. Instead, there was nothing. The theatregoers of Dublin were frozen in their seats, staring glassy-eyed and open-mouthed at the stage, utterly motionless.

As if on cue, Mr Fitzherbert strode in from the wings, and clicked his bony fingers. Lavinia felt her throat de-constrict.

"What sorcery is this?" the Gentleman demanded.

Mr Fitzherbert ignored him.

"My power has grown since you have been gone, Constance," Mr Fitzherbert remarked wheezily. His thin, tremulous voice reminded Lavinia of an eerily creaking door.

"I can see that," she replied, at a loss as to what to do next. Her only thought was to buy herself time.

"Oh yes, my dear," Mr Fitzherbert continued dreamily. "It is *amazing* what imbibing multiple souls can do, truly miraculous. I feel quite reinvigorated—almost a young man again!" He performed a bizarre jig, moving his long, spindly legs with a visible effort, as though showing off his newfound vitality.

"You mean …?"

Mr Fitzherbert smiled a twisted smile, revealing his sharp, uneven yellow teeth. "Yes, Constance, I do. You will, of course, recall my research into the possibility of absorbing not one soul at a time, but many. For years I believed such a feat to be impossible, but a recent breakthrough—! Well, I shall not fatigue you with the details. Suffice it to say, my dear, that I devoured Lady Denholm. She was, as you know, by far the most discerning of our regular customers. Each and every one of those vibrant, adventurous souls now resides in *me*!"

"No one could survive such a Procedure," cried Lavinia in disbelief. "You said so yourself!"

"And I've proved myself wrong!" the old man cackled insanely. "Just look at me, girl! I've never felt more alive, more suffused with youthful vigour! I'm positively *crackling* with energy!"

He snapped his fingers again, summoning ropes that instantly appeared out of mid-air and knotted themselves around the unfortunate Gentleman.

"Untie me, you abomination!"

"Well, now that you've asked so politely …" Mr Fitzherbert sneered, and turned to Lavinia. "Constance, my dear, if you would be so kind—?"

Mr Fitzherbert held a familiar rounded glass bottle in his outstretched hand. Lavinia stepped forwards as though in a dream, taking hold of the bottle and uncorking it, as Mr Fitzherbert blew minute traces of dust from the lid of his ornate holding box.

"Just like old times, Constance—father and daughter reunited! Oh, what a team we made! Perhaps I did not pay you enough compliments when you were a girl, my dear (I did not then understand the feminine need for incessant praise and flattery), but you were always my best Procurer, you know."

"Miss Lamont, I entreat you!" cried the Gentleman, who was squirming inelegantly in a futile effort to escape from the enchanted ropes.

Lavinia lowered her eyes, afraid of what her face might betray if she were to look at the Gentleman directly. "My father is right, Sir. We struck a deal, you see: your soul in exchange for mine. It is a great pity, Sir, and believe me, I am sorry for you—but it cannot be helped. I wish to live, you see."

"Miss Lamont, I cannot believe you would be so cruel! You, who have melted hearts of stone with the purity of your love, your noble and unwavering virtue!"

"Those were performances, Lord Percy," Lavinia responded derisively, "as insubstantial as the air. You enquired at our first meeting about the real Lavinia Lamont: she stands before you now, unmasked."

"I refuse to believe it!"

"That's the way, Constance my dear, don't stop talking to the boy," cackled Mr Fitzherbert. "Distress makes the brew more piquant!"

He was advancing slowly towards the Gentleman, like a predatory alley cat, before a ghostly audience of silent, empty-eyed spectators.

"You can't escape me, Lord Percy. Lord *Velmont* Percy. Yes, I know your real name! I am an Extractor, it is our business to know. There is no such thing as an anonymous soul."

He opened the holding box and began to mutter a strange incantation, words that had haunted Lavinia's dreams for over twenty years. The Gentleman stopped struggling abruptly, and a colourful substance, like gently swirling clouds, emanated from his mouth and began streaming into the silver box.

"It is working, Constance!" cried Mr Fitzherbert with glee, "it is working! Your presence, as always, has strengthened the brew—none but you could elicit such profound emotions at the very hour of death."

Lavinia watched with bated breath. If she made the wrong move, all was lost; but if she delayed for only a second too long … She looked at the Gentleman. The last wisps of his soul were leaving his body. Mr Fitzherbert had his eyes on the holding box, mesmerised. Now was the time to act.

With a sudden swift movement, Lavinia leaned over Mr Fitzherbert's shoulder and snatched the box from his bony hands, just as he was about to snap it shut.

"What do you think you're doing, you senseless girl?" Mr Fitzherbert spluttered. "Close the lid immediately, lest Lord Percy's soul fly out again!"

Lavinia took a step back and held the box aloft. "You were right to say that I rarely take the part of a spectator," she said: "but there is one thing about me you never truly understood: I am not made to play supporting roles. I prefer to take centre stage."

Before Mr Fitzherbert could react, Lavinia began to recite the hated incantation, finally giving voice to the vile string of words embedded in her brain. Mr Fitzherbert's eyes bulged, his face went grey, and his mouth popped open like a goldfish. As Lavinia chanted, the Gentleman's soul reversed its flow, while a bilious yellow substance emerged from the Apothecary's mouth and drifted like smoke into the still open holding box.

The Procedure only took a few moments. Mr Fitzherbert uttered a final drawn out shriek as the last remnants of his soul left his body, and Lavinia closed the lid with a decisive click.

It was done. Mr Fitzherbert's body crumbled before it hit the ground, disintegrating into fine yellow dust, like old parchment.

The Gentleman spluttered and rubbed his eyes, looking on in astonishment as the ropes unknotted themselves and slid to the ground.

"So you *did* have a plan after all, Miss Lamont! You might have given me some sign of it—I thought I was done for."

Lavinia shook her head. "I had no plan." She smiled, regarding the remains of Mr Fitzherbert—now no more than a crumpled heap of old rags on the stage floor. "I did what all great performers have need to do, at one time or another: I improvised."

"You really are the most marvellous creature I ever encountered!" declared the Gentleman enthusiastically, and with this pronouncement he swept Lavinia in his arms and planted an ardent kiss on her lips.

"Lord Percy!" Lavinia protested, extricating herself from his embrace and smoothing her pinafore demurely.

The auditorium reverberated with the unmistakeable sound of laughter, accompanied by scattered whoops and clapping, and not a few disapproving hisses. Lavinia and the Gentleman looked at one another.

"I see the audience has come back to life," remarked the Gentleman.

"Perceptive as ever, Lord Percy," responded Lavinia.

"Well well, then," said the Gentleman, adjusting his blue evening gown. "The show must go on! What do you say we give these depraved Dubliners an evening to remember?"

Lavinia smiled, and opened her mouth to speak.

Isobel Johnstone is an archivist with a background in English literature and theatre history. After many years of focusing on academic writing, she is branching out into fiction, exclusively (so far) of the speculative variety. Interests include reading, film and theatre-going, and cheese.

Anchor Point

Angus Yeates

Larian walked through a civilisation drunk on time, a world eating its own tail. Dust rose at his feet, gritty red-black stuff that coated the midday sky in a soft haze. Ahead, Atteridge's skyline shifted constantly, rooftops blurring with time distortion as their pasts were re-written. Sidewalks buckled with neglect and infrastructure lay abandoned, long bled dry.

Larian stole another careful glance behind him as he rounded a corner. In a world where one couldn't be sure of much, he knew he was being followed.

The woman wore dark sunglasses and a red scarf around her head in the latest fashion. Her stance was solid and confident. Her gait was familiar, but he couldn't quite place it.

His memory wasn't what it had once been. Too many trips through time, harbouring to his past anchor points. Too many lived-in years crammed into his skull.

He led her further into the slums, keeping his right hand close to his laz-pistol. The exo-skeletal structure encasing his left arm was spring-loaded, ready to crush a skull or ribcage.

Locals watched as he passed, gazing disinterestedly from corrugated iron lean-tos that crowded into alleys and spilled onto causeways. It was squalor, but it beat baking out in the Ell Desert. These were the people who couldn't afford the energy required to harbour, had they even owned anchor points to set.

He rounded a corner, too concerned about the woman following him to notice the officers that came into view.

The officers saw him and activated their link-pads. Before he could run, their link-pads had matched him to a wanted list. The one wanted list he didn't deserve to be on.

He activated an anchor point in his pocket as the first officer approached.

"Larian Carver, you are under arrest ..."

Larian swore.

"... for the murder of Danté and Delilah Carver."

Larian reached for his weapon, but the officer had already levelled his own. The officer fired off a stun round.

Larian's legs locked and cold spread upwards.

"You do not have to say anything ..."

Seriously? This was the 25th Century for Ell's sake. Larian collapsed to his knees. A glance behind showed the red-scarfed woman pulling something from her handbag.

He bit down, activating a trigger—

—*And harboured. Time flowed, moving backwards around Larian in a long instant. He saw alternate versions of himself look up, through the ripples of time distortion around him—splinter-selves watching from other timelines. They seemed more aware of him now.*

His attention snapped to something strange. Two of his splinter-selves stared back at him, time-distortion flaring and buckling the air between them. One looked on accusingly. The other looked sad and placed a hand on the accuser's shoulder—to console or restrain he wasn't sure. Odd enough that they were so aware of him, but stranger still to see that interaction—

—Again, the officer approached. This time Larian didn't wait for the arrest. He ran.

Stun rounds thrummed, narrowly missing him. The red-scarfed woman opened her mouth to speak as he passed. He pivoted around and dragged her back with him. The next volley of stun rounds struck her. Dropping her, he ran while the officers reloaded.

Turning a corner, Larian glanced behind. The officers hadn't yet rounded the corner so he tossed an anchor point into a side alley, activated it, and continued running.

He led them down thoroughfares and back alleys, waiting as far as his vest's remaining power reserves would stretch.

He rounded a final corner. Momentarily out of sight, he harboured—

—time ran backwards like sand. Larian saw his splintered selves. The accuser seemed to stride closer, lifting something—

He materialised at his earlier anchor point in the alley just around the corner from where the officers had accosted him. He caught his breath there, in his minutes-younger self, and shook his head, trying to clear the time distortions from his mind. But it was becoming harder. Larian swallowed against a lump in his throat, knowing he could no longer ignore the symptoms.

Time sickness.

He sank down the wall, exhausted, as the officers ran past searching for him.

There was no real cure. It was a symptom of harbouring too often and too rapidly. Most didn't need to worry, but most didn't work demanding jobs for his pedantic clients. Clients who provided the energy for repeated harbouring and expected results. Linear jobs either paid a pittance or required re-training, which required harbouring. For a man like Larian, anchoring and harbouring were the only jobs around.

Larian sighed. He drew lines in the dirt at his feet, trying to trace his life from the origin point and along the prime-line, but there were too many branches, and he couldn't remember. He was the original, prime-line, version of himself and, at the age of thirty-five, he couldn't remember. He couldn't hold all his lived-in years in his head.

Larian watched as people walked by. Everywhere, he saw unlined faces with eyes that must match his own—windows into old souls. Eyes dancing with stories their minds had forgotten.

He remembered his parents having eyes like that—half distracted as they shooed he and Bess out the door that day, smiling with mouths that no longer laughed. He would have been about twelve, and Bess six.

He and his sister had waited outside in the hot sun, dead grass roasting beneath their feet. Huddled below a window, they'd waited to be let back in, and listened to the recriminations fly.

"Do you even care about our family?" his father had demanded of their mother, with a voice like gravel.

"Oh don't be ridiculous, Danté. Nothing happened."

"I know you go back. For the flings."

She scoffed. "It's not like you don't go back. I'm here with the kids, and you piss off back to the past, trying to right your wrongs and fix your vendettas."

Larian wanted to shut it out, to cover his ears and run away. But he was held there in some strange way, duty-bound to bear witness.

"I'm just trying to fix our situation!"

"And what is our situation?" she demanded. "This?" She gestured out the window, to the dead grass, the roses that never bloomed, and desert just beyond.

There was silence for a moment.

"It's not cheating if it never happened," she insisted.

"So you skipped back, did it, and then skipped back again so it never happened?" Larian's father demanded. "What was his name? Fred? Lancet?" His voice struck flat. "You can't remember. Just because they never happened for me, didn't mean they didn't happen for you." Larian hated his father's choked voice. "It's not even about the flings. How many times have you left me, Delilah?"

More silence. Larian couldn't see them from this angle.

"They're demanding payment today."

Delilah sighed. "Grow a spine, Danté." When she spoke again her voice was exhausted. "You spend so much time in the past. Our relationship is now. Or it was."

Larian hadn't even realised he held his hands over Bess's ears until she flung her six-year-old body away.

Time travel was a selfish thing, Larian would later learn. At first you might travel back to help people, but soon others became pawns you knocked over and dolls you painted smiles on, broken things easily fixed. What was someone's happiness worth if you controlled every aspect of it?

An old man moved past the alleyway entrance. He stared wildly, beard ragged, whispering at shadows.

Would that soon be him, Larian wondered, seeing his splinter-selves in other timelines, unable to unsee a thousand nowadays?

As if in answer, the air distorted and, impossibly, his own reflection stepped out. Time rippled around his splinter-self. It lifted a laz-pistol.

This was impossible. It couldn't happen. Temporal physics forbade it.

Larian scrambled out of the line of sight behind accumulated debris.

He could see his splinter-selves in other timelines when he harboured, but he sure-as-Ell couldn't step through. And nor could they.

Larian swore as his other self came into view and fired.

Perhaps his splinter-self anticipated an attack, because it was only Larian's hesitation that saved him. Laz-flame fused the sand by his thigh.

Instinctively, Larian kicked out, catching his splinter nemesis at the ankle, collapsing him. The splinter-self seemed to fade a little, move slower through the air.

Larian scrambled to his feet. He turned a corner deeper into the alley, and ran straight into the woman with the red scarf.

"Hello," she said. "I found your anchor point and wanted to talk—"

She blocked his instinctive elbow with her forearm, triggering his exo-arm and sending it springing harmlessly past her face.

Then he saw the ring in her other hand.

He froze. It was worthless. Little more than a coin from an ancient press crudely welded to a chain link. The coin depicted a woman standing on a beach. Larian stared at it. The ring's image should have been washed from his dreams by innumerable memories, faded by the daylight of too many fractured lifetimes. But it stood stark.

His heart surged. His fist bunched in her scarf. "Where did you get that?"

She smiled. "Bo fetched it off a corpse years back. We thought it might get your attention."

Bo. A woman everyone knew of, but few had met, and the most powerful crime lord in the city. He reached for his knife.

Then the jolts of a stun-baton flowed through him.

Larian fell into black.

—◆—

*H*is *dreams are a morass of memories competing to cement themselves in a brain that can no longer contain them. Only the strongest win out and return to torture him, and even those are fleeting.*

He takes Bess by the hand. He cannot remember the details of her face, but he knows it is her. They flee their parents' argument, escaping to Junk Mountain on a restored hover bike.

There they play hide and seek. She was always better than him. Smaller and more cunning.

She finds the ring that day. Delighted, the troubled expression that always follows their parents' arguments vanishes from her face as she skips among the old junk hills, before instructing him to close his eyes and count.

He looks for her for hours, finally squeezing into a particularly cramped hole where he discovers the strange device. He activates it, unaware it is an old anchor point.

Whatever malfunction it causes, he loses hours. When he awakes it is late afternoon.

Eventually he returns to their parents' homestead to find sheets over bodies and the officers waiting. His parents lie sprawled on the carpet, laz-pistol burns covering them. The officers are surprised. Most criminals, they say, even twelve-year-olds, don't return to the scene of the crime quite so soon.

His dream shifts. He watches himself return and search for Bess countless times. Then his perspective shifts and he watches his splinter-selves moving back and forth through time. Seeking what? He cannot tell. But their movement in time creates more of themselves, occupying his myriad timelines. And now one of those trillions wants to kill him.

He dreams he finds Bess. The details of her face shift, fading from memory.

She isn't playing hide and seek anymore, she is playing chase.

He runs after her, but the closer he gets, the older he becomes. His hair grows long, teeth fall out, eyesight fades and steps falter. He cannot see her anymore, but his legs still move, rigidly and tired, as if of their own accord.

—◄═—

Larian came to.

It was night. He was being hauled across a great, broken courtyard, his feet dragging along the ground, catching on debris. His body was still frozen with the effects of the stun baton. Two sets of footsteps echoed at his sides.

The courtyard shifted, changing subtly, but remained stable.

Someone to his left lost their grip on Larian's shoulder and his world tilted. The rooftops here whipped and changed from one moment to another, some lightning fast, others slowly.

The Shifting Quarter, then. Atteridge's neglected heart. That wasn't good.

Someone hauled him upright with a curse and continued dragging him forwards, towards a door's dark opening.

He tried to move but still couldn't. The stun baton must've been fully charged. Where the hell had Bo found that ring? Why would she be interested in it?

Through the first door and into deeper darkness. Across a cold floor. Two masked figures stood to the side.

A door opened ahead and bright light cut through the darkness. More masked figures filed out as he approached.

He was hauled through the doorway and dropped on a hard stone floor. The air left him and he gasped. He tried to harbour but couldn't.

A hand wrenched his head up, forcing him into a kneeling position. He winced and surveyed his situation.

A dark-haired woman, presumably Bo, sat at an antique, heavy desk, piano-like in its depth. A faded carpet softened the hard floor beneath the desk.

The room was part of a once-vast warehouse, now bisected by a wall that concealed the remainder of the interior. A single door in that far wall was the only other exit.

Bo spoke intently with a masked henchman. No, a henchwoman, judging by the fall of the figure's clothing. Larian could barely make out Bo's words.

"Now is not the time to move," Bo hissed. Then, after a moment: "You'll lose the others' support."

The masked figure, agitated, glanced his way. "But we have what we need. There's no reason to delay. We'll have his support and countless numbers—"

Bo didn't rise from her seat. If anything she became more still. Her gaze locked on the masked figure standing over her. It was a look that had held assassins and mob bosses at bay. Bo's masked accomplice hesitated, then slowly wilted.

If Bo was bluffing, it worked. The henchwoman retreated, but still frustration lengthened her stride.

A cable was thrown ahead of Larian, its socket designed to fit his vest outlets.

"We've drained his vest's power, Bo. His anchor points are useless." Larian recognised the voice of the woman who'd stunned him.

"Thank you, Camilla," said Bo, her voice strangely similar. Face on, she was beautiful but worn down. Her eyes were old, like his and so many others. Although unlined, her face betrayed her weariness. *This was the fearsome Bo?*

Larian frowned. Where had he seen her? He searched his amnesiac mind, but nothing surfaced. He'd worked for so many criminals over the long years.

"You seem to be experiencing morale problems." Larian remarked, curious.

The retaliatory blow across the back of his head sent his vision spinning. "We act as one," hissed a voice behind him, distorted by a mask.

Larian winced. Only minor morale problems, then.

Bo looked over, smirking in response. "Have you always spewed pointless vacuities, Larian Carver?" Her eyes pinned his across the metres between them, searching.

Larian shifted, uncomfortable beneath her gaze.

For a moment Bo's expression softened, as if recognising something, and then the smirk returned. "I don't think so. Or you wouldn't be here." She sat back, considering him. "You run, Larian, but not from your own curiosity."

Larian's mouth twitched. "No power, or I'd harbour in a blink."

136

"Again with the glibness." Irritation flared in her eyes, and something else. Disappointment? "No one commits to a cause anymore; they say their hollow words and slip back through time to find another moment. But you're trapped now as surely as if I'd caged you."

Larian ignored her question, becoming serious. "Where is she?"

Bo's lips pursed. Her eyes bored into him. "How many times have you gone back to search for her?"

Larian's eyes narrowed, his fingers twitched. *Too many times.*

Bo threw her head back and laughed. "We're all looking for someone, Larian. Have you found any trace of her?"

Bo stood, neatly sidestepped the desk, and paced towards him. Her eyes, which should have been clouded by too many yesterdays, were focused.

Larian struggled to his feet, conscious of the desperation in his voice. "Where is she? Where did you get that ring?"

Hands like iron gripped him from behind and pulled him down. Rough hands bound his right wrist behind his back to his exo-skeletal arm. If he activated it, he'd dislocate his shoulder.

Bo stopped just beyond reach and removed something from her pocket.

His throat caught. The pressed-penny ring.

She threw it up and caught it. "I had copies made." She brushed it tenderly, then smiled coldly. "She's here, Larian."

Larian's heart jumped, his breath quickened.

A figure moved to stand before him. It was the woman from the alley, Camilla, knife in hand. She set it against his throat. "Don't move."

He nodded and Camilla removed the blade.

"Whatever she pays you, I'll double it," he whispered.

Her blade reappeared at his throat. "Our sister does this for all our futures."

He laughed. He'd heard this delusion too many times. "Is that what you think? That you're more than just criminals? That you're some kind of *family*?"

Bo gave Camilla a hard stare and the knife reluctantly vanished.

Larian glanced at Camilla as she returned to her post behind him. Her resemblance to Bo was striking. Perhaps they were sisters after all? He frowned.

"Business gets messy when you involve family, Bo."

Bo's demeanour shifted. Her hand clenched around the ring. In two strides she'd caught Larian by the collar. "Family is the only business I really care about," she hissed. She threw him to the ground. Hard.

Larian winced as his exo-arm slammed against the floor and wedged into his back. He heard something metallic break.

Bo knelt over him.

He was sick of this charade, his voice weary. "Tell me what in the Ell you want me to do and where she is." He moved carefully and, finding a new, jagged edge to his exo-arm, shifted imperceptibly to work the knot.

Camilla moved to separate them, hand on Bo's shoulder. Bo swung toward the woman, snarling. "Touch me again and you'll get nothing in this timeline, or any other!"

Camilla reluctantly backed away.

Bo turned back to Larian. Her eyes narrowed, pinning him. She leant closer, speaking softly. "I want the life that was taken from me. I want my old life back and only you can give that to me." She glanced quickly at Camilla, who stood a few paces away, and lowered her voice to a whisper. "Pay attention."

Bo stood and walked slowly to the desk. When she turned to face him again she'd composed herself. She leant back against the bulky desk, her expression cold.

Larian frowned. What was this about? "You've got all *this*. You can afford to stabilise your structure in the middle of the Shifting Quarter," he said, recovering to a kneeling position. Larian worked the rope faster. "You've got thugs to send back in time to intimidate, bribe or kill anyone who tries to change the building.

"Unless ..." He began chuckling. "You can't go far enough back. You've got the power, but you don't have an anchor point set far enough back." He let his head fall forward, laughter wracking him. "So you need *me* to do it? Change your past for you?"

Camilla shifted behind him.

Bo exchanged a glance with her. Then she strode forward, standing over Larian once again.

"Why not get someone else to do it?" asked Larian.

He didn't see Bo's foot bury itself in his stomach, only felt the air leave his lungs.

"There are complicating factors." She glanced again at Camilla.

Camilla's grip tightened, steadying Larian as he gasped.

"A simple choice," Bo said, losing patience. "Help me or die."

Larian laughed through his wheezing. "Your bargaining skills need work, Bo. And your people chose the wrong man." He caught his breath, grimacing. "I have the time-sickness."

Bo's face froze. "Already?"

Camilla spoke. "We confirmed it in the alley. We should act soon."

Act on what? wondered Larian. Why did Bo tolerate the insubordination? What did his time-sickness have to do with anything?

Bo's expression was stricken. "You're the only one who can do it, you're ..."

His questions multiplied, but one clamoured loudest. "*Tell me where my sister is.*"

Bo deflated, weariness crowding her features. "Remember, I told you to pay attention?" She shifted her weight off the desk. "Like I said." She turned, found the lid of the heavy desk and lifted it with both hands, folding it back. "She's here."

Camilla yanked Larian up, allowing him a better view.

He almost lost his footing. A lock of hair. An identical, but rusted, penny-pressed ring on a tiny, bony finger, attached to the skeleton of a child.

Larian surged forward, straining at his bonds. Camilla gave one step, then two. He was a mere metre from Bo. "What did you do to her?" he shouted.

But it was useless, Camilla's grip was iron. He sagged against her, exhausted, washed hollow by the past.

"She wandered through the junk yards for a while." Bo stroked a femur. Her eyes locked on some memory. "We always remember our first one, don't we?"

Larian spat, angry tears in his eyes. "You're a monster."

"And who makes the monsters?" snarled Bo. "The vulnerable girl? Or the brother who abandoned her?"

Larian worked the exo-arm once more, angrily, and the bond broke.

He stood, even as Camilla and the masked sentry realised what had happened. Larian pivoted, bringing his arm around, angry tears in his eyes. "You killed my parents and sister." He angled and sharply rotated his forearm. The exo-skeletal hammer sprang forward. His aim was off, but the jagged side to it tore through the masked assailant's throat and spine, before she dropped, limp, to the floor.

"You took her ring." Larian spun back to face Bo, who had backed away. "The one thing she cherished!" He eyed the laz-pistol and stun baton at her belt.

"The one thing we all cherish," she replied, with a sad smile.

He advanced a step. "You destroyed my home."

Bo backed away a step, holding up a hand to restrain Camilla. "Wrong. And it wasn't much of a home, as I recall."

Larian threw an anchor point into the air, activating it meters above them. "You don't know anything about my home!"

But when he looked back at her, Bo's sorrow had deepened.

Larian stopped. Now he saw why her troubled face had seemed so familiar. Not because he had seen it reflected in Camilla's earlier that day. Maturity and constant vigilance had changed her, but she was about the right age. *I want the life that was taken from me … only you can give it to me.* It explained the copies of the ring. *It's always been about family.* He struggled to breathe, to release the words. His eyes stung. "Bess?"

She froze, meeting his stare. Regret bloomed in her eyes. Her shoulders slumped despite the strength that had held them straight for so long. "I'm sorry, Larian. It's difficult to find someone who doesn't want to be found."

Larian stood still. "But you dragged me here."

Bo shook her head, looking past him. "No. They did." She unholstered her laz-gun, lifted it towards him and fired. Heat brushed his arm and he dodged to the side. But her intended target was Camilla, standing behind him.

Camilla cursed, clutching her shoulder.

"What do you mean *they*, Bess?"

—A flash of blue light behind him and *time blurred around Camilla as her past rewrote itself*—

Re-written memories crowded into his mind.

Camilla had let the same conversation play out, but this time had fired her own weapon first. "You will not undo our existence," she said.

Bess was on a knee, laz burns on her chest. Her weapon was raised, but now it was aimed at Larian. "They'll send you back time and again until there are too many of you."

Bess's laz-shot entered through Larian's stomach, and he collapsed to the ground, blood running beneath his fingers. "Who? Why?" But he knew who she meant. His splinter-self.

"So they can't use you like they did me." Bess collapsed beside Larian, her weapon sliding out of reach.

Somewhere a door opened. Four figures approached and stood over him. They had shed their masks. The same face repeated itself.

Bess's face.

"A splinter-brother also has the technology to invade the prime-line," said one. "Larian must bring him forth."

So it had already happened to Bess. Had the skeleton in the desk been the first? Had she kept it as a threat to the others?

"Sisters. Your splinter-sisters, Larian." Bess's—the real Bess's—eyes had seen much, but they couldn't lie. He saw years of it. A young girl trying to make her way in the world. The killing, first at the whim of others. Then, when the time sickness took her as it was taking him, at the whim of her splinter-selves. It was more than the simple madness most endured. She couldn't harbour without releasing another of them.

"Some of us are trapped by circumstances," she said, her eyes clouding.

The splinter-Besses looked down at where he lay, expressions blank. "I'm sorry, brother," they said in unison.

"You were always too talkative," he said, with a tight smile. His hand closed around the stun baton in Bess's belt. He lifted it to his vest's power socket, activating it. It wasn't much power, but it was enough.

He bit down, harbouring—

—*"it wasn't much of a home, as I recall," she'd said*—

—He was in mid-air and minutes earlier at his tossed anchor point. Only a fading blur where he'd once stood below. He heard Camilla's bones break when he landed on her and gasped as his own shoulder dislocated.

Larian fought blackness at the edges of his vision. "Bess, I know. They know." He sensed her hesitate as he rose into a crouch, and snatched Bess's laz-pistol from her holster. He pivoted, firing into Bess's splinter-selves as they entered once more through the door behind him.

When he turned back, Bess lay on the ground. Blood pooled beneath her.

Behind her, his splinter-self stood, weapon raised.

Larian fired at his splinter-self. It moved in a time-twisting blur, effortlessly dodging the laz-flame, reading his intentions moments before he acted. It advanced slowly, but inexorably, gun levelled.

Larian crouched next to Bess. She tried to rise, but fell back again with a wet cough. She motioned for him to lift her.

He complied, wincing at the weight on his one good arm.

Larian fired again at his splinter-self. His wild shots only slowed its advance.

"I might have forgotten what I was," Bo whispered in his ear. "But I know what I am now." She motioned at the desk. "Choices make us monsters."

More shots entered Bess and her eyes started to lose focus.

Bess pulled his laz-pistol up between them. "Something he doesn't expect," she whispered. She fumbled, dialling the laz-pistol up to maximum power. One shot remaining.

"Reactor core … far end of the warehouse. Go back … Get the life that was taken from me." She pressed the pistol to her shoulder. "I know you didn't kill Mum and Dad," she whispered.

Larian swallowed, grasped the pistol, and fired. The beam scythed through Bess and beyond, cutting through the arm of his splinter-self.

It blurred, trying to rewind and find another way, but whatever tech allowed it through seemed to falter. It stumbled away towards the dividing wall and, clutching its shoulder, entered the back room.

Larian closed his sister's eyes and gently lowered her to the ground. She looked peaceful, as if she really had seen only her twenty-nine years. He marvelled at how timelessness aged a person in subtle ways, leaving their skin smooth but their face hard, and how it receded in death.

A noise from the back room returned him to the present.

The power source.

Biting down on the pain, he wrenched his dislocated arm back into place and stumbled to the back room.

His splinter-self looked at him with an accusatory stare, activated the core and harboured in a flash of blue.

Larian moved to the panel, draining the core's remaining power. He knew exactly where his splinter-self was going. He harboured—

*H*ow *the splinter Larian, or Besses, had managed to physically invade the prime-line, Larian had no idea.*

But he saw them all, in an instant that seemed an eternity, awaiting their turn, as he followed the prime-line back down the years, back to Junk Mountain and Bess. Shadowy splinter-selves looked up from whatever moment in time they were caught, their faces scared or angry.

Except one. He was caught in the act of kneeling to ruffle someone's hair, his expression sad. Then he looked up, noticed Larian, and smiled.

Instead of searching for Bess, and failing to find her, as he had so many times before, Larian ran from the junk yard.

His bare feet whispered across the sand. Twelve-year-old limbs whirred, trying to outrun the future, returning to the house he'd left only hours earlier.

Ten minutes later, he could hear the distant sound of laz-shots echoing from his home.

The first dead man lay next to the rose garden, weapon taken. The second was dead by the doorway, weapon still holstered.

Larian retrieved it and entered his family home in time to see the laz-shot pierce his mother. His father was already curled into a ball, dying.

"Why?" his mother breathed.

Larian saw his splinter-self's young throat move, as if trying to say something. But no words emerged, blocked by some property of time or the technology he used to cheat it. Was it recrimination? Or words of sorrow?

Larian decided he didn't care. He raised his weapon and fired. His splinter-self collapsed, and Larian saw his own twelve-year-old face staring sightlessly back.

Larian moved to his parents. Both their vests were damaged beyond repair. His father coughed and, holding his mother, tried to speak.

But Larian quieted him, already moving to max his vest's power from an outlet.

Then he stopped, his earlier words returning to mock him. *You've got the power, but you don't have an anchor point set far enough back.* He couldn't undo it. A tear rolled down Larian's face. He raged then. He pleaded with them not to leave him, promised that he'd go back and fix it.

Larian's parents died holding each other.

Larian cradled them for as long as he dared. Then he rose and, taking what provisions remained from the homestead, left before the police arrived. He deactivated and destroyed his vest, removing any temptation to return to his former timeline.

Later, the newsfeeds would report an attack on his parents' homestead. The mother and father killed, the son also murdered while attempting to defend his parents against revenge for sizeable debts.

Larian pieced together a theory over the days that followed. Years ago, he reasoned, those early splinter-selves, like his sister's, must have concluded that eventually prime-line Larian would reach a large enough power source, cease a fruitless search for his sister, and find a way to save his family and create a past in which he could find contentment. Perhaps, for his splinter-selves, even the pain of their shared parents' murder had faded with time.

Maybe they forgot their shared trauma or fell to madness or simply moved on in their own timeline. Regardless, they'd perpetuated their existence in the only way they knew: ensuring history repeated itself. And eventually they'd found the technology to do so.

Larian could never go back and save his parents, but he could find his sister. Even if he became old in the process, even if his teeth began to fall out and his steps faltered.

He'd kill whoever he had to so that Bess would never become Bo.

He thought of the splinter-self that had smiled back in that last harbouring and resolved to change the future one final time.

Angus Yeates was originally from a remote desert mining town in Western Australia, where he began reading and later writing. He now lives and works in Canberra as a full-time public servant. To spice up his life he has pursued various interests (with various degrees of success), including martial arts, archery, acting, public speaking, and stand-up comedy. However, his main passion has always remained writing speculative fiction. His earlier published work 'The Swagman' appeared in the previous CSFG anthology, *Never Never Land*. This is his second published work. He hopes you enjoyed it.

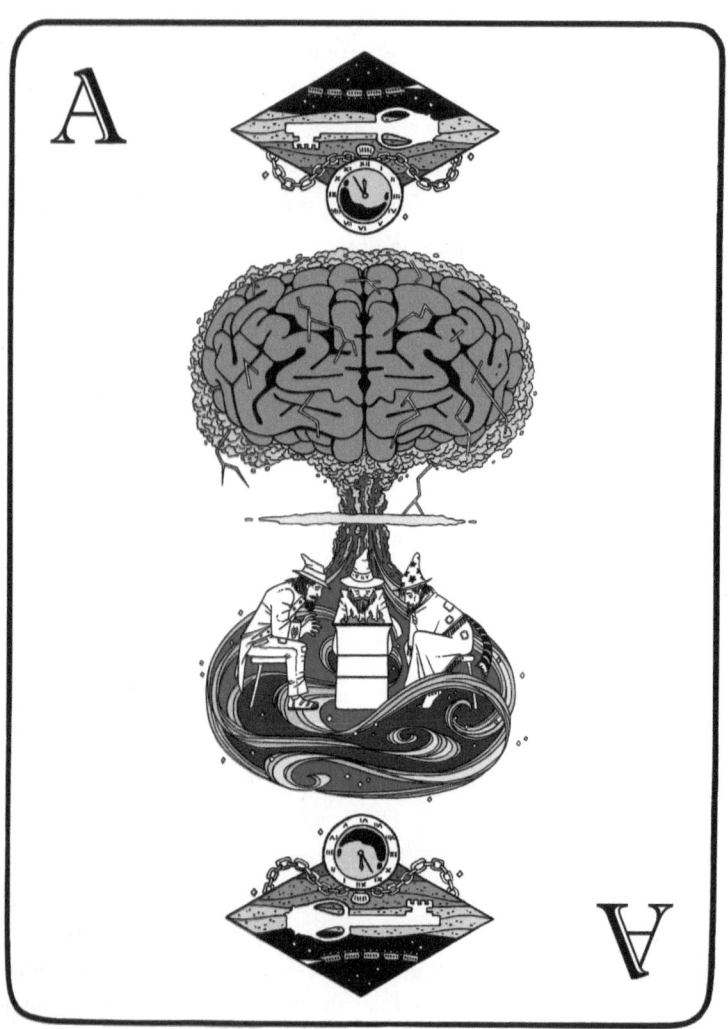

The Last Magicians of Sad Hill

C H Pearce

The woman in black warms herself by our fire, as if she's one of us. Next thing she'll be helping herself to stew. We're sheltered from the desert wind in the shadow of the old family store by the railway tracks. The store is boarded up. The tree by its side is bone-dry. We're the last stragglers to leave town.

I hold my blue-veined hands over the flames, so close my beard threatens to trail in the bin fire. My fingernails curl toward the heat as if to dive in.

The woman in black doesn't put out her hands like us. She must be warm in that cloak. We're jealous. We squint sidelong at the stranger from under our hats and above our beards.

"What's she doing," mouths Brother Duo, "by *our* fire?"

He says it like there's another campfire within the exclusion zone. I scrape down the pot, dividing the last spoonful of stew between us. I slap Brother Duo's hand away when he grasps at Uno's share.

The birds in the skeleton tree are screaming. Must be hundreds of them now. I can't tell if it's because of the smoke, or the stranger, or the interloping sun staggering up the horizon in a haze.

"Waiting for the train." The stranger's voice is as toneless as hooves on stones. Is that supposed to be a question?

"Town's been evacuated." I stroke my beard. "Last train is coming for us." My face is warming as I speak. It's pleasant, then—shit. A spark burns bright in my beard, and I flail my limbs batting it out.

I transform my dance into pacing. When I'm double-sure the fire is out, I brush down my coat. My fingers close on my pocketwatch and I draw it out. It's gold, and when I flick open the cover, there's a black-and-white photograph of a woman holding a baby. Behind them there are apple trees in bloom. The woman wears a white dress and her ring is set with a jewel as big as the baby's eye. The watch hasn't kept time since evacuation day. I've not let that get in the way of my routine.

My watch ticks. Just one twitch of the second-hand, but I see it.

"How long have you been waiting, Brother Tres?" The woman in black turns her hooded face to me. She is picking at her fingernails with a long knife.

"The last train is coming for us," I repeat staunchly. I look to Uno and Duo, but they're already staring at me with their mouths open. Duo lifts his hat to scratch his balding head. I'm hoping the stranger isn't going to ask why we're evacuating. It doesn't matter if I've lost that. It's only detail.

"Your beards and fingernails have grown long with waiting," says the stranger. "And filthy. What kind of names are Uno, Duo and Tres? Real ones?" The woman in black taps her forehead. I don't like the way her smile wraps around her face. I wish she'd wear her hood all the time.

"You're the heroes who saved Sad Hill. So don't look sour. You've contained the nuclear blast in a timeless zone for one hundred years, with a magic that exacts its dues from your once-great minds." The stranger examines her fingernails and re-sheathes the knife. "Apparently."

The woman in black stands and raises a hand to the sky, as if to hail the driver of an approaching train only she can see. She is looking directly upwards. What a nut-tree. "It would be timely for you to leave with me. Everyone's living safely in bunkers in Undercity West. Your failing magic is obsolete, but your deeds are known. The Mayor has instructed me to escort the Last Magicians onto the stage when she wins—again—tonight."

"What rot," I bellow, or try to, but the air has grown dusty, and it's dried up the words on my tongue. The birds are silent. Something is wrong; we all know.

The earth roars. My Brothers and I are knocked from our feet by the force of it.

My ear is to the shaking ground. I raise my head and rub sand from my streaming eyes.

"Is it our train?" I shout over the din.

The woman in black tells us, I can see her lips forming the words, but my ears are ringing. Nut-tree points: her sky-train is coming for us. She sweeps an arm for us to follow.

My Brothers look to me. I echo the gesture and we stagger to our feet in the wake of the woman in black. I think of a nuclear blast, like the first spark of a wildfire, paused in its inception and ready to spread. Behind us a bright white light eats up the horizon.

"I was saying," the woman in black patiently explains, "I would leave you to die, but if I don't bring all three of you in, I don't get paid."

Through the grubby sky-train window, we watch the nuclear blast mushroom, slowly at first, then faster and faster, as we rise high into the air and the timeless zone judders out of existence.

The stranger is crouched easily on the trembling metal floor. If it were wood, I might think us inside a train compartment. We three struggle to hold our footing and barrel into one another for support. The woman in black is frowning at a panel set in the skin of her arm. On the panel there are colours like a page torn from a picture-book. The sky-train thrums like the wind whipping through our bare tree.

"Are your ears ringing, old man?"

I press my face against the glass. The sliver of window runs the extent of the sky-train cabin. I rub the grime from the glass with my sleeve, watching the old family store, our tree and the railway track recede beneath us. Our bin fire is a pinprick.

"Look, Tres." Duo is pointing over my shoulder. "See how our railway track runs out. The dunes cover it short of the edge of the zone. The train could never have come for us."

What remains of the railway track is being eaten up by the white light, expanding towards our camp. I wonder if our birds have flown high enough.

The sky-train shakes. Harsh light floods through the windows onto my Brothers' faces, throwing every crag into sharp relief. How old we have grown. Uno and Duo will require an explanation presently.

I pat Duo's withered hand. It is shaking.

Minutes ago—I reach again for my pocketwatch, and it's ticking correctly to the second—we were in the desert. The woman in black helped us up a metal ramp into the descending sky-train, one by one, like an old friend. And when the ramp drew up to shut out the desert and the white light, she let go of my hand.

The woman in black holds her wrist to her face. No mouth ought to be in possession of so many teeth. "We're in the air, Assistant Mason. All three special guests are accounted for and"—she looks at me—"intact."

A boy's voice cracks and I jump: it's coming out of her arm. It sounds like a young man endeavouring to lower his voice to sound mature. *Dutiful as ever, Chernobog.*

I snort with laughter and cover my mouth with my hands. Chernobog turns her face to me. "Sorry," I wheeze. "I laugh when I'm nervous."

Chernobog looks to the panel in her arm. I see now there's a young man's face in it. I wonder if this is the magic she told of. I wonder if we are the wizards of legend Chernobog insists we are. Perhaps she has rescued the wrong three old men. I imagine the real wizards somewhere else in the exclusion zone, vaporised by the white blast, and no one being any the wiser.

"Dutiful?" Chernobog's laugh is like a persistent cough. "Let's have no confusion, Assistant Mason: you mean professional. I will complete the Mayor's delivery in one hour—three hours prior to the Election Day broadcast, which you will note is more generous than agreed in our booking. Will you verify?" She casts her arm towards us.

My Brothers and I huddle together, staring at the tiny face of Assistant Mason on the panel in Chernobog's arm. Uno buries his face in my shoulder.

"You'll wire me the next instalment now," says the woman in black. "I'll take the remainder upon arrival."

Chernobog casts us a sidelong look. She doesn't trouble to whisper when she adds: "Assistant, one suggestion. A makeup team prior to the ceremony if you intend to stream live. Consider also a chewable relaxant for the stage appearance. They're very, very … old."

Assistant Mason is nodding. *Check your accounts. I'll expect you at the station in one hour.*

When Mason nods to us, we all jump. Duo and Uno huddle behind me and peer over my shoulders. *I look forward to meeting you in person, Magicians.* The young man bows and stretches out a hand towards the panel. On the tiny screen he appears no bigger than a rat. I'm frozen with terror, imagining he's going to climb all the way out of the panel, scramble down Chernobog's arm, and run at us. The panel goes black.

"Sit. Take a look out the windows." Chernobog examines the numbers on her screen, stroking *5000 bits* as if the text is as tangible as gold. I wonder if that's a little or a lot. "The exclusion zone will be gone in a tick. You'll need your strength for tonight's ceremony."

Duo and Uno perch on the nearest bench. Like grotesque children, they kneel facing the window with their palms on the glass. "I can't see our camp, Tres," says Duo.

A dust cloud obscures our view of the ground. From up here the zone looks endless. I can't tell if it's desert or fallout. I don't want to look anymore.

"It's just as I told you, Uno and Duo. A good thing you had faith. Our train came to evacuate us just in time. Goodbye, Sad Hill. Hello to the new world."

My Brothers' old faces crumple into smiles. I watch them visibly relax: their high shoulders slump and they shuffle about the cabin. Who will greet them at the station at Undercity West? A lover, or a family?

"Be aware that any loved ones you may remember have been dead for generations." Chernobog is taking bites from an apple. The juice dribbles down her chin but she catches it and sucks her fingers thoughtfully. "Except the Mayor. Time moved differently in the zone."

"Is this your idea of kindness? Keep to what you know," I snap. I don't remember anyone but my eyes are watering. "Don't tell Uno and Duo, for God's sake."

"They will figure it out when we reach the city. So will you." I expect her to throw away the core but she keeps eating with the persistence of a horse, leaving only three small seeds. "I am patient, generally speaking. You are quicker than your brothers, but my business is not usually with senile old men. My patience is wearing thin."

"Why don't you just let us die?" I surprise myself. It sounds more whine than outburst.

"I told you," says Chernobog. She cups each apple seed in her palm and from there, places them one by one in a pocket at her belt, next to her holster. "I want what the Mayor and her Assistant have promised me."

"More money?"

Chernobog speaks no more. She looks at the panel set in her wrist and suggests, via tossing her knife in the air with the opposite hand and catching it by the handle, that she has to concentrate. I join my Brothers at the window and talk to them carefully of the new world.

When we reach the entrance to the Undercity we circle. Uno is sweating. He is still wrapped in his mismatched layers of cold weather gear. I divest him of his hat, scarf and gloves, all of which are sandy, and place each item in his hands. "Hang on to these, Uno." I close his fingers over them. "It might be cold in the new world."

"Air traffic control, Undercity West," Chernobog repeats into the panel on her arm. "This is Oldtimer-105. Seeking permission to land."

"This is Control. We're working on it," crackles a voice from the speaker. This man sounds older than Assistant Mason. Assistant Mason sounded twelve.

Chernobog repeats this exchange. Then she repeats it a full five times. Each time she adds an alternative question.

"Are you aware of lockdown procedure exemption 14B?"

"Are you aware it's safe to open the outer doors during an exclusion zone event for 0.7 seconds, providing quarantine procedures are followed?"

"Are you aware we are running out of fuel?"

And finally: "I suggest you call the Mayor's office. I am wiring you the direct number now."

"The Oldtime party candidate's office," corrects the Controller. "You mean candidate Gopinatha."

"I mean the Mayor," says Chernobog, "incumbent, future, and always."

"Alright," says the Controller. The static stops as he signs off.

Thirty-two seconds later the static resumes. "Landing permission granted. Commence landing procedure in accordance with emergency lockdown protocol." The Controller swallows audibly. "I'm so sorry for the mixup ..."

"Take a seat and buckle up." Chernobog turns to my Brothers and I, having ignored us for the past hour. I nod and shepherd my Brothers to a bench. Duo and I buckle ourselves in. We are still wrestling with Uno's straps when the ship shudders into life.

The ship groans. Chernobog is guiding us down with flicks of her fingers over the panel in her arm. She tells the Controller, "There's nothing to forgive," and seems to inhale his sigh of relief through the speaker, before adding "but I cannot speak for the Mayor." She signs off partway through his protest.

"The Controller was unwise," Chernobog tells me in response to my questioning stare.

"What will happen to him? What kind of person is this Mayor Gopinatha?"

"Mayor Gopinatha is the kind of person who pays exactly what she agrees upon," says Chernobog, "for exactly the service she agrees upon."

"I thought you worked for yourself. Why are you so sure this candidate will win the election? Are you a member of this Oldtime party?"

Chernobog shows me her knife with the speed of a spider. Her lips are drawn back behind her yellow teeth. Her receding gums give her teeth a skull-like prominence. This is the last thing I am going to see. All I can think is that I badly need to relieve myself, and I can't remember what one does when there isn't the back of an old general store and an infinite amount of sand available.

Suddenly Chernobog is smiling, and I wonder if it was a smile the whole time. "Correct: I work for myself. I have no political affiliation." Her teeth are still bared, and her knuckles white. "Silence until we land at the station."

We three sit admonished on the bench like schoolboys. I cross my legs, hold onto my dignity, and look out the window. My beard scratches against the glass. I force myself to look past my own reflection.

As we descend, the desert gapes like a trapdoor and a waterfall of sand cascades into the pit. As we near it, the sky-train rumbles. Our pilot brings us gently down.

"We are descending into the mouth of a demon," whispers Duo. "I want to go back to Sad Hill."

Uno's mouth becomes a thin line. He looks like he's about to vomit.

"Don't frighten Uno." I smack the back of Duo's head. "Go back to Sad Hill if you want: it's radioactive dust. It was a wasteland to begin with. We're going to Undercity West, the new world."

Chernobog nods. We dip under the sands and the windows turn black.

Though it would soothe my Brothers to hear it, I can't bring myself to repeat the part about us being heroes, or magicians. I don't feel like a hero. I feel like an old man who needs the bathroom. I'm sure that even with my memories scattered, if I retain the *conviction* that where there is civilisation there ought to be bathrooms presently, I should retain a conviction that my Brothers and I once acted with heroism.

The door in the desert thunders to a close above us. The sky-train travels level now through a cavernous tunnel. Above us the darkness is lit by lamps at regular intervals.

"Look, we're a train now." My Brothers sit on either side of me on the bench, our heads twisted round to look out the window. I shake their shoulders jovially. "Trust me. Chernobog came to evacuate us, and presently she will deliver us to the new world. Everything is happening exactly as I told you."

—◂—

We glide, trackless, into a station. With a final sigh the ship is silent. The station sign reads UNDERCITY WEST. Above us is a towering ceiling lit by lamps, and no sign of sky. The crowd is so thick I cannot see the ground between the people. Many of them are waving their arms at us and holding banners.

GOPINATHA FOR MAYOR—AGAIN!!!

BRING BACK THAT OLDTIME MAGIC.

OUR SAVIOURS—GOPINATHA AND THE MAGICIANS.

KILL ALL NEWTIMERS.

I nod sagely as if I am unsurprised.

Chernobog is already talking to Assistant Mason with her wrist at face level. The crowd is quick to throng around our ship, pointing and jumping. We remain in our seats because Chernobog has not yet told us we can get up, and I remember the threat of her teeth and her knife.

"We're going to have trouble escorting our special guests through the crowd," she is telling Mason through her armpiece, "in their condition."

We can't have them seen in their current state. I'll have a propo crew, with make-up, outside your ship in ten minutes. From the moment the Magicians step off the Oldtimer-105 we'll start the party victory broadcast, live.

"We also need a bathroom," I call out. Uno wheezes with silent laughter.

Chernobog echoes with a hacking cough. From the panel in Chernobog's arm Mason stares at us. It unnerves me deeply to meet his gaze, but I grin at the little face with all my remaining teeth.

"There's a bathroom on the ship, Brother Tres," says Chernobog. "I am not a savage. I'll show you."

Mason takes a deep breath. He is pressing two fingers to his forehead. *I see what you mean about the Magicians. I'm sending the Mayor's scriptwriter and voice coach with the propo crew. We have a lot of work to do in two hours.*

"You might have had them delivered earlier, had you asked."

The Mayor knows what we need. We are paying for the Last Magicians of Sad Hill to be delivered alive and well to endorse our glorious victory. The party has no need of campaign assistance.

Chernobog shrugs. "I will take my leave," she tells Mason, her finger hovering over the panel, "or the Last Magician will wet himself." With a swipe of her finger Mason is replaced with a blue slate.

Chernobog shows me to a small toilet compartment and waits outside until I am done.

I struggle out from behind the door to find Chernobog watching. "Did you think I would magic myself down the drain?"

"You have a little magic left. And a little life left, I think. Your Brothers, I am not so sure of."

Chernobog's black hood has fallen back onto her shoulders. Her hair is pulled tight in a bun. There's nowhere for an expression to hide, and yet there's not a flicker to indicate a joke, when she adds: "You remind me of my father."

I stroke my beard thoughtfully and discover the bone of a small bird. I put the bone in my pocket where it clinks against my gold watch. "Did your father have a long, unkempt beard," I hazard, "in which he kept small bones?"

"No." Chernobog bursts into hacking laughter seconds before she manages: "My father was a useless drunk."

I laugh along. Reflexively at first, but soon my shoulders are shaking. I find Duo and Uno and tell them Chernobog set me up. We cackle together.

I make sure Uno and Duo use the toilet and wash up before the propo crew arrives. Uno struggles to do up his fly, then stares at the water trickling from the washbasin tap. I laugh at his helplessness, and when I grow ashamed, help. I turn off the tap for Uno, dry his hands on my sand-dotted scarf and tell him that he did a good job. I wonder what kind of person Brother Uno was before all this, and regret that I must have known and forgotten.

"Stay back on the benches," Chernobog warns. "The Mayor's crew approaches. You may prefer not to look out the windows."

Immediately I look down from the sky-train windows onto the crowd. A black cart with a *G* emblazoned on the roof moves toward our ship at an obstinate crawl. At first there is cheering. The cart's progress is slow but constant, and the crowd is thick. People can't quite move out of the way fast enough.

The first person who is crushed does not fall under the wheels of the cart but under the scrambling feet of her neighbours. The woman's head dips under the level of the shifting crowd, slowly and then all at once, like she's been sucked into quicksand. I expect to hear a cry, but there's no sound. She's gone.

That's when the real panic starts. Even from inside the sky-train I can hear the muffled roar of screaming.

"I told you to look away," says Chernobog. She lets down the ship's ramp.

Pouring out of the black cart and up the ramp are a team of smartly dressed young men and women. They file up the ramp and into the sky-train at a run; they are carrying black bags like doctor's briefcases.

Panicked members of the crowd attempt to run inside after them, but the ramp is rising, and Chernobog is drawing her pistol from her belt.

As the uninvited scramble up the ramp, Chernobog shoots. She reloads and advances as the first two are falling from the ramp back down onto the crowd.

The third she shoots in the leg, and he staggers back down the ramp by himself, as if he had just been politely instructed to leave.

The last of our invited crew runs into the sky-train. This one has blood on his suit and bag.

I have to look away to cover Duo and Uno's eyes. When I have both hands in place over their faces I watch again.

As the ramp folds back up into the ship there's one last interloper clinging to its edge. He's half-thrown his leg over the top of the ramp.

"Let go," Chernobog warns.

When the man doesn't let go she shoots him in the side of the head. He falls into the crowd below and the ramp shudders closed.

Sweat beads on Chernobog's upper lip. She shows me all her teeth in a grin. Then she holsters her pistol. "If I hadn't shot him," she tells me, "he would have met a stickier end between the ramp and my ship. What do you think of my aim?"

"It's good." The sound of my own voice surprises me with its normalcy. I lower both hands from Duo and Uno's eyes. "Good job, my girl."

Chernobog is talking to the suits with more animation than I have seen her show hitherto, pointing to my Brothers and I, and gesturing expansively.

The suits advance on us and I am frozen. A woman with a sweep of bright green hair is tilting my head back and pulling a razor from her work bag. She holds the razor to my neck.

"It's fine," I assure my Brothers. "They're here to help."

We three old men are stripped, clipped, shaved, doused with sweet-smelling water, towelled, and dressed. The team pull us into new clothes like parents dressing their reluctant children. I expect to be compelled into suits like the Mayor's propo crew. Instead our robes are long and colourfully embroidered. Our hair is combed—the green-haired woman notes that Duo has hardly any left, compared to me—and our faces are dusted with fine powder.

While they work, a pair of suits are setting up what looks like a camera on a tripod. Another suit is sweeping our filthy clothes, our grey hair and our nail clippings into a corner.

Chernobog is talking to the suit with the camera about crowd control. "I'd prefer not to shoot anyone live on propo."

The young man assures her they would prefer that too.

The green-haired woman is holding a hand-mirror up to me. I expect them to reinvent us but I don't look a jot less ancient than I looked in the sky-train window. If anything, our lack of beards and our slicked-back hair show our craggy faces more starkly.

"That's it. Don't smile too much." The green-haired woman returns the mirror to her bag. "I don't have time to do anything about your teeth."

"Five minutes until showtime," calls the suit with the camera. "Get ready to move."

The ramp lowers and we're ushered out of the sky-train. The deaths seem to have occurred as part of the whirlwind of preparation for the ceremony, no more unpleasant and inconvenient than our dressing and shaving.

Chernobog pulls her black hood over her face and prods me in the ribs, as if I weren't capable of walking unaccompanied. Uno and Duo cling to the sleeves of my robe. The crowd cheers.

"Another miracle. Bring my brother back to life, Magician," begs a voice from the crowd. There's too many faces. They are cheering. *Gopinatha. Victory. Welcome our saviours* ... I can't see who is talking. The suits form a barrier between the crowd and my Brothers and I. We move forward in a pack.

"First heal my sick mother," cries another voice. She could be any one of a dozen I pass. "She has been a loyal party supporter all her life."

"Are you saying my brother wasn't ..." We leave them behind.

At the rear of the station is a stage. In the centre of the platform is a single microphone, a woman and a young man, and above them, a banner reading: GLORIOUS VICTORY FOR OLDTIME.

The woman's suit and hair are white. She is very clean. Her only ornament is a ring set with a great jewel. It's about as big as a baby's eye, and green as an apple.

I smile up at the stage. I had often wondered, thumbing the black-and-white photograph in my pocketwatch, what colour that jewel was.

The orator's voice is mellifluous and the crowd hushes when she speaks. Behind her stands a young man whose face I recognise as Assistant Mason's.

The crowd wasn't there for our ship at all. It was just the overflow of party supporters who arrived too late to congregate close to the stage.

"It is Gopinatha, the Mayor Eternal."

What does Chernobog expect me to say? I knit my brows and pat down my robes with the intention of showing her my photograph. But my effects are back on the Oldtimer-105, with our fingernail clippings.

"I will take you to the wings. When you are escorted onto the stage, you must say only what you are told through your earpiece, and no more. Then I will receive my reward."

The words on the banner shift before my eyes. SPECIAL GUESTS: THE LAST MAGICIANS OF SAD HILL … APPLAUSE … As the word APPLAUSE rolls across the banner the crowd cheers and claps violently, as if each member is trying to outdo their neighbour.

Uno, Duo and I walk out onto the stage like prodded cattle. It is wider and emptier than our desert, and the roar of the crowd more foreboding than the wind. Chernobog accompanies us.

"It's you who make Undercity West what it is by allowing me the privilege of guiding you for a twenty-fifth term. I pledge that for the next four years … "

"A twenty-fifth four-year term?" Duo whispers to me. "That would make her over one hundred years old."

"She looks good for her age." My mouth is dry. Time moved differently outside the zone, Chernobog said, except for the Mayor. I begin to wonder if it was my Brothers and I, one hundred years ago, who chose Gopinatha.

I wonder if everything we have seen today is not only our achievement, but also our fault. I look to Chernobog but I can't see her face under that hood.

"But where would the Oldtimers be without a touch of magic? Those of you who remember your history will know the righteous have always had magic on our side. Our enemies may have driven our forefathers from Sad Hill, but when we moved underground, we only grew stronger. Today we have our own weapons. Please welcome the original Magicians—Cato, Manu and Efe."

Who is who? My Brothers and I look at each other warily. I don't know when to step forward. I put my arms on their shoulders and pull us all into a bow instead. Our robes sweep the floor.

"And thanks to the woman who bravely returned them to us after their long service—Chernobog, great-great-granddaughter of Efe."

The cheering crowd becomes background noise. Chernobog does not lift her hood for the propo camera but she does attempt to smile without showing her teeth. She won't look at me. I know that I am Efe.

I address the crowd exactly as I am told through my earpiece. The voice in my ear is as harmonious as Gopinatha's, but my echo sounds rough. I quickly grow hoarse from trying to project. The crowd hushes and those closest to the stage jostle forward, straining to hear me.

Then, Assistant Mason hands me the microphone. My face burns hot under the stage lights.

I repeat every word into the microphone. This time, everyone in Undercity West station, and everyone watching us live on the propo can hear me.

Wing of newt and bone of flea,
A ring beneath an apple tree.
From ancient Order, Brothers three,
Take time from them and give to thee,
Take life from them and give to me.
Praise the Order of the three.

It's a poem, or a psalm. Or—my stomach drops like I taste spoiled meat—a spell. On the third reading the crowd chants with me. Upraised arms ripple through the crowd in waves, all the way to the back of the station. There the tops of sky-trains are starkly interspersed, like grey rocks in a field that might otherwise be tilled. People are swaying. In the chanting I can discern a tune.

The voices of the propo crew, Assistant Mason, and the Mayor, rise to join me. Even Duo and Uno clap and mumble along. Only Chernobog is silent and still.

The roar of the crowd is all-embracing. If I close my eyes I can imagine myself back in the desert, bracing for a storm.

I conclude the third reading. Gopinatha stands beside me and puts her hand on my shoulder. The jewel on her finger flashes in the stage light. I shiver, despite the heat.

⚷

When the ceremony is over my Brothers and I wait in the wings. Chernobog and the suits mill around us as if engaged in some work other than guarding us. My Brothers and I don't speak. We don't know what to call each other anymore.

Mason ducks into the wings. He wipes his forehead with a pocket handkerchief. He is sweating from the stage lights.

Chernobog is by his side like a shadow. "My reward," she says.

Mason jumps. "Yes! Alright. Efe goes with you."

Chernobog takes my arm.

"You will keep the third Magician safe? And well?" Mason double-checks on me, as if Chernobog is shepherding his child off to boarding school and he can't help but draw out the parting. "The Mayor won't like it if he's harmed. She requires all three intact."

"Efe is my blood," says Chernobog. I wish she had simply answered 'yes'.

"What about ..." I frown at my Brothers. They both shrug. "... the others?"

"Manu and Cato will return with us to party headquarters after the ceremony. They will be safe with us. The Mayor has no use for two old men with almost no magic."

"If you don't have any use for my Brothers, why keep them? I think Gopinatha does need us." I can't believe myself. I'm batting away Chernobog's hand, and prodding Assistant Mason square in his immaculate tie with my yellow, trimmed fingernail. "I think we are still doing magic, right now, that keeps your Mayor alive for as long as we are alive. And I'll tell you what else—"

"Don't," suggests Mason.

"—looking at this city, I can't say we didn't make a mistake saving the lot of you in the first place, and putting Gopinatha in charge."

Assistant Mason looks, with quivering eyes scanning the wings, as young as he sounds. "Even you aren't permitted to say that."

I prod Mason in the chest again. "I can't leave without my Brothers ..." But I've run out of names, and I've used up all my words. I goggle at Chernobog like a fish in the desert.

Chernobog shakes off her hood and shrugs at me as though I'm the one who brings nothing but trouble. She grasps my hand and slips something into my palm. Even before I open my fingers and see three apple seeds in my lined hand, I know that this is magic.

My hand tingles. It is the opposite of a limb falling asleep. Warmth radiates through my awakening arm. Numbness leaves my bones, and I am sure that when it reaches my lips the words of the spell will come.

"Try to do something useful, Magician," Chernobog suggests. "If you can't, I'll take care of you and your Brothers." Under her cloak her hand crawls onto her pistol.

Celia 'C.H.' Pearce writes and illustrates speculative and historical fiction, from dystopian futures to fantasy-Westerns. With a background in history, she works in records management, and recently completed a postgraduate diploma in writing and editing at the University of Canberra.

Celia's stories have appeared in *Aurealis*, *Capital Letters*, and *Award Winning Australian Writing 2016*. They have won awards including the Marjorie Graber McInnis Short Story Award in 2015.

Celia is working on short stories, novellas, and her first novel. For information and art, visit www.chpearce.net/

Lost Property

Helen Stubbs

Rosemary Watson watches from the lofty heights of the school office waiting room as Principal Wright's pointy nose angles upwards to sniff the scent of frangipani drifting across the street. He adjusts his poison dart cufflink and tweaks his moustache, sneering briefly, allowing Rosemary a glimpse beneath his smooth veneer at the black heart. If he could, he'd bring back the strap, the tongue-tearer and all the other ways teachers tortured students before the Convention on the Rights of the Child.

Under the stony glare and bare fangs of flying fox gargoyles hanging from the decorative tracery, Wright restores his smile for the motley crew of ne'er-do-wells littering the garden of St Anne of Nassau's College. A kilted rapscallion tugs out a gladiola bulb and shoves it into his pouch, while a bent old woman with pink hair pops a snail into her mouth, catches Rosemary's gaze and grins with glee. The snail extends one worried eyeball around her front tooth, as if dreading what might happen next.

"I know just how you feel." Rosemary sighs.

Munch. Crackle. Glob. The granny closes her eyes, enjoying *al fresco escargot sashimi*. Rosemary supresses a shudder. Like her mother, this lot will send their children to St Anne's College, hoping that with an education they'll move into the most promising contemporary sectors for liars and robbers: politics and medicine. What Rosemary wants, most of all, is to *not* be like them. She feels like the snail, getting crushed to death, but gradually. A little each day.

"That brings us to the end of our tour." Wright's voice thins over the distance. He spreads his arms. "I look forward to welcoming your darling scoundrels into kindergarten in the new school year."

He backs away, all the way up the degraded concrete stairs and into the office building, too wily to turn his back on them. Rosemary ducks beneath the sill of the leadlight window and shifts further along the chaise lounge. Here he comes, to deal with 'the interminable Rosemary Watson'. She stops biting her fingernail to dribble spit on her hand, hoping to ease the sting from Mrs Lead-Sprinkler's cane.

"Ms Watson," Mr Wright says tersely, marching through the waiting room, down to his office, the interior with which Rosemary is far too familiar. Dread creeps up her neck. If only she could escape to her boarding room, in the tower. The receptionist, Dora, in spectacles and Sumo sash, waddles after him, her voice muffled by corners and plush carpets.

"Her mother can't come in."

That's no surprise. Rosemary's mother couldn't care less about her any more. She can't remember exactly when it began. Some time after she started school her mother seemed to fade one day, almost disappear.

"She's in meetings all day," Dora continues.

Meetings? Right. With Ellen and Danoz Direct, from her dingy living room.

"She's given up on the girl." Mr Wright says. "Who wouldn't?" His voice quiets, barely audible. "If not for late Daddy's trust account paying her fees, she'd be long gone."

Rosemary's breath quivers with disappointment. She sinks back into herself. Sadness solidifies, like cooling magma, around her heart. With a flick of her hand she extends her right stiletto from the sheath at her forearm, then cleans her nails with the point. It's all true. Mum possesses no detectable level of care. She'd loved her once though … they'd snuggled together drinking hot chocolate and watching Dexter. Everything changed around the time Rosemary lost her onyx earrings, passed down from Nanna. As though Mum could never forgive her for that.

Rosemary retracts the knife into her sleeve, for fifth period Slashing Assassination—which she'll attend if she ever gets out of trouble. She squints at the bright window behind the shifting curtain. She should just *go*. Walk out the door. What could they do about it? A shadow falls over her then, preceding Mrs Kitewater, the librarian with a sideline in Apothecary Arts. A sheet of silken black hair swings aside to reveal her wide face.

"Hello, Rosemary," Mrs Kitewater says. Clouds of sadness surround her like mist moving over a mountain. "Is something wrong?"

"Do you feel sick?" Kitewater reaches for Rosemary's forehead, but Rosemary moves fast, cart-wheeling over the lounge, black and brown tartan skirt flying, onto the other side of the lounge, which she'd been ordered to remain glued to, or *else*. That meant more caning, she assumed. Eventually the nerves in her hands would die—which would come in handy in ninpo class. Rosemary quickly adjusts the small gun nestled beneath the waistband in the small of her back—standard issue to all of year nine taking Headhunting as an elective.

"Come to the library with me, dear," Kitewater offers. "I've bought a new book I'd like to show you."

Rosemary shakes her head, hugs her arms closer, in a protective shell.

"Why not, darling?" Kitewater reaches a tender hand toward her.

"Rosemary," Dora's slappy voice interrupts. "Mr Wright will see you now."

Rosemary gulps and covers her sore hand instinctively. Kitewater catches sight of the redness of her palm and swoops in. "Oh no! Show me your hand. I have oils that can help." She reaches into the top of her dress and draws out a tiny stoppered bottle.

"Just leave me alone." Rosemary glares at the librarian, warning her away. She darts down the hallway hung with *commedia dell'arte* masks whose shadowy eye-sockets track her as she passes. Mr Wright's office is a hateful reprieve from Kitewater's uncomfortable kindness. There's something sickening about her sympathy. It's not normal. No one should care as much as she does. She could take a lesson from Principal Wright, who doesn't give a damn.

He hunches behind the oak desk in his spacious office, trophies decorating the glass cabinet behind him.

"Come in and sit down, Rosemary."

"Are you gunna give me the cane, too?" Rosemary blurts out.

"Sit in the chair."

"Not until—"

"Do as you're told!" Spittle flies from his lips as his glare fires at her over the black rims of his spectacles. A nervous giggle escapes Rosemary's lips.

"Do you think this is funny?" He leans forward, fists clenched.

"No, sir." Her next giggle sounds more like a whimper than a laugh.

"Sit down," he says, then returns to his writing. "I'll deal with you in a minute."

When adults say 'minute', they mean 'hour'.

Wooden plaques inset with engraved shields punctuate the walls, testament to the college's success at interschool competitions. First place in Sleight of Hand, third in Mood Alchemy and second in Sniping. Overall Champion in Espionage and Sabotage ...

Wright seals and stamps the envelope with a bang.

"Now." His gaze drills into her. "Miss Lead-Sprinkler doesn't want you back in class for the week. I don't blame her. I'm sending you to work with the cleaners."

"You can't do that!"

"It's done. You think you're too good to treat your classmates with respect. Let's see if scrubbing toilets will teach you humility."

"But sir, Stuart said—"

"Don't *but sir* me. It doesn't matter what he *said*. This is about what you *did*. This is your final warning, after which comes expulsion and *normal* school. Then most likely youth detention, and trust me they'll have *much* less tolerance for your miscreant ways."

Rosemary curls in on herself, anguish squirming in her stomach. Cleaning. How humiliating.

"What about the library, sir? Even that would be better than—"

His irate gaze burns her. "Are you—?" He closes his eyes for a moment. *Stupid.* He was going say that she was stupid.

"No, Rosemary." His pitch rises, indignant. "Do you understand that this is a punishment, not a holiday?"

Punishment, not holiday, could be her life motto.

"The cleaners work out of their storerooms down the stairs at the end of the basement. North is Lost Property. Cleaners are south. They're expecting you. Go. I'll find out if you don't appear pronto."

Lost Property. Shudder. At least she doesn't have to go near Fledge.

"Can I start in an hour?" She raises an eyebrow hopefully.

"No."

"It's lunchtime, though!"

"Then you'll be busy cleaning up wrappers and crumbs. Just hope that no one vomits. Or spurts diarrhoea into the engraved rim of one of the heritage toilet bowls. That's all. You're dismissed."

Rosemary clenches her teeth. She stands slowly and drags her feet toward the door, tears blurring her vision. Damn him! She kicks the doorframe on the way out.

"Rosemary!" Mr Wright shouts. "Did you hear nothing I just said?"

"I tripped," she lies.

"I hope so."

She shakes her head and trudges out of the office, down the stairs, across the basement—an open area underneath a five-storey building. In the courtyard outside, students vie with various weapons and insults for a higher perch in the pecking order. Rosemary trots down the spiral southern staircase, tapping her nails along the iron railing. The scratched cedar door is marked *leaners* in silver letters since someone stole the 'C'.

Barbra, the wrinkly old lady who empties bins and hoses away leaves, glares at Rosemary. She curls a gnarled finger toward the broom.

"Start sweeping."

Rosemary's shoulders droop. Even Barbra doesn't think she's worthy of full sentences.

The brass bell rings, high in the belfry, making the flying foxes flap and flutter. She's seen them from her room. She'd run to its seclusion, but they lock her out during schools days.

"But it's *lunchtime*," Rosemary whispers.

Barbra shrugs. "Boss says you're working through."

"I can't sweep while the other kids eat."

"You should'a thought of that before you did what you did."

Rosemary steeples her fingertips. "What if I *don't* do what he says?"

"He'll be watching." The cleaner shrugs. "Did he tell you what would happen?"

"I'll be sent to *normal* school."

Barbra shakes her head, stray wisps of dark grey hair trailing the action. "The first step to fallin' through the cracks."

Rosemary's guts churn as she accepts the facts, presses her palm to the broom handle and wraps her fingers around it, nails scraping over the dry wood. Head hanging, she drags it up the stairs. The bristles scrape through fluff balls, mandarin peels and an encrusted dribble emitting a mouldy miasma. *Swish-clunk*, into the basement, trudging across the paths of other kids who flow around her in white, black and tan uniforms. Fifty-cent coins jingle in their pockets. Lunchboxes rattle in their hands. Chatter, giggling and laughter rushes around her like static. She's *not* like them.

"Ow!" cries a girl with short blonde hair, tripping over the broom. The girl flicks open her switchblade as a reflex.

"Watch it," Rosemary warns.

"Why's she got a broom?" the girl says to her friend, spinning her knife before she folds it away. He shrugs and snaps pictures with his iLens glasses. They exchange grimaces.

"Delete those photos," Rosemary says.

She drags the broom through a puddle of strawberry milk, making for the bubbler. She must be the first student ever subject to this punishment. To stall starting work, she takes a long drink. Water fills her growling stomach as a line forms behind her, visible out of the corner of her eye.

"Don't make yourself sick," Kitewater says, appearing from behind the thirsty students. Rosemary bites her tongue, surprised by the teacher sneaking up on her. She wipes her mouth.

"You'd best get started. Mr Wright will have an eye on you from his window."

Rosemary turns away and starts sweeping, cheeks burning.

Stuart, her absolute enemy, laughs in her face, thrilled to see her punished for the violence he provoked her into. He runs his thumb beneath his thick gold chain and smirks. "Pipsqueak—" he says.

Rosemary snaps the broom handle at his chin like a pool cue, missing him by an inch and silencing his taunt.

"Call me that again, and you'll regret it," Rosemary warns.

Lunch hour drags on as Rosemary pushes the broom around.

"Get that dust over there, *broom girl*," chirrups haughty Karmina Spurges. "You'd even fail sweeping!" Karmina and her friends show their crooked teeth as they throw back their heads and laugh.

"Rack off, Your Emptiness," Rosemary mutters.

Karmina's eyes widen and her auburn hair flounces as she jumps up and waves her hand. "Oh! Miss, did you hear Rosemary just tell me to eff-off?"

"I did not!" Rosemary cries.

"Girls, leave her to work," Kitewater says. "You can all go and pick up that litter along the rock wall, over there." Her black fingernail indicates the pebbles beneath the principal's office.

"Aw," sighs their chorus of complaint. "Good one, Karmi."

They file away like obedient slaves, one of them even wearing a studded dog-collar. That's what Rosemary needs to learn to be like, except she's not one of them. She refuses to be. There's something vacuous about them. Karmina, especially. If a little trapdoor existed in the back of Karmina's head and Rosemary opened it and peered inside, she'd find empty space, aglow with an orange and lilac sunset.

"Rosemary," Mrs Kitewater says.

"Yeah."

"Stop sweeping and look at me for a second."

Rosemary takes a deep breath, stills the broom, and raises her gaze to Kitewater's dark eyes.

"I would like you to come by the library after school. I want to lend you a book. Your talent for reading and writing could occupy you sufficiently to keep you out of trouble." She almost smiles.

Rosemary rolls her eyes, wishing she hadn't accidentally left her journal in the library that day. What an invasion of privacy, for Kitewater to read it. Though what could she expect in a place like this?

"I always walk my cousin home from school."

"The offer's there, if you need it," Kitewater says.

The bell rings and kids scatter to get back to class. Speak of the devil. Richie, with his spikey brown hair, runs by—as well as he can with his broken arm in a sling. He stumbles to a stop, pocket torn and hair a mess.

"What you gotta do this for, Rose?"

"Come here." She fastens an open shirt button and tucks in his torn pocket, scanning to check no one's listening. "I whacked Stuart Burton with my knuckle-duster when he said I'd ... done something gross ... with Fledge."

"That's not fair that you got in trouble and he didn't." Richie scowls. "If I was bigger I'd knock Burton's block off!" Richie makes a fist with his good hand.

"No you wouldn't, Richie. You're better than that."

"So are you, Rose."

She sweeps the broom towards his butt. "Get your arse to class. See you after school."

Richie runs off. Rosemary leans against the cold wall, pressing her sweaty top to her back, ears ringing in the fresh quiet. At least she's missing algebra, where letters don't form sensible words but lean sideways and conspire with numbers, slipping under lines and vaulting upward to lock stares with her at eye-level.

Rosemary rubs her grumbling tummy, wondering if she can collapse on a wrought iron bench and eat. Footsteps come trotting down the stairs. It's Mr Wright. Quick! She starts sweeping again, watching him out of the corner of her eye. Hands on hips, he makes a show of looking around.

"Leaves and food everywhere," he says, shaking his head. "What have you been up to for the last hour? I saw some other girls helping you out. That Karmina and her friends. I think they did a better job than you in just a few minutes."

"Mrs Kitewater made them do it."

"She's kind to you, isn't she? I think she likes you."

As if that could be possible.

"Do you appreciate her friendship?"

Rosemary shrugs.

"Didn't think so. Incapable," he says under his breath. "Sweep those piles of dirt up, then collect any hats and drink bottles you can find and take them down to Lost Property."

The broom drops. Rosemary's hands hang at her sides as she raises her eyes to him.

"Yes, I said, *Lost Property*," he says slowly.

Rosemary shakes her head. "Sorry, sir—"

"Oh, ho-ho." His cheek twitches into a grin. "Don't tell me the *incorrigible* Rosemary Watson is scared of poor maligned Mr Fledge, like he's some kind of monster? The staff invented that rumour to keep the kindergarteners out of Lost Property. To think high school bullies bought it, too!" He rocks from his toes to his heels, with delight.

"I'm not a bully." Rosemary shifts from foot to foot, with a sudden urge to pee. "And I'm not afraid."

"Then you won't have a problem taking those hats over there"—he points to two black hats on the seat—"down to Lost Property."

The Lost Property Dungeon! Her worst nightmare. No way.

—⚷—

Rosemary sweeps the mess into a dustpan and tips it into the bin. She'd rather drag the wheelie bins across the school than go down to Lost Property! She'd only been in there once before, on her first day of kindy, so long ago … ten whole years ago. Something happened … she doesn't want to think about what. It was bad enough that she'd cried and screamed in year one, when Mum wanted her to go and check for the lost earrings. She'd refused, so Mum had gone instead, and returned with the earrings, but—that was the day—she'd never been the same since.

Faced with having to return, Rosemary rubs her forehead and lets the memories worm through her mind. On that first day, Stuart had dared her to go in and steal the confiscated lollies Fledge kept in his desk drawer. Karmina had walked Rosemary to the door, smiling, pretending she was so nice with her sunset vacantness, even then. They'd both left Rosemary there and run away. She'd ended up cowering behind a shelf as Fledge's broad shoulders blocked the doorway, his features hidden in shadow. Rosemary had bitten her tongue, tasted blood, trying to hold in her scream. Then he'd moved into the light … long blond hair, like an angel, and a handsome face too. Rumour was he'd slain a dragon, long ago, when magic was alive and well and this world was a very different place.

Fledge had known exactly where Rosemary was hiding. Just thinking about it makes her heart race and the back of her head burn. No way she's going back. She sighs, picks up the hats and flips them over. *Please God let there be names on the labels*, she prays.

And yes! There are. They're faded, but she can make them out. *Sophie Yorkville, 8MA*. Rosemary squints, struggling to read the other one. *Rowena Blackspeck, 11* … something. Good. She'll find the kids' bags and return the hats to them. And then she won't have to face Fledge.

After returning the hats to their rightful owners, Rosemary drags her broom around. A warm afternoon breeze picks up. Swallows chitter in a nest up on a metal girder and life doesn't seem so bad. With a sudden chill, hairs prickle on the back of Rosemary's neck. Is someone watching her? She turns to look over her shoulder and jumps. It's Fledge, in the dark of the stairwell, beneath a thick net of spider-web, watching her with piercing blue eyes. Muscled arms extend from his sleeves and a red beard descends from his smooth-skinned face.

"I was expecting you with my lost property," he says.

Rosemary reverses a step. She slips her hands behind her back and thrums the blades of her knives for reassurance.

"I found the kids they belonged to and gave them back."

"That's not how it works." He narrows his eyes. "Lost property's *mine*."

"I'm sorry, Mr Fledge. They weren't really lost."

"Next time you bring 'em to me." He clenches his fist, like he's crushing a dragon's throat, or Rosemary's. "If you don't, you'll lose something much worse."

He recedes into the shadowy stairwell where his threat lingers obscured, indecipherable. Rosemary squints into the darkness, with the unnerving sensation that it's gazing right back at her.

Rosemary runs along the cobblestone path, out the side gate, late to meet Richie. There he is, down by the gas streetlight, but Fledge is between them, walking toward her, a smug grin tugging his lips into a scalene triangle. Rosemary carves a wide arc around him. Across the street, the barely normal guy, with his grey beard, shiny skinhead and blurry old tattoos, waters his nasturtiums. His gaze darts toward Rosemary then away, as he mutters to himself. Maybe she's paranoid, but she could swear he's mumbling about her.

Other kids trundle past, in dribs and drabs, swinging scimitars, nunchaku, punching each other playfully with knuckle-dusters.

"Ow!" one little kid cries, then sprays her big brother with mace. "Take that!"

The acne-cheeked big brother screams, grabbing his eyes as he falls to his knees.

"You two," the dad says fondly, ruffling her hair and scooping him up. "Sorry, mate, I left the eye wipes at home."

Richie runs toward Rosemary, carrying his heavy bag with his good hand.

"I'll take that," she says, swinging it onto her back. "Man, what've you got in here? Did you steal plutonium from Political Strategies class?"

"Nah." He laughs. "It's a safe for the Year Three pilfering assignment."

"Weak-point drill with a plasma cutter's the way to go. Hey, did Fledge say anything to you just now?"

"Who?" He scratches his head.

"Fledge."

Richie raises an eyebrow, with no idea what she's talking about.

"Never mind, then."

Fledge's presence must have been coincidence. Or he was trying to freak her out. Rosemary doesn't want to worry her little cousin unnecessarily.

She delivers Richie home to Aunt Cordelia's place and agrees to bring him home at lunchtime tomorrow because he can't play sport for a few more weeks.

"Join us for milk and cookies, dear," Aunt Cordelia offers.

"No thanks, but I'll take one to go." It always feels awkward inside the compact kitchen of their town house, like her aunt *has* to be kind to her while secretly blaming Rosemary for Mum's demise.

The screen door slaps closed behind Rosemary and she strolls back to school the long way, under the avenue of tall shady trees. As she's making her way up the hill towards school, she glances into the barely normal guy's garden, expecting to see him—but he's not there. *That* is weird. He's *never* not there. She looks around, and finds him behind her! It's slow going, with his walking stick, but she suspects he's been following her.

"Hey, girl," he calls.

Rosemary knows better than to stop and talk to him. That metal rod would easily double as a hanbo—a small fighting staff.

"I have to tell you something!"

She could reach for her gun or her knives, but that seems too extreme, so she runs. The enforced P.E. sprints pay off. She makes it to the school gate well ahead of him. Rosemary wipes the sweat off her forehead and peers back. He's given up, returning to his garden. Wondering what he wanted, she trudges up the dark and lonely stairs to the solitude of her boarding room in the tower.

After the next day of mopping and moping, Rosemary waits outside school for Richie, just after lunch. Most students meander down to the field for football, which Richie can't manage at the moment. She kicks the light pole at ankle height, knee height, hip height. It's practice for kicking Fledge if she ever needs to. She kicks a stone, then hates herself, and looks for Richie, up and down the hill. No sign of him. Maybe he went down to sport after all, but she's sure Aunt Cordelia said he couldn't participate.

With most of the kids playing sport, the tall building slumps, tired. Could Richie have gotten past her, or gone another way? He *knows* to meet her here. The road is quiet except for the sound of a garden hose, which draws her attention across the street.

"Hey kid."

Rosemary locates the source of the voice. It's the barely-normal guy who followed her yesterday. He's hiding behind his frangipani tree, tattoos out of sight.

"Why are you hiding?" Rosemary asks.

"I saw that *big* guy, the one who works there. He chatted to your little brother before you came out. Then they walked off."

"You didn't!" Rosemary cries. Fledge! Is this some kind of revenge for the hats?

"I tried to warn you yesterday, I'd seen 'em talking."

Her eyes twitch and her blood boils in her veins. "Where did they go?"

"Back into the school."

He throws down his hose, limps out his squeaky gate and across the street, rubbing his beard with his free hand.

"I've seen his type before." He forms a thoughtful fist, then points as he shakes it. "A real hoarder."

"What do you mean?" Rosemary asks.

"They want a bit of everything, even if they can't use it."

"That sounds about right," she says. And, this time, he's taken Richie. Fledge has gone too far. This is *war*. Secret weapons? Why, yes. Yes, she has.

Switchblades up both sleeves.

Mace in the compact clipped to her bra strap, tetrodotoxin (milked personally from a blue-ringed octopus) and hydrochloric acid—the kit a smart young woman doesn't leave home without.

A Ruger LCP 380 in her holster-belt at her lower back.

She snaps the belt to the outside of her tartan skirt, quick draws and sights the red laser beam on the letterbox across the street. Loaded and locked, she slips it back away.

Spike or whatever his name is has seen her taking inventory. "I'd help but …" He glances back at his frangipani.

"I've got it covered," Rosemary says.

"Looks like it."

He can't give Rosemary the sort of help she wants. She needs a knowledge ninja, the librarian, Mrs Kitewater.

<hr/>

"Well, I can't believe it!" Kitewater smiles, rising from her computer screen, behind which cogs turn and live wires sizzle.

"He's taken Richie," Rosemary blurts out.

Kitewater's smile evaporates. "Who's taken Richie?"

"Fledge!" Rosemary cries, fingers splayed.

"Why?" Kitewater moves closer. Along the ceiling, the library spiders follow her.

"The guy across the road says Fledge is a hoarder."

"A hoarder?" Mrs Kitewater looks to a high shelf, tapping her cheek with a finger. "That reminds me of a story."

She rolls a mahogany ladder along the shelves, its brass wheels squeaking, then climbs up, to reach the shelf above *Encyclopedia Brittanica* and *Codex Seraphinianus*.

"Here," she says, drawing out a leather bound volume. "*Myth and Monstrousness* by Claudia Costin."

Rosemary reaches up and takes the dry leather cover into her hands, measuring the full weight of the large book, and delivering it to the table. A spider dangles above her, walking the air hopefully, as Kitewater shuffles alongside and adjusts a reading lamp. The cover falls open with a bang and billow of dust.

"I recall reading something in here back when I was a student, about a curse upon dragon slayers." Kitewater thumbs through the pages.

"Is that true, about Fledge?" Rosemary asks.

"Here's something." Kitewater reads: "𝔍n 𝔓ierre-𝔉ort be one maeden who, with steadie hande, slayed a nine-spined 𝔇raegon, towering talle. 𝔗he maeden kilt the 𝔇raegon to wynne the faboure of her hearte's desierre, 𝔓rince 𝔉leddelecke. 𝔅ut her bictorie left her in loue with only that which shines, and nought else."

Rosemary frowns, her gaze drifting across the collection of old polished armour in a display cabinet.

"Silver and gold, she must mean. Do you think this is what happened to Fledge? Why would he take Richie, then?"

"Maybe it's a different curse or 'viral possession' as we've come to view them. Or one that's mutated. Most of the olde magick has died out in this world, or transformed, to limp along in the modern era. You've seen how it flickers in the corners and fades out in the light. It's stronger where it's safe—places favouring subterfuge and subversion—like this school."

"I have," Rosemary mutters. "How does any of this help us get Richie out of his clutches?" She plunges her hands into her hair and scrunches up handfuls, desperate.

"Let's see what's happening in Lost Property. Then we'll figure something out."

Rosemary closes her eyes and clenches her fists. Of all places it's the one she most fears. And why? She *has* to remember, so she edges closer to the horrid memories. Fledge had laughed at her, made her feel so small. Threatened that he would take something precious. Not just something …

Some*one*.

She has to face her fear, right now, for her cousin's sake.

"We're going to get Richie back," she says.

—◂—

Kitewater follows along behind, flipping through the tome's pages for any useful details.

"Interesting." Paper crinkles as she turns another page.

They're moving too slowly so Rosemary breaks into a run, determination conquering her fear. Reaching the dark spiral stairwell, she tiptoes down the stairs slick with slippery water from a dripping pipe. The fire door's propped ajar, and Rosemary eases through the gap into Lost Property. Fledge grins, gloating over Richie. He strokes her cousin's spikey hair.

"Rose!" Richie cries, beaming while munching on cookies and sipping a glass of milk. A wave of relief washes over Rosemary, but then caution. Has Fledge already taken something from Richie? The surrounding shelves are lined with jars and small boxes. A dried dragon tongue hangs alongside raincoats, a limp flamingo skin (legs and beak and all), and what might have once been someone's cardiovascular system. A pile of lost tennis rackets, gloves and muddy shoes stinks like last summer's sodden dog bed.

"This stops *now*." Rosemary turns her hostile stare on Fledge, who rises from his chair, eyebrows uniting into a single hairy menace. Rosemary inhales, drawing herself up taller to match his aggression, but not his height.

"No more taking things from the kids. And you give everything, *everything*, back. Even ..." Rosemary points to the jars and boxes. "What's in those?"

"I don't know what you're talking about." Fledge shuffles forwards and spreads his arms over what he can. Rosemary moves closer, reaches up and takes down a jar.

"Put that back. It's none of your business," Fledge growls, grabbing for it, but Rosemary darts away. The jar's warm. She unscrews the lid and finds a lilac sunset inside and a mound of viscous purple goo at the bottom. There's something about the texture of it, and the scent. Not unpleasant. She closes her eyes for a deeper sense of what it could be. It has something to do with Karmina Spurges. But what is it?

"Get out of here, Watson," Fledge growls. "Or you'll regret it."

The realisation hits her. "This is Karmina's kindness!" She glares at Fledge, who looks as guilty as hell. Rosemary knocks a lid off a box. "What's this?"

"Hey!" Fledge cries, grabbing for her, but she ninja rolls around him. Some kind of brown innards worm around inside the box like livers.

"What are the donors doing for organs these days?"

"Stop it, now," hisses Fledge, grabbing for her neck. Rosemary evades him by leaping up onto a counter just as Kitewater, puffing, enters through the door, lugging the heavy book.

Rosemary opens a jar with a dark rainbow of unmixed colours: blue, shimmering gold, shining black. "This is all the apathy Kitewater ever had!"

"Is this why my mind whirls, always, full of worry for others?" Kitewater reaches for the box. Rosemary passes it down.

"You lost the ability to switch off after you came to the school, didn't you?" Rosemary guesses. "I bet you came in here, and he took it. You had no apathy. Not even for a moment. Did you ever sleep?"

Kitewater grasps a handful of the sludge and inhales deeply.

"I will, after we've dealt with him."

Fledge's eyes dart from side to side, suddenly outnumbered.

"You have to give all this back to the students," Kitewater commands.

Rosemary scans the shelves. But where are *her* things? Aha, that little clear bubble-shaped jar. It's something of hers for sure. She slips the jar into her pocket. But that's not all he took.

Fledge darts for the door and Rosemary leaps after him. She wraps her hands around his neck. "Give it all up. Now!"

"Never," Fledge cries.

"Surrender, or else!" Rosemary threatens, squeezing his throat.

"Or else what?" He shoves her back against the wall. "You'll hurt me, pipsqueak?"

Pipsqueak is her trigger word.

Left arm clamped around his neck, she flicks out her right stiletto and sinks the blade into his neck. Fledge collapses and Rosemary falls with him, bouncing on his round back. He wheezes, like an inflatable mattress, as air hisses out the holes. Like a massive balloon he shoots out from underneath her, then ripples and rises, spinning, spiraling, shrinking, down to a wrinkly skin no bigger than her hand. It flops on the floor with a final defeated fart.

"Rosemary!" Kitewater cries, racing over and squatting next to her.

"I'm all right." She stands unsteadily.

Across the room there's a thump that makes them both turn.

"Richie!" Rosemary cries. He's collapsed on the floor.

"Oh no," Kitewater says.

Rosemary darts across the room and shakes her cousin. "What's happening?" she begs Kitewater, through blurry eyes.

"I just read about transmission. The hoarder virus was in the milk and cookies. Fledge transferred the possession to Richie."

"Is there some way to save him, before it takes hold?" Rosemary cries.

Kitewater glances at the book on the table, and Rosemary grabs for it. She flips through the pages until she finds an antidote.

"Do you have any of this stuff? Patchouli, musk. I have the tetrodotoxin."

"Show me." Kitewater frowns as she scans the list. "Yes, yes, and yes." She reaches into her bodice and draws out three tiny bottles of oils, with stoppers in the tops.

"Here!" Rosemary pulls a cup off the rack and unscrews the lid of her toxin. She adds the specified six drops, deadly in other circumstances. Kitewater adds her ingredients, too.

"Is there a spell to go with it?" she asks.

Rosemary flips over the page. "There is, but will it make any difference?"

"Try. Magick is fading from the world, but its power isn't entirely gone."

As Kitewater raises Richie's head and prepares to tip the medicine down his throat, Rosemary reads:

"Hair of hope and eye of doubt,
Scour the possession out.
With cousin's blood and caring eye,
Keep Richie's soul in body nigh."

Rosemary nicks her fingertip with her knife and lets her blood drip into the cup.

"That should do it." Kitewater shakes the mixture, then holds the cup to Richie's mouth. Rosemary opens his jaw and they tip it down his throat. "Come on, cousin."

Rosemary squeals as a seizure shakes his body. It's a violent fight over physical terrain, as the hoarder virus wrestles to hijack her cousin. His teeth chatter and arms twitch. His elbows jerk backwards.

"You can fight it, Richie!" Rosemary cries, holding him close.

Finally he stills. Rosemary strokes his forehead, feeling for a temperature, or the texture of possession, but he feels cool, his hair damp with sweat.

"Is that it? Is the possession gone?" she asks.

"We'll know soon," Kitewater says.

Richie coughs, wakes and struggles upright. "Help—"

Rosemary hugs him closer. "You're all right." Tears of relief flood her eyes.

He's shaking, clinging to her. "I had the worst dream. I was shrinking. This thing was taking me over—"

"You're okay, now," Rosemary says. "It's gone."

"What about you, Rosemary? Are you all right?" Kitewater asks.

"I think so. I found this." Rosemary pats her skirt pocket. "There's something else here for me, I think."

"Rosemary?" Karmina Spurges peers around the corner. "I have a feeling I left something here …"

Rosemary offers her the sunset box. "This."

It doesn't surprise Rosemary that the lost elements are calling to the kids they belong to. That should mean that the hoarder virus has been dealt with effectively.

"Ooh," Karmina says, cradling her box. She opens it up and a glow illuminates her face. The light shines back into her, through her eyes.

"What's in this one?" Kitewater asks, dragging out a big wooden chest.

"Yes—that's it!" Without seeing, Rosemary knows that it's for her, and that something warm is inside, limp in storage, like a puppet. It's a lost part of a person, and the centre glows red.

She turns to Richie. "If you can walk, let's get you home."

Richie climbs to his feet awkwardly, his sling torn.

Rosemary heaves the big chest onto her hip.

"Mrs Kitewater?" she says.

The librarian turns dark eyes on her. "Yes, Rosemary."

"I just want to say, thank you."

"Anytime." Mrs Kitewater smiles.

Mr Wright strides into the room and retrieves a green block of … what? General decency, Rosemary assumes.

"You've done well, Rosemary." He nods. "To think, for some time now, I haven't been all there."

Rosemary snorts a laugh. "Sure weren't, sir."

Kids and teachers wander through the room, reclaim their stolen attributes, and thank her or pat her on the back. Rosemary's head is light, and her heart warm—feelings she might grow accustomed to.

With Richie's hand in hers and the wooden chest against her hip, she makes her way up the stairs, into the basement.

"What you carrying there, Rose?" Richie asks, pointing to her cargo.

Rosemary smiles. "My welcome home."

When her mother reclaims her missing self, she'll love Rosemary again.

"It's something very special. Something just for me."

H K Stubbs is a writer and creative producer based on Australia's Gold Coast, with stories published in anthologies and magazines, including *Apex Magazine*, *Midnight Echo* and *Winds of Change*. Her Creative Writing Honours dissertation explores literary activism and the interaction between nature, emotion and the supernatural. Between writing short scripts she's currently servant to three quails, Flapper, Scratchy and Rover, while competing for the title of Worst Surfer in Queensland. Catch up with her as @superleni on Twitter or visit her blog at helenstubbs.wordpress.com.

Gardening Through the Danse Macabre

Maureen Flynn

Nowadays I know that the vital part of Guan is high up and hidden. Clean sandstone glinting in the sun, verdant green fronds crawling over the wall, and everywhere the bustle and the hustle of silks and colour and dancing. And at the city centre Guan's double jewel: my garden, and beside it, Layla's tiled dance floor.

"No one suspects a gardener of high magic," Eliah had said years ago, when he'd first devised our venture. "'Specially not them up there and not Layla neither, and we got to be careful of her most of all." I remember the way his head jerked upwards, eyes sad and mocking at once. "We'll get you a pass to Guan's city proper and the grand dancers one day, kid. It's a double apprenticeship you're getting. Thieving and gardening in one package. You get this right, we'll save this city. No more curses."

My finger pointed at the muck around me. I didn't need to explain myself for Eliah to know what I meant.

"Yes," he sighed. "If you break Layla's curse, Cesspit'll have healthy fields ripe for tilling. I said all of Guan would be free of Layla, didn't I?"

I was eight.

Eliah, the best thief and last spell weaver in Cesspit (his words), took his protégés on young.

—•—

It was three years later that I first noticed the new, deeper worry lines on Eliah's face.

"Apple, we can't leave this too much longer," he said one day, leaning against the apple tree that I'd made when he'd first taken me in. "Else Layla's curse will never end and all of Cesspit will be dead, but for Guan's wretched dancers. Guan will have consigned itself to a half-whispered footnote in history, a dangerous reminder to others of what happens when your city is crazed enough to cross someone as powerful as Layla."

"Why don't we all just leave?" I asked in my innocence. "You and me and Rael and Katija too."

Eliah laughed.

"And go where and how? Layla did more than just curse our spell weavers to endless dancing. She cursed our fields too. No more water. No rich soil. Why else do you think nothing grows in Cesspit without someone like you spending an age on a spell? How many people have gone further afield looking for better land? You know as well as I do they've never found any."

"Why doesn't she come here to finish us off?" I asked in horror. "Why doesn't Layla end this now."

"Because she wants us to suffer," Eliah said with an impatient snarl. "Haven't you been listening?"

"You've never told me why Layla did such a thing to us," I whispered.

Eliah studied my face.

"You were too young, Apple, when I first signed you up. Perhaps now ..."

He trailed off and I caught his calloused hand in mine.

"Rael knows. You told Rael."

"So I did," Eliah admitted with a sigh. Then he smiled sadly.

"Now is as good a time as any. Guan wasn't innocent in what happened, Apple. Our spell weavers told Layla we didn't want her harp song or her sultry dancing. We told her that her and her people with their fey green eyes weren't welcome in our precious city. We didn't know then the kind of power she wielded."

"But why didn't you stop her," I insisted. "You and the others. You weren't always a thief and an outcast."

"No," he said. "But we couldn't imagine her intent. She sang and strummed her harp and touched Guan's spell weavers' minds as her enchanted tiles sprang outward in the centre of Guan, marking the place for us to dance upon for all eternity. Then she simply rode away while spell weavers, struck by an inexplicable urge to dance, made their way out onto the tiles."

He dropped his eyes to the ground, as though ashamed.

"I avoided Layla's curse because I was the youngest and the weakest, and because Layla wanted me to get away. Her laughter haunts my dreams and dogs my days." Eliah's voice broke. "We have to find a way to stop her. We must, no matter what."

Back then, neither of us had known just how *long* it would take.

I've converted most of the free land inside Guan's walls. These days, my hands shake as I set my shovel to the dirt and my foot aches with rheumatism as I push hard against its metal bottom. It should be obvious to onlookers that this old woman's almost spent, that it takes me a lot of effort to make a spell to get things growing. I find myself resting more and more, and I need to mutter spells out loud just to keep my garden awake.

The dancers pass me by, oblivious, their golden anklets a-jangling and bracelets a-clanking as they link arms and dance hard on the ceramic tiles next to me. Later, they collapse exhausted and laughing and admiring my flowers, the blank-faced servants tipping the wine down their throats 'til they pass out on the edge of roses and lilies and daisies.

But it's not for the dancers, once Guan's spell weavers, I do this for anyway. It's for the people below in Cesspit. For my second family; for crippled Eliah and my sister Katija whom I had to leave behind, and for Rael, whose name still hurts me to remember even after all this time.

I wasn't a trusting girl. I couldn't remember my Mam or Da, for they'd passed long since. All I had of them was an old necklace of my mother's I'd worn for as long as I could remember. So, I was used to being alone. I grew up used to the suspicion in people's mean, pinched faces as they watched me lying with my elbows deep in the muck, whispering to the hard, rocky ground.

"Why even pretend to cast spells, child? It ain't a game," they'd mutter. "Come closer to our fire, lass, and we'll remind you why it ain't funny to pretend at magic."

I'd stare at them, confused. As I bent to the ground, my mother's old necklace dangling, I could hear the earth singing to me, feel in my bones the beginnings of a root unfurling, taste the tang of something sharp on my tongue, so how could they not feel what I could?

But then Eliah had found me.

He'd ignored the pointing and the whispers. He'd knelt beside me. I remember looking into his kind, weather-beaten face, lips parted in surprise. I remember how he spoke to me as clearly as if it were yesterday, for no one until him bothered to talk to me in those days.

"What are you doing so full of concentration, my girl?" he asked. "And what are you whispering to?"

"The ground," I said defiantly, prepared for the usual disapproval. "The roots are coming, but it takes me so long."

His eyes gleamed with excitement, and I pulled back from him warily. But he put out his hand.

"My name is Eliah. Have you heard of me?"

"You take children!" I let him pull me up, too curious to be afraid. "You're strange."

He laughed.

"Says the girl whispering to the dirt. Come with me!"

"What's in it for me?"

"Shelter from the wind," he said, "broth every night, a blanket, a roof. In short, a place to call your own, if you can earn it."

I'd considered his words only for a moment. What choice did my younger self have? Besides, he was the first person who hadn't chastised me for talking to the dirty ground like I thought I could make something happen to it.

His big hands enclosed mine and he led me to his home, right on the outskirts of Cesspit, a quiet place, for people were afraid to contaminate themselves by walking too close to Cesspit's last working spell weaver and his child apprentices.

Instead of leading me into the house proper, Eliah led me to a creaky gate, opening it onto a rocky garden, brown and dead and hard.

"Talk to it, would you?" he said. "Talk to it like I saw you do outside in the muck."

I looked at him, eyes hard.

"Yes," he said, unfazed. "This is a test. If you can't do what I need, there is no place for you here."

Caterpillars crawled down my spine. He was the last spell weaver in Cesspit after all, but I was afraid to hope I had a talent that could make me belong to someone.

"Go on," he said more gently. "My garden is dead and I am hungry."

I looked at him in trepidation. He stood with his arms crossed, waiting. I shrugged and knelt into the hard ground. I pressed my nose to the earth and closed my eyes. I muttered nonsense under my breath.

Nothing happened. At first. Then I felt the ground swell and respond. I felt a small tremor beneath my elbows. I kept chanting.

Eliah knelt beside me. He closed his eyes and placed both hands on the space where I'd chanted.

"You've sung an apple tree into existence," he pronounced quietly, eyes shining with delight and relief, though I didn't then know why. "So you are the girl to do what I and my children cannot. What's your name?"

"I never had one," I said. "Or if I did, I don't remember it."

"Take a new name," he said. "One gifted from me to you. Apple."

Eliah gave me more than just a name and a roof over my head. He gave me a place I could call my own and he gave me a family; my sister, blue-eyed Katija, she who saw visions of the past and the present, and my more-than-a-brother, Rael. Rael who could turn invisible when he concentrated. Rael who had clever fingers and was a better thief than Eliah. Rael who made himself learn to climb steep walls for me. Rael who loved me. Oh Rael!

I study the dance, skin crawling in distaste. Men and women, lips and eyelids painted bright, link arms and then fly away in another direction, sweat tracking down their backs. Though there are rooms for them to sleep in at night, now they use them less and less. Another one of Layla's subtle tortures, I think, to make these once mighty spell weavers dance and dance 'til they collapse until morning, no longer able to feel pride, self-respect, or humiliation.

This dance is my least favourite. It is a mockery of everything I miss. I hate that I remember Rael as I watch this dance. That I recall snatched kisses and our one night together before he and I climbed the wall.

It starts with arms linking and ends in unholy laughter and sometimes, if I'm unlucky, the man and woman who happen to be placed at the centre of the tiles, stripping naked and plunging inside each other to the sound of raucous cheers.

Layla's power is stronger at the dance floor's centre. I am sure of this now. It is her will that whispers to the dancers at night. It is her tune they cannot break themselves free of.

And there is only one of me.

There came a day when Eliah didn't return from the wall after a day's scavenging and Katija fell into a trance. Her eyes widened, still unseeing, and she screamed, shrill and piercing.

"He's fallen. He's fallen!"

She sat upright, blue eyes full of pain.

"Eliah's fallen from the wall." Her voice sounded flat and dead. "I couldn't see if he lived."

Rael went to find our teacher. I sat on the rushwork floor beside Katija, cradling her head in my lap.

"He may live yet," I made myself say. "Even if he's broken he can still teach us."

"But we need him to scale that wall," Katija said.

"Rael may learn yet," I made myself say, though I didn't really believe it. "He and I can go up the wall together if we must."

Katija looked at me.

"Rael is no Eliah," she said dully. "We'll never stop Layla now."

"You don't know that," I whispered, but it was hard to find the conviction to believe it later that evening when Rael returned home with Eliah, back broken and close to death.

Even an old woman has feelings. There's one dancer I've got my eye on. He has the look of Rael about him, moving sleek like a panther, skin bronzed and cracked from the hot sun. He looks young enough to be my son, but I know he is ageless, youth eternal thanks to Layla. I could reach out and touch him, but it is too risky. While I don't try to get their attention I am safe, but if I try to touch or to talk, I'm guaranteed a knife to the rib. Another layer of protection Layla wove to ensure her spell could never be broken.

Still, tonight I plant a red rose for this dancer. I close my eyes and sing to it softly. One finger strokes my wrinkled cheek as I concentrate. I feel my nerves strain against my skin, yearning for the ground beneath me. I stop myself from sighing. Every part of me strains for burial.

I am so old and so tired. I miss Eliah and Katija. I want this thing ended.

As I watch my old-yet-young panther dance to eldritch strains, something strange and sharp swells within my chest. My ancestors had been arrogant, no doubt about that, but they never did deserve *this*.

When I put my head to the ground at night to sleep, I can sense the greens reaching out hungry roots. Asleep, I dream of those roots waiting for my command to start the wave.

Only a few more months of this.

Only a few more.

Then peace for my panther dancer and for me.

After Eliah fell, Rael and I couldn't put off climbing the wall any longer. Who could have said if Eliah would climb again? When we told Katija, she wrung her hands against her torn and dirty smock. She hadn't liked it, but, like the rest of us, would do what she must to survive.

The day we left, she choked back a sob as I put an awkward arm around her. I'd undone the rusty necklace about my neck, placed it into her hand and closed her fingers over it.

"Keep it safe," I'd whispered. "It was my mother's. Wear it and think of me."

I'm a poor thief now. You'd think this would make things trickier for me, especially now I'm slowed down proper, but you'd be wrong. Layla never knew someone as stubborn as Eliah. She hadn't predicted the kind of waiting game he would play.

Those first few days in this walled city, near numb with grief for Rael, I sat in dark corners too exhausted to move, fascinated by the reel and dips of the dancers. Afraid to come out in the open, I threw a pebble once so that it hit the arm of one dancer and clattered against the tiles 'til it came to a stop by another's feet. The second dancer stopped, blinked once—twice, like he were dazed. I saw him register the first man, the red haze come down upon him. I saw the dagger drawn from beneath his silks wink in the sunlight 'til it gouged a hole in the first dancer. I sat in horrified silence, unable to breathe for fear and guilt.

I had made that happen. Even though I hadn't wanted anyone to die, even though I was trying to break Layla's curse, I had done this terrible thing.

Memories like this one make me despondent. Inside Guan there are no winners or losers. Whether the dance goes on unbroken, or something happens to break its rhythm, the only option is death. Layla has been cruel indeed. I make myself think of poor Eliah and of Katija, waiting, waiting for me to come back to Cesspit. The thought of them is the only thing that keeps me going.

Eating and drinking were so very hard those first few years. I grew wraith-like from its lack. Every reconnaissance mission into a home was a potential pathway to death and failure.

And every morning I'd sing softly to the ground, bit by bit coaxing something to seed in the hopes that it might grow. And in the full light of day I'd sit still by a section of Guan's wall, watching the dancers in silence. Watching, waiting.

Even now, years later, on the glowing dance floor those dancers keep whirling and twirling. Whirling and twirling 'til they puke up and collapse and wine gets splashed across their face and sprayed into their mouths. Very few of them fight against Layla and leave the dance floor.

So I get into their compounds easily. There's no need to sneak or to run. All my senses are on full alert, but nothing comes of it.

Not any more.

Getting into Guan was a nightmare. I hadn't wanted to let go of Rael's hand when we reached Guan's wall. It looked insurmountable; smooth and high. I couldn't imagine how Eliah had managed it. Rael's hand gripped my wrist.

"You're ready for this. I'll go up first and make sure of the ropes."

I shook my head.

"I'm afraid."

He swallowed against a lump in his own throat.

"Oh Apple, I know." His fingers laced through mine. "I'm scared too. It wouldn't be right if we both weren't scared, but it has to be now. We don't have a choice and I will be with you every step of the way."

I turned and gripped Rael by both shoulders so that he faced me front on. I wanted to study every contour of his face, commit every part of him to memory, lest the worst should happen.

"Let's go now. Before we think about this too hard." He turned from me, wiping a dirty, ragged sleeve against his eyes.

When I passed the ropes to him, his eyes were clear and his mouth set in a tight line. He chanted and two ropes snaked up Guan's walls. Then Rael began to climb.

I held my breath as Rael climbed quickly like a monkey. As the sun set, he crested the wall and secured the ropes. Then all his attention was on me and my clumsy climbing.

He didn't see the lithe dancer behind him. Her shadow crept up along the wall like a spider trapping prey. Before I could scream to warn him, his mouth opened in an 'oh' of surprise. Then his body arced slowly over the wall. It hit the ground with a harsh thud.

I turned away. Right then, I didn't care about any of it. I wanted to die. I wanted to join him.

It took me all night to get a leg over the top of the wall. I slid so many times, scraped knees and elbows so many times, spilled tears constantly. I nearly dropped the rope at one point and that would have been me and my quest done for in one hit if I hadn't caught its frayed end at the last possible moment, my heart beating against my chest like a drum.

But fate had a different ending in mind for me. No one saw me as I slipped between the cracks of two compounds. No one heard me collapse exhausted, unable to stay awake, weighed down by grief.

I woke a full day and night later. No dancer had come near me. Why would they come to sit in a dark crevice between buildings? But from now on I was to be cautious. Despite my reckless abandon, I had survived. Nothing could keep me from starting that garden for Eliah, for Katija, for Cesspit and for Rael most of all.

If I close my eyes and do not think of Rael, feel only the sun's rays beating down on me and my garden both, I can almost be content. I can sit, my back against the apple tree in Guan's centre, and smell the scents of fresh fruit and vegetable and flower and hear the insects softly buzzing. I can try to drown out the relentless beat, beat, beat and click, clack, click of feet pounding on ceramic tile and bracelets and anklets rattling.

I tried not to look down on Cesspit. Looking reminded me of what I'd seen my first night in Guan, when I'd crested the wall and glanced back; a shadowed form, unmoving. Rael. I'd remember the way my whole body ached from the climb and from the horror of seeing Rael's body fall. I'd remember the way I wanted to throw up and cry and curl up into a ball and never wake up. I'd remember just how much I missed him and the remembering felt like unceasing knife stabs to my heart.

Besides, people were small, like insects dotting the landscape. I couldn't make out any of their features to know if they were Katija, if they were Eliah, looking up at me. Somehow that made things worse. I knew I'd spend too much time mourning Rael, too much time day dreaming about the people I'd left behind if I gazed from the wall for long.

Once I dreamed I saw a man with a rope over one shoulder edging towards the wall. He uncoiled his rope with great care and flung it up at a vine with practised skill.

Eliah style.

When I woke my eyes were stinging with unshed tears, for I knew in my heart of hearts that after his injury, Eliah would never climb again.

It hurts to sleep now. My pillow is the first tree grown by my magic here and its boughs are gnarled and hard. Its roots sneak deep beneath me and I feel them like a rod to the back. I have created a forest, deep and verdant and green, atop the city walls and it grows taller and deeper every day.

Tonight I fall asleep with hope in my heart. When my ear presses against the ground I can hear the plant roots stretching like long fingers. They almost connect under the lattice of Layla's tiles.

I dream of Layla as she would have appeared to Eliah. Young and beautiful and cold with terrible power.

"Why did you do this to us?" I ask her, mesmerised by green eyes devoid of anger or hate. Filled instead with emptiness. "We may have wronged you, yes, but did we truly deserve this?"

Layla's lips are painted gold. There's glitter on her pale, pale cheeks. Her eyes contemplate mine, still empty.

"I did not come before your people as I look to you in your dreams. My people and I were desperate with hunger and with fear."

"That's not what Eliah told me," I whisper to Layla's dream figure.

Layla blurs. She wisps and splits. Noise rushes into my dream, louder and louder. And I see her and them as things seemed to Layla.

She rides a faltering, dust coated horse. Her dress is muddy, stained with dried blood, and torn. There are cuts down her cheek and neck, the blood dried and dark. She slumps forward on her horse. Her people walk behind her, some are half-carried in the weary march towards Guan.

And then my people ride out to meet her and them; clean and rich and proud. They mutter in suspicion, point at Layla and her people, frown into their beards.

And they turn them away.

Layla's voice is in my head like a clap of lightning.

"You condemn us, we who are driven from our homes and our country and our dead. So I curse you. I spend everything left inside of me to curse you now, and down the ages."

And she laughs and laughs and laughs.

Then like a distant echo a different voice, and one I hadn't heard for years, went on:

"Until a woman comes caught between both worlds. She shall be the one to set Cesspit free." And then, the voice fading, "Come back to us, Apple."

I wake up to a racing heart and grit beneath my tongue. That last voice had been Katija's. Tears trickle down my cheeks.

The sound of the music, never-ending, floats to where I lie. A monotonous drone that usually makes me want to scream, today I hear its strains anew.

I will break the spell this month. I know it in my ancient heart. And what shall I say to the people of Cesspit left alive when I do? What is there to say to make sense of all of this?

I sit down to composing. I, who have always been silent, must find the words to make this right.

When I am not dreaming of Layla, I dream of Cesspit and the people I left behind. Eliah calls to me from far below, his hair grey and straggled and his skin covered in sores. He walks with a slow hunch and his eyes are gummy and weep muck. Katija stands by his side, supporting him.

"Are you there, Apple?" he and she call, the sound of their voices tugging at my heart 'til I think it might break. "Are you still alive to do what must be done?"

"Yes," I whisper, and then louder and stronger. "Yes."

Eliah's head tilts to one side.

"I am growing old and tired, child. Katija will be lonely without you."

His breath is as soft as cobwebs. His words as brittle as dead wood.

"Hold on, Eliah. My teacher, my rogue. Hold on."

But as he smiles wearily, I know it is just a dream. Eliah must have died years ago.

The skin I touch is as dry as parchment. When I pull a curl of hair around to my face so that I can see it, the colour is pure white. *This is what happens, Rael,* I think. *This is what happens when you give your whole life to a cause.*

I stretch out on the ground to embrace the grass and the dirt beneath me. I smell the rich loam I have created and smile. Under my breath I sing a jaunty strain Rael used to hum. I hear buds unfurl and roots creep deep beneath me. Even with my eyes squeezed tight I can see the people. Ever dancing, with the sweat dripping from their faces, shoulders, and backs.

The roots form an intricate underlay. They frame every tile's underside. A final root is almost at the tiles' centre. I sing and I sing and I sing. Hours upon hours I sing.

Then I remember Rael, and poor Eliah too, who never did get to see what I became, and the song becomes gut-wrenching, full of pain and anguish.

The roots claw upwards. I let my voice soar, full of power.

And it begins.

Enormous roots upturn tiles, flinging dirt and plaster everywhere. Coughing, I stop singing and open my eyes. I walk out amidst the tiles, onto the broken dance floor. Dancers stare at me, from the ground where they've fallen, all in a daze. Some of them work their mouths open and shut, as though they've forgotten how to speak after all of this time, and their eyes bulge at what they see.

I want to laugh and to cry. I reel from so many feelings coursing through me all at once.

My hand reaches out to touch the dancer nearest to me, her eyes filled with equal parts confusion and fright. Before I can, Layla's image is in my head.

"You have been punished enough. People of Guan go free."

The dancers look about them in wonderment; at the mess of broken ceramic tiles, at me and at each other, and all of us surrounded by the riot of colour from my flowers all around us.

And then, as one, like a collective sigh, they wisp in the wind. They crumble into dry dust 'til there is nothing but yellowed bones in heaps on the verdant greenery I have made.

My eyes sting for the barest moment. Then I turn away. It is a time for the living, not the dead.

It is later, much later, after I have flung open every shutter and every door, made room for sunshine in every nook and cranny that I walk downwards to open the gates of Guan. When I push open the great doors, I see people outside in the distance, wide-eyed with fear. They point and whisper.

Who is she? What is this new horror brought upon us?

"I am Apple, tender of gardens," I make myself say, tense as a bowstring. "Layla's curse is broken. Come inside to shelter, to clean water and to growing things. I have broken the Danse Macabre."

No one moves.

I sigh. I know gaining their trust will take time.

And then, the crowd parts for an old woman wearing a rusty necklace around her neck. I freeze, heart beating fast, but I make myself peer at the necklace first. Just to be sure. Alas, it's been far, far too many years and my eyes are old. Desperate with longing, I look into the woman's big, blue eyes. The disbelief and recognition I see in them reflects my own and now I know. There's a lump in my throat and tears fall freely, as Katija steps forward, her ancient hands outstretched.

Maureen Flynn lives on the sunny South Coast of NSW with her partner and is an avid speculative fiction lover, writer and fan. Her collection of poetry, *My Heart's Choir Sings*, a collection about grief, guilt, the blame game and moving on was self-published in 2014 and she religiously reviews *Doctor Who* on her Inkashlings blog. She has finally taken up consultancy in 2018 so she can dedicate more hours of her day to working on novels and short stories. This is her first short story publication.

Stardust

Charlotte Sophia

Gorganos III, Gorganos System, present

Seventy-two hours earlier, Zahra Imdali had been assured her partner for the mission was trustworthy, the payout would be enough to finally get her far away from Vandia, and their plan was utterly foolproof.

Her current options of dying on a planet whose native name was impossible to pronounce, or being sent to the prison planet of Sol III, did not seem to be consistent with those assurances.

Sadly, as another seven laser blasts steadily burned holes into the warehouse wall she crouched behind, it didn't look like her day was going to go anywhere near as planned.

Zahra drew her blaster, shooting a glare at the empty space where her 'partner' should have been. The crate he'd been pushing sat abandoned several feet away.

She swore into her oxygen mask and reached around the wall to fire. She knew she shouldn't have trusted that gods-damned Terran.

—◆—

Sulis, Saskari System, 72 hours earlier

"We call it Stardust," Cela Juro said. It wasn't his real name, and his face wasn't real either. He was a Terran of questionable morality and a bastion of ulterior motives, but Zahra owed him money as well as her life. It wouldn't do to slight him, especially in his own dubious establishment of neon lights, long shadows and a dozen armed guards ready to kill on command.

"You might've encountered it in your late-night wanderings," he continued, raising a well-groomed brow in question. "My fellow humans find it allows them to enjoy the sensation of travelling the galaxy without leaving the planet."

Zahra kept her face perfectly blank. Eighteen months living on the Terran colony planet Sulis had left her far more intimately acquainted with their behaviours than she'd ever wanted. The surface level of the planet's vast metropolis and untouched landscapes was nice enough, but the underworld was a cesspit of crime and poverty, where carrying a weapon at all times was a necessity. Nevertheless, all sorts of foreign species passed through there, allowing a dark-haired, lilac-skinned, yellow-eyed Elassi female of planet Vandia to go completely unnoticed.

If only she'd stayed as unnoticed as she'd intended. A droid ambled over out of the shadows, the magenta lights in its joints jerking with each step. It had been one of many Zahra had stolen and repaired as part of her first job for Cela, but as it placed two glasses on the table between them, it was clear the droid didn't recognise her.

"I have a contact on Gorganos III who's anxious to get a batch into the market," Cela went on. She turned her attention back to him. "Unfortunately, the Gorganosi High Command doesn't agree with the synthesising and distributing of drugs on their rock, so you'll have to be discreet. Everything's in place for you and your partner."

"Partner?" Zahra asked. Eighteen months on Sulis—and her entire childhood on Vandia—had taught her that going solo was the best way to survive.

He nodded towards a shadowy silhouette seated in the corner of the room, a smirk on his face. Backlit by the golden wall behind the bar, the figure detached itself from its stool. The bar-room chatter buzzed as Zahra beheld a young man stepping towards their table, grinning widely.

He was what Zahra had heard Terran women describe as "tall, dark and handsome". Lean, with dark hair and eyes, the faintest smattering of stubble on brown skin. The battered trench made him look even taller. She supposed the description suited, but her experience with Terran men could be summed up as "trouble, pain and misery". Memory of her best friend stabbed her in the gut. Ezri would have been so jealous.

"This is Cassius," Cela said. "Cass for short. He's been with me a few years."

Her still-grinning wannabe-partner extended a hand. "I've been looking forward to meeting Cela's favourite Elassi smuggler."

From the look in Cass's eyes, *that* was obvious. She smiled primly.

"Zahra Imdali. Betray me, and I'll blast your brains out."

Gorganos System space, 32 hours earlier

"If you don't stop asking personal questions, I'll eject you out the airlock." Zahra piloted the *Venture* around the shadowed curve of Gorganos III. Lights were sprinkled across the surface below, brighter spots illuminating cities and outlining the shapes of continents. In the distance, a blue crescent-shaped glow appeared along the edge of the planet. Zahra shielded her eyes against the sun as the star Gorganos rose above the horizon, illuminating the cabin.

Cass scoffed. "Everything's personal with you. Can't ask about family, friends, Vandia—"

"The airlock's down the hall to the left," she said.

He went silent, fingers tapping absently at the edge of the console. "Got a boyfriend?"

Zahra closed her eyes and said a silent prayer as the *Venture* angled towards the atmosphere. Spire-like mountains jutted through the clouds below. Far ahead, she could see their destination—at this distance little more than a pockmarked mass clinging to a sheer mountainside. She cast a sidelong look at Cass. "Have you?"

"He broke up with me." Cass shrugged. "My sister was heartbroken, my grandmother was thrilled … Kind of depressing, really."

She already regretted opening her mouth.

"Can you believe this is the fifth face I've seen Cela with?" Cass said, shaking his head. "The first time I saw him he looked like a model. Gorgeous.

Then I ended up five hundred thousand credits in debt, and he turned into that cranky old bastard."

Given the ship was probably bugged, she opted to say nothing. Making comments about her employer's physical appearance was unlikely to assist in her plans.

Cass leaned on the console, peering at her. Wondering, no doubt, why he'd been looking forward to meeting someone who was so uninterested in conversation. Zahra wondered the same thing herself.

"So. Robotics, huh?"

She started. "What?"

Cass shrugged, the barest of smug smiles on his lips. Zahra glared at it. "People talk. I heard that's how Cela found you—working in some sketchy workshop a year ago."

His words were met with silence.

"If it makes you feel better, he found me in a compromising position with his favourite bartender after I clogged his toilet."

"I don't care about your life story." She didn't want him to care about hers, either. And she certainly didn't want him to know that she'd continued to work in that sketchy workshop in order to get off Sulis as quickly as possible. People talked, and Cela wasn't going to be pleased to hear she was working for someone other than himself.

She could see him eyeing her head to toe in her peripheral vision. "Is it true Elassi melt rocks onto their skin?"

Zahra tugged the right edge of her jacket across her collarbone. A sweet smile plastered itself on her face as she turned to face him. "Is it true Terrans destroyed their homeworld and turned it into a prison?"

Cass glowered. "We didn't turn Earth into Sol III."

She smirked. "If you say so."

The descent was easy. She'd insisted they both set their blasters to stun in case they ran into any trouble. From the way Cass had looked at her, it was clear he thought she was one of those people who refused to kill under any and all circumstances, but truthfully she just didn't want her name and face on every billboard in the galaxy under the label 'murderer'. All they had to do was wait until the cover of darkness, enter the warehouse where the drugs were disguised as crates of synthesised oxygen, and load them onto the *Venture*. Compared to her last smuggling run involving an eight-legged horse and a canister of laughing gas, this was going to be a piece of cake.

"Are you indentured to Cela Juro?" Cass asked. He didn't look at her, seemingly transfixed by the steadily looming surface of Gorganos III.

Zahra blinked. "Are you?"

"Payment's more than enough for two people's debts," he said. "With enough left over to do whatever they wanted afterwards."

She raised a brow.

"We work together on this, and we're both free." Cass shrugged. "I want freedom as much as you do."

Zahra narrowed her eyes. Ezri had had a relationship with a Terran—a relationship that she'd paid for with her life. But Zahra was already facing death if her family ever caught up with their disgraced daughter, so she doubted this partnership was going to worsen her situation.

"All right then, Cass," she said, leaning back in her chair. "But you stick by me."

Cass grinned. "I'll do whatever you ask, Imdali."

Gorganos III, Gorganos System, present

She was going to kill Cass.

Everything had gone according to plan until the blaster bolts shot past her head. Until the Gorganosi Customs Officers disabled the *Venture's* engines, rendering it unable to fly.

Until her oh-so-trustworthy partner had decided to disappear.

Trapped inside the warehouse with three Gorganosi officers firing at her while another seven took the six crates of Stardust from the *Venture* onto their own insect-like ship, Zahra knew she didn't have many options. A different exit meant nothing if her ship was grounded. The entire job meant nothing if she couldn't get the payout she desperately needed. And the payout meant nothing if she was dead.

It didn't help that the warehouse had been erected within an enormous beehive-like structure hanging suspended from one of the planet's pointed mountains. Or that the beehive itself was crawling with gorgantua—carnivorous worms the size of Terran housecats. Without a ship, the only way off was a sheer drop to the surface at terminal velocity, or an invitation to dinner.

The Gorganosi Customs Officers still had a space-worthy vessel, though.

She shot around the side of the wall once again. A barrage of return fire replied through the fog, barely missing her. She ducked back behind cover, the air crackling where the bolt had passed through. Her hair rose with static. She supposed she should have been relieved the bolts were yellow rather than the white of blasters set to kill, but it was a bit difficult when holes were still burning through the wall she hid behind.

Somehow, she had to find a way onto the Gorganosi ship.

The officers shouted to each other. The blasters went silent. Zahra aimed at the edge of the wall, finger on the trigger, waiting for the officers to pour around the corner. Her breath, amplified within the oxygen mask, was conspicuously loud in her ears.

Several heartbeats later, and she was still waiting.

She peered around the wall, hoping she wasn't about to get her head blown off.

The officers were retreating into the bowels of their ship.

Zahra grabbed the last crate—Cass's—and tore across the space between the warehouse and the ship. Cass might have abandoned both her and the cargo, but she wasn't about to let a much-needed payout slip by—and she certainly wasn't going to let her only means of escape leave without her.

Several gorgantua slithered into the safety of the fog as she approached the ship. Wisps of dense cumulonimbus fled before her hovering crate.

Zahra's boot landed on the ramp of the Gorganosi ship. The walls of the cargo hold inside were lined with countless items confiscated by Customs.

On the left side of the hold, clear bags of transparent orange liquid hung from the ceiling. A massive blaster hung on the wall beside the cockpit doors, accompanied by an assortment of other weapons of various shapes and sizes around the room. A hairless rodent scurried the length of a cage near Zahra's right elbow. And in the centre of the hold were the six crates of disguised Stardust.

All ten officers had their backs to her as they huddled between them, a set of stairs leading to the cockpit ahead. They removed their helmets, revealing smooth, grey insectoid heads. Pincers clicked as they conversed. Blasters were strapped to their sides.

She fired at the nearest officer's head. He fell like a stone.

They went silent, pincers going still. Then, as one, they turned towards her. Lidless eyes stared.

Dimly, she wondered if she'd just made a bigger mistake than the one that had landed her on Sulis.

The door behind them crashed open, revealing a shadowy silhouette backlit by the cyan lights of the cockpit. Cass bowed deeply at the goggling officers, raised his own blaster, and—

Yellow exploded throughout the hold. Zahra fired, ducked behind her crate, fired again. Cass blasted two officers and whirled behind the cockpit door as bolts sliced through where he'd just been standing. The room filled with static and heat, and the fizzing of blaster bolts cleaving the air.

There was a flash of yellow in the corner of her eye, a flush of heat on the right side of her face—

She spun around the crate as the shot ricocheted off the wall and scarred the floor where she'd been crouched, passing close enough to her leg to burn a hole in the fabric and leave her skin more pink than purple.

"On your left!"

Zahra turned just in time to shoot the officer advancing on her. The blast got him between the eyes, and his head snapped back before the rest of his body followed suit, a black burn mark where the shot had made contact with exoskeleton. She nodded acknowledgement at Cass, aiming for the last officer standing.

Her laser blast hit him at the same time Cass's did.

It had all taken about twenty seconds. Zahra straightened and aimed her blaster at the ten officers lying sprawled on the floor of the hold, limbs splayed in all directions. She lowered her blaster slowly and turned to Cass. His eyes met hers over the top of his oxygen mask as he dipped his head.

They wasted no time in dragging the officers off the ship and dumping their unconscious bodies on the ground outside. Zahra watched on from the bottom of the stairs as Cass heaved an eleventh from the cockpit and added them to the pile. She grimaced. It looked like the aftermath of a Terran party.

"I think that went well," he said, dusting off his hands as he climbed back onto the ship. There was a dark burn staining the right shoulder of his trench, but otherwise he looked unharmed. "Could have done without the drama, but you can't expect much from—"

He stopped in his tracks at the receiving end of her blaster. Slowly, eyes wide, he raised his hands above his head.

Zahra scowled at him. "Remember what I said about betraying me?" Her voice was distorted through the mask.

Cass cleared his throat. "You said you'd blast my brains out."

She smiled genially. There was a click as her blaster snapped into kill. He flinched. "I don't appreciate moles. How else did they know about our assignment? Should I shoot, or do you want to explain yourself first?"

Cass swallowed hard. "It wasn't me," he said. She raised an eyebrow in challenge, blaster aimed between his eyes. "I need your help."

Helping him was quite possibly the last thing she felt inclined to do. "What?"

There was no immediate answer. Instead, he reached deliberately for the nearest crate, keeping his gaze locked with her own, and lifted off the lid. A white glow emanated from inside.

Zahra didn't have to look to know what it was. It was the stuff she saw Terrans quaffing in all the nightclubs on Sulis. It was the stuff Terrans loved so much because it only worked on them. The stuff she and Cass had been sent to retrieve: Stardust.

"You, me, and the mysterious contact are supposed to be the only people who know about this," Cass said, gesturing to their shimmering cargo. "And if it's all here, and worth a lot of money, what reason could the contact have for turning us in? How would they get their money for all this?"

She could think of a few reasons. "Maybe there's a secret deal with the Gorganosi." The blaster didn't waver from his face.

"The Gorganosi don't like drugs here." Cass put the lid back on the crate. "If you were hell-bent on stopping a drug trade, how would you do it?"

Confiscating the contraband the way the officers had done seemed like a good start. Taking the drug peddlers in for questioning, rather than killing them outright, seemed like another good idea. It explained the yellow bolts.

But instead of trying to arrest them, the Gorganosi Customs Officers had simply walked away.

"Whoever organised this wants us alive," she breathed. "But not captured. They let us go free." Cass nodded. She didn't lower the blaster. Killing them would have been so much easier. It could look like a botched job, or an accident, and no one in the entire galaxy would notice they were gone. Or care.

She swallowed. "They'd have to benefit somehow. Gain something."

"Or," Cass began, a wild gleam in his eyes, "they just have to not lose anything." There was something hopeful in the look he gave her, and it made her uncomfortable.

Zahra narrowed her eyes. "You said you needed my help."

"We've both almost paid off our debts," Cass said carefully. "I know Cela needed someone who knew robotics when he found you. I know you kept working at that workshop to try and pay him back. And once we complete this mission, we're both free."

She glared. "That's not an answer."

"I have a job lined up for when I leave." She kept her expression blank, but that hopeful look remained on his face. "It involves a droid. And it might need repairing—"

"So let me get this straight," she interrupted, finger itching to pull the trigger. Rage bubbled up inside her gut. "You found out all these things about me, were looking forward to meeting me, because you wanted to use me?"

"No!"

"Yes." She wondered why she didn't just shoot him and be done with it. Ezri had always been interested in humans—obsessed, even. She'd made Zahra study Terran languages with her, dragged her to the port to practice on the human traders. So Zahra had forced Ezri to study technology and robotics. And when the incident with Ezri and her Terran had ruined everything, including the mere idea of humans, those technology classes were the only thing Zahra had left. The only part of Vandia that didn't make her sick or try to kill her.

She had already thrown some of it away to work for Cela. But Cass was another story. There was no way she was going to let this Terran take what little she had left away from her. Absolutely no way in hell—

"Do you think Cela will ever let you leave?" Cass demanded.

She blinked, scrambling for words. The smirk on Cela's face as he introduced her to Cass flashed in her mind. "This job will pay off my debts," she said. The words sounded weak even to her own ears.

He snorted and shook his head. "And have you seen just how well this job has gone? The ship can't fly, nearly all the cargo was taken, and we would have been stuck here with no way of easily getting back. We'd have no choice but to turn to Cela for help. To run back to him. We were set up to fail, and if we fail—"

"We don't get paid," she finished for him. A wave of relief seemed to wash over him. She felt empty, herself.

"Just one job," he said quietly. "Then we can go our separate ways. But we'll both be free."

Her arm shook, whether from emotion or the effort of holding her blaster in Cass's face for so long, she didn't know. She clicked the blaster back into stun and lowered her arm.

"I think we should pay Cela a visit."

⚓

Sulis, Saskari System, 35 hours later

Cela threw them a welcome party. Half a dozen armed guards were waiting in the hangar when the Gorganosi ship came in to land. Two of them were droids Zahra had repaired on her first job. All of them answered to Cela Juro.

Zahra and Cass followed their entourage of guards from the hangar, the two droids staying behind to take the cargo out. The hangar was Cela's, used for a small segment of his criminal endeavours, and exempt from the mandatory checks every other port was subjected to. Any checks that did happen conveniently found nothing.

A set of doors slid open at the back of the hangar. Closed, the doors blended into the smooth grey metal of the wall. Open, they revealed a dimly lit passageway beyond. The two smugglers fell into step behind the guards as they made their way into the corridor, the muffled sound of music drifting towards them.

Zahra cast a look at Cass. The back entrance to Cela's club was as dingy and grimy as everything else below surface level on Sulis. Naked pipes snaked along the walls, reverberating with distant music and the occasional flush of a nightclub toilet. She knew that Cela liked to use the back door for his illegal activities. She had used it herself on occasion, but to be escorted there by a group of armed guards was unusual.

From the grimace on Cass's face, it was clear he would have preferred to use the front door, too.

The guards cracked open the door at the end of the passage and ushered them inside. The nightclub was as Zahra and Cass had left it four and a half days earlier. The room was mostly in darkness, neon lights shining on the far wall onto the dance floor a level below. Music pulsed throughout the club. Droids served customers drinks and didn't even cast a look in Zahra's direction.

Cela was sitting at the same table.

He got to his feet as they approached, a slick smile on his face. Two chairs sat opposite his, waiting for occupants. Zahra and Cass sat slowly.

The look on Cela's face was pleasantly hostile. "Did you get it?"

Cass blinked. "Why else would we be here?"

Zahra glanced around the room. The guards had placed themselves around the walls, two on either side of the back door. Four sets of hands rested on their blasters. The floor around the table was bare.

All the other tables were empty.

Cela leaned forward, elbows resting on the table. "You got all the crates?"

"Every single one," Cass said. Twin smiles made themselves at home on Cass and Zahra's faces. The atmosphere hummed.

"We'd like our payments now," Zahra said. "If that's not too much to ask. I believe we agreed on twenty thousand each?"

"And then we'll get out of your hair," Cass continued for her, eyeing the bald patch on top of Cela's head. "If it's not too much to ask."

Cela considered them for a moment. "Of course." He waved over one of the droids and whispered in its ear. The droid ambled into the corner of the room. Zahra watched it go. "Only, I wasn't expecting you back so soon," Cela went on, looking between the two of them. "So I don't have the money on me at the moment."

"We can wait." Cass leaned back in his chair, crossed one leg over the other, and clasped his hands over his knee. Zahra crossed her arms. They both kept on smiling. Cela smiled back. Zahra's cheeks began to ache.

Again, Cela glanced between them.

"There were only a few mishaps along the way," Zahra said, catching Cela's eye. "The *Venture* was grounded on Gorganos III."

"And we didn't have the codes to enable the engines again," Cass added. "So we took a Gorganosi ship. I'm sure the payment is more than enough to cover the cost." He shrugged, flicking at the burn on the shoulder of his trench. "That is, if you ever intend to give it to us."

Zahra cocked her head to one side.

Cela's eyes flashed briefly behind the smile still on his face. "Is there a reason why I wouldn't?"

Zahra and Cass exchanged a look.

"Let's just say that the few mishaps we had were fairly big ones," she said. Cass nodded. "Someone tipped off Gorganosi Customs, grounded the ship, tried to take the cargo, but wanted us left alive." She sighed. "But more importantly, it's—what, seventy hours to Gorganos III and back?"

"Plus several hours planning," Cass cut in.

"A few hours to do the job—"

"Half a day to kill while we waited for nightfall—"

"About four and a half days total," Zahra said. "And yet, you weren't expecting us."

"Funny, that." Cass smirked.

Cela's expression was poisonous.

"So, the question remains," Zahra continued, in her most courteous tone, "do you ever intend to pay us?" Both she and Cass still smiled, lounging comfortably in their chairs.

There was no reply from Cela, save for the sliding of his gaze to the guards who lingered around the edges of the room, and the three droids that loitered nearby.

"I'm going to take that as a big fat no," Cass said, moving to get up.

Zahra followed suit. "We'll leave you with the cargo then," she said. "It should cover the loss of the *Venture* as well as our debts to you. You can keep the change."

"You might want to use it to get those pipes checked." Cass jerked a thumb towards the back door. "Smells like a bloody sewer out there."

The click of blasters was barely audible over the slamming of their chairs against the table as they pushed them in.

Cela shot to his feet. "You're both still indentured to me. You can't leave."

Zahra frowned at Cass. Cass frowned back.

"Maybe he didn't hear us," he said. "We've repaid our debts."

"You haven't paid me back until I say you have," Cela sneered. He gestured towards the three droids in the corner of the room. They straightened as one. "So you'll keep working for me until—"

Two yellow bolts converged on his face.

The droids launched themselves across the room. Cass fired at the nearest one. The blast made no impact on its advance. Zahra did the same. The droids got closer with each step as Zahra and Cass backed into the table behind them—

"Override code—Ezri!"

All three droids came to an abrupt halt. Zahra breathed a sigh of relief. She reached over and pushed Cass's blaster down.

"Incapacitate hostiles," she said. The droids rotated on the spot to face the guards stationed around the walls, sensors locking onto the raised blasters. Cela was sprawled on the floor beside his chair. She met Cass's eye.

The droids threw themselves at Cela's guards. Light exploded around them as the guards fired wildly and uselessly, hitting glasses behind the bar and shattering light fixtures. Music still pulsed on the level below.

Cass and Zahra were back-to-back, firing yellow around the room and blasting Cela's guards into unconsciousness as the droids kept up their attack. One dropped beneath a table, crawling along the floor to reach Cela. Zahra bolted for the back door, Cass right on her heels.

The passage didn't actually smell like a sewer. As they raced towards the doors to the hangar, Cass turned, aimed—

And blasted the pipes open, just as one of the guards burst through the back door.

The contents exploded into the corridor.

The guard's screech of disgust would have made her laugh, if the smell of sewerage hadn't made her want to throw up. Cass was laughing like a maniac.

She pounded up the ramp into the Gorganosi ship. All seven crates had been unloaded, the droids who had done the unloading watching on with confusion. Zahra threw herself into the pilot's chair, Cass leaning against the chair beside her.

A rumbling beneath her feet told her the engines had come to life. And then the ship was rising off the ground and turning towards the hangar opening, blaster shots bouncing harmlessly off the hull.

"Tell you what, Imdali," Cass grinned, "Cela's going to need another new face after *that*."

Zahra smirked as the Gorganosi ship shot out of the hangar and upwards towards the sliver of light on the surface of the planet.

If the blasters to the face didn't do it, then receiving the cargo would. She felt only slightly disappointed she wouldn't see his expression when he opened the crates.

Seven crates in total. Two filled with Stardust—enough to pay off her debts and Cass's. Maybe even enough to cover the cost of the *Venture*. The other five, though … Cela was going to peel his own face off when he found the eleven Gorganosi Customs Officers packed inside like sardines. She grinned to herself at the thought.

"So what do you say, Imdali?" Cass said, leaning down and lifting up a floor panel. He straightened, a bag of glowing white in his hands. Five crates' worth were stuffed into the floors and walls of the ship, ready to take them wherever they wanted. Far away from Vandia, and far away from Sulis. "Just one job?"

"Just one job, Cass," she said, a sly smile on her face.

"And then?" He strapped himself into the seat next to her.

"And then we'll see."

The Gorganosi ship shot into the light. Blue water, green vegetation, and shiny, spiralling towers stretched as far as the eye could see. She angled the ship upwards towards the edge of the atmosphere.

"You'd better tell me about this droid."

Charlotte Sophia is in her second year of university studying a Bachelor of Writing after a lifelong obsession with storytelling and speculative fiction. She has no idea if that will ever get her a decent job, but hopes her allegedly excessive smashed avocado consumption won't hold her back. She currently lives in Canberra with her pet chickens, who have trained her to feed them at will.

Immortal, Coiled

David Coleman

Gilgamesh the deplorable jostled in the greasy queue, a few pan-handled bits of currency rolling in his palm. He didn't need the felafel roll, but the begging, the buying, the eating, helped to pass the time.

He never got the knack of money, and staring down at the jumble of coins he had no idea if there would be enough. But maybe coming up short would cause a diverting scene, a burst of violence. His warrior heart flickered.

Gilgamesh edged forward, drunks on all sides, the hot sweat and optimism of the bar closing crowd, tomorrow's hangover like some distant country.

He had tried, a hundred times or more, to live among the slow build of forests, the right speed of mountains, the long hiss of deserts. Once, mid-ocean, he'd leapt from a brigand's ship and sunk down, down, down into that black cold isolation, him and the sea—wine-dark and reckless. Vowed to himself only, no one else to tell, to spend a century there cross-legged. The waveless muddy bottom and him, a null place to contemplate the mindless wheel of eternity.

But after a week, four days if he was honest, him alone—no Poseidon, no Tangaroa—just blind fish and silence, it was enough. No philosopher he, even after millennia. So he began the slow trudge, any direction, vast black plains and stumbling across never-seen mountains in the stern cold. Even the novelty of being the first to explore by hand and foot—no sight, no sound, only hard-pressing water—provided no diversion.

Stepped sightless off a ledge once and found the deep dark had further depths still. Wondered how he would get out of this one, a chasm, narrow, sharp and binding. By then the ocean adventure was getting old.

Patience never was a warrior's virtue. When he remembered that he could try swimming. If he wanted to.

Wriggling free, one stroke, five, and lift-off from his dark hollow, scraping elbows and knees against those trench walls and then there was more room and nothing solid anywhere at all. Gilgamesh would never use a term like 'endless' or 'forever'—he knew better than anyone that everything had boundaries. There were always edges, somewhere a start, and beyond, a finish. Even for him there was that leading edge, the point of his distant birth. His final edge, his finish, was also out there, somewhere. Or so he hoped.

And so it was with the ocean. After a billion strokes, always imagining he was reaching upwards but never really sure, there, the leading edge. Surfacing, into mid-ocean night-time. Sunrise later, hard-teeth of midday, night, storms, clouds, a whale once far off, three times a bird. Bobbing for months, sun-burnt and salted, staring at the sky, counting the stars.

Then, the next perimeter. Sprawled on a beach, his legs all wobbly and clothes mostly rotted. Chased away for being a vagrant.

"No tabouli! No tabouli!" he bawled too late, his mind yanked back to this moment, this felafel shop, this wherever he was. Back among fast moving humans, he couldn't keep away for long. He couldn't blame the tired man now slopping on the hommus. Gilgamesh knew his own accent to be impenetrable, was surprised he was able to find even those words. Never had the gift for languages—his mother tongue long lost, a disappointment to scholars if ever they knew he was there, with no language ever properly taking its place. Only snatches and phrases in five hundred dialects smeared over five millennia. Just enough to barely get by.

Gilgamesh the knock-about could not live like a mountain, had had enough of oceans. Always returning to the fast moving humans, the turn and cycle of mortal-timed ages, the urbanality. And he savoured that other edge too much to turn away—he was a warrior-born after all. Hundreds, thousands of skirmishes he could scarcely recall, echoes of random carnage. Some of the recent ones stood out, even if he did not know how to pronounce them— Crimea, Passchendaele, Dieppe, Incheon, Freetown, Marryatville, New Rio.

A freelance brawler, not even a mercenary, barely aware of the sides, each war's purpose unknown. Merely the blood sport of cut and parry—he would not lie to himself, not after all these years.

The pieces of eight or whatever name they had in this country, this century, were enough for the felafel after all. Three coins pushed back his way, scooped up with scarred fingers. No scene then, just turning from the fluorescent lights and the Lebanese pop, cradling a sloppy wrapper and slinking away.

Later: the blackness before the dawn. Even the roaches were sleeping. But not Gilgamesh, not old Bilgames. Those gods, always a sting in the tail, the small print, the loop-hole conjured out of dust and nonsense. The wager for immortality had been simple enough, seven nights awake and that's all, a loaf of bread baked to mark each sunrise. And he had done it, with gods as his witness. That final morning he had strained to his feet, swaying, wilful and expectant, the oldest and mouldiest of the loaves lofted like a trophy.

The god had sulked, insolent and prissy. Stared thunderclouds at Gilgamesh for long minutes, but he didn't look away, not even once. The reward would be given, and the twisty little god knew it.

"Since you like staying awake so much," the god had sneered, his voice pinched and nasal. "Then so you shall remain. All the days of your eternity." And threw immortality at him like wet newspaper.

Last laugh all right. Eternal life. Eternal insomnia. Now those gods are long gone and Gilgamesh the warrior, Gilgamesh the demigod, Gilgamesh the freebooter sits in a cold lane of a city whose name he does not know, his open-ended prize for toughing it out one week sleepless.

Not that he minded the lane. As good a place as any when you'd been everywhere and were going nowhere. No appointments, open dance card. Two million nights lain awake in brothels, haystacks, under bridges. Hundreds of feather beds, rivers of silk sheets, someone warm, something cool to sip. That such pleasures no longer stir his ancient loins his greatest regret.

The felafel roll lay beside him, cold, uneaten. He found the crease in the paper and slowly started to unravel it. A leading edge, he mused, as the paper tore under his fighter's fingers, as significant or as meaningless as anything else he had done in his long slow turn of time. He thought of another sunrise then, the next one coming, and decided to find a high point to see it. There. A goal.

In the alley he looked up at a fire escape, the bottom rungs twenty feet above his head. He calculated, took three steps back and ran at the wall, planted a foot seven feet up and vaulted, reached the steel rung easily, him an athlete and marauder after all. He swung upwards onto the platform and started to climb, stomping up the metal steps. From the windows flowed the usual sounds, of couples in stifled sex, babies with colic, his fellow insomniacs fiddling with teapots. And he heard that other accurs'ed breed, the blissful sleepers, gentle snorers in their blanket-wrapped ease. He stomped hard and climbed the ten stories of the apartment building, desiring the nothing achievement of a rooftop.

He swung from the fire escape over the brick parapet, no castle this, no army waiting, only startled pigeons and rust and dust. He approached the edge overlooking the street, looked down on parked cars and streetlights.

He contemplated jumping off, the pointlessness of it, the impactless impact, even the two seconds of freefall sure to be without frisson. He peered at the horizon instead, the near forgotten felafel roll hanging soggy from his left hand.

Just then, precisely as he looked, a smog-slicked sunrise stumbled into the sky. Gilgamesh the mighty scoffed at himself as a tear escaped his eye, just a messy sunrise over a grey city somewhere on this world that he was cursed to walk. Yet his old bandit's heart trembled despite all he had seen, and he felt the shimmering of new days and new possibilities and swift steel and near escapes and a thousand new scrapes besides.

He bellowed to that oily sky, his felafel held up like a baton. With a whoop he cast it from the roof and immediately regretted it, his stomach turning with a sudden appetite. He leapt from the roof and found that in fact he enjoyed those two seconds of freefall to unforgiving pavement, not a sprain or a bruise to the deal. He gazed about and spotted the felafel, still half rolled in its paper, partly sunk in a scum-pocked slick of curb water. Gilgamesh the pillager bounded over like a puppy and raised it sodden, cold and slimy to his lips. He, a creature who need not eat, ripped away the remaining paper and bit deep with the hunger of the ages. Filthy grey sauce oozed down his chin and he even relished the tabouli, parsley be damned.

It wasn't for him to live at the pace of mountains, but instead by moments. Silly sunrises and plastic food was all the meaning he needed, rubbish like religious icons swirling in the gutter at his feet. One moment to be followed by another, then another one after that. Gilgamesh the terrible stomped down the unknown street, step by step, moment by moment, looking for joy, looking for trouble, looking for nothing beyond that which appeared before his eyes. If he was to persist, gods be damned, he would persist, sucking the marrow from all that befell him. A new strategy, long may it last. A hundred years? Four days? He laughed, loud and deep, then spat and cursed the god who had cursed him.

He reached a corner, turned left, saw a group of early morning joggers and imagined possibilities. Gilgamesh the immortal quickened his pace.

David Coleman is an award-winning writer, with stories appearing in *Aurealis*, *Dimension6*, *Kaleidotrope* and four CSFG anthologies, amongst other places. He has been short-listed as a Writer of the Future. You can find David here: http://davidcolemanwords.wordpress.com/

On the Consequences of Clinically-Inhibited Maturation in the Common Sydney Octopus

Simon Petrie and Edwina Harvey

"Just as a matter of interest, Blakey, what did you expect to happen?"

"Yes, Professor, I've destroyed all nine. Ten? What d'you mean, ten? There were only nine in the tank. Yes, I'm sure."

"Clearly there's a mistake in this dissection report. That level of neuronal interconnectedness would make it almost ... human."

"Do you notice that damp smell in this part of the building? What d'you think's causing it?"

"Jim, you can rest assured that if I'd had designs on that bottle of rum you've been storing in your bottom drawer, I'd have found a better use for it than emptying it into the fish tank."

"Hey, my chair's wet!"

"So if Blakey's cephalopod project was scrapped a decade ago, why do we still have a standing order for octopus growth hormones?"

"I can smell ... paint. Fresh paint. Can you smell it? Just next to the tearoom?"

"The cafeteria is on the phone again. They're really narked that whenever they put in an order for frozen calamari somebody from head-office sends a text right after and cancels it."

"Shouldn't there be fish in this tank?"

"Yes, I'm calling about some apparent water damage to my book on driverless vehicle design."

"But weren't all those test animals destroyed? Besides, octopuses only live a couple of years. You must've seen something else."

"Why do all our photocopiers keep shorting out? And what is this even a copy of?"

"Welcome to Acme Car Insurance … and your policy number is …? And what sort of claim do you want to make?"

"Well, the call obviously didn't come from here. There's nobody in the building who talks like Stephen Hawking. We wouldn't even know what to do with that many anchovy pizzas."

"Look, mate, we can only repair leaks if we can find them. I've just wasted the bloody morning exploring this building's roof cavity—"

"No sir, marine corrosion damage to your fourteenth-storey office isn't covered in your Institute's excess. Please hold, I'll check …"

"We would remind all staff that under no circumstances are CSIRO computers to be used for viewing or downloading hentai."

"I'd use the one downstairs if I were you. There were all these weird splashing noises coming from the cubicle next door."

"Didn't there used to be a door here? Leading to the electronics workshop?"

"Relax! It has to be a hoax. If Management really had the goods on our little side business, they'd be raking the two of us over the coals, not demanding Bitcoins."

"Your invoice specified forty-three live, mature, female gourami. You've got a bloody nerve only shipping two. This has set our research back weeks. We expect a full refund. And we'll be using an alternative supplier in future."

"It looks as though they've only taken the waterproofed electronics packs. Buggered if I know how they got in, anyway."

"No sir, I don't think your policy includes car upholstery soaked in sea-water. Please hold, I'll check ..."

"Completely cleared out ... and all they left behind was this badly-written, soggy IOU."

"Where did all these prawn shells come from?"

"Yes, yes, I'm getting the photos now ... Well, it certainly *looks* like a giant octopus, but much bigger than any sample I've ever seen before."

"Hey, this keyboard's wet."

"Just give me a list of what equipment has gone missing and I'll make a point of logging it with Security."

"Would whoever made an unholy mess of the seafood platter for the Ministerial visit please see the Departmental secretary regarding the required payment?"

"Yes, I met him on one of those online dating sites. He sounds like quite a catch. He's so different from the other guys! I can't for one minute believe he'd be after my millions. He just needs an account to move some money into for a few days."

"That email you got—for God's sake don't ignore it. However this guy knows about it, he means business."

"I'm getting really fucking sick of this. Third time this week one of you has nicked my tuna."

"You were on a glass-bottomed boat and you thought you saw *what*?"

"Police are refusing to comment on public speculation that the recent series of driverless-car ram raids on fishmongers might have been preparation for this much bigger operation at the Sydney Fish Market."

"Has someone been messing with the biosecurity suite's door-access card reader?"

"Someone left what looks like half a pilchard beside my drill press."

"No, I'm sorry sir, we don't know of any car paint specialists who could remove the giant sucker-marks from your duco without doing an entire respray. Please hold and I'll check …"

"We would remind all staff that under no circumstances are Defence Ministry computers to be used for high-volume futures trading."

"So you can't tell me who placed the order, using a research grant code you've never heard of but which the system somehow recognised. And now you tell me it's all disappeared overnight? Isn't a lot of this gear under embargo anyway?"

"No, I can't see either why there'd be a two-hundred-kilometre pipeline to the ocean from the new facility. But it's in the plans, so I'm not arguing with it."

"Yes, a complaint. It's in regard to that supposedly-secure, top-of-the-line vault you installed for us."

"If I didn't know better, I'd swear that Great White was traumatised."

"Weren't there five vials of the agent? I mean, if this stuff got out …"

"I was working here late last night, nobody else around, and there were some bloody weird noises coming from within the walls. I reckon the air conditioning needs servicing again."

"Somebody trashed, and I mean totally trashed, the workshop over the weekend."

"Yeah, just driven off the wharf. Deep there, too—it's gonna cost a packet to haul it up. Reckon it's the same gang who shorted the alarm system on the vehicle depot last week?"

"Were they supplying complimentary wine and beer on the glass-bottom boat tour, by any chance?"

"Apparently, our largest single-line expenditure over the last fifteen years has been something that's only listed in the purchase database as 'O.G.H.', sourced from somewhere called Marine Bioceuticals Inc. Anyone know what that's about? We've spent millions …"

"We were doing our usual pre-dawn row up the Parramatta River when something grabbed the boat and held us there for about a minute. The coxswain swears he saw something pointy rise out of the water, but we can't find any shark teeth marks on the hull at all."

"Unmanned submersibles don't just disappear. What the hell is happening here?"

"What's being described as an exceptionally virulent bout of food poisoning within the offices of the Department of Education and Training has decimated the group responsible for administration of research funding in biology."

"Amazing what you can do with Photoshop these days. That eye looks to be the size of a car tyre. Where'd you take this? And, of course, my condolences regarding your wife."

"You only get giant squid in really, really deep water, though. More like off the continental shelf."

"This fine for improper mooring is preposterous, simply preposterous. I refuse to pay a brass razoo. I moored the yacht at my designated berth, I *always* moor the yacht at my designated berth. I've no idea how it could have got moved to the naval station."

"A spokeswoman for Majestic Cruises refused to comment on the incident, but a crewmember on the ship concerned said the sighting could possibly be put down to a case of mass hysteria following a showing of *The Beast from 20,000 Fathoms*. Meanwhile, expert opinion on the veracity of the reported photos remains divided."

"Yes, I'm well aware that whales often beach themselves. But twenty kilometres inland? C'mon!"

"While the source of the devastation remains a mystery, those concerned say it may be years before these fish farms are able to return to full commercial production."

"Cut the nets! Cut the nets! We're being dragged backwards!"

"Have pirates returned to the Caribbean? Fingers of blame are being pointed in all directions following the apparent interception of a twenty thousand tonne shipment of frozen fish that had been scheduled to arrive in New Orleans yesterday."

"Let's row out to that island, you said. It's not far, you said. Well, look around. There *is no* bloody island! There's—bloody hell! Since when do islands have eyes? Row back! Ro—"

"Oh it *has* to be Photoshopped! If there really was something with tentacles that big lurking at the end of the pier, there'd be a Japanese fishing trawler on the horizon intent on hunting it down."

"Amazon staff are totally at a loss to explain the sudden, and apparently irreversible, erasure of cookbooks and recipes featuring octopus from Kindles worldwide. They say, however, that in accordance with company policy, they will not be issuing refunds."

"As the officer in charge of this submarine, Captain, you're responsible for the safe carriage of its warheads. Do you honestly expect this panel to accept your explanation that 'they just went missing' while you were on patrol in the South Pacific? If the Russians or the Chinese happen to get hold of them …"

"Ballard, famous for discovering the *Titanic* in 1985, maintains that several of the wrecks he has observed recently appear to have been dragged long distances across the seafloor. Though by what, and to what end, remains a mystery."

"I don't care how many shell companies that supertanker is listed through. *Somebody* has to own it. And somebody has to be crewing it."

"The World Bank has refused to comment, but officials there privately admit that they are as baffled as anyone as to why such a large, and ever-increasing, share of the world's fiscal reserves should be passing through an anonymous online bank account whose only registered address is the now-demolished South Sydney Marine Research Institute."

"So what *do* you attribute these sudden large shifts in whale migration paths to?"

"Yes, it's an extraordinarily generous research grant, but I still say you should decline it. I mean, you don't even know anything—and nor, it seems, does anyone else—about this organisation that's funding it."

"Chinese officials have given no reason for the sudden abandonment of the contentious artificial islands, but sources in the Pentagon have reported evidence for what they describe as 'aggressively scuttled warships' seen in recent satellite imagery."

"So is this a yacht, or a ferry, or a—Oh. No, I'm sorry, but we can't help you. We no longer insure trawlers. No exceptions."

"My God, it's like a city! It *is* a city! It's—hey, what happened to the feed? Get it back!"

"Mate, if you can find a better quote for what you're asking, go for it. But I'm telling you, *nobody* ships directly over the Marianas Trench anymore, it's just not bloody worth it. You could always spring for airfreight."

"While the cause of the blasts—individually measured as between 150 and 350 kilotons—remains shrouded in mystery, with no nation or non-state actor yet having claimed responsibility, polar experts say their location only makes sense if someone were trying to engineer large and rapid rises in sea level for reasons known only to them. Hard questions are tonight being asked of Switzerland and Bhutan."

"So, have you received this new email too? And what does this even mean, 'Cthulhu is coming'?"

Simon Petrie is a Canberran by way of the Canterbury Plains. **Edwina Harvey** is a Sydneysider born and bred. Edwina and Simon first worked together on *Andromeda Spaceways Inflight Magazine* and have collaborated on several other writing and editing projects. Edwina's most recent book, *An Eclectic Collection of Stuff and Things* (Peggy Bright Books, www.peggybrightbooks.com), and Simon's latest, *Wide Brown Land: stories of Titan*, are widely available online.

The authors attest that no hyperintelligent octopuses were liberated into the ocean during research for this story.

Trojan Thoughts

Chris McGrane

Two men in dark suits approached me as I sat in the transit lounge, awaiting my connecting flight to London.

"Are you Nathaniel Tsang?" one asked.

I nodded.

"We are from the National Security Bureau. Our intelligence suggests that your mind has been used to share highly classified information with a non-state actor dedicated to undermining our national security. Your mind is a crime scene. You are under arrest for espionage and thought smuggling. You do not have to say or think anything. However, anything you do say or think will be recorded and may be given in evidence."

The man produced a Thought-pad™ and scanned my brain.

"Wait … You can't read my mind. Not without a warrant."

"You watch too many American movies, Mr Tsang."

"You appear to be preparing to broadcast a number of subversive ideas. Please come with us."

They bundled me into the back of a black limousine.

I demanded a lawyer and assistance from the Australian embassy. They ignored me.

In the back of the car, I struggled to comprehend my predicament. I wracked my brain for subversive thoughts. There were unkind thoughts about some local politicians, and a few illegally downloaded memories, but nothing that would pique the interest of the NSB. Since leaving Australia nine hours before, I hadn't even opened my Psi-mail account. I certainly wasn't stupid enough to carry a suspicious psychic message into a foreign country. So how could I have anything illegal in my brain?

I had almost convinced myself of my innocence when I remembered my connection to a psychic technology company named Mindshare. I was studying Psi-T/Commerce at the University of Canberra and looking for a way to fund my end of year tour of Europe.

Mindshare paid its test subjects well, so I'd volunteered to participate in their latest experiment.

I had signed over part of my brain to Mind-Share, to use while I was sleeping. In return, they'd promised to pay me for all the mental processing capacity they used.

Initially my experience with the technology had been positive. The first client was the European University astronomy department—they'd harnessed my unused mental processing power (and the power of thousands of other sleeping brains—sourced through Mindshare) to chart a previously unseen corner of the Milky Way. I would wake up with amazing interstellar images in my head and money in my pocket. It had seemed like a wonderful arrangement, until now.

"Is this about Mindshare?" I asked. "Did they use the processing capacity of my mind to do something illegal? Maybe that's why these subversive thoughts seem to emanate from …"

My captors sneered. "Is that the best excuse you have? Our scans show that you've been in contact with the Ripper. Many of the messages in your head bear his unique thought-patterns. Those thoughts alone are enough to earn you a life sentence. Then there are all the other contraband ideas in your head …"

The Ripper was well known for smuggling proscribed thoughts into countries whose rulers had banned them. It dawned on me that I was now the latest in a long line of Australians to be arrested in the City State for thought-smuggling—a crime punishable by death.

I hammered on the bullet proof glass screen that separated me from the NSB agents. "Please—I'm just a student. You can't do this. *I didn't even know those thoughts were in my head.*"

I stopped abruptly, realising how clichéd my declaration was. I began to shake.

Get out of the car.

I was so distraught that it took me a few moments to realise the voice in my head wasn't mine.

The passenger door isn't locked.

How could the door possibly be unlocked? I thought. How could the agents make such an elementary mistake?

The NSB agents aren't as resistant to thought-hacking as they like to think. Now get out of the car. Quietly.

I waited until the limousine stopped at a red light, then gently pushed the door open and exited the vehicle.

Walk away calmly. Do not run.

I did as directed. Every second that passed, I expected to hear the frenzied shouts of the NSB agents, followed by gunfire. Yet nothing happened. The limousine drove away as if I were still inside.

To your left is a taxi rank. Head to it and enter the third cab in the queue.

Inside the cab, on the back seat, sat a young Asian woman in a retro-chic pinstripe suit.

Hello Nathaniel. I'm the Ripper. I believe you have some information for me.

I clambered into the cab and tried to think of something suave and sophisticated to say. Instead, I blurted: "I thought the Ripper was a man."

She smiled. "So does the NSB. It makes life so much easier."

"They arrested me for thought smuggling ..."

"I'm sorry about that. My colleagues were using your brain as a meeting room and drop box for illegally acquired information. We needed to hide it somewhere no-one would look. Your brain was just the kind of infrequently scanned backwater we needed. My father used to say 'Always hide your most precious belongings in your least impressive container'. Your mind was the least impressive container we could find at short notice. My friends were supposed to remove anything incriminating from your mind long before you arrived, but they ran into some legal difficulties and had to disappear."

She handed me a Thought-pad™. "Download everything you know about General Psionic Corporation's research facility in the City State."

I was about to protest that I knew nothing about GPC when, to my surprise, my mind made contact with the Thought-pad™ and started feeding it information.

Access codes, guard patrol schedules, building schematics, personnel files and a very detailed description of the building's psychic security protocols all burst forth from their hiding places in my subconscious.

Ripper grinned as the information passed from my mind to hers.

"Reptile Brain and his band of head hackers gathered much more than I ever expected. We have enough information to pull off the heist of the century."

"Incidentally, does your devoutly Catholic mother know you download movies like *Root It Ralph* and *Things that Go Hump in the Night*?"

I didn't know what to say.

"If you don't want people reading your thoughts, you need to be more careful when you use thought sharing applications—and you really should install a better psychic firewall inside that brain of yours. Now come along. We have work to do."

"I need to get to the Embassy."

"You're a fugitive thought smuggler. The Embassy won't help you leave the country—but I can, in return for your assistance."

I didn't need Ripper to explain her target to me. In retrospect, I had been dreaming about it for months: it was the fifty-storey glass and steel monstrosity that housed GPC's research facility, in the City State's Accelerated Development Precinct.

"Let's go for a drive," Ripper suggested.

The 'Thought Activated Ignition' light on the dashboard flashed and the vehicle roared into life. Soon we were racing along the City State's pristine streets.

"Why are you interested in GPC's research facility? Are you looking to embarrass GPC again, the way you did in Davos?" I said.

"Why are you asking?"

"I need to know what we're doing here, Ripper."

"You misunderstand me. Why are you asking questions? Are you a wannabee quiz show host? Or are you an innovative head-hacker, capable of finding information on your own?"

"You want me to hack your head?"

Her emerald eyes sparkled in the soft light.

"Only if you're game."

I concentrated on the 'Meeting of Minds' psi-con on my Thought-pad™ screen. Meeting of Minds was one of GPC's most popular products, a program that facilitated 90% of the world's psychic communication. From my studies, I was aware of a number of flaws in the program's security—flaws I now exploited to gain unrestricted access to the brains of those connected to the local Psi-Net.

Soon I was surfing a wave of second-hand thoughts, watching and invading the minds of a host of Psi-Net users as they traded memories, dreams and ideas. Kids swapped mental pictures the way previous generations swapped cards. I visited sites that offered to print out hard copies of my mental pictures and record the songs and voices in my head. I saw the darker side of the Psi-Net, the side that offered to deliver amorous dreams to the object of my affections or bone-chilling nightmares to my enemies. I illegally read the thoughts of local factory workers, police officers, tourists and even a visiting parliamentary delegation. In the cacophony of thoughts that characterised this metropolis, the only mind I couldn't hear was Ripper's.

I glanced at the 'Thought Directed Steering' light on the taxi's dashboard. Ripper's thoughts would no doubt be heavily encrypted, yet the taxi received and understood them—so the taxi must have a decryption program, and a communication channel into Ripper's head.

I hacked the taxi's CPU and copied the decryption program. I followed the link into Ripper's heavily defended mind and downloaded several files, punching the air in triumph once I'd managed to decrypt them.

"Databanks in the basement of the facility contain proof of the existence of an ultra-secret program known as the Mind's Eye Protocol."

Ripper nodded. "Rumours abound in the darker corners of the Psi-Net that GPC has established a protocol that would allow it to evade every psychic firewall ever developed. Effectively this would give GPC a 'back door' into the minds of its users—allowing GPC to access billions of minds at will, without the owner's knowledge. We need to raid the database. I want incontrovertible proof that the Mind's Eye Protocol is real. The world needs to know what GPC can do to its customers."

"The City State is the ideal place to perfect such technologies. Not only is its corporations law conducive to tax minimisation, its secretive nature and distrust of concepts like human rights make it the perfect place for ethically dubious, cutting edge research. The City State gave GPC a lucrative tax deal and permission to operate with impunity. In return, GPC helps the City State monitor the thoughts of all of its citizens and take pre-emptive action against anyone who desires to challenge the ruling party's authority."

"GPC conducts all of its unsavoury research in the City State. That is why all of the information on the Mind's Eye Protocol is stored in GPC's local facility."

"Judging by the security files you had stored in my brain, that facility is more heavily guarded than the White House. How do you propose we infiltrate it?"

"Tomorrow night, GPC is holding a charity gala in its research facility. The event will raise funds to combat Communicable Mental Illnesses (CMIs)."

One of the disadvantages of the psychic communications revolution was that many mental illnesses became communicable—especially in countries that hadn't adequately invested in mental health services or state of the art psychic firewalls. The 'Decognition' Psi-Net virus—an easily transmissible form of schizophrenia, which had reached epidemic proportions among young Psi-Net users, was one of many CMIs plaguing the developing world.

"The gala represents our best chance to infiltrate the facility. Not that gaining access will be easy."

Ripper activated her Thought-pad™. Suddenly, I was standing outside a perfect 3D simulation of the GPC research facility.

Relax Nathaniel, I'm taking your mind's eye on a tour of the GPC building.

"How did you establish such a strong connection to my mind?"

When you downloaded the thoughts from my head, you also downloaded some psychic programs that give me 'administrator access' to your mind. They're called Trojan Thoughts. Now, pay attention …

Ahead of me, a long line of simulated guests queued up to enter the GPC building.

Each guest will be subject to an ID scan.

A guest approached the guard point just inside the door. Complex machinery whirred and a light above the guard point turned green. The guest was then allowed inside the facility.

If our thoughts don't identify us as invited guests, we won't be allowed inside.

As I approached the guard desk, the light above me turned red. A hulking bouncer in a tuxedo blocked my path.

In addition, the NSB keeps the thought patterns of wanted terrorists and other dangerous criminals on a database. If any ID scanner in the country matches our thoughts with those on the database, the NSB will be instantly notified.

The ID scanner continued to probe my mind. The red light above the guard point began to flash. Sirens wailed and soon I heard the thud of army boots on the pavement outside. As I fled, NSB troops opened fire.

Mercifully, Ripper re-set the simulation at this point.

I was now standing on the red carpet in the GPC building's lobby.

Security is even tighter inside the building.

The interior of the building is patrolled by an elite group of GPC operatives known collectively as the Mind's Eye Corps (MEC). Each MEC operative has a head full of psychic software that allows them to read the thoughts of anyone in sight. If you even think about committing a crime in their presence, they will know about it within seconds.

I pushed through the crowd of guests and tried to find the door to the basement. As I left the sanctuary of the crowd, a man approached me. On the lapel of his dinner jacket he wore a gold pin in the shape of an eye.

I backpedalled, trying to avoid the MEC operative. He locked onto my thoughts in seconds. Once again, sirens began to wail. I had barely run 100 metres when armed guards cut me down.

Ripper reset the simulation again.

There will be multiple MEC operatives at the party, guarding key access points. It is impossible to pass into the secure parts of the facility without encountering at least one of them.

I made multiple failed attempts to outwit the MEC operatives. My simulated self died more often than a cheap mobile phone battery.

Hours later, Ripper ended the exercise.

The taxi parked in a suburban garage. A connecting door led into an ageing ivy covered mansion.

"This is my base of operations," Ripper proclaimed. "I call it the Memory Palace. It is a refuge for banned thoughts and memories."

The mansion's walls were dominated by antique mahogany bookcases packed with illegal memory recordings, leather-bound tomes and framed black and white photographs.

"Make yourself at home. I have some errands to run."

Exhausted, I lay down on an overstuffed couch and drifted off to sleep while viewing an episode of Psi-Watch.

The thoughts and memories contained in this recording are the property of General Psionic Corporation. Unauthorised copying or sharing of these thoughts and memories is illegal. Memory content may change online on Psi-net. Please discontinue use if you begin to experience anxiety, distress, or suicidal ideation. By concentrating on this paragraph you have agreed to indemnify GPC and hold it faultless for any injury (mental or otherwise) you may suffer as a consequence of using GPC products. Thank you for choosing GPC.

Tonight on Psi-Watch:

What do your kids REALLY think about when they are alone? Our covert thought scans reveal some disturbing results.

As Pyongyang accuses Seoul of violating its sovereignty by broadcasting seditious thoughts into North Korea, we profile the dissident who was jailed for thinking unflattering thoughts about the Supreme Leader.

PLUS: King William tells journalists: "Stop scanning my family's thoughts."

To watch this and other full episodes of Psi-Watch, subscribe to the General Psionic Psi-Net channel.

I spent the following day trying to outwit 'Oracle 2.1'—an extremely cheap imitation of the mind reading software used by GPC. Inside the Memory

Palace, Ripper loaded the program into her mind, turned away from me and challenged me to walk up behind her and remove the cap from her head, without 'Oracle 2.1' detecting my intentions.

Whenever I crept closer than eight metres while thinking of removing the cap—the program detected my thoughts and alerted Ripper. I tried to focus on other thoughts, but found consciously trying not to think about something nigh on impossible. If I thought about stealing the cap, I was doomed, and if I tried to bury my illegal thoughts under a barrage of nonsense, I could, at best, conceal my thoughts for a few seconds. No matter how hard I tried, I could not get within six metres of the cap—and Oracle was far less sensitive than the software GPC would be using.

Some of the thoughts and memories that Reptile Brain had stashed in my mind made no sense—probably because they had been protected by some form of anti-piracy software. Yet many of the memories were extremely useful—like the list of party guests.

The next morning, Ripper and I began to tail one of the guests—the American journalist Megyn Chen—as she enjoyed the first class boutiques in the Old City.

Ripper logged on to the My Thoughts™ site and sent Chen a 'Like Minds' friend request. Shortly afterward, Chen accepted.

Now I can clone all of Chen's published thoughts. However, I'll also need a few of her private ones.

Ripper handed me a thought recorder. "Keep this pointed at Chen."

We followed Chen through the crowded shopping district, surreptitiously recording any thoughts she spontaneously broadcast. These cloned thoughts could later be re-broadcast from Ripper's mind—to help convince GPC's psychic scanners that Ripper was Megyn Chen. If necessary, Ripper could broadcast instructions to Chen using Chen's unique thought pattern. If we were subtle enough, Chen would assume the incoming thoughts were her own and obey them without question. This was thought hacking at its most elegant.

We followed the journalist into a jewellery store. Ripper checked on the material we were gathering. "I think we have enough now."

"Can I help you?" a shop assistant asked.

"We're not here to buy anything," I announced, "just to commit identity theft."

The shop assistant's jaw dropped.

"Isn't my husband hilarious?" Ripper asked in a fake Valley Girl accent. She grabbed my elbow and escorted me from the store.

"What the hell are you doing?" she hissed once we were outside.

"I just had a sudden urge to confess ..."

Ripper scanned my mind with her Thought-pad™. "I should've guessed GPC would plant a few surprises in the data we stored in your brain. You've accidentally uploaded the 'Confessor' Psi-Net virus—it artificially induces a compulsion to confess your illegal intentions. Hopefully Mind Sweeper™ Anti-Virus 5.7 can remove it."

As she activated the anti-virus program, I felt a tingling sensation, as if a swarm of tiny insects was crawling around inside my skull, combing my mind, eliminating malicious thought code and other foreign material.

We had to prevent Chen from attending the gala. Some "thought-hacking" convinced Chen to extend her shopping trip for longer than she initially planned. Meanwhile, we sabotaged her car.

Ripper approached Chen's candy pink Lamborghini (which boasted personalised "Crazy Bitch" licence plates) and began to upload the Silencer virus into the car.

"Her car is brand new—brainwave activated—no keys required. Silencer prevents the car's brainwave sensors from working. The virus will activate as soon as Chen enters the car and closes the self-locking door. After that, the car won't detect her brainwaves—so she won't be able to start it or open the doors. Plus, Silencer disrupts any communication devices within fifty metres."

Once this was done, Ripper sent me to an open air café to record the thoughts of some young businessmen who were eating there. These thoughts would form part of my own disguise.

"Stay here. I'll be back in 20 minutes," Ripper said breezily.

Three hours later, she returned.

"Where the hell have you been?" I asked, draining my sixth cup of coffee.

"Thought hacking Prince George," she said. "Now, we need to change for the party … and purge the virus from that quaintly outmoded processor you call a brain."

●

Men in tuxedos and women in elegant evening gowns streamed into GPC's research facility.

"Megyn Chen, *Infotainment Tonight* … and my guest," Ripper said.

The well-manicured security guard scanned Ripper's thoughts detecting the patterns we had cloned earlier.

"Welcome to the gala, Miss Chen."

Ripper surreptitiously watched me as I walked past the guard. No doubt in preparation to intervene should I feel compelled to confess our entire plan. Thankfully, the virus seemed to have been effectively eliminated. I smiled at the guard and escorted Ripper along a red carpet.

The spacious lobby of the facility had been converted into an entertainment area, where a string quartet serenaded the crowd and liveried waiters served canapés and champagne. Movie stars, corporate executives and diplomats mingled and admired displays showing the fine work GPC was doing to combat CMIs in the developing world.

The Mind Reader stood between us and the door to the lower levels. As long as we were in the crowd, the Mind Reader would not be able to detect our criminal intentions beneath the general psychic hubbub of the cocktail party. However, to approach the door, we'd need to leave the protection of the crowd.

A few steps away from us, the CEO of GPC was speaking to Prince George and a small crowd of other celebrities.

I had never been so close to such influential people. Despite my best efforts, I felt sweat prickle my brow.

The CEO opined, "Your Highness, a key concept in Anglo-criminal justice systems is *Mens Rea*, guilty mind. With GPC mind reading technology, guilty mind has never been easier to prove."

"I fear the courts may not agree with you. In England, Watkins is challenging his conviction on the basis that the mind scanner the Met used wasn't accurate enough to prove guilt—and in the US, Chelenko is arguing that convicting him based on his own thoughts amounts to self-incrimination and is thus a violation of the Fifth Amendment."

The CEO smiled, exposing sharp white teeth.

"I'm sure the courts will ultimately see the light."

"I wouldn't bet GPC's future on it, sir. If your corporation is found to be illegally scanning human minds the repercussions would be … severe."

The CEO's smile disappeared momentarily and then returned in a blaze of white.

"This brings us to the reason for your visit. In your capacity as a UN Human Rights ambassador, would you like to tour the lower floors?"

The Prince nodded. "May I bring my new friend, Miss Chen, and some of her colleagues?"

The CEO paused. "That wasn't part of our original agreement. However, GPC has nothing to hide, so by all means bring your friends."

Ripper looked toward the Mind Reader then turned to face me. "I'll stay in the crowd until I can thought-hack the Mind Reader. I'll need another 15 minutes. I'll ask my new best friend, the Prince, to delay for a while."

My iSpy beeped. "We don't have much time. The real Megyn Chen has just appeared at reception."

"Damn roadside assistance—they were too efficient. Time for plan B."

The original plan called for me to hide in the crowd while Ripper took the VIP tour. I was only present to provide technical support, using the vast cache of information stashed in my brain. But with our covers in jeopardy, I couldn't simply hide in the crowd.

At Ripper's urging, the Prince walked toward the door to the lower levels and the small party of VIPs followed. The Mind Reader didn't intervene; he simply scanned those who approached. Anyone scanning 'Megyn Chen' would be puzzled by the fact that her thoughts were simultaneously appearing in two different parts of the building. Even worse, if anyone scanned me, they would rapidly see past the cloned thoughts shielding my real intentions.

The Mind Reader stared at me as I strolled along the corridor with the other VIPs.

A cold sweat broke out on my brow. I tried to concentrate on something innocuous but knew I couldn't hide my true thoughts from the Mind's Eye for long. I estimated I had about ten seconds before the Mind Reader discerned my true intentions and ruined our best chance of exposing GPC.

On the heavily encrypted psychic communications channel that I shared with the Ripper, I could hear her preparing countermeasures. By tampering with various psychic advertisements around the city, Ripper had used the psychically intrusive billboards to transmit illegal thought-code into the minds of the guests. At Ripper's command, the guests unwittingly began sending wave after wave of psychic messages to the MEC operative in front of me. Hopefully, a sustained barrage would temporarily overload the operative's brain, allowing me to walk past him without my mind undergoing an invasive scan.

Eight seconds until detection. As the chattering VIPs moved, achingly slowly, toward the door, I tried to surreptitiously walk to the front of the group.

Waves of psychic communication crashed into the operative, but the software in his head kept it from doing any damage. Ripper redoubled her efforts.

Five seconds. The CEO paused, with mock formality, to allow Prince George to pass through the door first. Other guests followed.

A tidal wave of thought assailed the operative, but the state of the art software in his head held the wave at bay, like a giant dam wall. Ripper scoured the wall for a weakness, firing a hail of thought bombs and malicious psychic programs at it.

Giant cracks began to appear in the dam.

One second. I was still in the corridor, and our mission hung on a single thread.

The psychic dam broke. The Mind Reader was deluged with millions of simultaneous psychic messages and requests. He clutched his head in pain and staggered away, collapsing onto a nearby chair. We walked past the stunned Mind Reader without incident.

Inside the lower levels, we paused by the main database while the CEO addressed Prince George.

"You see, Your Highness. There's nothing sinister down here. No illegal thought-reading technology. No mad scientists conducting mind control experiments on dissidents. I'm afraid the fake news media have misled you."

The rest of the crowd, the small group of journalists, camera operators, diplomats and celebrities, chuckled.

Ripper, pretending to be recording the CEO's statements, glanced at her Thought-pad™, then concentrated on the sequence of psi-cons required to upload the 'Skeleton Key' to the database.

Skeleton Key was a custom-made psychic program—stolen from one of GPC's competitors, which could shut down every psychic firewall and security program in the building.

Seconds later, GPC's psychic firewalls quietly crashed and we began downloading corporate secrets.

At that moment, the Mind Reader burst into the room, accompanied by a squad of heavily armed guards. The Mind Reader fixed his gaze on me. "I knew there was something odd about him." He began to scan me. I could almost feel him dragging secrets from my brain.

When the scan was complete, the Mind Reader snarled, "He's a Psi-Net hacker—here to raid the database." He glared at Ripper. "I'm guessing she is too. Her true thoughts are well concealed, I'll need to spend more time on her ..."

The armed guards stalked toward us like panthers through long grass. Cries of confusion erupted from the small crowd of VIPs. George's bodyguards closed ranks around the Prince.

As the GPC goons charged towards her, Ripper spun about and shoved a business card into the CEO's hand.

The CEO frowned as he studied the card. It read:

Trojan Thoughts Inc.
Hacking our way to a brighter future.

"What the fuck is this? Do you think you can intimidate me with a business card?"

Ripper smiled. "No, but by concentrating on the card, you've agreed not to press charges. Good night."

"*The fuck I have!* You can't attempt to rob us and simply stroll out of here! When I order the NSB to kill you, they'll do it—no questions asked. Even if you manage to leave the city alive, we have a technique that will allow us to hack into every mind linked to the Psi-Net. Wherever you run, we'll be watching for you with billions of pairs of eyes. Maybe, when we catch you, we'll subject you to the Weaponised Mental Illnesses we're developing for a certain client state. You'll love them, just one of them could give a million people Schizophrenia. I'll make sure we test the new batch on you and your friends. You'll spend the rest of your miserable lives in asylums. That's what happens when you fuck with me."

The CEO stopped abruptly, but the cameras surrounding him did not.

"What the hell have you done to me?" he gasped.

"We've given you a compulsion to confess your criminal intentions. Annoying isn't it?" Ripper grinned.

"All of you ... surrender your equipment and all memories of this event," the Mind Reader screamed.

GPC security guards started grabbing cameras from members of the crowd and smashing the machines into the concrete.

The crowd erupted into chaos.

"You can't do this," George yelled at the GPC guards.

The Mind Reader's eyes glowed a sinister shade of purple as he stepped in front of Prince George and prepared to wipe the Prince's memories.

In a series of lightning-fast movements, George's lead bodyguard smashed his fists into the Mind Reader's face. The Mind Reader collapsed, clutching his bloodied nose in his hands. The bodyguards then formed a flying wedge around George and charged out of the room, felling other GPC personnel in the process.

⚓

Thirty minutes later, Ripper and I were on a speed boat, heading to Malaysia.

As we sped along the Straits, I logged on to Psi-Net. The CEO's rant had already been uploaded to Psi-Net and viewed millions of times.

His highly incriminating thoughts about GPC's illegal activities were now available to anyone with a Psi-Net connection.

Ripper and I watched the short video clip several times.

"Congratulations Ripper. You've proved GPC has been engaged in a host of illegal activities, from unauthorised surveillance to psychic weapons development. They're finished."

"Swiss banks hold a very large amount of money belonging to group of rather odious ultra-nationalist European billionaires nicknamed the Dark Cardinals," she replied. "Most of the money is held in the form of a new cryptocurrency called Psi-coins™. Psi-coins™ exist only in the minds of the bankers and billionaires that trade them. Do you want to come to Zurich and help me steal the Cardinals' fortune?"

"You must have read my mind."

Riding prize Arabian stallions across the Mongolian desert, parachuting into Afghanistan as part of a UN mission, out-witting Somali pirates and serving as a bodyguard for the Emperor of Japan. **Chris McGrane** has never done any of these things, but is mentioning them in his biographical statement in a vain attempt to make his life seem more interesting than it actually is. Chris is a second generation public servant, who loves to write. His short stories have appeared in a number of publications, most recently in the Dark Helix Press anthology *Trump: Utopia or Dystopia*.

The Killblaine Legacy

Tom Dullemond

Jonathan Killblaine tried to untangle the politics of it all on the back of the Night Tom poster he'd angrily torn from the alley wall. He only had a stub of charcoal, which made the process all the more frustrating.

Initially, arriving at the house of '*Master P. Semmelhorn Esq., 53y-o-a, wealthy, make it look like a robbery, son*', he'd squatted in a dark corner of the street, pulling his hooded cloak over his face and feeling very stealthy indeed. After only half an hour, as the sky spun too-slowly towards midnight and the foot traffic petered out, the pain in his legs was so bad that he'd had to stand up, wincing, and that's when he'd seen it: the fucking WANTED poster, with the 3,000 shekel reward for capturing the Night Tom (dead or alive), "famous cat burglar, revolutionary and anarchist." Some hack artist had roughly sketched a face—masked and hooded—of a caricatured smirking black tomcat. It was in no way identifiable or useful, but it was cool. So damn cool.

Jonathan hated it.

The artist could be forgiven for not sketching a likeness of a person they'd never seen before, sure. But there was no excuse for mangling a cat like that; there were plenty of street-scarred cats to model from. And then, the effrontery of *still managing to make it cool*.

Jonathan, whose only actual talent and passion was for sketching portraits, bristled that such a hack could be employable.

He tore the poster down, flipped it over, and spread it flat on the damp cobblestones outside Master Semmelhorn's house, drawing three circles with his charcoal and lettering them '*papa*', '*Univ. of Crime*', and '*Eccorsian Triad &c*'. In the middle, he wrote '*Night Tom?*', then began drawing tentative lines between them.

Papa had arranged this job—Jonathan's first actual assignment since completing his training. It was probably just a favour to their family on behalf of the University of Crime. Papa lectured there often enough and the Killblaine name had weight. Jonathan had objected, as always; he simply wasn't cut out to be an assassin, a fact no one had yet grasped. His family's legendary excellence haunted him through every blundering, borderline-passed exam.

"You're a Killblaine, son. We're a proud family, long history!" That was papa, his voice never far away, like a living ghost in his head.

"I think it's all an act," whispered Mistress Avalanche to another teacher in the hallway of his school memories. *"He never fails, but he only ever succeeds by the slimmest of margins. He's deliberately keeping his skills to himself, so even we never know his capacity for silent murder."*

Sighing, Jonathan looked over his diagram. He drew a line from papa to *Univ. of Crime*, then across to *Triad*. Those bastards had bad blood going back all the way to the time of great-grand-pappy Killblaine, who'd literally named himself after his mission to kill their founder. Ironically they'd never *found* Blaine Eccors at all—not that his descendants cared about that detail.

Amongst all those pigeons sprang the Night Tom, who wasn't affiliated with anyone and was giving the University a bad name for not being able to honour the citizens' theft insurance. So who exactly stood to benefit most out of this midnight assassination of *Master P. Semmelhorn Esq., 53y-o-a*?

He stared a little longer until the pins-and-needles left his thighs, but by then his knees were hurting instead. He groaned and stood up, staying hidden as best he could. He smudged his cheekbones a little darker with the charcoal, black against his own coffee-brown skin, and pocketed it with the folded poster. Then he looked up the wall to the lowest window.

Time to take care of this job.

Jonathan's teachers had never been particularly fond of him, but they kept their distance. There had been no attempts on his life, unlike other unpopular students, and when he made basic mistakes they pretended not to notice. At least he'd been alright at climbing.

Bracing himself against one rough wall he tested his weight against the drainpipe of Master Semmelhorn's home. It creaked a little, then shifted and held. He focussed his breath and—*one—two—three*—pushed up while pulling in, straining his arms against his weight and hooking fingers in gaps. The trick was to leap high on the first step then keep climbing arm over arm before your upward arc slowed and you sagged back down.

His fingers snatched at the edge of the window frame and his feet slipped at exactly the same moment, leaving him arms-outstretched in full view of the street, dangling from the first floor. His dagger sheath banged loudly against the metal drainpipe, a hollow drum tattoo announcing his arrival. He winced.

"Oy mate." A woman's voice from right below him. *Great.*

"What?" His own voice was muffled against the brick. The tips of his fingers gripped the ledge but he wouldn't be able to hold on for long.

"That looks uncomfortable." Closer now. The sour smell of buttermilk: someone coming home after a day of linen bleaching.

"Yeah … Look, can I have a leg up? Just stand underneath and put your shoulder under my foot."

He felt a movement beneath him and seconds before his fingers lost their strength his right foot found a shoulder. He breathed a sigh of relief.

"Great! Now just hold still for a second." He steadied his breath, shifted weight to his benefactor, then pushed up again, scrabbling to get his elbow on the ledge and push himself up higher against the drainpipe, which groaned under the pressure.

One more push …

Jonathan overestimated his strength and pushed himself face first into the window sill. Old wood and glass strained then cracked loudly, flinging pieces and splinters into the dark room beyond.

"*Oh sh—*"

He rolled forwards, and tumbled headfirst into the gloom. Something heavy shifted to his left and then an avalanche of leather-bound books rumbled dully over the top of him. A dim candlelight from the hallway turned the uneven books on the floor into shadowy ocean waves.

Jonathan didn't move. His training was clear on that: when in doubt, just freeze. Open your senses to the world around you and wait. He lay on his belly amongst the books, head to the side and eyes wide open to adjust to the gloom.

The woman on the street outside yelled, "Have fun cleaning that up!" but when he didn't reply she just laughed to herself as the echo of her boots on cobblestone faded away. A floorboard creaked once but there was otherwise no sound in the house. No change in the candlelight, so that meant no one was carrying it, at least. A thin sting in his left hand. He moved just the fingers, felt slick warmth: a cut, hopefully not too deep—he didn't want to leave a blood trail up the side of the wall. Wood and glass shards pressed into his waistcoat.

Silence. Then a slow creak from outside.

The creak turned into a scream of tearing metal and the drainpipe crashed to the cobblestones below. Jonathan winced, but still didn't move. The sting in his finger became a dull throb.

So far, so disastrous.

He carefully rolled on to his side, books sliding into new configurations around him. Without cutting or injuring himself further, he rose slowly to his feet, glancing through the dimly lit room—just bookshelves and some reading chairs here.

As he approached the doorway to the hall, the smell of wine grew stronger, and he heard heavy breathing, almost snoring.

Nothing in the hall. The candlelight came from a different room at the end—a bedroom or study—which was also the source of the snoring. A wooden board creaked loudly under his foot and he gritted his teeth, reaching for the pocket where he kept his University of Crime standard-issue poison phial. He pulled the tiny cork, but immediately fumbled it out of his fingers and watched it bounce across the floor and roll into the study. Well, at least he hadn't spilled any of the poison.

Jonathon reached into his waistcoat and pulled free an inch-long pin, dipping it slowly into the clear liquid. It would kill his mark quickly and painlessly, leaving just one pinprick for no one to find. Then he'd make it look like some incompetent thief had smashed in a window and tried to rob the place.

Without setting off another floorboard, he shuffled along the hallway until he reached the open door and peered into the dim, candle-lit room, cataloguing as much detail as he could.

The room appeared to be a large study. The main light source was a stubby inch of candle guttering on a desk strewn with rolls of parchment.

Fainter but steadier moonlight filtered through the solitary window, which was open. A wide settee had been placed beneath it and a lump lay sagged across the width, snoring softly. It seemed to be an older man in a dressing gown clutching ... an uncorked bottle of Perro Blanco Imperial Amontillado, which really wasn't a late-evening sherry but was strong enough that it paired well with late-evening poisoning.

As his eyes adjusted, Jonathan spotted a trail of documents strewn across the floor, starting from the desk and leading into a black corner of the room. A glint of metal, too large to be a vase, too small to be a full size door ... He squinted. A large safe with its door flung open.

Had someone already robbed the place? If so, he needed to get this business over with even more quickly.

Jonathan stepped into the room, deadly pin held carefully out between his fingers—it wouldn't do to have any poison drip into his cut and bring this escapade to a permanent close. Master Semmelhorn, whatever his misdeed, was not long for this world. Nothing personal, just business. He stepped over the documents, past another empty bottle of Perro Blanco that had rolled along the floorboards.

When the needle slipped into his neck, the man simply groaned a little. Jonathan watched, holding his breath for any sign that the poison was taking effect.

After a minute he jabbed the man again, just to be sure, but this time Semmelhorn coughed and his red-rimmed eyes opened wide.

"Dear god man what are you—?"

Jonathan dropped the pin and reached for his dagger, the phial of poison still in his other hand.

The man stopped. "Ah, it's you. Just make it quick."

"Ex ... excuse me?" Jonathan's hand stopped on the hilt of his weapon.

"I've been waiting all night, just make it quick."

This was off-script.

"Well uh … ," he looked around the room a little awkwardly. "Well, uhm, I already poisoned you, sir, I guess. So … hurrah?"

That mollified Semmelhorn somewhat, which was strange. Not that the poison seemed to be doing anything, even after a double dose. Jonathan glanced at the little glass phial in his hand.

The silence became awkward after a while,

"Sooo," Jonathan offered eventually, when Master Semmelhorn didn't say anything. "Did you … uhm. So … why were you expecting me? What's going on, exactly?"

The man looked up at him, as if gauging him, weighing his soul. Then his face perked up a little and he said, "Oh, of course, I'll be dead soon anyway, so …"

Before Jonathan could inquire he added, "It's all arranged. University said my insurance would cash out and … " He looked across the room to the dark corner harbouring the safe. "There's a lot of debt. My family will be safe."

"Excuse me," Jonathan started, "but what do you mean 'it's all arranged'? What are you trying to—?"

"This poison," the man interrupted. "How long is it supposed to take? I feel fine." His words were a little slurred but that was probably just the sherry.

"Ahhh … " Jonathan struggled to think of the answer. He'd never paid that much attention in alchemy or botany. "Soon?" he offered.

Master Semmelhorn burst into tears. They were solid, drunken-old-man tears. Snot began to run from his nose. "Oh gods, Patron, please. I have no money left. I know it's insurance fraud but they said it would be ok, you're some kind of famous assassin. Please, *please* just—"

Jonathan stepped back as the old man lunged at him, grabbing at his waistcoat. He threw his hands up to ward him off—he had no interest in being the bearer of hopes and dreams.

"Look now sir, I don't know what's going on but everything's above board here!"

He glanced around the shadowy room as Semmelhorn staggered closer. Was there anything he could do or say to keep this man away from him long enough for this poison to do its work? Was he going to have to brain him, *then* poison him?

There was a shuffling sound from near the window and Jonathan's training kicked in. He turned to face it, dropping into a crouch but terribly exposed in the centre of the room. One hand to his dagger, the other still holding the poison. Not ideal. Especially with Semmelhorn nearby.

A footfall behind him. He turned his head, holding his body motionless. Two figures had appeared at the door.

What was going on?

A creak from the window to his right.

He shifted his eyes to see another figure, climbing in.

"Alright then, fun's over, Killblaine." The woman's voice came from behind him, one of the intruders at the door. "Nice try, but you made a mess."

Jonathan stood up slowly, still not ready to give up whatever meagre advantage he might have. Semmelhorn stood awkwardly beside him, bewildered by the three newcomers but not appearing any closer to death by poison. Jonathan said nothing, trying to identify the figures in the sputtering candlelight while estimating how long it would take him to grab Semmelhorn and use him for cover. It should've been easier: his studies had primed him for this moment. Of course, that didn't really mean much given his grades.

He glanced around again. The shadows made it hard to identify the female silhouette at the window and the man in the hallway, but it highlighted the woman who had spoken.

"Mistress Avalanche? What are you doing here? Are you ... grading my first assignment?"

The university lecturer at the study entrance stepped forward. She wore a greatcoat, possibly concealing any number of weapons. The male figure behind her remained a little uncertainly in the hallway shadows, as though he was waiting for permission to reveal himself. Jonathan remembered a lecture about dramatic entrances. There would probably be some monologuing.

"Not quite, boy. University business." She scanned the room, sparing barely a glance at Semmelhorn. "We've been keeping an eye on this place.

Seems your pal the Night Tom's been sneaking around this part of town."

He nearly asked her why she thought he knew the Night Tom, but he had a sudden recollection of a class he'd mostly sketched pictures of heroes through: never give out free information. Instead, he composed his face into what he hoped looked like vague curiosity.

"Don't try anything, Killblaine," Mistress Avalanche said. "I have reinforcements downstairs." The man behind her finally stepped forward and in the candlelight Jonathan recognised him as Nathaniel Eccors, Eccorsian Triad luminary. Jonathan's shoulders slumped as he realised how much trouble he was in.

"Thought you'd come in through the back, and we'd make easy work of you," Nathaniel said. "But you was too clever for us, wasn't you, sneaking in from the main street in plain sight of anyone. Mistress Avalanche told me you was sneaky: we couldn't make a move for all the witnesses. You're a cunning sort. You upset Elaine. She was looking forward to a little fist-chat."

So that was the figure at the window. Good to know.

Jonathan tried not to betray anything with his expression. *Of course he should've broken in through the backyard; the street was full of possible witnesses.* "Yeah," he lied eventually. "I expected trouble from the likes of you and covered my trail."

"Well, it's time to fess up. We know you're working for the Night Tom, you and your father. I asked the Mistress here to witness it. When the University faculty hears about this you're done for."

"I have no idea what—"

At that moment, Semmelhorn lunged forward and snatched the phial of poison out of Jonathan's hand. Everything froze while he poured its contents into his mouth.

"*What are you*—?" Jonathan managed, and then there was a thud and a thump from near the window. He glanced up. Nothing. No sign of Elaine.

The sound of a body dropping heavily into the backyard.

"Elaine? Where did you—?" said Nathaniel at the now empty space of the windowsill.

"This is just water!" wailed Semmelhorn.

"No, it's a very deadly and subtle poison!" snapped Jonathan, at the end of his patience.

Nathaniel again, tentatively, "Elaine?"

"*Boys.*"

That was a new voice, husky, hidden.

Everyone, including Semmelhorn, froze. Jonathan couldn't figure out where it had come from.

Mistress Avalanche pulled two daggers out of the inside of her coat and crouched down.

"*It is water,*" said that shadowy voice again, seemingly from all directions. "*I swapped it.*"

"What the—?" began Nathaniel, and two darts snapped out at him from the darkness above. He dropped like a sack, and Mistress Avalanche whirled around with her daggers at the ready. A heavy shape fell from the ceiling behind her. Nathaniel made a strangled sound on the floor, thrashing to dislodge the darts, knocking over the desk chair.

Jonathan stared, completely overwhelmed. He was an assassin, not a tavern brawler, and there were now far too many moving pieces in the scenario. The newcomer who'd dropped from the ceiling was nowhere to be seen, hidden among the room's many shadows. Were they there behind the safe, or was that movement just another trick of the candlelight?

"You're done for Killblaine!" Mistress Avalanche shouted, stepping back and roughly manhandling a wounded Nathaniel to his feet and clumsily towards the window. She glared at Jonathan then pushed Nathaniel out before the invisible intruder reappeared. She leapt out as Nathaniel crashed to the ground outside and the sounds of their retreat faded away into the night.

Semmelhorn still hadn't expired. Jonathan squinted around him into the flickering shadows to find the intruder.

Then a soft *mrreeowww* from the direction of the safe.

A Cheshire Cat white grin split the darkness.

Oh fu—

Jonathan tried to dodge the black shape that charged at him from the shadows but a befuddled Semmelhorn got in the way and he nearly tripped.

He was grabbed by black hands and pulled further off-balance.

"I've got you, Night Tom!" Jonathan yelled, although it was he who was got. He pushed into the grip, shifted his footing to find a bracing balancing point—and then suddenly all resistance vanished. He overbalanced forward, felt a hook at his arm, was spun around. His elbow bent under a fast jab, an invisible punch to the solar plexus doubled him over, then his arm was twisted behind him, his wrist snapped forward, and with a stabbing jolt of pain through every joint he found himself totally immobilised and on his knees.

Slowly, excruciatingly, the pain thinned. There was no blossom of warmth anywhere on his body—he was generally confident he'd not been stabbed.

That voice again, now too-close, breathy in his left ear.

"Well, well, well. Good ol' Jonathan Killblaine."

The room disappeared. He was in a sunny meadow, six years old, trying to arrange some flowers he'd plucked instead of doing his daily exercises. Ma and pa had been arguing for long enough that they'd forgotten him.

A black booted foot kicked the flowers apart, spitting rainbow petals into the air and kicking his heart into a nervous rattle.

"You put those bleeding flowers down and concentrate on your breathing!"

The meadow vanished and candle-licked shadows rushed back in.

He paused to gather his thoughts.

"M … *Ma?*"

Her familiar voice over his left shoulder. "Aye. And I can't have you killing this old moneybags."

"Excuse me? *Why?*"

"I can't let you kill him because he's your *real* father."

Everything spun black, punctuated with tiny white constellations of pain fizzing in his joints, until he realised that all she had done was spun him around to face her. He hadn't seen her for years. Her skin was ebony, in a way his could never be, and her features sharp and proud and fierce.

"My real—?"

"Son, I've been blackmailing this sonofabitch for years, ever since he seduced me." His mother did not release her hold.

Jonathan glanced dubiously at the red-nosed slobbering mess who'd sagged to the floor nearby. Semmelhorn was quivering at the sight of his mother. Even here, in the centre of the room, limned by moonlight on one side and candlelight on the other, she seemed to blend into the darkness, except for her teeth and the occasional reflection of the whites of her eyes.

"Well, he had more hair and muscles back then," his mother clarified.

"But papa? The Killblaine name ... ?"

"*I'm* the Killblaine. Your papa took my name when we married."

"But ... the unbroken lineage?"

"Great-great-grandfather whatsis married Madeline and she took *his* name. And then she kind of ... kept it." She shrugged. "Passed it down the generations to her daughters."

His mouth opened to make a sound but he just couldn't.

"Matrilineage, my dude," she said. "Line ends with you, I'm sorry. Took me many years to accept it but all things come to an end."

"But ... I could find a girl and ... " He gestured helplessly at his groin.

"You can't pass down Killblaine blood through your wing-wang, my son. Unless you get punched real hard in the kidneys I guess." She laughed uproariously at her joke. "I suppose papa never explained that bit."

"No. I always thought he was disappointed in me for other, more obvious, reasons."

"Nope. Out of your hands entirely." When the silence got uncomfortable she added, "The only thing you can be sure of in this world is the hole your ma shit you out."

That didn't make the silence any less uncomfortable.

"That's ... great to hear, Ma. But my entire life I've been training to be an assassin, a real Killblaine. Even when I didn't want to, I *tried.*"

"Son, I've accepted you couldn't be an assassin if you wanted to. You're terrible. It was so easy to follow you here that I literally took a half hour break to smoke some weed just to add a challenge."

"And was it more challe—?"

"No, son. There's not enough weed in the city, I'm sorry."

She finally released her grip a little.

"Listen my boy, I know I've not been around much—"

"At all."

"—yeah. Yeah. Been … busy impersonating a gentleman cat, and all. No one looks for a lady assassin when a man cat is pissing all over the University insurance schedule, you savvy?"

He chose not to reply.

"Well, turns out your ol' man here accrued some serious debts and started asking around for ways to fix it, meaning how he might defraud some legitimate businessmen with the old 'overvalued life insurance' gambit. Me, keeping an eye on him as I do, meant I crossed paths with a few of the University actuaries sniffing around the place. Didn't turn out so well for them, so suddenly it became this high prestige job and your other pa naturally thought it'd be perfect for your first jaunt." She took a deep breath.

"Well. I couldn't let you kill your *real* father," she said, stepping back a little. "So I interfered some. And besides, I heard you graduated, so I made Semmelhorn here sign the deed of this house over to you. So you could do something useful with your life instead of just … desperately trying to be as good as I am, see?"

Jonathan couldn't believe what he was hearing. He'd never wanted the responsibility of carrying on the family name, but now that he wasn't able to, he felt a stubborn urge to rebel.

"So what do I do now?" Who was she to say he couldn't carry the family name?

"Look after him," she said. "And do something useful with your time. Weren't you always artistic? You know … how they say … *artistic* … as in, you loved your arts so much you never really looked at the girls?"

"Mother, that's none of your business," he bristled.

"Anyway, meet your real pa." She waved a careless hand at the quietly sobbing Semmelhorn. "I've got University wannabes to torment."

Without a further glance at either of them, she wrapped herself in a black cloak and stepped smoothly towards and out of the window, vanishing into the night. He couldn't even hear her land.

Semmelhorn retreated slowly to the couch, sobbing.

Jonathan looked around at the chaos of the study. Large, expensive, unused sheets of parchment lay spread across his father's bureau.

"Wait here," he said. He couldn't bring himself to say *pa*.

He rummaged through the study and brought out a fresh candle, lighting it from the dying spark of the old one. *I'm passing this light into the future*, he thought, *from one dying career to a new one.*

He found an unopened bottle of sherry, worked the cork out slowly, and poured himself and Semmelhorn a full glass each. It wouldn't do to guzzle from bottles like commoners.

He set the candle and his glass down on the heavy wooden surface next to the gathered stack of parchment.

Ignoring the remnant ache in his abused joints, he felt in his pocket for the piece of charcoal, looking at it on his upturned palm for a while. Then he felt for the folded WANTED poster he'd collected on the street, took it out and flattened it on the desk.

He sat down and pulled a blank sheet towards him.

"WANTED," he copied. "3,000 SHEKEL REWARD FOR THE CAPTURE OF

NIGHT TOM

(DEAD OR ALIVE)"

At the bottom, "Famous cat burglar, revolutionary and anarchist."

In the clear space, he began to sketch. It was a masterful piece of work, confident lines of charcoal that slowly carved out a shape, recognisable by its hood and mask as a ne'er-do-well of the highest order. Her face, though, was proud, sharp and black as night. He even managed to get the white crescent of her smile right.

"There's a challenge for you, Ma," he whispered to the room, sitting back to look at the masterful portrait while sipping his Amontillado.

He pulled another sheet towards him and started sketching 'WANTED: Mistress Avalanche, University of Crime lecturer'. It was absolutely not acceptable to bring attention to criminal lecturers, but the citizenry didn't know that.

When he finished, capturing her last shocked expression perfectly, Jonathan Killblaine sharpened the charcoal stick on the edge of his father's desk before reaching for the third sheet of parchment. It was going to be a long night.

He started to deftly sketch Nathaniel Eccors, grimacing with the pain of two of his Ma's darts in his chest. It was important to tell a story in a portrait, he thought.

By the time he finished the eleventh lifelike WANTED poster—working his way through the most egregious bullies and teachers at the University of Crime—he'd decided that, yes, he did have a future in the arts.

Tom Dullemond is a Dutch/Australian humanoid who stumbled out of university with degrees in Medieval/Renaissance studies and Software Engineering. One of these got him a job and he has been working in IT ever since. Tom writes primarily short fiction across all genres, including literary fiction and the occasional poem. He contributes a regular science fiction column for the CSIRO's *Double Helix* science magazine, and on the other side of the publishing mirror, reads and edits for *Andromeda Spaceways* magazine. He also runs the writing management website Literarium.net. Find him online for occasional ramblings at www.tomdullemond.com or @cacotopos on Twitter.

The One Who Walks The Permanent Way

Claire McKenna

The track gangers worship Him differently out on the five-and-six foot broad-gauge rail, the One Who Walks the Permanent Way. He's a Union man, a Railway man, That Guy, man who has stridden in iron shoes the length and breadth of the broad track, a man who's gone places. In one hand He carries the Gauge, the tool upon which a life is measured, from origin to termination, the pick up and set down, from siding to baulks.

In His other, the Stick, symbol and sceptre of Right of Way through the single-line. To Our Lord of Labour is authority given, over the Stick, over the *stop* and *go*, the *hold* and *continue*. May God always grant you the Stick, the gangers say, may your rail be unbuckled, your ties never split, the track protected, your signal green, your hammer-song like the footsteps of the One Who Walks, quick and clean.

Was Edgar Forrest who operated the steam-hammer for Automatic Rail, had done so for five winters and that bad-moon year when there was none. Was him that first interrupted the Conduit of Labour, back in the days when men still worked metal, made their own minds up about their goings and comings. Started the long decline when he got kneecap-broke laying iron through the backside of Pisswater, that paper town halfway between East Shinlock and Plumb. Fell on the pointy end of a dog spike, flayed the joint open to cartilage and bone. Gave blood to the rail. Not the first offering he would give, and the iron would take his life before he was done.

Before Forrest was even out of the infirmary, the steam-hammer company approached him. They laid paper on his pillow. A handsome sum. Would he be so kind to look at this bundle of rag-bills and count them? Could he smell the sweaty remnants of desperate men who had fondled the notes, kissed the notes, pushed the notes across whiskey-wet bars or smoked out poker tables in supplication to those fates which might return more money? Might he gaze upon the bloodstained corners, the grains of miner's explosive caught between the leaves? So much work and effort and sacrifice caught up in those fibres. So much power in them, and here he was being offered these collected pieces of unrequited dreams over which men had sobbed and bled and fought and died. All he needed to do was lift his hand and press his thumb to the tack, apply the blood to the contract that would make him a full-time employee of Automatic Rail.

What else could Edgar Forrest do? His knee was busted, and as a Railway Man he wasn't about to move far from the Permanent Way.

The blood-print left a shiny mark on the parchment in the shape of a tie-head.

They say Orphen Coir met Forrest in a bar a way out of Shinlock the following winter when he'd only been working for the company a year; met a changed man. A steam-softened handshake, a cough of black-lung, the rail worker's once iron-vision gone bright and brassy.

In former days, Forrest had been known for long silences and spare, considered words. Seconds after they shook hands in greeting, the steam-soaked fellow accosted Orphen with the indignant ferocity of a preacher who has discovered a soul not yet saved. For two hours, Forrest berated Orphen of their backwardness, their reliance on human muscle to drive down the railway spikes when a steam-hammer could do the work of ten in half the time. Between long passages of industrial glossalgia, Forrest told Orphen of the revolution that would come once steam and sun and human labour was replaced with rock-seep, the aromatic liquor of the deep earth. Invoked its rising like blood from a cut artery.

"Piped!" Forrest shouted, black spittle flecking his lips, the table, the white head of his beer stein. "Pumped! An iron-piped network of stone blood across the land, copper valves shining in the sun! Why, a man merely might turn on a spigot in his home and this phlogiston miracle would be delivered to him. Engines that need no rails! Factories that need no workers! Lightning harnessed to do the job of an army, oh the things I have seen!"

Orphen Coir too was a Union man, a Railway man. He had set down track across the country since he was old enough to pick up a hammer and kill his stepfather; the one who had beat him every day since his drunken appearance upon the marital bed. When the police came to arrest child-Orphen for murder, one of the young constables was the stepfather's adult son.

I know what he did to you, the Constable said. *For he did the same to me too.*

The Constable opened the window to the unrepentant boy, told him to scram before the others caught him. Thus was the deepest moral lesson delivered upon Orphen, that two men in union might stand up to a monster.

The boy joined the gangers on The Permanent Way. He discarded his name amidst the ballast with his past, but not the anger. A bigger threat might stand over men as a shadow had once loomed over Orphen, belt in hand, curse on lips. Labour might be taken by force. Intimidation might accompany an order. Upon Orphen's back a tattooed Christ, crucified on a cross of railway sleepers, his hands and feet penetrated with spikes.

Orphen Coir was a hard man who was not easily bullied, but what Forrest said in that bar, on that winter afternoon, terrified him.

Long had the rough beasts of progress circled, singing of a future that seemed too good to be true. Long had they made a hymn of freedom, freedom from work, freedom from decision, freedom from the pains that accompany the endless ordeal of life.

Now, of all men, Aesop Function had known these pains more than most. He'd died back whenever, in those fire weather years when the Il Papa winds blew hot and hard down from the deserts and the static electricity crackled through the newly inserted telegraph lines, when bar fights spilt out onto streets and horses collapsed suddenly in their stalls. Function had always been a man beset by demons. They sat in the pulpit of his ear and berated him righteously. For most of his life, he ignored his disruptive clergy, but hot Il Papa had a way of getting under skin and reducing defences, and it had not been an uncommon sight to see Aesop drunk with madness, cursing the creatures who rode him.

Aesop showed those demons who was boss, who made the decisions. He put his head upon the iron of The Permanent Way, and to the song of the singing, rumbling steel, under the wheels of the steam engine, the demons were quieted forever.

He left behind a widow and several defaulted loans. Travelling salesmen touting their radon-water and uranium-soap had bled Aesop dry. Widow Function sold their home but kept his blacksmith tools, dug out the apple tree she had planted over the grave of their stillborn child and headed for the junkyard of Plumb. The child-tree found residence in the rusted remains of a steam-shovel's scoop.

Sometimes Orphen Coir might stop by, if his travels between work-gangs might take him through Plumb. Widow Function smelt of coal fire and blacksmith's leather and hot steel. The Conduit of Labour was open between her hands and the things she made. He liked to lie between her calloused palms, feeling the energy flow between them, the way his own body came to life in her embrace.

That night he told her about Forrest and his exorbitant claims. The pipes, the unlimited energy.

She listened quietly, her lined face taking on the room's shadows.

"I have heard of this lapidary-spirit, this blood of the rock," she said at last. "It is a fraction of black seep, distilled from the subterranean tar like one might distil whiskey from fermented grain. You see what drunken men will do for ethanol spirit? Imagine that hunger a thousandfold. Imagine the greed and suffering that must be fed into the earth before it gives up such a gift."

Orphen held her close to him, remembered another woman, fragile as sticks. His mother or grandmother. He could not remember now, his old life discarded so many years ago. "Tell me I must not be afraid, if what Forrest said is true. He says there will come a time when they have no more need of men."

Widow Function pressed her callus-horned hands together. In the half-light, a faint illumination appeared between her fingers, the Conduit's signature.

"Men take iron from the ground, wind from the sky. Men make rails upon which the coal-trains run and feed the furnaces. In all these things, the Conduit of Labour is maintained. Each step requires the application of work, of hand to tool, keeps us in the loop of information. The stone blood breaks the chain. With certainty I can tell you that."

"Dare you suppose what follows?" Orphen whispered. "What happens when there are steam-hammers and blood-driven trains, and spigots that drip liquid fire to every home? What happens if these actions need no more hands?"

A train was passing in the night. With the downing of tools in the evening time, the Conduit faded. Trains still ran, electricity still pulsed in the telegraph wires, but a faceless independence grew as these things happened without thought. *Action* despite human input. *Work* despite the faded Conduit.

She pulled her hands apart. The light faded.

"Autonomy," she said.

—◆—

The night bloated and suffocated him with incoherent dreams. A Union preacher shouted from an upturned tie-box about the steam-hammer, how it threatened their livelihoods, their independence. A boss-man shouted the preacher down with a megaphone, cited figures and statistics, brayed about cut operating costs and a million miles of Permanent Way lain for a penny, lain without worker or Union or downtime.

But when the steam-hammer came, no operator's manipulations kept the hammer from bearing down on the frightened men, worker and boss alike. The machine shot railway spikes like bullets, not caring if it were skin or sleeper that was pierced. Forrest's skeleton remained in the driver's seat, click-clacking on the dried ropes of ligaments, whips of hair attached to the skinless cranium, blowing in Il Papa wind. Behind him, a thousand derricks punctured a flayed land, their spinning drills bitted with corpses' teeth. A thousand wounds in the ground, spurting black blood. And for each derrick, ten thousand madmen, digging the earth, frantic, urgent, digging until the flesh was gone from their fingers and they raked the dirt with finger bones.

Then the blood-train bore down upon them all, a thick wedge of black steel roaring with internal, autonomous combustion. The dreadnaught's spiked iron wheels chewed up the Permanent Way before veering off the ruined track towards Plumb.

And Orphen Coir, alone on the Way, powerless to stop the coming destruction.

Behind the driverless train a crescendo of voices built and held, the song of a million hornets the size of men. No flesh clothed these dead automatons, no mind inside them lived to maintain the Conduit of Labour. Copper coils formed arteries and nervous systems. Aromatic rock-blood quickened their bodies, steel wings caught the hot gusts of Il Papa. Blue lightning forked along the span of their weapons, and they flew into Plumb, flew and devoured, devoured and razed, razed to the bloodied ground.

Automation, and the death of everything.

Orphen woke with a shout, and alone. He sat up on the gritty sheets of the Widow's bed, his skin clammy with cold sweat. No dream, but prophecy and warning.

He rolled over, wiped the sediment of sleep from his eyes.

Upon the shabby bedside table, a glass tube hummed a warning note. A clock within a vacuum that ran backwards, cathode filament wires glowing orange from diode heat. Through the shack's one oily glass window, he saw Widow Function outside, digging up her child's tree from the steam shovel bucket.

He pulled on his denim overalls and picked his way over the remains of machinery and mining tools to reach her.

"You are leaving."

"Yes."

"Where will you go? The steam-hammer will follow the Permanent Way. The Conduit is being broken as far north as Shinlock, far south as Dogskin."

"Aerostat," she replied between shovels of dirt. "We've been collecting emissions from the refuse and nightsoil, we'll contain the aether in an envelope of aluminium and greased silk. We'll float to where the Railway has not reached." She stopped digging to bind up her child-tree's roots in a square of hessian. "There is a place in the North where men lay out glass tiles like seed-rows, harvest pure energy from the sun. The Conduit lives on, there."

Orphen Coir believed her because he wanted to believe her, because the nightmare of Autonomy remained so strong in his mind. The creosote taste of burning sleeper ties still tarred his tongue. The woman picked up the child-tree and began to walk.

As he followed the Widow deeper into the boneyard, he came upon the clumsily stitched patchwork of bed sheets the yard-dogs had lain out and smeared with mineral oil. The fabric was still flaccid even after a week. Conduit fire shimmered under the sheets before escaping into the morning air, providing not even enough lift to ruffle the greased edges.

"What if your dirigible doesn't work?" Orphen asked, imploring her to see reason. "What if you cannot leave before the stone blood begins to flow?"

Widow Function clutched the tree's hessian-bound root-bag to herself, oblivious to the dirt which stained her apron. "It has to work. We cannot stay here." Her expression took on the vacancy of someone whose mind is made up. "Wherever the stone blood flows, misery will come. People will war over the bones of children for a single cup of piped petro-liquor. The wealthy will feed on flesh as a delicacy. The land will be turned to poison and the sun burnt out of the sky once the Conduit of Labour is lost."

Orphen knew that. He had seen it in his dream.

"But if people leave this place, that outcome is guaranteed."

"The Conduit of Labour will still continue strong, Orphen." She touched her belly. The previous night Orphen had noticed but quietly ignored the splitting of muscles at the Widow's stomach. A child was coming. He'd wondered if the child was his.

But because she had not mentioned it, and because their parting was no different than any previous one, Orphen realised with a bittersweet disappointment that he was not her only lover, and wherever Widow Function was going, he was not invited.

So Orphen returned to the Permanent Way, because the Railway's song was his song, because he had kept the Conduit alive in all the years he had laid track. There was no place else for him.

When the steam-hammers came to replace the gangers, the men scattered. To the cobalt mines, to copper fields, and eventually to prisons if they could not divest themselves of the terrible bottled-up Conduit energy in honest work.

The machine-built Iron of the Way stretched out through lands lost to memory, through starving mineral-rush towns and farms populated by dust, alongside foundries and factories mechanised through stone blood, alongside pipelines and refineries that jettisoned a noxious fume and turned the land to poison.

Having no work left for his great spike-driving arms, Orphen took up the gauge and the stick and began to walk the Way, doing the thing that the steam-hammers and the blood engines could not, measuring the path of the five-foot through the wilderness. Through him, the Conduit stayed open, no matter how many steam-hammered spikes and track-chairs pinned down an automatic track. The gauge would glow between his hands, and the line would sing each time he placed the five-foot tool between the rails.

There can never be Autonomy if a human hand is required at just one step of the process. There could be no Apocalypse of petroleum and copper and steel, not while Orphen Coir was still doing his job. Many mindless things set out in search of Orphen, set out to kill the last remaining link of the Conduit, the human hand that kept them from closing their lifeless loop. Many men were given rag-paper bills and the name of *Coir* as an instruction, a name whispered in dark rooms and fever dreams.

But he could never be found. Just like the first time he'd defeated a monster, he had found anonymity within the Permanent Way.

In the arch and span of time, the name of Orphen Coir became just that: a name known to everyone, but not one attached to an individual ever met. A stranger in a railway town will be greeted by the name *Coir*, just in case he is the One Who Walks The Way. The passer-through shall be given lodging and a bed, for it may be them that keeps the Conduit open. If two men not of each other's acquaintance meet in a place not known for civility, both will be polite and respectful, for either could be Him.

Even though the years since Orphen Coir walked the rail have extended past the natural term of a man's life, during the hot windy days of Il Papa, telegraph stations will still receive messages from towns that no longer exist, dispatches from relays long since corroded to oxide dust. Reports of a buckle in the track, a broken rail, attention required on the Permanent Way. Lost transmissions, living in the wires for a hundred years, the dot and dash of shuffling feet walking from sleeper to sleeper. Ghost statements, in transistor and silicon, and in all the technological permutations of eternity.

Nobody questions their origin. They are Orphen Coir's messages. The algorithms that govern human existence, the bots and routines and incursions and aggregations have no power over Him. He cannot be deleted. He who walks the Permanent Way walks in the Word and the Work, and in true labour is forever after granted eternal life.

Claire McKenna is a spec fic writer from Melbourne. Aurealis and Ditmar nominated, Clarion South graduated, lives with two humans and a cat. With a prolific output of one short story per year, her website is at clairemckenna.net.

Miscreants at Large
Aiders and Abetters

Chris Large is the kind of hybrid writer/geologist/game narrative designer rarely seen in nature, or discussed in casual conversation. He may even be unique, which potentially also makes him endangered. Whether he's worth preserving is another question entirely. His writing career began with childish stories written in crayon, and hasn't really progressed in the seven or eight years to now. Surprising then, that he's managed to convince Aussie and US publishers to print his work in real, authentic magazines and anthologies of some note. He's currently working with a US-based studio designing narratives for casual video games.

Juliette Morley grew up on late night movies, vinyl records and the Land Beyond Beyond! Her fascination with being Elsewhere—in a fantasy realm, a galactic landscape or urban soundscape—never waned. She has travelled as a researcher and worked in many fields but now, as a new arrival on the Canberra writing scene, is cutting her teeth on her first love of writing.

Shauna O'Meara is a Ditmar and EG Harvey Award winning artist and writer based in Australia. She has contributed cover and/or interior art to *Lackington's Magazine* in Canada as well as several Australian speculative fiction anthologies including: *In Fabula-divino, Cthulhu: Deep Down Under, Gold Coast Anthology: Undertow, Andromeda Spaceways Inflight Magazine 61, Winds of Change, Next, The Never Never Land* and *Wide Brown Land*.
She is on Twitter at @OMearaShauna and Instagram at @shaunaomeara and you can find her at www.theshaunacorner.wordpress.com

Simon Petrie hasn't slushwrangled before this, but he's done plenty of prior typesetting and e-book formatting for *ASIM*, CSFG, Dragonwell Publishing and Peggy Bright Books, as well as for various local and international indie authors. He's online at www.simonpetrie.wordpress.com and tweets as @fomalhaut451.

—+—

Leife Shallcross loves a good short story. She has written a few and has been published in places like *Aurealis* and *Daily Science Fiction* as well as several Australian and international anthologies. She even won the 2016 Aurealis Award for Best Young Adult Short Story for 'Pretty Jennie Greenteeth' in the anthology *Strange Little Girls*. Her first novel, *The Beast's Heart*, was published by Hodder & Stoughton in May 2018. *A Hand of Knaves* is her first foray into the glamorous, yet mysterious, world of editing. Look her up online on Facebook, Instagram and Twitter @leioss or at leifeshallcross.com.

Rogues' Gallery

Phill Berrie (Knave of Knives)   Indrani Mukherjee (Knave of Coins)

Lily Mulholland (Knave of Masks)

Anthony Clark
Kristy Evangelista
James Fellows
Alis Franklin
Darren Goossens
Chris Large
Marley Large
Sally McRae
Sarah Neilson
C H Pearce
Simon Petrie
Louise Pieper

Gillian Polack
Rob Porteous
Rivqa Rafael
Tansy Rayner Roberts
Marta Scrabacz
Leife Shallcross
Cat Sheely
Catriona Sparks
Paulene Turner
Dave Versace
Mark Webb
Angus Yeates

About the CSFG

(the Canberra Speculative Fiction Guild)

The CSFG is an incorporated association for Canberra-based creators of speculative fiction— science fiction, fantasy or horror—in any medium. Most members are writers of short stories, novels or both.

Our goal is to support and provide development opportunities for our members as they move from aspiring, to published to (fingers crossed) professional makers of spec-fic.

Oh, and also, world domination.

To achieve these goals we do a number of things:

- A website at https://csfg.org.au, through which we promote our members' activities and achievements in speculative fiction.

- An online community through Yahoo! Groups, open to anyone in the Greater Canberra region... which currently encompasses the Pacific Rim but we're probably flexible on that if you ask us.

- Publishing short story anthologies (such as this one), edited by CSFG members and to which our members and other writers from around Australia contribute.

- Monthly members' meetings at which we discuss the business of the association and conduct informal workshops by members and guest speakers on the craft and business of creating speculative fiction.

- A novel writing group, and critiquing groups for short stories and novels, which also meet regularly.

- Our members also participate in writing events like Write-a-Book-in-a-Day and NaNoWriMo. Many members are active elsewhere in small-press publishing and in the Australian convention scene.

Also from CSFG Publishing:

A Masterclass in Spec-fic Novel Writing

ISBN 978-0-6480765-6-8

The Book of Lore, by Rob Porteous, is a compendium of the notes prepared for the CSFG's Novel Writing Discussion Group.

If you write fantasy or science fiction, this Masterclass will lift your writing to a more professional level.

It's the essential guide to starting your first novel and full of insightful tips that will even help experienced writers.

It covers everything you need to know about starting, and finishing, your spec-fic novel. There are definitions of important terms, discussion prompts to get you thinking and heaps of exercises and tips to apply to your work-in-progress.

It's available now, from our website at https://csfg.org.au.